Blood Prize

Blood Prize

By

Ken Grace

Published by

M@KTUB *it is written*

www.maktubitiswritten.com.au

First published in 2014

Maktub It Is Written
Freeburgh VIC
Email: info@maktubitiswritten.com.au
Web: www.maktubitiswritten.com.au

Cataloguing-in-Publication details are available from the
National Library of Australia
http://catalogue.nla.gov.au

ISBN 978 0 9924265 1 4

Cover design by Ilian - http://ilgeorgiev.elance.com

Acknowledgements

Thanks must go to Katie Grace, for her editing and publishing talents and her marketing expertise.

To my wonderful mother and father, Wanda and Arn Grace, who never gave up hope in their son.

To Jenny Bouda, another wonderful woman who never stopped offering her belief, support and knowledge.

To Jane, Michael, Cassie, Adam and Nic Fenton, for endlessly suffering my ideas and for their support.

I extend an extra thanks to Nic Fenton for his expertise in producing the trailer film for *Blood Prize.*

For Katie

I dedicate this book to a woman of raw courage and loyalty, who never stopped believing. My beautiful wife, Katie.

Prologue

Professor Alexander Fox turned and glared at the men behind him, silencing their chatter.

"That's not a pretty sight, is it, gentlemen?"

He turned and sighed as he looked out over the plain.

Incompetent bastards. They don't give a damn.

His ground-penetrating radar equipment rippled in a vast lake of heat-haze distortion, one hundred metres to the west, with no operator in attendance. He spat a globule of saliva into the sand and faced the two men following him.

"What on earth is wrong with you? We find the remains of a large carnivorous dinosaur and you both go back to the shed for beer."

The professor tilted his head and stared at them over the rim of his glasses. He expanded his lungs and let out a long resonating groan.

"Get going the pair of you. We'll talk about this tomorrow."

He watched the two men retreat. They shuffled along with bent backs and drooped shoulders, making small clouds of dust as they dragged their boots through the dirt.

"Idiots."

Finding an unidentified Tyrannosauropus species from the late Cretaceous period justified all of the toil and the dollars, yet for some unknown reason, his well-paid moronic staff didn't bother to inform him. He felt like wringing their necks. A unique find in the Winton region of Queensland rated as a significant story; a tale worthy of a press conference, not a drunken boast from some seedy bar.

As he watched the two men shrink and then disappear from sight, his dark thoughts became a rant; his voice sounding angry and bitter.

"I'm surrounded by a sea of morons. I'll just have to take over the dig and get this baby out of the ground myself."

He studied the information sheet that he wrenched from his staff. A layman could have compiled a better report, yet it contained enough information to suggest that the skeletal remains could be dated to at least sixty-five to seventy million years ago and that the creature measured nine metres in length and weighed in at over a tonne. He also determined from the report that the horned skull contained more than eighty curved and serrated teeth, in jawbones that appeared to be longer than any previously recorded specimen.

The professor tensed as he lowered himself into the old steel-framed chair. He proceeded with caution. He knew from experience that the lack of padding exposed several bolt heads that protruded towards his advancing buttocks. After managing some degree of comfort, he fixed all of his attention onto the high-definition monitor of his Farrow and Fraser imaging equipment.

He began by studying the nature of the subterranean environment.

There doesn't seem to be anything unusual here.

He widened the coverage area and recalibrated his equipment. This time he did see something, so he reduced the field of vision, captured the identified target area and magnified it, tightening the images for the best possible focus.

You're kidding me.

The professor pulled away from the monitor in confusion. He felt stunned. He tried to stand, but needed the support of the machine to steady himself.

"Bastards."

He turned away from the screen and glared into the empty horizon, as if daring some offender to come forward.

"What the hell's going on here?"

His staff lived for pain-in-the-arse party tricks.

Could such an elaborate ruse be possible? No. No, it couldn't.

He slowed his breathing in an attempt to calm himself. He needed to think, to understand. He wanted to believe what he just witnessed, but how could he? Below where he stood, the ancient rock sheltered a sealed environment that just happened to contain the absolute over-the-top impossible.

You're a scientist ... Come on man. Act like one.

The professor forced himself to take another look at the screen and his breathing became ragged. He could see seven intact skeletons in one section of the cavern and something else that he found truly disturbing. To his knowledge, nature didn't produce square containers with precise measurements and especially ones that included handles.

He blinked, shook his head and spoke to the machine as if he expected an answer.

"These are manufactured items."

He knew his hypothesis created more dilemmas than answers. For one, solid rock surrounded the objects in question.

How could any kind of manufactured item turn up in a naturally enclosed space?

This problem required clarity, which meant focusing his brain cells towards some degree of professional comprehension.

He held his breath and rechecked the screen. The images remained precise and clear. Not something he imagined.

"This defies logic ..."

The professor knew that differing perspectives could be deceiving. Two years ago, in 2015, he heard a story about a group of Aboriginals who lived not far from the dig site. In all of their years, this group of people never got the opportunity to experience rain and when it eventually fell on them, after a lifetime of dry, they ran in all directions shrieking, as if the melted sky fell in droplets around them. He knew how they felt.

"Like I do now ... Shit-bloody-scared."

He closed his eyes and tried to relax.

Could this be the hand of man or a natural occurrence?

He knew that God fashioned most of our reality, leaving the rest of creation for humanity. Technical equipment existing in a time-sealed space as old as the dinosaurs didn't fit into either scenario, it just didn't make sense.

The professor rubbed the sting of perspiration from his eyes. His shirt sleeve acting as a facial mop.

Come on man ... Focus. Start with the skeletons.

The depth and age of the surrounding sedimentary rock meant that the bodies must be at least many millions of years old; information that went against all teaching from big bang to now.

He considered the skeletal remains to be humanoid in structure with little to no deterioration of the bones; noticing that they lay along the cavern's floor in a perfect row.

It's a burial site ... Behaviour determined by culture.

He compared their size against his own.

"Bloody hell ... They're giants."

At close to four and a half metres in length, they measured more than twice his own height.

This is remarkable. It changes everything.

The professor closed his eyes and took in a long slow breath.

He knew what it meant to have giant, technologically advanced humanoid beings existing here millions of years before us.

Every-damn-thing I've ever believed about where we came from is wrong.

Chapter One

Tom glanced into the murky surroundings of the Old Royal. Ten steps in any direction and a person's features began to disappear and he suspected that this remained the reason for the pub's popularity at five in the morning.

He slowed his breathing and listened.

He could hear fragments of conversation from the shadowy booths along the far wall. He squinted into the gloom and noticed the cautious glances of the occupants.

Bloody scoundrels ...

He grinned at his thought; this group of crooks invested in the commodities that didn't find their way onto the London Stock Exchange.

Tom sat close to the rear exit, facing the entrance. He knew the local police often raided late-closing establishments in the hope of raising their wages, so he needed to determine an escape route; a good strategy, except that an attractive female shared his booth and blocked any chance of a speedy getaway.

He didn't know her real name so he called her Jacqueline. Her need for secrecy made him feel a little uneasy, but he liked her anyway, even though the giggling and the constant need for eye contact distracted him.

No ... Don't make stupid comparisons. Don't even think about it.

He wanted to enjoy the moment and not have to consider her as a possible partner, which meant judging her; weighing up all of her positive features against the inevitable negatives.

It's ridiculous. No-one ever weighs up ... I'm not sure I'll ever find her.

Where other males got off on alcohol or drugs, his one obsession wore a dress. All the men he knew seemed to love football and violence, but he loved women; all women, and especially one very specific kind of woman. He often wondered if he conjured her in his mind, or if God placed pictures of her there; giving him glimpses and clues so he could find her in the immensity of it all.

Why this constant need? It drives me crazy.

He didn't understand; only that coming close to any dark haired super-slim women with a certain face and body shape made his physiology change, causing perspiration, trembling muscles and involuntary heavy breathing.

What kind of dark magic could bring someone to their knees with a glance?

Unfortunately, his obsession devalued everyone else, which seemed unacceptable when he viewed it logically.

He felt her staring at him so he cleared his thoughts and decided he needed to focus on her; a real being of flesh and blood who deserved his attention, rather than a phantom who drove him insane.

"Tom, can I ask you a personal question?"

He winced, but nodded.

"What do you want? Outta life, I mean."

Tom looked away from her towards the ceiling to hide his discomfort.

"To be happy, I suppose. What do you want?"

"Money. I'm sick of being dirt poor."

"The whole world's poor. Only the Church and the ultra-rich have money."

"They're revolting. I hate them. Why do they have everything and I have nothing?"

"The Church controls everything; even our bastard politicians. It's supposed to be evil to want money."

"Then why do they have so much?"

"You're asking the wrong person. I'm as poor as you."

She pursed her lips and looked away and Tom felt a moment of relief; thankfully, the 'do you ever think about having a family?' question, didn't eventuate.

When she turned back, her smile made him shiver.

"Tom … Hold me."

He obliged, wrapping an arm around her soft shoulders and feeling the warmth of her back ease against his chest. He sighed as she turned and raised her face towards his, closing her eyes and slowly parting her lips. Tom accepted the invitation and her kiss felt soft and wet, and full of promise, so he ignored the stale breath and the unruly blond hair that tickled his face.

Her boldness surprised him as she took hold of his hand and began to guide it. He closed his eyes and let her take control, allowing his fingertips to become the sole agent of his understanding of her. He sighed again, this time more loudly, as his fingers fired the language of her body up an ascending pathway to his brain, sending shivers through his body; even his blood felt hot, as it rushed towards his extremities.

Tom held his breath. His hand slid up under the cup of her loosened bra and grasped the weightiness of her breast; the touch of its erect nipple sending shockwaves through the palm of his moving hand.

"Tom …"

She moaned and placed his right hand under her skirt. He needed no further encouragement. He stroked the inside of her thigh, easing his hand slowly upwards. Her legs parted as he felt the tops of his fingers brush against her panties and the mound of her Venus. He felt the hair bristle against her underwear and the muscles of her right leg clench and unclench, then she stiffened and pulled from his embrace.

Tom followed her movements; she stood with her back to him; patting down her attire.

"Is something wrong?"

She giggled.

"I've got to go to the toot. I'm about to burst."

Tom fidgeted with impatience as he watched her disappear towards the toilet. Every moment waiting for her return, felt like an hour of tension.

He slid across the bench, until his back rested against the wall. This way he could see her coming back, but nothing happened. Ten minutes dragged by and his apprehension increased.

Where the hell is she? She couldn't have left, not without a word of goodbye.

Another ten minutes dragged by and Tom continued to fidget. The idea of going into the female loo didn't thrill him, but it seemed like the only way to discover her whereabouts.

Tom made a quick decision. He slid across the bench, stood and tried to flatten his own clothing. He remained crumpled and unruly and snorted his disapproval as he turned and walked towards the restroom doorway.

I felt a connection ... She couldn't have gone.

After several steps, he noticed someone watching him from a booth beside the exit. He stared back at her wild auburn hair and beautiful face; his stomach contracting as he attempted to hold her gaze. Their contact felt intense and sexual, yet without any sense of flirtation, or attraction. He thought about saying something, but her cruel smile kept him silent. As he turned and walked away, he recognised the sick feeling in his stomach as alarm.

He refocused and entered a hallway with several doors. A sign above the left one read: Hen's WC. Tom felt apprehensive as he reached the entrance. He knocked and called out, but no-one answered. He waited for several seconds before slowly pushing on the door with his index finger. It creaked open.

Alright. I have to do this.

Without waiting any longer, he slipped through into a brightly lit room, the harsh light forcing his eyelids to compress; his pupils contracting as he adjusted to the glare.

As he slowly became aware of his surroundings, he began to notice the whiteness of the tiles, and the walls and the ceiling. He also noticed three cubicles against the far wall, a sink with a hand towel dispenser and a waste paper basket to his left.

He walked towards the centre of the room and felt something soft move under his boot. Without meaning to, he kicked the white leather shoe further into the room. Only when he bent to pick it up, did he notice the discolouration. From a crouched position, he could see under the middle cubicle door, to where red liquid pooled out towards him. He could also see two feet; one without a shoe.

Tom ran to the partly opened door. He held his breath and forced his head into the gap.

"Jacqueline?"

He stared at her in disbelief. His date lay back against the cistern with her partially severed head resting against the wall; her throat slit wide and gaping; her eyes open, as if she still focused on her killer.

Tom cried out and backed away from her.

"No."

He fell against the door, his back sliding down its surface until he crouched just above the bloodied floor tiles.

A rush of nausea overwhelmed him and he vomited.

Tom's head pounded and his eyes blurred with moisture as he forced himself to rise.

My God ... What the hell am I going to do?

He couldn't wait for the police; not around here. It might have been the year two thousand and sixty one, but time didn't change the facts. His piece of London represented extreme danger. In the East End, police dished out their own idea of justice, especially the

9

hated Special Religious Police. Over the years he witnessed so many beatings and even worse; summary executions.

Like everyone in his part of the world, he knew the penalty for disobedience. He hated that neighbours ratted on neighbours. The SRP ruled the streets with networks of informers; exploiting everyone's fear. Billboards everywhere declared that by being above the law, the legal system remained unclogged; keeping gaols from spilling over, but he knew this rubbish meant nothing to the mothers of those that went missing.

Calm down ... Breathe ... Think.

He closed his eyes and tried to compose himself, drawing a fitful breath as he took a last look around. He knew he shouldn't leave incriminating evidence at the scene, but survival took precedence. Then he noticed his reflection in the mirror and baulked at the drained face staring back at him. He looked shrivelled and bent; ancient for a twenty-year old.

I can't believe this. It's ... so senseless.

The nausea came back; rising with his fear. It felt debilitating and instinctively, he knew he needed to push through the panic. He felt wretched. He looked back at the mirror, clenched his fists and willed his features to transform themselves. He pulled back his shoulders, puffed out his chest and straightened his body to its full height.

Instead of a stranger; a tall young man with unruly blond hair and a gammy elbow stood before him. Would this person be tough enough to survive? The expression on the face in the mirror seemed unconvincing.

As he re-entered the hall and hurried to the rear entrance, he thought about who might have seen him in the bar. He remembered the striking auburn-haired woman and his fear intensified. He couldn't see a solution other than luck. The only plan he could think of required him reaching his parent's house undetected, gathering some gear and laying low somewhere, until he could figure out what to do.

Tom ... From here on, you need to run.

He moved away from the pub as quickly as possible, following the network of narrow alleyways that stretched to the south.

Darkness and fog made visibility difficult. Despite his urgency, each step required careful attention. Worn soles skated across slippery cobblestones and stumbled over heaped garbage. He slowed. He couldn't compromise his mobility; an injury might prove fatal.

When he reached the first intersection, he heard footsteps behind him and his fear returned. It couldn't be a coincidence. The person following moved at a similar pace and stopped when he stopped.

Tom ran and the muffled sounds behind him paralleled his own. He felt exposed and vulnerable as he reached the first of several lit crossways. He staggered out under the cone of light, with his collar up and his chin on his chest; just another drunk on the way home to his hovel. As soon as he reached the safety of the darkness, he pushed himself against a wall and waited to see who followed him. Someone committed bloody murder and he needed to avoid it happening to him.

Footsteps … Keep still.

Tom held his breath and flattened his body harder against the wall. He saw a shape appear, lurking at the far edge of the circle of light and a man stepped out into the open. His collar stretched up to touch the brim of his hat, hiding any facial features from view.

Tom ran; softly at first for the benefit of stealth, then faster, as he outdistanced the possibility of his hunter hearing the sound of his footfalls. He thought he held an advantage with his knowledge of the alleys, yet that remained an assumption better served by speed. Fear affected his thinking, yet in a moment of clarity, it occurred to him that if the killer knew his identity, could he ever be truly safe? He needed a way to determine what this scoundrel looked like; a place where he could view him from close quarters, yet a place dark enough that the man didn't need to hide his features.

Tom slowed and allowed his pursuer to catch up. An old, barely legible sign marked: 'Lane's End' revealed his chosen hiding place.

His plan depended on this narrow cul-de-sac and he hoped that the man following him didn't know the way over and through.

Hopefully he's not from around here.

Most locals knew that this area once contained parkland and little else, but a severe shortage of housing thirty years earlier, turned the place into a shantytown with tiny streets. Over time, the tin dwellings became brick and mortar, but the maze of narrow alleyways remained.

Tom hurried towards the rear wall. He joined his hands around a water pipe and used his arms as a sling, pulling himself up until he reached the safety of the building's roof. He hid himself behind a row of dripping pipes, with enough of a gap for him to see down into the alley and remain hidden.

Down on the street below, the only illumination came from several undraped windows, where local East Enders readied themselves for another day of labour. The uncovered bulbs providing enough light for him to discern the small area of cobblestones and grimy walls, and hopefully the face of a determined killer.

Keep still ... He's coming.

Tom noticed movement. A swirling of the mist and a shadow by the far wall, yet his assailant remained hidden, which left him little choice. He must wait until the man made his move, but just as he thought this, the shadow walked into the light and became form.

The man removed his hat and looked up at Tom's hiding spot.

"I know you're up there. I'm not going to hurt you. I just want to talk."

Tom knew he only needed to slide backwards across the slate for several feet and run along the rooftop to safety, but something about the man in the trench coat caused him to remain.

Tom judged him to be young; maybe only seventeen or so and his voice didn't seem to hold the slightest bit of malice. The lack of any visible blood on his person eventually persuaded Tom to remain.

"Keep your hands out where I can see them and don't move. Then we can talk."

"I have no intention of harming you, Tom. In fact, quite the opposite."

"Yeah right. You knife my girl and follow me out here for a nice little chat?"

"You're half right, old son. Actually, I'm your guardian angel and believe me, you need to be protected."

"Rubbish. Start making sense or I'm off."

The young man below raised his hand, slowly moving it to the pocket of his coat. Just as slowly, he took out an envelope and held it up towards Tom.

"This letter will explain everything. My boss sent me here to give it to you, but then things happened."

"Yeah, you killed her?"

"Nah, not me. I've been outside that bar all sodding night, waiting for you to come out. I only went in when I heard some patrons screaming. When I did, I realised that you'd already left, so I flew out the back and got lucky. You weren't that far ahead of me."

Tom wanted to believe the youth. He needed help, but it seemed far more sensible at that moment to run.

"Who killed her then and why the hell are you so interested in me?"

The young man below didn't answer. He stiffened and raised the forefinger of his right hand to his lips. Tom noticed him take a step backwards towards a darkened doorway and heard two muffled metallic sounds in close succession.

Tom pulled back from the water pipes in surprise, as the young man fell to his knees, moaning and clutching at his side.

"They shot me ... Go ... Get outta here ... Now."

Tom arched his spine and began crabbing backwards on his hands and knees, but stopped when he noticed a flash of movement below him. A figure entered the cul-de-sac with astonishing speed.

Tom's body tightened. The tiniest of movements might give up his position. Only his eyes followed the dark shape, as it grasped the young man's hair with one hand and pushed down with the other; forcing the youth into a kneeling position.

Tom heard laughter. It sounded harsh, cruel and more surprisingly, feminine. He felt confused as he tried to absorb and understand this information.

What the hell?

He stared unblinking as the woman wrenched at the young man's hair, pulling his head up and to one side; revealing the neck. She laughed again as she lowered her head and sank her teeth into the exposed flesh.

Tom heard the young man's cries for help and felt his stomach heave. He saw the woman jerking her head from side to side, tearing through the skin, until a chunk of meaty tissue tore from his neck. Then the killer straightened and pulled her victim's head up by the hair; blood pumping from the grizzly wound below his ear.

Tom tensed. The woman looked directly up at him and removed her cap, shaking her curly auburn hair loose around her shoulders. She smiled at him with bloodied teeth and the remaining contents of Tom's stomach exploded out over the side of the wall.

Tom's eyes blurred with tears, but he saw the women release the corpse, letting it flop onto the pavement. Then she turned and concentrated on the other end of the alley. Tom could see people emerging from doorways and he heard a car's engine rev into life.

"You'll never get away from me. I know who you are. I'll find you no matter where you go."

She smiled up at him, spat a spray of blood onto the cobblestones and vanished into the darkness, as quickly as she arrived.

Tom spun around onto his back and tried to calm himself. He forced extra oxygen into his lungs and attempted an understanding of the night's events. Jacqueline murdered, now this. None of it made any sense at all.

He rolled over and raised himself onto his knees. More lights shone into the alley and he could see well enough to confirm the devil-woman's departure. He knew he needed to run; over the roof, where no-one would see anything. He took a last look down at the macabre scene. The corpse lay face up on what appeared to be a pillow of blood.

What a waste of life.

Tom felt disgust and almost turned away when he noticed a tiny portion of white sticking out of the victim's coat pocket.

The Envelope.

Chapter Two

Father Dominico Rossi disembarked from his British Airways flight, thirty-five minutes behind his intended schedule. He tried not to frown or show suspicion, even though he considered the cancellation of his Costa Corporation jet, to be a warning.

He felt even less amused suffering the traffic from Ciampino Airport to central Rome, with an over-talkative taxi driver.

He smiled at the man and it felt as unpleasant, as he supposed it looked. 'Don't sweat the small things'; a lesson remembered from his childhood, but enough small things put together make a big thing; his anxiety seemed justified.

"At Rezzale delle Provincie, take the second exit onto Via Catania and this time pay attention."

"Yes Padre, but as I was saying, my poor Mama ..."

The priest moaned as they turned from Via Francesco Crispi into the heavier traffic of the Via Sistina. As the hotel came into view, he felt his heartbeat increase. Trouble lay ahead. It could mean a step towards success or possible disaster; he didn't know which to expect.

A nervous looking concierge greeted him on arrival at the Intercontinental De La Ville and rushed him into an austere looking boardroom. He knew the purpose of this space. Every word uttered, every nuance of expression, every movement relating to body language, created a picture of what lay behind each individual mask; allowing little chance of anyone deceiving his employer.

He understood the Church's need for control and their hatred of science.

They think it betrays God.

This justified a world where the average man knew nothing of technology.

They're afraid of course. Knowledge is a dangerous thing in the wrong hands.

Only religious-controlled governments and trusted affiliated organisations acquired permission for technical expertise.

The Assembly keep their boot heels on the neck of the poor. The amount of money these bastards spend on technical security could feed thousands.

He started to shake his head, but stopped; realising that Assembly personnel scrutinised his entrance.

It's all about control. When the threat of Hell isn't enough, violence is the next best thing.

His masters in the hierarchy of the Church believed that mass-produced comforts polluted the world. They admonished the population with proclamations of a future Heaven, in great peril of remaining empty of man for eternity … Unless humanity became totally obedient to the will of God and as such, His administrators, the Church.

And, they employ the Assembly and their Special Religious Police to make it happen.

As he stepped further into the room, he tried to improve on his smile. It seemed fake, yet better than his last attempt. He directed it at the two well-dressed men rising from their seats, holding out hands in greeting.

The chairman and larger of the two, returned his smile and embraced him.

The priest forced himself to stifle a laugh.

Politicians employed the same phoney conviction hugging babies.

Frederick Vogel, the shorter man, returned to his chair and looked away; his welcome being courteous, yet frosty.

As always, the priest avoided staring at Vogel. It required an effort on his part. The man's looks offended him, no matter how often the two men came together. His hair resembled the pelt of a leopard, being close-clipped and red, with several patches of darker hair and two prominent blotches of grey.

The priest risked a glance at the man's angular, sallow face and winced; overall, he considered him a grotesque and dangerous creature.

The clergyman looked away when he spotted Vogel's eyes darting in his direction. He noticed him moving forward on the edge of his chair and despite the obvious animosity, the priest recognised the man's grudging acknowledgement of the hierarchy that existed between them. In Vogel's world of security, he continued to be the Assembly's top man, but here, he seemed cunning enough to know his place, at least for the moment.

The priest turned his attention away from Vogel and attempted to engage the larger man, returning his exuberant expression. Father Dom tried to remain calm; outwardly confident despite the danger. Antonio Costa owned the world's largest private corporation and chaired the Assembly of the True Faith. He dominated everyone with the power of his position and the fear that standing evoked.

"It's been a long time, Dominico. Rome isn't the same without you."

The priest kept his facial features neutral, while his brain once again registered a warning. He knew the tactic. Overdoing the pleasantries kept the quarry from running and as a consequence, at the Assembly's mercy. He played along, stretching his lips into a more convincing smile.

"Now to business, Dominico."

The old chairman ran his fingers through his thinning hair, gathering the strands where they fell to his shoulders. Then in one motion, he swept them up and over his bald peak with the back of his hand.

The priest hid his disgust.

The chairman seemed oblivious to the priest's thoughts, as he captured the last unruly thread from in front of his face. He used both hands to pat the oily mass into place, before turning his attention toward the other seated man.

"Mr Vogel, if you please."

Frederick Vogel coughed and as he spoke, a nerve twitched above his left eye.

"There's been a breach of security. In the early hours of this morning, two different parties approached Fox and an incident occurred. Fox escaped unharmed."

The priest raised both of his arms towards the heavens.

"What? Why wasn't I contacted about this earlier? Who the hell are these two parties?"

Vogel didn't initially respond to the clergyman's questions. The priest noticed the muscles around his jaw, bunch and clamp, and for a brief moment, his teeth flashed between thin, bloodless lips. Then he frowned at the chairman and waited for his barely perceptible nod before answering.

"A member of the PMSG made contact with Fox. They're a group of subversives known as ..."

"The People's Movement for Secular Government. I know who they are, but that's absurd ... Impossible. Fox is dead, officially and we've gone to a great deal of trouble to keep it that way."

"Well, not enough trouble. Someone eliminated the PMSG contact as well as the girl with Fox. The deaths seemed brutal and purposely obvious; we think it's some kind of warning, or scare tactic."

"By who, Vogel?"

"We've been unable to determine the perpetrator. No witnesses and nothing left for identification purposes. A professional job."

"What about Fox? You say he escaped."

"He's hiding; safe for the moment."

The priest squeezed his fingers into a fist to stop them shaking as he struggled to contain his composure.

"This material is for the board's eyes only, Mr Vogel. Perhaps you'd like to explain, how you've become privy to this information and the lad's real identity, when Fox himself doesn't know?"

The Assembly chairman cleared his throat and both men turned and faced him.

"Frederick has my confidence, Dominico. He runs a plant in the PMSG, a spy who's helped us in the past."

The priest studied the chairman's face and his worry began to escalate.

Why would the high and mighty, Chairman Costa, answer for an underling like Vogel? Be careful ... It's another warning.

"I don't have to tell you how serious this is, Dominico. Decisions have to be made and quickly, for the good of our sacred order."

The priest tried to slow his breathing in an attempt to remain calm. This project required absolute secrecy; the responsibility belonging to him since its inception, yet the Assembly Council proceeded without him, preferring Vogel's murderous skills over his diplomacy. He knew his survival depended on his next words; he needed to be convincing.

"Mr Chairman, I assure you, nothing's changed. There are only two choices available. You either eliminate the threat by killing Fox, or you take a risk and go after the Prize."

He glanced at the chairman; the man's complexion turning as pale as the collar of his crisp white shirt.

Good. A little stress to push my point.

"So, what's it to be? The status quo, or is the Prize worth pursuing at any cost?"

The priest felt his power returning and with it control.

"Tom Fox is the key. His existence alone could destroy us all. Murder him. Throw his mutilated body into the Thames and we can all rest easy. However, if you do this, you will lose the greatest of opportunities. Don't misunderstand me, Mr Chairman. Right now, Tom Fox is the most dangerous human being alive, but he also represents power beyond all imagining. Use him effectively and you rule everything."

No-one spoke. The priest allowed the silence to settle around them as they considered their positions.

After several seconds, the Assembly chairman frowned and raised his left eyebrow, creating an expression of disapproval. The priest thought it contrived; his decision already made.

"I believe Fox is the one, we all do, but he's young and untested. I have your report, Father Dominico, but I'd like to hear your personal assessment of him."

The priest nodded and tried to relax his shoulders. Testing Fox meant putting him into action with all the possible ramifications that could follow.

"As you are aware, we created surrogate parents for Fox after the death of his own. We used these people to control his childhood development, creating the kind of individual that could achieve our goals."

The chairman interjected, waving his right hand around in circles.

"Your report indicates that Fox has some dubious sources of income, which you've described as illegal. He also seems to be particularly aggressive with little semblance of empathy?"

The priest nodded his head in agreement. He manipulated these reports. More accurately, he lied in every one of them. He achieved this by omitting certain facts pertaining to behaviour. Fox remained complicated. When it came to violence, he reacted in the extreme; aggression returned times two.

At ten years of age, he grappled with a group of young Lebanese migrants who tried to rob him. He fought bravely against five much larger boys and almost died as a result. He received a knife wound on his left cheek, a fractured skull, a deep stab wound to his right buttock and an arm injury, inflicted by a metal bar; the perpetrator repeatedly smashing his left arm and elbow, which resulted in multiple fractures.

The on-duty emergency registrar at Chelsea and Westminster Hospital ran to the point of exhaustion that night. With little to no help, he couldn't cope with the human flotsam and jetsam from that Friday evening's fight-club. He stemmed the blood flow and took x-rays of Tom's skull and arm, but the patient waited a further six hours for treatment on his fractures. The doctor plastered the arm, but didn't pin it. Tom recovered, but could never fully straighten it again.

The priest sighed as he remembered the damage.

The knife wound to his face healed quickly enough, but it left him with a three centimetre scar, which changed his otherwise gentle appearance; adding a hint of danger.

After that incident, the priest secretly made arrangements for Tom. He just happened to meet a young man known as Jimmy Omagra; an up and coming star in the world of martial arts. They became friends and trained under the direction of the same man; Sensei Martin Omagra – *Fifth Dan*, Jimmy's father. After seven years of Shorinjiryu instruction, Tom refused to participate in any official events, but reports indicated that he could defeat his friend and every other member of the Dojo, including the Sensei. The priest knew this to be no easy task with Jimmy Omagra recently winning the 'British Open Karate Championships', for the eighth year running; rating him second in the world.

You're an enigma, Tom Fox.

Despite being compelled to stand up for himself and others, against any bullies, the priest knew the truth about Tom's fighting abilities.

He's all courage, but, like me, he hates violence. The murder of your parents will do that to a person.

"Yes, Mr Chairman, he's as aggressive as we need him to be. He's ready."

The chairman nodded and raised the Fox report; waving it at the priest.

"And what about his intellect? You indicate that everything depends on his capabilities and our ability to manipulate him. Some of the information in this report conflicts with those needs. For instance, it says here that he is exceedingly bright, yet his grades over the years don't support that assessment."

The priest remained expressionless. The truth regarding Fox's learning and cognitive abilities remained a significant negative, which might unduly influence the Assembly Council; this he didn't want.

Early IQ scores rated Fox in the highest echelon of intellect; only a significant brain could produce a score of one hundred and sixty five, yet he continued to struggle academically. The priest quickly determined the extent of this dilemma; information he never included in any report to the Assembly.

He hired a private psychologist by the name of Doctor Robert James, to determine the specifics. His report showed central nervous system dysfunction in the form of specific learning disorders. He found that head trauma may have caused some cognitive impairment at an early age. A subsequent lack of academic support, from all aspects of his environment added to this situation. He didn't appear to have a problem with input or integration; only the storage and output areas seemed affected. This meant his memory could sometimes cause problems in processing his thoughts into language.

Doctor James classified Fox as having a disorder referred to in an overarching way as Dysphasia, which he classified as a partial degree of impairment. The diagnosis also included Dysgraphia, which explained Fox's inability to spell correctly on one day and not on another, and Anomic Aphasia, which caused him intermittent problems with remembering the names of buildings, movies and frequently used items.

Tom Fox understood the deepest complexities of philosophy and scientific theory, yet on many occasions, couldn't remember the name of a friend.

Doctor James explained that Fox's subsequent emotional, behavioural and social problems might well be a negative consequence of his Dysphasia. He quoted *Zebat & Hibrow (2042)*: In the case of the British prison population and in particular violent inmates; twenty four out of thirty suffered from learning disorders, which were not in any way related to IQ.

The priest closed his eyes and nodded; happy with the summation of his thoughts.

"Yes, Mr Chairman, Fox could be defined as street smart. This is a reflection of his upbringing. His poor results are primarily due to a severe lack of parental reinforcement with regard to academics. I believe his abilities are worth our level of risk. Fox is the perfect conduit to our success."

"Yes, yes, but can we realistically achieve this? Given these current incidents, the board needs to be assured that our goal can be safely accomplished."

"If Mr Vogel's spy has your trust, Antonio, then yes, it can be accomplished and earlier than we'd previously planned. It's an opportunity that we can't easily discard.'

"I disagree, Mr Chairman."

Both men looked at Frederick Vogel with surprise.

"This is not an acceptable risk. We must remove this threat at once. These incidents tell us that our opposition are now aware of his worth."

The priest squeezed his lips together. The Assembly's head of security remained a servant in this company. He knew the required protocol, which meant he interrupted with a purpose. Vogel played the opportunist. If he got to Fox first, then he could own the information himself and only God knew what might happen, if that cold-hearted bastard discovered the location of the Prize.

Chapter Three

Tom hurried through the thick morning fog and it swirled around him. He could hear people and vehicles, and at times caught brief glimpses of them through the murk. This suited his purpose. He didn't want to be recognised and no-one could follow him.

He continued walking until an imposing red-brick building emerged out of the mist. As he approached, the expansive double archway rose above him with a metal sign attached to the top, which read: 'Squatter's Flat Station'.

Tom remembered the decrepit state of the entrance. Eight years of disuse, scattered clumps of pigeon droppings, and the refuse from countless vagrants, caused a lot of filth.

Come on, Tom. Keep concentrating, just for a little longer.

He searched about for the tunnel entrance and any signs of danger. Everything remained the same as his last visit. Old slabs of timber and rusty sheets of corrugated iron covered the doorways, windows and ticketing booths.

He crept towards the east tunnel and tugged at the tin barrier at precisely the right place. It moved just enough for him to push through. He fumbled in the darkness for his miniature Mag-lite, twisted the metal shaft and the tunnel became visible. As he looked around, he realised that his body ached from tension and his brain felt as foggy as the dank environment outside.

He looked up at the dripping walls. Graffiti covered most of the surfaces. Just above his head, a religious slogan claimed God to be a murderous despot, only loving the rich.

He stifled a laugh.

The rich of London acted like Gods, so he supposed it held some semblance of truth. His neighbourhood's only blessings involved violence, depravity and suffering.

Tom found the driest piece of concrete not covered with faeces or broken glass and tried to make himself comfortable. As he lowered himself to the floor, he wondered about that; the idea of being comfortable. It didn't seem to fit with his reality; a double murder, probable gaol and the possibly of his own, violent death.

Yeah. Very comforting.

His chest hurt as he sucked in a breath. He tried to stop the unwanted thoughts, but the same images kept returning; his date, Jacqueline and the youth in the long dark coat; their eyes searching, questioning, asking him why.

He took another deep breath and tried to think of something else.

Then he remembered the letter. For the past hour, every time he moved, he felt it like a hypersensitive part of his anatomy.

He removed the envelope from his pocket and brought it out into the beam of his torch. Despite his impatience, he opened it and removed the contents with reverence. As he unfolded the paper, the memory of bloodied teeth filled him with revulsion.

Tom,

My name is Noah. We need to meet. I have something of great interest to you. There is a bookshop near your house, on the corner of Queen's Avenue and Lawrence Street, called Bartholomew's Books. Be there tomorrow at precisely nine in the morning.

If you think to ignore this message, then consider this; you are not and have never been Tom McKnight. That is because your entire life is a lie and I can prove it. Don't be late and don't let anyone follow you.

Tom felt let down.

Adoption ... Really?

He couldn't stand his angry, mindless parents. Only the law kept him under their control, forbidding him to leave their care until he reached the age of twenty-one.

Tom allowed the letter to fall to the ground.

Damned nonsense.

Killings didn't generally happen over long-standing adoption issues, which meant the deaths must be random and unrelated?

He remembered her words, 'You'll never get away from me. I know who you are. I'll find you no matter where you go.' She knew him. That made it related.

Why did the woman reveal herself? Hell. Why kill someone for delivering an impotent letter?

A more pertinent question remained; what could he do about it?

I can't leave, that's for sure.

Friends or the ability to sustain himself didn't exist outside of the East End. This left him with only one choice; stay and discover his enemies.

Tom stiffened. He heard a scuffling sound.

He raised the torch, reached out and sought a piece of broken concrete, which he launched in the direction of the noise. A thud and a screech echoed down the tunnel, as the rat scurried for the cover of darkness.

Tom grinned and tried to refocus his thoughts.

This Noah may have the answers.

He sent the young man to warn him. He wrote the letter. Despite the risk, Tom knew he must attend the meeting.

Chapter Four

The priest held his breath as he watched the chairman raise his hand for silence.

"Yes, the danger's real, Frederick, but I agree with Dominico … In principle. We are the protectors of our Mother the Church. As such, we cannot forget our sworn undertaking. The return of God's True Ordained Order for this world is our mission and I believe that Tom Fox is the pathway to that end. That said, if I take this to the Assembly Council, I need something tangible. I need proof of success."

The priest perceived the chairman's true meaning.

If it all goes to shit, the bastard needs someone to blame. Alright, it's about time I delivered my coup de grace.

"Let me make myself perfectly clear, Mr Chairman. It can be done and with minimal risk. Our original plan required manipulation and enforced coercion, but the spy in the PMSG presents us with a unique advantage. We can be reasonably sure that this subversive group is trying to recruit Fox. So we use them. We even help them."

"No. You're joking. You're suggesting we help the enemy. They could destroy us."

The priest felt his shoulders tighten; Vogel's interjections continued to disregard long-standing protocols and the chairman did nothing.

"Calm down, Frederick. The PMSG are the perfect vehicle. Through your spy, we'll have the opportunity to instantly monitor all outcomes."

The priest glared at both men, before continuing.

"We'll drive Fox into total dependence on them. We can then direct every movement from then on, forcing them to find the Prize for us."

"And, if anything goes wrong?"

The priest recognised the threat behind the question. Vogel's hatred for him remained palpable; as obvious as the man's ambition.

He turned away from the security man and focused his attention on the chairman.

"If anything goes wrong, we can instigate a thorough clean-up operation. We simply utilise Vogel's spy and eliminate the problem from the inside."

The chairman adjusted his great bulk and thrust his head forward in concurrence.

"I agree, Dominico, and I'm sure my colleagues on the Assembly Council will also agree. We must find the Prize. However, if we lose control, then Frederick has my full authority to clean-up any mess."

The three men nodded and exchanged parting pleasantries without conviction.

———

Vogel scrutinised his two superiors as they left the room. He despised them, particularly the priest. He knew both of these men served only themselves. Like him, each grasped at this unprecedented opportunity. Tom Fox remained a treasure beyond reckoning. If he could capture him without the Assembly's knowledge, it would only be a matter of time before he forced the truth out of him.

As he pondered this, a flutter of movement broke his concentration. A Red Admiral Butterfly floated to a stop on the table in front of him.

"How-the-hell …?"

He watched with amusement, as it flew toward him and landed on the back of his hand. Without any fear, it opened and closed its wings and Vogel noticed the deception in colour; dull brown on the underside, yet the upper portions portrayed markings of white and black, and glowed with vivid red and orange. He coughed out a rasping laugh of appreciation. Like him, this organism chose what personality it presented to its enemies.

"You've defeated my entire security network, little one."

With exceptional speed, he flipped his hand in a clockwise direction and caught the butterfly between his thumb and forefinger. He squeezed and smiled, as the tiny creature's life oozed out between his fingers.

"Nobody defeats me."

He laughed again.

Fools.

They thought they owned this game, but he refused to be a servant. When Fox became his, then no-one could stop him … He'd own it all.

Chapter Five

Tom noticed the dilapidated state of the bookshop as he edged his way in past the proprietor. A thick layer of dust covered every surface including the floor, which carried so much grime that it appeared to be natural earth. He couldn't see anyone else inside the building, so he pretended to fill in time, searching through the mishmash of bookshelves that stretched up all the way to the roof.

"Tom."

As Tom tried to turn, he stumbled and pulled several books from the shelf in an effort to rebalance; one striking the new arrival in the side of the head. He looked back at the man as he brushed the dust from his clothing. He expected him to be white. In this world, black men rarely held positions of power.

"You're Noah?"

The man nodded towards the rear of the building.

"Follow me."

Noah turned, swinging his powerful shoulders around in the opposite direction. He moved quickly, despite the beer belly that hung over his bandy legs.

Tom felt anger redden his face.

"No. Not before you tell me who killed her."

The man turned back and frowned.

"Don't stop. Just keep moving to the back. Then I'll tell you as much as I can."

"Yeah, like I'm not supposed to be Tom McKnight?"

"We can give you back your true identity, but from here on your choices become difficult."

"This is such bullshit. My parents aren't real and I'm not who I think I am?"

"Yes."

"Hey look, I'm not worth ripping off, alright. I don't have anything you'd want."

Their conversation ceased, as several people entered the store and sidled their way into the adventure section.

A tense silence fell between them.

Tom held Noah's steady gaze, but allowed his peripheral vision the opportunity to scrutinise the shorter, stockier man. He seemed likable. Streaks of grey coloured his dark hair, which receded above the temples, making his jovial looking face appear bulky. A prominent beak-like nose dominated his features, with large black eyes and long feminine lashes adding a softer contrast. Tom discerned a gentle nature, yet the man's entire persona conveyed strength.

"Alright, lad, let's get to the point. The people you know as your parents are impostors. They're not your real family. You were born in Australia. Your mother's an Aussie and your father's a Yank."

Smiling, he held up both of his hands with the palms up and shrugged his shoulders; as if this gesture proved his statement.

"Your pretend father and his sister are illegal immigrants. They're remnants from a bad time in Ireland and wanted over most of Europe."

"Brother and sister …? How do you know this?"

The man handed Tom several sheets of official Europol mug shots. One for his surrogate father and another for the man's sister; the woman he'd known as his mother. The third sheet contained lists of their unlawful behaviour, including terrorist activities and murder.

Tom felt his face flush. He became aware of a hand squeezing his shoulder and he pushed it aside. Terrorists? Murderers? These words didn't belong in his world.

"So if they're not my parents, then who is?"

"You get that information when we have an agreement."

"Yeah, right. Just tell me who they are and what you know about the killings."

Tom experienced a moment of desperation. He needed answers. Not being a McKnight didn't bother him; it felt like relief; a kindness, yet an irrelevance compared to his current situation.

Another two shoppers drifted into their aisle, which only added to his frustration. He looked over at Noah, who nodded towards a smaller area to their left; a section provided for readers.

"I'll give you some of the information, but it comes at a cost."

Tom closed his eyes and shook his head.

"Here comes the rub."

"Wake up, lad. You're in trouble. Yes, the courier belonged to me. He's dead … because of you."

Tom tried to shut out the images, but the memory of the young man's terrible demise forced its way back into his mind.

"My organisation is willing to give you protection, but you'll have to earn it. We'll need your assistance with certain matters."

"And what if I don't?"

"I know what you're thinking, Tom. You'll just forget the whole thing and hide. That's a mistake. Whoever killed your friend and my man, knew their business. They'll find you, use you and kill you, lad. If you want to survive, your only real choice is me."

"Bullshit. I don't have a clue what you're talking about."

"Don't play games, Tom. You've seen it with your own eyes. Killing means nothing to these people."

"You've got to be joking. Why me?"

"You get your answers when we have an agreement."

"Come on, help me out here."

Noah began to speak and Tom shifted closer. Simple answers, that's all he needed. The idea of an agreement made him suspicious. This fellow sounded convincing, but he could just as easily be his enemy.

"Alright, Tom, I'll give you this much. Your real father had an involvement in a restricted project. We're talking about weapons development that superseded everything else; it provided the ultimate power for its owner. That's why they want you so bad. You're connected to these weapons."

Noah stopped and looked around, as another reader drifted by.

"Make up your mind, Tom. I can't tell you any more than I have. Not here; we've stayed too long already."

"It sounds like crap to me."

"For God's sake, lad ..."

"Alright then, tell me who you are; who you represent. And, I want to know exactly why you're helping me and what you want in return."

Noah leaned further forward and lowered his voice.

"We're a group called the PMSG, which means 'The People's Movement for Secular Government'."

"I've heard of you. You're that anti-government group that I read about in the news ... because of ...'

Atrocities.

More words appeared in Tom's mind.

Stupidity, mistake, danger.

"Surely you realise that the papers are government owned, Tom. They only print what serves them."

Tom stood and looked around. He felt anxious. Anyone in this shop could be one of them.

"Look, you're probably right. They don't seem to be my real parents, but I'm no radical either. Please. Don't contact me anymore. I don't want your help. I don't need anyone's help."

Tom hurried out of the store and set off along the familiar putrid streets that led to his old residence. He knew of several places to hide, but first he needed to confront the people who pretended to be his parents. They knew something, or they knew someone who did. He needed answers. Even now, that hellcat of a woman could be following him.

Chapter Six

Isobel tried to duck away from the wet leaves that evaded her scarf and attacked the only exposed portion of her face. She retaliated; flaying an open hand at the intrusion. She hated the wind. It penetrated through every layer of clothing, freezing her skin.

What the hell happened to spring?

As she tried to imagine gorgeous sunshine warming her face, the youthful countenance of another filled her vision.

"Good morning, Isobel."

The young man stumbled in his haste to open the door for her. She gnashed her teeth and tried not to frown. Men acted so foolishly in her presence. 'Your eyes are like jewels; you're so beautiful'.

Bullshit.

Rampant hormones made her attractive to men. She knew what they wanted; what all men wanted.

She looked for her reflection in the glass door and winced.

Damn freak.

She recalled her mother's comforting lies. 'You're petite, my dear. Not tiny'.

What a load of rubbish.

She weighed only thirty-nine and three quarter kilos. Even as a woman of nineteen, strangers treated her like they might a ten-year old.

She remembered standing naked in front of her bedroom mirror; never feeling beautiful, never feeling sexy; just hoping for a transformation; a miracle. She conjured many tall, curvaceous women, always imagining herself bursting with confidence, but when her eyes opened, there stood the same 'twig' with the tiny breasts and the protruding ribs.

She felt almost ill comparing her imagined self with the fleshless body beneath her clothing; a creature whose skinny legs created a gap between her thighs, a hand's width apart. This made her pubic bone seem larger than what she considered to be normal. She looked prepubescent, with almost no pubic hair and noticeable weblike veins flowing under her translucent skin.

I'm grotesque and horrible.

She glared at the young man as he opened the door for her.

"Look, I'm paying you to be a technician not a dim-witted doorman."

Isobel ignored his mumbled reply and entered. She allowed herself a moment to take in her surroundings.

God, I love this place.

The old Sydney Road building remained a link to her past; to her parents. It once accommodated a small furniture factory, with some offices and a showroom in the front upstairs portion and a production line operating on the ground floor.

Her father and his partner converted the two storeys of decaying red brick, exposed hardwood beams and rusty corrugated iron, into a high-tech fabric-testing laboratory.

"Excuse me, Miss Kite …"

Damn it … Leave me alone. I don't want your attention.

Isobel headed towards the back of the building, avoiding all conversation with speed. She maintained an angry expression as she proceeded, ignoring everyone in the room. As she reached the rear of the building, she allowed her eyes to follow the low ceiling and exposed pipes to where they turned upwards, disappearing into the heights of the interior. She began to relax. Here, her staff tested fabric strength and durability; it felt like a second home to her.

She mounted the steps to the mezzanine platform, which ran along the back wall of the building. It once housed spare parts and unused equipment, but she cleaned it up, glassed in the front and added the necessary equipment for an efficient office.

Efficient ...?

She frowned at the thought. She couldn't stand the accountancy side of the business, nor could she stomach the endless river of administrative duties.

"You're late, Isobel Kite."

The woman standing by the door smiled, but meant it as a rebuke.

"We'll need to work through some of these figures before my appointment at the bank."

Isobel tried to return her accountant's smile.

"Look, Mrs Cooper, is this really necessary? I've given you all of the paperwork and I'm really busy this morning."

"Yes. I'm afraid it is. You can't put this off any longer, Isobel. We need to talk about your financial situation. Frankly, these figures don't present the business particularly well. I need to know your reasoning around some of your financial decisions, so I can try to negotiate your position with the bank."

"Great."

Isobel unlocked her office door and offered Jan Cooper the only chair other than her own.

Old cow.

She blamed her accountants for the demise of her company's finances; sacking her previous advisor in favour of her latest financial hope. She needed good advice; guidance that never seemed to eventuate. A condescending shake of her head remained Mrs Coopers only contribution.

Isobel attempted to ease past her visitor towards her side of the desk. She felt dazed and unfocused and she didn't notice the obstacle. At the last moment, she tried to stop her momentum by turning her body, but couldn't avoid crashing into an open filing cabinet drawer.

"Ow, that hurt."

She tried to back up and rebalance, but her wet shoes gained no traction and she went down.

"Oh God, Isobel, are you all right?"

Isobel hung off the cabinet drawer; her watchband caught on its edge. It held and her arm stretched down to a body sprawled across the floor.

"Help me up will you, I'm stuck."

Isobel tried to laugh, but her composure gave way to anger.

"Bloody hell. This isn't a particularly good omen is it?"

She fell into her chair and attempted to rub the pain from her wrist. She knew what Mrs Cooper intended to say, but she didn't want to hear it. She preferred denial rather than suffering the guilt associated with her inadequacies.

"Isobel, I know how much this place means to you, but you just can't afford the past anymore. Your present contracts got tendered at ridiculous prices and now there's not enough equity, or possible future income to stop the inevitable."

"The inevitable. That's blunt."

Isobel noticed her hands shaking. She pushed them further under her desk.

"Surely, it's not that bad. There has to be something you can do?"

"I'll try, but based on these figures, I don't think any bank is going to offer you another overdraft. I'm sorry."

Isobel continued massaging her swollen wrist. She couldn't give up without a fight, but the *how to proceed* eluded her. Her position seemed hopeless. Poor management skills hindered any real opportunities for success. She excelled at science and mathematics, but as an administrator … she knew her failings.

Isobel sighed with relief when her accountant finally left. Alone, she could think. She belonged here and she couldn't see herself anywhere else. Eviction removed her only remaining connection with her late parents, especially her father.

She lifted her wrist to catch the light and her arm began to throb. She could see a red welt, but the skin didn't appear to be broken.

"Stupid ugly thing."

She tried to smile. Her father presented her with the broken timepiece not long before he died. Looking at it usually made her laugh.

Bloody worthless rubbish.

The watch; a Seiko, belonged to her father's business partner. Her father asked her to wear it until his partner's son arrived to pick it up. If nothing else, she remained faithful to that promise. She wore the awful thing every day and wondered about its owner. It embarrassed her sometimes. She spent so much time imagining him that he became a fully-developed fantasy in her mind.

She needed decent project funding, not an imaginary man. She felt silly believing he might come.

She sat back in her chair, sucked in some air and sighed.

"Ah, Mr Fox, my imaginary knight in shining armour."

She frowned at her depressing recurrent thinking.

She knew these to be strange thought processes, considering her distrust of men; even approaching the periphery of her memories regarding any male other than her father, made her tense and sick with loathing.

She remembered her thirteen-year-old self; so inadequate, just a baby girl compared to her female acquaintances and classmates. She hated the 'in girls', they collected boyfriends so easily and teased her with the secrets of their liaisons. She understood the bullying in their embellishments. They elevated themselves by keeping her in her place. It made her feel worse than nothing.

Then a miracle occurred. Jenna Jovanovich, one of the prettiest girls in her school, befriended her; a boon that instantly inducted her into the same 'in crowd'. She didn't care that her new glamour-girl status arose out of association only.

The following week, Jenna invited her to an impromptu, after-school party, which Isobel accepted without hesitation. It meant that she could be late home and have some explaining to do, but she couldn't turn down her first invitation; she might never receive another.

When she arrived at Jenna's house, there didn't seem to be any party, just two boys drinking Vodka Cruisers and no parents. Isobel felt scared, wanting to leave, but Jenna pulled her by the arm, pressuring her to join them. After only one glass, she felt tipsy and began to relax; the alcohol creating feelings of excitement.

A boy held her hand and stroked her neck. She recalled Daniel's nice even features and sandy hair; a hunk interested in her. She also remembered his good-looking friend, Roberto, lying on the lounge room floor kissing Jenna.

The rape took place in the Jovanovich's master bedroom.

It began with a kiss that made her tiny body shiver. Then everything changed. Somehow it felt wrong, which the boy confirmed when she attempted to pull away from him. The more she struggled the more violent he became.

"Please ... No ... Stop."

Daniel's placid features morphed into a grotesque angry mask, as he pinned her to the bed and tore at her clothes. Isobel screamed when he entered her. The pain burnt like alcohol rubbed into an open wound. She tried to fight him off, but couldn't move. Then she remembered Roberto and Jenna materialising in the room and she called out to them for help.

She heard them laugh at her. Then she heard Jenna's shrieking encouragement to her lover.

"You give it to her, Robbie. Hurt her. Hurt the little bitch."

Isobel tried to roll away as the participants changed position, but couldn't break free. Now Roberto grunted above her, holding her down with a hand squeezing her throat; his sweat and saliva dripping over her face. She felt too numb and tired to continue fighting.

Isobel reported the incident to the local police, but the humiliation hurt her almost as much as the attack. She discovered that victims of rape didn't exist here. Sydney's Special Religious Police viewed such cases, as promiscuity escalating out of control. She remembered the comments and the mocking smirks; women who 'led men on' got what they deserved.

They think I'm common. They think I'm a slut.

She felt dirty saying it. She forced her eyes closed and attempted to remove the memories. In her more generous moments, she accepted the theory that some men were good, but she struggled to maintain her optimism. The world seemed to conspire with her darker beliefs and prove them right every time. Despite this, she knew her father to be a wonderful man, which she supposed provided some hope for mankind.

I don't want anyone's help.

She knew that no one person, other than herself could make a difference to her circumstances. Nothing could change the events of her life, especially someone she didn't know. She placed her forehead into the palm of her hand and examined the old timepiece.

"You're as ugly as I am. We're meant for each other."

She smiled bitterly.

Her heart and the stupid watch held an unwanted bond; neither seemed to work after the death of her parents.

Chapter Seven

Tom stood in the shadows, taking in every detail of the tenement houses lining each side of his street. Every home looked identical on Queen's Avenue. He couldn't see a single street number under the layers of grime. Only subtle differences of filth announced each residence to their owner.

He felt tired; anxious. He needed to confront the people masquerading as his parents; he needed answers and he couldn't wait any longer. Keeping alert for possible danger, he eased out into the sunlight towards the gutter, but hesitated as a car jerked to a halt in front of him; the rear doors flying open as several men jumped from inside. Within seconds, they surrounded him, blocking any chance of escape.

They know already? How?

Waves of adrenalin surged through his body. He felt like a trapped animal; panicked; desperate for a means of escape, then he heard a voice coming from the dark interior of the vehicle.

"My name is Frederick Vogel. I'm assisting the Special Religious Police with their investigation."

"Yeah, so what?"

"So, either you get into this vehicle right now, or you suffer the consequences. One way or another, you're coming with me."

For a brief moment, the police waited, as did the man in the car. Windows opened all along Queen's Avenue and people began to gather on the pavement.

"Get in Fox. I'm not going to ask you again."

Tom noticed a tough looking man alight from another vehicle and strut towards him.

"Piss off. I haven't done anything wrong."

Their moment of bargaining ceased. Surrounded and outnumbered, Tom gave up any notion of a possible escape. He took two quick steps to evade the nearest policemen and climbed into the car.

As they drove away, he noticed the crowd of people on the street. With the SRP vehicle a safe distance away, they jeered and shook fists at the air.

Very brave ... Thanks for your help.

They travelled west through the mid-morning traffic along the M4, which allowed Tom some time to consider his current circumstances. His demise appeared the most likely scenario. Death via the noose, or delivered by a sinister woman with auburn hair; either way, he could see no future. He shuddered; overwhelmed by a feeling of terror.

"What's this about? Why the hell have you picked me up?"

Vogel turned towards the policeman on Tom's right.

"Shut him up."

The policemen slapped the back of Tom's head with the palm of his hand; creating an explosion in his brain and a gush of nausea.

Tom glared back at the man in charge.

"Asshole."

This time Vogel twisted around in his seat and returned the young man's stare. The eye contact made Tom feel uncomfortable.

Just one look into Vogel's indifferent grey irises confirmed his opinion.

This one's dangerous in the extreme. I'll have to be careful.

"What do you want from me?"

Vogel didn't answer for some time.

"Officer. What did I tell you?"

A fist cannoned into the side of Tom's head, causing pain and disorientation, and a detached feeling in the brain.

"No more talking."

Their tyres screeched. Tom bounced off the shoulder of a policemen as their vehicle veered off the motorway, heading south through Harlington and into an area being suffocated by pollution-puffing factories and smoke stacks.

Tom noticed a road sign with the heading: 'Heathrow', but as he twisted around attempting to read the rest of it, the driver braked hard, throwing him forward against the front seat. They seemed to have arrived at their destination. Tom followed everyone's gaze to the warehouse at the end of the driveway. It looked dilapidated. Every window appeared to be broken and rust covered most of the tin surface of the building.

"Get out and follow me."

Vogel strode ahead and entered the building first, followed by Tom and the three remaining men. They shoved him through the door and into the darkness. When his eyes adjusted, he noticed that the warehouse seemed larger from the inside. Light streamed in from holes in the ceiling and upper windows, which highlighted the broken glass littering the floor.

"You. Wait. Don't move."

Tom turned back towards the doorway. He felt a moment of confusion; the SRP wore earmuffs and goggles with dark lenses.

"What's going on?"

No-one answered.

A hand grasped the back of Tom's neck, forcing him forward and he stumbled further into the interior of the shed. He tried to straighten, but another push drove him to his knees amongst the broken glass.

He became aware of movement. A flickering of light appeared in his peripheral vision, to his left; reflecting off the tin. He turned towards the source.

Am I dreaming? Could this be real?

He gawked at the glowing shape suspended high above the floor at the southern end of the shed; monstrous in its proportions. He tried to turn his face from the light, but some kind of force prevented him from moving.

He went rigid. The creature behind the radiance beamed malice at him. It raised its arms and the light around it sparked and crackled; growing in intensity; overwhelming him. Behind the glare, its lips parted and it screamed with a keenness that drove Tom backwards onto the broken fragments of glass.

Then hands grabbed his ankles and dragged him across the warehouse floor. He felt stunned and lifeless when they lifted him and threw him into a smaller room.

Tom heard laughter. Somehow, he sat at a table across from a smiling Frederick Vogel and an enormous older man with oily hair.

"I see you've met our glowing friend."

Vogel's smile dissolved; his expression turning hateful. Tom recognised his sneer as viciousness; it conveyed danger, like standing too close to the edge of a precipice.

Tom thought about saying something like, 'why the hell am I here?' Instead, he just stared straight ahead at nothing.

"It's a shock, isn't it?"

He waited for Tom to respond and became annoyed when he didn't react. He banged his fist on the desk.

"We know who you are."

"I don't have a clue what you're talking about."

Vogel eased back into his plush leather chair and tapped his fingers on the desk.

"I've got you by the balls, Fox. You're the son of a traitor; a co-conspirator and we've caught you consorting with an anti-government group."

Tom noticed Vogel's teeth appear through his smile, turning it into a grimace.

"You've made a mistake. I'm not the person you think I am."

"Don't be smug with me. I can have you hanged."

Tom didn't respond, he didn't know how to. This day became more surreal by the moment.

"Well?"

Again, Tom didn't answer.

"We know you're working on behalf of your late father. All you have to do is give us what we're after and you can go free."

Tom's thoughts felt like swirling water. Reality followed patterns that he could accept and understand, but this ... He looked at the man accusing him from across the table and realised that he hadn't mentioned the killings.

Good. Something positive.

With an effort, he staggered to his feet and his wooden chair crashed to the ground.

"Look, I can't even remember my real father. You can't hold me. I'm outta here ... I'm going home."

Home ...?

He remembered ... Home didn't exist. He felt completely drained. Defeated, he stooped, picked up the chair and sat back down.

"You're a clown. You're going to give me what I want, or ..."

Vogel ceased talking as the enormous man beside him rose to his feet with a series of grunts. As he straightened, he attempted to gather the few escaping strands of hair that hung in front of his face.

Vogel stood and nodded as the man left the office.

He remained standing for several seconds staring at the door, before turning his attention back to Tom. Then he leaned across the table, smiled and slapped him across the side of his face.

The shock came in stinging waves. Tom rubbed at his face and felt his anger rise.

"Do your best. I've got nothing else to say to you."

"Really ...?"

As Vogel returned to his seat he slid his hand inside his jacket pocket and removed a pre-World War Three, Beretta automatic pistol, putting it on the table just out of Tom's reach. He placed a single nine-millimetre bullet beside the gun and sat back in his chair. Then his face bunched into a smirk, as he made a pretend gun out of his hand and pointed it at Tom.

"I'm going to make you an offer. So listen carefully."

Tom tried to hold Vogel's stare, but couldn't. He felt powerless and looked away.

"You've got three days to deliver your father's plans. If you back out for any reason, I will personally take up that bullet and blow your stupid brains out. Is that clearly understood?"

"Yeah, whatever …"

Tom hadn't understood at all.

Plans. What plans?

"You don't seem that eager to please me. Perhaps some time with our friend out there, might change your attitude."

Vogel nodded and without a word, his men replaced their goggles and re-covered their ears.

"If you manage to survive, don't forget our arrangement."

Tom didn't resist when they dragged him from the office. Nor did he fight back when they beat him and threw him onto the warehouse floor. How could he fight the inevitable? Death remained the one truth that no-one could deny.

He rose to his feet, turned and searched for the glowing figure.

"Alright, you bastard …"

The creature remained in the same position, hovering fifteen metres from where he stood.

"Let's get it over with."

The colossus shrieked; pulsing brilliant light and without perceptible movement appeared right in front of Tom. It captured him before he could manufacture a single thought.

An electrical current engulfed him; tongues of blue lightning inflicting agony; pain that tore through him with no resistance. He could smell his flesh burning and his torso shivered, like a fish on a line.

Tom didn't feel his body hit the floor. His eyes opened on impact and he saw a shimmer reflecting off the shattered glass. He could also see smoke rising from his clothing and blood pouring from his cut hands. Then his eyes closed and the blackness came.

Chapter Eight

Noah struggled through the small opening in the fence at the rear of the building. Every year, keeping fit became increasingly difficult. Despite the rigours of his life, he estimated that he remained a good fifteen kilos over his preferred weight.

He hated his beer belly. He understood the calories equation well enough. If he ate more than his body could burn off in the course of a day's energy usage, then his system stored the excess as fat and deposited it around his middle.

There appeared to be an easy solution. Stop drinking fabulous red wine in large quantities and refrain from eating anything that tasted terrific and he would soon look like an athlete.

He shook his head in disgust.

That's not likely.

His communicator began to buzz and a flashing green light appeared above its screen. This warned him that his team followed Vogel and the SRP from the warehouse.

Noah closed his eyes and relaxed his shoulders.

They're coming. Just hang on a little while longer, young man. I've got no use for a corpse.

He sat in the shadows, scrutinising the target area from a second story window at the far end of Queen's Avenue. Hidden inside the disused building, he focused his Tasco field glasses, clarifying the targeted image that lay seven hundred and twenty-one metres to the north.

"I've got you, young man."

He spotted the black SRP vehicle arriving in Burrow's Street; a narrow lane running west off Queen's Avenue. It jerked to a stop, directly adjacent to Tom's old residence.

"You're as predictable as ever, Vogel. You've got nasty blood in your veins."

He felt anger grow hot on his face. Dumping Tom like that demonstrated his adversary's sick sense of humour. Local people distrusted anyone surviving an SRP interview and treated them accordingly.

Noah discerned movement. The rear door of the black Ford Ventura sedan opened and a body flopped to the pavement.

"Well done, lad. You made it."

The enemy sped away as the young man tried to stand. Noah could see smoke rising from his burnt clothing. He could only watch, as Tom limped away.

He heard a beeping sound and felt for his communicator.

"Noah. We think he's heading towards the abandoned railway station at Squatter's Flat. The team will be in place before he gets there."

"Good. Keep alert and don't make contact. This could be a setup."

Tom's choice of location created a predicament for Noah. Until they could eliminate the possibility of enemy involvement, they couldn't make a direct approach for fear of a trap.

"Also, monitor all traffic and search for any type of electronic signal in or out of the area."

A solid darkness permeated the east platform. Noah ordered several members of the PMSG to spread through the tunnels on both the western and eastern side of the station.

Only the faintest light from the stairwell, allowed Noah to see Tom creeping towards the old Station Master's Office.

The boy seemed to be a good choice. His job required him to deliver a secure mobile phone to the room. This enabled Noah to have direct contact with Tom, without fear of detection.

"What are you doing? You silly boy?"

The youth pulled on the door of the hut several times, turned back in Noah's direction, shook his head twice, then pelted the phone at the small office window. Noah could hear the pane of glass shatter from his position.

"You little ..."

The street boys could be useful, but not always reliable. He began dialling.

"Come on, Tom. Pick up the phone."

"Hello. Who is this?"

"Tom, yes. It's Noah ... from the bookshop. Are you alright, lad? Tell me about your injuries."

Tom sighed. Even sympathy from a wanted activist, seemed better than suffering this alone.

"I'm burnt and bleeding, but I'm alright ... well, apart from something sharp in my chest. It hurts when I breathe."

"Tell me what happened."

Tom sat up, using his elbows for leverage; his hands still contained shards of glass. He attempted to explain his meeting with Vogel, but the pain in his lungs made it hard going.

He frowned with an unwanted realisation.

I'm trusting a radical, a fugitive.

He tried to smile, but his entire being hurt. He didn't care anymore, no matter what Noah's motivation might be.

"You have to come to us, lad. You know they'll kill you if you don't."

How could a lifetime of running from the police, be a sane choice? Yet, these same police threatened his life and caused this pain?

"Yeah … Great. I haven't got a choice other than you."

———————

Noah guided Tom west along the east tunnel, until they reached the entrance to an adjoining maintenance shaft; its red steel door left unlocked and ajar. They entered and climbed up a steep stairwell with several landings, before finally reaching the surface. From here, Noah directed a smaller team to an old blue Toyota sedan, with faded, powdery oxidisation on the boot, roof and hood. Several small dents on the bonnet and left front fender, added to the look of disrepair, helping to make it nondescript enough to dissolve into the normality of the daily traffic.

They left London, taking an erratic route through the suburbs, as a precaution against a tail. Tom sat beside Noah, while two other people rested in the back seat; a pretty blond with hair cut short like a boy's and a large man with dark features.

Tom felt embarrassed each time he cried out. The vehicle's jerky movements caused him pain.

"I'm sorry, Noah. I …"

"Just hang on, lad. The drugs will cut in soon and you won't feel so bad."

They travelled along the M3, heading south-west towards Winchester. On the outskirts, they waited forty minutes in a hidden lane for a contact to arrive. Then, after receiving further instructions, they headed into Dorset via every lane and back road imaginable.

"We've been to this lane before. We're going in circles."

"It just seems like it, Tom. Close your eyes and try to relax, and let me do the driving."

Tom felt sceptical until he spotted Noah pointing towards an increasing brightness through the front windscreen. With an effort Tom raised his head just enough to see the sign for Romsey glowing in their headlights.

"This is it. We're nearly there, lad."

Tom felt dizzy and disorientated as they headed down another obscure road, north towards Salisbury. Fifteen minutes later, they drove down a boggy driveway and arrived at a farmhouse, surrounded by enormous English Elms.

After helping drag some of the group's gear into the house, Tom slumped into a chair beside the kitchen table. He looked up at the whitewashed walls and dark timber ceiling and then across the table at Noah.

"You promised me the truth once I became committed, Noah. Well, I can't get any more committed than this ... Can I?"

"It's late and we're all tired, Tom."

"Can I, Noah?"

"No ... I suppose you can't."

"Then tell me. You seem to know more about my life than I do."

Tom saw Noah's face scrunch and crease with concentration. He looked anything but happy.

"Alright, Tom. Your father's discoveries started this whole godforsaken business."

Noah looked away from Tom and softened his voice.

"And your mother ... Well, she's still one of the most wonderful women I've met. Everyone loved her."

"That's great. Where is she, Noah?"

"She's gone, Tom. They're both gone."

"Gone? What do you mean?"

"They're dead. They've been gone from us for many years now."

Tom detected the sudden change in the room. Everyone's attention centred on him. Presumably, to see how he handled such devastating news.

What are you all looking at?

"You should've told me this before, Noah. At least give me their names."

Tom noticed the apprehension in Noah's expression; a hesitation punctuated by darting eyes and a nervous fluttering of his lashes.

"Katherine and Alexander Fox."

"*The* Alexander Fox?"

"Yes."

"We're talking about *Professor* Alexander James Fox?"

"Yes."

Tom's brain throbbed with an increase in blood flow. His eyes lost focus as did his ability to understand his feelings.

"Alexander Fox, the Satanist?"

He tried to remember how the Church described him.

"The Antichrist. The Devil's entrepreneur. The modern-day Hitler. *That* Alexander Fox?"

"Yes."

No ... This can't be true. Even little children knew this man as Mr Evil.

"Is this what you dragged me here for? To tell me my mother's dead and my father's a monster."

"There's more to this. Much more, son."

"I'm not your son. I'm no-one's son."

"Tom ..."

"No. You conned me. You made me think ..."

The room began to swirl and Tom felt like he might vomit. He jumped to his feet and sent his chair tumbling over the polished wooden floorboards. He heard the sound of glass breaking, but he didn't understand what that meant.

He staggered backwards as his mind began to spin round and round; a black vortex sucking him in.

"Tom ... Tom ... Tom."

He heard someone calling his name, but it receded and vanished, as he plummeted into a black pit of unconsciousness.

The abyss.

Chapter Nine

Two accidents in one morning brought traffic on the Sydney Harbour Bridge to a halt. An hour and a half later, Isobel reached her office; a journey that normally took thirty-five minutes.

Perspiration trickled down her spine, as she walked from the car park. She felt drained of energy. It seemed weird that winter could turn into summer in just a few short days without any semblance of a spring.

She rounded the car-park corner into Sydney Road and stopped.

What's all this?

A large group of people slumped about in front of her building. Isobel attempted to identify their faces, but the angle of the mid-morning sun, hurt her eyes.

She recognised the uniforms.

Hold on. They're mine ... My staff. Why the hell would they be out here in this heat?

She raised a hand to shield herself from the glare and noticed two police vehicles parked up on the curb.

"Let me past."

Isobel pushed through a group of technicians sheltering in the doorway. She entered, spotted a police officer and signalled for him to come over.

"What's going on? Who's in charge here?"

"This is a police matter, young lady. Staff are to wait outside."

"I'll ask you again. Who's in charge here?"

The man sneered and nodded towards a woman who appeared to be twice Isobel's size in both height and girth.

"The sergeant's busy, so if you could just …"

Isobel ignored the constable and strode towards the woman.

"You must be Isobel, the owner."

The sergeant extended her hand.

"Do we know each other?"

"I've already interviewed several of your staff, they described you well enough. Please, come and sit down and we can talk. It's only natural to feel a little overwhelmed."

The sergeant led Isobel through a chaotic mess of overturned furniture, fallen racks of fabric and spilt chemical drums. The policewoman lifted two chairs from amongst the mess of broken equipment and sat down.

"I'll ask the obvious first, Isobel."

She withdrew her notebook and made a place on the only upright table, to write.

"Do you know anyone capable of doing this? Enemies or rivals perhaps."

Isobel shook her head.

"No I don't. Who would do such a thing?"

"According to your staff, there doesn't appear to be anything missing. It seems to be some sort of threat, but if that's the case, you'd have to know something about it, wouldn't you?"

"Oh please … A threat?"

The sergeant sighed.

"Not revenge then?"

Revenge. Isobel stiffened. The note of cynicism in the policewoman's voice meant she knew something.

"What do you mean?"

"Oh, I think you know exactly what I mean. People don't take this kind of risk to threaten someone without a reason."

Isobel scowled. It smelt like Jenna-bloody-Jovanovich and her pack of rapists.

"Look, Isobel, I'm not the SRP, but even an ordinary New-South-Wales coppa like myself, has a few good contacts. I know about the rape, unofficially that is, and I also know about your conviction for grievous bodily harm. A permanently scarred face and a wired-up jaw are bloody good reasons for revenge."

Isobel tried to stop the images that raced through her mind, but she couldn't hold them back.

Many months after the rape, some of her dorkier female classmates invited her to a birthday party. She accepted, not expecting any danger, but within minutes of her arrival, Jenna Jovanovich showed up with two other pretty looking vipers and set about baiting and insulting her.

"Look at my nose, bitch. The SRP did this, after you dobbed on me about some bullshit rape."

"You know it happened. You made it happen."

"That's a joke. Who'd want you?"

Isobel felt adrenalin surge through her system, but instead of moving, she froze; her body shivering with fear and embarrassment. Her mind kept screaming. Move. Escape. Run.

Oh God ...

Too late. Daniel and Roberto stood blocking the doorway. As Roberto entered, he threatened the seven other invited girls at the party.

"No-one moves and if any one of you talk, we'll kill you."

The boys took hold of her and Isobel remembered feeling a lump in her chest, the size of a fist. She tried to pull away when Jenna stepped towards her, but she couldn't move. She turned her face away from the first punch, but the second struck her on the tip of the chin, causing a sickening pain to reverberate through her head.

Jenna laughed.

"How's that feel, bitch?"

She moved in again, but before she could deliver another blow, Daniel removed his right hand from Isobel's arm and thrust it down her pants. She screamed with pain as he brutalised her. Even now, her reaction to his abuse shocked her. In that moment, all of her fear and embarrassment exploded into something wild and uncontrollable.

Isobel's scream sounded like a roar. She twisted and broke free, striking Roberto with the back of her hand. He fled from her, retreating several steps, before staring back with an expression of bewilderment. Only Daniel hung on; his silver bracelet momentarily caught in her underwear. He pulled hard and it came away. With both hands free, he reached forward, grasped the back of her dress with his left hand, and punched her in the back of the head with his right.

Isobel remembered the feeling in her head; her thoughts burnt, as if they swam in acid and her vision blurred with pain.

He screamed abuse at her and she recoiled from the strange high-pitched tone of his voice.

"I'm going to take you right here, you whore. Then … I'm going to smash your ugly head in."

Isobel reacted without conscious thought. She felt her hand make contact with a heavy rounded object that turned out to be a Vodka bottle belonging to Roberto. In a wild panic, she lashed out and the impact jarred her arm. She felt the crunch of breaking bone, as Jovanovich collapsed at her feet. The next blow struck Roberto on the crown of his skull, which broke the bottle and covered him in a spray of raspberry coloured vodka. He fell to his knees, clutching his head.

She remembered seeing Daniel in a similar position to Roberto. He knelt with his hands covering his face in a futile attempt to stem the flow of blood. It spurted through his fingers and pooled in his lap. He kept screaming the same words.

"You bitch … You rotten bitch …"

Only when she looked away from Daniel, did she notice the blood on the end of the broken bottle, which she still held firmly in her hand.

Isobel sighed and tried to shake off the loathing that came with her memories. She took several large breaths before addressing the sergeant.

"Look, lady. I picked up rubbish every weekend for a year and spent another one digging graves. They even kicked me out of school. I finished my studies through some shitty correspondence course. I think those bastards already got their revenge, don't you? This is just a coincidence. Just some morons trashing the place for fun."

Without a word, the sergeant stood and led Isobel towards the rear of the building. They climbed through the scattered debris, until they reached the entrance to Isobel's office stairwell.

"Look behind you, Isobel. There's something you should see."

Isobel turned and looked back in the opposite direction. High on the wall of the second story, were a collection of bitter words written in red paint.

Oh God ... It's the same hateful garbage they put there before they killed my father.

BEWARE TOOL OF SATAN.

Chapter Ten

An ethereal glow of golden beams streamed in through the shuttered window and in that moment just before wakefulness, it felt to Tom like the afterlife.

"It's time. Get dressed and come down stairs."

The man standing beside his bed, grinned and extended his hand.

"My name's Luther."

Tom's hand disappeared into the bulk of the man's grip.

"Don't dally, Noah's waiting."

Tom noticed the fresh bandages covering his burnt torso and lacerated hands, as he struggled from the bed. His chest hurt as he tried to stand; each breath, feeling like metal grinding against metal.

He entered the kitchen and Noah marched over to greet him.

"How are you feeling, lad?"

"Look, about last night, I felt tired and angry and ..."

"Not last night, Tom. You've missed more than a day.

A smile grew on Noah's face as several people trundled into the room. He stood and embraced each of the new arrivals.

"Come and meet the team, lad. We can talk privately later."

Noah opened his arms, encompassing all in the room.

"Tom, this is the British Group Elevens, or G11's for short."

Noah's belly shook as he began to laugh.

"You've met Luther. You also know Petra and Julius from our ride here in the car."

As he spoke, another figure strode into the room and Tom stiffened with recognition.

"Ah, Tom. This's Uta ... The Raptor."

Tom nodded towards the woman, but took a protective step backwards. The moment he saw her, his mind screamed *murderer*. Yet, no. It might not be her. Tom studied her features. This one stood slightly taller than the auburn-haired woman and her raven locks hung straight and long.

Tom looked into her eyes for any sign of recognition, but the woman didn't seem to know him.

Don't say a word. This coincidence might have unwanted consequences.

"And, this good fellow is Surat."

Tom struggled to drag his eyes from the woman and over towards the tough looking man, leaning against the doorframe.

"He's the one you run to when everything turns to shite. He's our security expert and the best in the business."

Surat straightened and glared at Tom with obvious disdain.

"I hope you're worth it, Fox. You better deliver or else ..."

Tom hated being threatened.

"Or else what?"

Surat spat on the carpet, turned and took a step towards the door before answering.

"Or else we're all dead."

Chapter Eleven

The priest examined the dark timbers and white walls of the interior without enthusiasm. The new Dead Rat Hotel on Kings Road, deceived many of its patrons, most believing the building to be hundreds of years old. He knew better.

The priest nodded his approval. He could see the man's claustrophobia in his erratic movements.

Good. He's bent over like an arthritic old woman.

The low ceilings and lack of light inside the Rat created exactly what he sought for his meeting with Vogel. The late venue swap from Rome to the southern English city of Brighton, avoided Vogel's territorial advantage.

The scoundrel can't rely on security monitoring, or intimidating assistants here.

Father Dom arrived earlier than necessary, choosing a black leather booth near the open fire, with a fine view of the white-capped waters of the Channel. This provided him with time to think and plan, and to indulge himself with a pint of Tui Pale Ale, his favourite imported New Zealand beer.

He could see Vogel wandering around the main bar area, his face downcast and anxious as he attempted to find the correct booth; his expression tightening into a sphere of scrunched lips; a pout the priest associated with cruelty and hatred.

Nothing new ... Wait ... There we go.

He spotted Vogel's eyelids blink in rapid succession, revealing uncertainty, even fear, which enhanced the priest's position. His security chief needed a lesson in compliance. Despite his dislike for the man, he needed him; his improvised plan depended on his spy. The man's obedience remained a priority.

"Nice trip, Frederick?"

"Hardly. Why here priest? What's so important?"

Father Dom glared at Vogel with as much malice as he could gather.

"You are, Frederick. You're the reason. The chairman and I are worried about your loyalty."

"Rubbish. The chairman knows where I stand."

"Don't feign innocence, Vogel."

"I don't know what you're talking about."

"You need to understand a basic truth if we're to move on and continue this arrangement."

"Is that a threat?"

"Yes, Frederick. It is."

Father Dom noticed Vogel's pupils widen and lose focus. He sat stiffly; his anger becoming greater than his phobia.

"Fool. Endangering Fox could have destroyed our entire project. You are this close to being eliminated, Frederick."

To accentuate his meaning, the priest raised his right hand, holding his thumb and forefinger close together.

"The chairman isn't a fool. After he left you at the factory, you thought to play Fox for your own advantage and he knows it. The only reason you're here and breathing is because of your spy ... and, because I believe you're still the best man for the job."

The few beams of brightness streaming in through the lead-glass window, betrayed the dampness in the visible areas of

Vogel's multi-coloured hair. He removed his grey hat, pulled a hanky from the interior of his matching grey suit and patted at his forehead.

"I don't understand you, priest."

He continued to dab at the perspiration on his brow and his teeth appeared between his lips.

"Why support me?"

The priest tried to smile and regretted it. Instead of sincerity, he could see his fake grin materialise as distrust in Vogel's reactions.

"It's our objective that's important, Frederick."

"Bullshit."

"Alright, here's how it is. I don't trust you Vogel. Not even for a minute. What I do know is that you won't be that careless again. You of all people should know the cost of betraying our employer."

This time Father Dom didn't smile at Vogel's anomaly. The man visibly relaxed; believing and feeling comfortable with the priest's distrust of him.

"Now that we've finished with that unwanted business, we can move on to more operational matters. Tell me about the girl."

The priest noticed Vogel's body begin to unstiffen and sag, as the presence of the roof once again bore down on him. His voice sounded curt as he explained the tactics they employed to recruit the Kite girl; the laboratory trashed and the slogan planted.

He stopped talking and the priest discerned his change of expression. The lines and creases in his face softening and drooping from cruelty to petulance.

"No. I don't like this plan. It's obvious. Too open. We don't need outsiders becoming involved in our business."

"The plan requires control, Frederick. We're the puppeteers. We create their actions."

The priest continued speaking to Vogel, as if instructing a child.

"We always win, because we're the ones pulling the strings."

Vogel began to raise the pitch and volume of his voice.

"No. It puts my spy in serious jeopardy. Do what you like with the Kite girl, but don't risk my spy."

"You will do what I tell you to do. Is that understood?"

Vogel scowled and didn't move.

"You have your job and I expect you to do it exactly as prescribed."

The priest maintained his eye contact with Vogel, until the security chief gave a faint nod of assent.

"It's important at this early stage that they fall for the ruse. We have to push them into complete dependence on the PMSG. There can be no way back to a normal life for either Fox, or the girl."

Father Dom sat back and quietly ignored the man opposite him. He watched the rain come in from offshore, ordered another beer and some hot chips, and collated his thoughts into a cohesive working plan.

"In every library, Frederick, there are newspaper archives. If you were to look back, you could find many articles about the Professor Fox situation. Some of those articles mention a colleague ... A priest."

The clergyman stopped talking and frowned. Vogel looked annoyed and perplexed. The priest needed to be more specific.

"Find one of those articles, Frederick. Get in touch with your spy and be sure that the old newspaper is left where Fox can find it."

The priest despised the man in front of him. He felt like reaching over, grabbing him around the neck and squeezing the life from his sour face. How many people wouldn't die if he did it? He took in a deep breath and relaxed his fingers.

"The PMSG will be compelled to make contact. Now that they have Fox, they won't know exactly how to begin. I'll be that beginning."

———————

Tom sat at the dining-room table, watching Noah stomp around the room.

"We don't go around killing people, lad."

With a wave of his arm, Noah gestured towards the other members of his team.

"Nor do we rob banks. We have benefactors that support us. Not openly, just financially."

"Does what you do make any difference?"

Tom noted the group's reaction to his question. The room became quiet and the expressions, stern.

"Yes, we're extremists. We destroy. We're here to annihilate unconscious enslavement."

He sat down at the table and looked across at Tom.

"Let me ask you a question. All the rules you live by in your life, your beliefs, where do they come from?"

"Me. They come from me."

"Yes, but where did you get them from? Think about it, Tom. Most of what you believe wasn't your idea. It came from government controlled media and fake parents. It's a manipulation; a tool for control."

Tom wished he hadn't begun this conversation.

"My thoughts are my thoughts. I've got to go and start dinner."

He wandered into the kitchen, privately contemplating some of Noah's ideas; plutocracy: a life predetermined to serve the rich and the powerful. An interesting idea believed by most of the masses.

We live in a prison of rules to serve our masters.

"Get out of my way, Fox."

Her kick struck him on his left knee and he fell sideways against the kitchen bench and on to the floor. Before he could twist out of her way, she straddled his waist, leant forward and placed a knife at his throat.

Tom experienced searing pain and he roared his displeasure at the woman on top of him.

"Get off me ..."

As he struggled with her knife hand, he spotted Noah running into the room.

"What's going on? What happened here?"

He glared at Uta and then at Tom; his eyes following the blood trail that flowed down Tom's neck until it disappeared below the collar of his shirt.

"I think she just sliced a chunk out of my ear."

Uta got to her feet, as other members of the group arrived. The woman looked on the verge of attacking them all.

"What? He got in my way."

Noah's face flushed red with anger.

"Everybody out. Uta … I'll deal with you later."

They made way for her, as she strutted out.

So much for their macho persona. They're all scared of her.

"Petra, bring the first aid kit and something to clean up this mess."

Noah only stopped pacing the room, when Petra returned carrying an old wooden box with a faded red cross on its lid.

He rummaged through the contents and removed antiseptic, gauze and a sticky bandage.

"Wait …"

He stopped his search. Without thinking he began stroking the yellow stained newspaper that lined the under section of the box.

He read the newspaper article with his hand in the air, palm up, lest somebody interrupt.

"I think we've found the start of our trail, Tom."

"What do you mean? Where?"

"Australia … Your birthplace."

Noah felt a moment of anger and uncertainty. Coincidences often occurred in life, no doubt, but when they forced his team into a direction, strategically good for their opponents, it made him feel uneasy and suspicious, yet what choice did he have other than this?

Noah relaxed the tension in his face, as he carefully removed the old newspaper from the box.

"You'd better read this yourself, lad. The priest it describes is dangerous, but we can't ignore the opportunity. He wouldn't talk to us in the past, but this time we have you. Father Dominico Rossi won't deny the son of Alexander Fox."

Chapter Twelve

Isobel enjoyed being at work on her own. She liked her weekend's people free.

This particular Sunday, she spent the morning sprawled on the office floor, sorting through piles of invoices and dozens of other registers and data reports.

You've got to be bloody joking.

She shook her head in disgust as she looked up at the large clock on the wall. Eleven thirty. Three tedious hours and not a single outcome achieved.

This is a nightmare.

How could she find any order in the chaotic mess of filing scattered about the office?

"What's that …?"

The sound of metal clanging against metal made her flinch. She stopped filing and sat still; suspending her breathing so she could hear more clearly.

It's just your stupid imagination.

Isobel thought she saw movement out on the factory floor. Without thinking, she crawled over and pulled herself into a kneeling position behind her desk.

Then she noticed a column of uniformed men making their way through the factory floor, towards her office.

Oh God ... They've broken in.

She watched from behind her desk as the men spread out and checked the staff kitchen and laundry area.

They've nearly reached the stairwell. I've got no way out.

Isobel made a decision.

She took a deep breath, raised herself into a standing position and left the office to face the threat.

She stood in front of the men with legs apart and hands on hips. Despite her bravado, Isobel's body trembled and she couldn't stop the quiver in her speech.

"Who are you? What are you doing here?"

Isobel cringed and took a step backwards, as a slovenly looking man stepped forward; his belly and shirttails hung out of his cheap brown suit.

"Hey, look at this yappy little poodle. Maybe I should tie her up and give her a bone."

He grinned back at his men and reached out towards Isobel.

"Don't touch me."

She slapped his hand away without thinking and watched as his face flushed red with anger.

"Take her and hold her still."

Isobel fought, but with little effect. The men seemed to enjoy their power over her.

"Stop. Let me go. I've called the police. They'll be here any minute."

The group's leader reached around and grasped her ponytail, jerking her head back until her chin pointed towards the ceiling. He moved in close and brushed his lips against her cheek, using his free hand to stroke her face.

"We are the police, little love. We're the SRP and we want answers."

The men on either side of her loosened their grip and she pulled away from them.

"Take what you want and leave me alone."

"Does that include you, sweetheart?"

She sneered at him. She felt like throwing up.

"Me? I don't think so. Why don't you just piss off?"

The leader scowled. He looked about to strike her.

"Just remember what happened to your father."

He nodded and smiled at his men.

"I'm going to give you the same chance, so let's be smart."

Isobel's shoulders drooped and she felt tears running down her cheeks.

"Tom Fox has shown up, but you already know that, don't you?"

He reached over and grabbed her face between his thumb and forefinger, forcing her to look into his eyes.

"Your father left you information didn't he?"

He pulled her to him and kissed her limp mouth. To break his grip, Isobel dropped towards the floor and he released her.

"Listen to me now, sweetheart. When Fox makes contact, I want the information his father left for him. He'll know what I mean. I'll be back here next Sunday. If you don't show, I'll find you … and you'll pay in other ways. Got it?"

He pulled her from the floor by the hair and leant forward; his lips approaching hers; confident of her capitulation, but she slapped him across the right side of his face.

"You skinny little …"

He glowered with anger.

Isobel saw him move, but didn't have time to react. His right hand made contact; the slap knocking her off her feet and onto the concrete floor.

"You've got until Sunday. Then I'll be back."

Chapter Thirteen

The G11 team split into three separate units; Tom, Noah and Petra in the first, Julius and Luther in the second, and Uta and Surat in the last. Noah made sure they travelled with different itineraries, to eliminate the chance of capture as a group.

Tom considered the logistics of transporting seven wanted activists on a journey of around eleven thousand miles, without anyone noticing.

He nodded to himself and mumbled his growing admiration for their leader.

Noah, you're very bloody clever.

Tom's group set out first, travelling overland on a range of country roads and lanes, towards South Wales. They utilised an old grey Land Rover for the trip; the vehicle left purposely dirty with dried faeces splattered over the fenders and wheels. Only a farmer drove such a vehicle. Noah registered the four-wheel drive in the name of Tait & Sons Pty Ltd; a fictitious farming business with a genuine address.

The deceased estate, entitled, John's farm, a legitimate property and residence, lay on the Wells Road, in Totterdown, just south of Bristol. Noah instructed Petra to hack the UK Births, Marriages and Deaths database and swap the previous owner's title with their own. With slightly less difficulty, she also hacked into the UK Driver and Vehicle Licensing Agency and repeated the process.

After an incident free drive, they arrived at their destination early, then spent twenty-five minutes waiting in their vehicle in a side street, not far from the port of Cardiff. Ten minutes before the scheduled departure, a representative of the Alexander Line approached Noah.

"Theodore, you old goat. It's good to see you."

"Ah, Noah, I didn't recognise you with that barrel above your balls."

Tom could imagine the two men getting drunk together and sharing bawdy stories in some seedy bar.

"Theo, this is Tom Fox."

He looked at Tom; evaluating him from head to foot, before nodding without enthusiasm.

"We haven't much time. Follow me."

Theodore ushered them aboard a freighter, bound for Istanbul, via Italy and Greece. Tom followed the group down several stairwells and as many corridors to a tiny cabin in the bowels of the ship.

"You don't have to worry about being noticed. As you can see, there are no portholes and no-one will hear you above the noise of the engines. Farewell and good luck, my friends."

Tom heard the metallic click as Theodore left the cabin.

They locked the door ...?

"At least we'll all drown together, if this old bucket sinks."

No-one responded. No-one heard him above the noise.

At one point in the seemingly endless journey, Tom saw Noah check his watch, stand and then gather his rucksack. Almost immediately, there came a knock on their cabin door and without being bidden, a sailor entered.

The man led the group back up to the starboard gunwale where Noah checked his watch once more.

"It's five past bloody seven. Where are they? They're late."

Tom heard a low growling noise out through the darkness and felt Noah's hand on his shoulder.

"Alright, Tom, you'll be the first to be lowered down. Then Petra. I'll come down last."

Tom swung out into the darkness. Half way down he could hear men below him radioing instructions to the sailors at the top. The ocean remained calm and the operation smooth. They repeated the process until they all stood together aboard what appeared to be a large speedboat with a wooden hull.

They shared the boat with three other men. Tom overheard Noah referring to them as the Corsicans; one in the bow at the controls, while the other two guarded the stern. Both carried automatic weapons.

For most of the trip, Tom didn't see much of anything, except darkness and the occasional dot of light. After an hour of travel, Noah grabbed his shoulder and shook him.

"Tom, we're heading into the Strait of Bonifacio. There's to be no light of any kind and no talking, alright?"

Tom nodded; too cold to speak.

"There may be other boats and we don't want to be seen. We're pretty close to the bottom of Corsica, but we'll be travelling in Italian waters. We're staying just off the northern tip of Sardinia to avoid the French patrols."

They didn't speak again until they crossed the Tyrrhenian Sea. To the north, on the Italian mainland, Tom could see a few lights from the town of Fiumicino.

"As soon as we hit the beach, Tom. We have to change into these overalls."

Noah held up a plastic bag, covered in tape.

"We'll be driven by our people to the cargo terminal at Leonardo Da Vinci Airport in Rome. There, we'll be given staff identification and papers, but don't say anything to anybody. Just stay near me and nod. Got it?"

They boarded the Alexander Boeing B940 – 2000 cargo carrier, in the half-light before dawn. After a fifteen minute wait they taxied onto the tarmac and began their flight. Tom endured twenty-two hours in an area not much larger than a toilet, before he met up with their contacts and the rest of the G11 team in Sydney.

Chapter Fourteen

From the deep shade of a waratah tree on the opposite side of inner city Oxford Street, Tom found what he looked for; a narrow lane running alongside a restaurant called the Jagat Palace.

He headed for a gate at the rear of the building, which allowed patrons access to an outside eating area.

A bearded man with a white collar sat alone at the far end of the courtyard, surrounded by a climbing pink rose. He seemed to be the only person willing to trade the restaurant's air-conditioning, for the heavy heat of the flowered patio.

"Father Dominico Rossi?"

The priest looked up from his abundant serving of curried vegetables and dahl-fry, and frowned.

"Yes. What can I do for you, young man?"

"I need to talk."

"As you can see, I'm having my …"

"It's about Alexander Fox."

The priest sat back in his chair and regarded him. The annoyance in his expression barely concealed by the thickness of his black beard.

"Who are you?"

"I'm Tom Fox. His son."

"That's nonsense. What's this about?"

Tom attempted to answer, but the priest raised his hand and continued to speak.

"Don't start young man. I'm not interested in anything you have to say. I don't care who you work for. I won't discuss this with you. Is that clear?"

Tom felt his stomach tighten; his allies might reject him if he returned with nothing.

"Why did they kill my parents? Tell me. I know you know."

"Lower your voice."

The priest looked up at the profusion of flowers above him and shook his head. Without another word, he looked back at Tom, nodded towards the restrooms and headed for the entrance. Tom hurried to keep up.

"If you're Tom Fox, you'll have a couple of identifiers. A birth mark shaped like a butterfly and a scar from a stab wound."

They entered the men's toilet; cramming themselves into one of the cubicles.

"Drop your pants and hurry up. I don't want to be seen in here with a half-naked … Well, just get on with it will you."

Tom lowered his trousers and turned his buttocks to the man.

"Oh, my Lord … They're both there. Don't say anything else, just do as I say. You could have been followed."

Tom shadowed the priest as he moved away from the restaurant. As instructed, he kept the clergyman in sight, utilising a slightly different route up Oxford Street, through the three adjacent areas of parkland that ran south to Bennelong Point and on towards the Sydney Opera House.

They met again at the pool of reflection, at the southern end of Hyde Park and joined the crowd descending into Museum Station.

"Don't look at me and keep quiet. We can be seen and heard from a long way off."

They entered the train through different doors and sat one behind the other, as far away from potential listeners as possible.

"How did you know me, Tom?"

"I saw a picture in an old newspaper. You haven't changed much."

Tom lied. The priest didn't look like the young man in the picture. Thick black wavy hair, bushy brows and a roughly pruned beard, hid some of the deeper lines in the priest's worry-worn face. He appeared to be half again as heavy as the person in the picture and the greying around his ears and below his bottom lip, only accentuated the difference.

"Why have you come here, young man? My involvement with your father ended many years ago."

"I need information about what happened to my parents and about something called the Prize."

"Tell me what you already know, but keep your voice down."

Tom rushed through a well-rehearsed story. Noah had tutored him on what to say and what to omit.

"This is no place for a thorough discussion. You may have been followed."

"Please ... I have to know."

The priest looked around, adjusted his collar and continued.

"You can ask a few questions, but the rest will have to wait until I can arrange a safer meeting."

"Who killed my parents?"

"A very dangerous organisation known as the Assembly of the True Faith. If you value your skin, don't have anything to do with them."

"And the Prize, what is it exactly?"

"It's a form of technology. An alien substance that will allow its owner to play God and ... pretty much control humanity indefinitely."

"Shit ..."

"Exactly."

"But, why are they after me? I didn't know my father, or his work."

"They're after you because he discovered the Prize. He kept it from the Assembly and wouldn't give it up, so they eliminated him."

The priest tilted his head and stared at Tom through bushy eyebrows.

"He could've destroyed them, as you could now."

"I keep hearing this rubbish. How?"

"The Assembly tore the planet apart looking for your father's research, but then they realised their mistake. They held the key, all along. They controlled you."

"Look, this is starting to piss me off."

"Let me explain, Tom. The Assembly knew your brilliant father wouldn't destroy something so scientifically important. So they went after his partner, Professor Kite. They tortured him and before he died, they got what they wanted. Your father left a trail to the Prize, a trail for you, Tom. That's why they're after you."

"Bullshit. I'd have to know something about it."

"You asked me and you got your answer. Believe what you want."

"Alright. Alright. So how do I find this trail?"

The priest scribbled a name and address on a small piece of paper, and handed it to Tom.

"It's your father's old laboratory. Isobel Kite, the daughter of his murdered partner, owns it now."

"You think this ... Isobel knows something?"

"She might. Her father knew a lot about this business. It's a start."

Chapter Fifteen

The G11 team placed themselves out of sight around the warehouse, creating several defensive positions and three backup escape routes, well in advance of the time schedule. Petra remained one street to the north-west, occupying an overlooking third story rooftop terrace with a view of all access to and from the target area. The position also acted as an emergency point of communication.

"Our enemies can't know about the girl, Tom. No matter how distasteful, we have to break in and confront her."

"Won't she reject us?"

"We'll have to be convincing."

Noah knew that initial failure meant an end to most operational missions. Not many received a second chance in the field.

Nobody liked working on Sundays, particularly in the city and not because of any pious observance of the religious holiday. Visibility mattered. On Sunday mornings, the CBD quietened; no business people, which added an extra, unwanted dimension to their work. People became more obvious if they couldn't blend into a crowd.

"Let's go, Tom. The girl's left the rear door ajar. We'll go in through the back."

"Doesn't that seem strange to you?"

"Yes, but it'll help when we confront her. At least we can claim that we didn't break in."

Tom and Noah entered the yard at the rear of the laboratory at exactly ten o'clock, as instructed by the priest.

The creaking sounds that emanated from the laboratory's testing area made Isobel uneasy. She could have stayed at home, but she felt just as vulnerable in her small north-shore apartment.

She felt a little more comfortable verbalising her security measures.

"Ok, I've left the back door open."

Possibly not the wisest of decisions, but she believed it might give her a second or two, if she heard someone come in.

"And, I've got the local police on speed dial."

Isobel determined that her biggest worry involved her not hearing an intruder, leaving her no time to run, so she accustomed herself to every sound in the laboratory, no matter how miniscule.

"Oh no ..."

She heard something. A muffled thump from inside the laboratory. In one awful instant, Isobel became aware of her worst fears. This time she didn't wait. She bolted from her office and down the stairs.

In her panic, she slid off balance and her momentum drove her against a bench and she fell.

Isobel gulped at the air, trying to fill her lungs. She attempted to rise from the debris and run, but she couldn't coordinate her movements. She looked up and focused on the back door.

The door ... It's only metres away.

Tom led Noah through the gate and on towards the laboratory. They worked their way through neat stacks of drums filled with inflammable chemicals until they reached the rear door.

He listened. No-one.

Tom squeezed his head through the gap. Still no-one. Satisfied, he quietly slipped inside and left the door open for Noah.

"It's clear."

Tom turned away from the door and took several rapid steps forward before becoming aware of a flash of movement in his peripheral vision.

"Noah. Stop. Look out."

Tom twisted his torso and head out of the way and struck out at the attacker with his shoulder.

"Oh hell ... It's the girl."

A young woman lay stunned at his feet. He bent down, lifted her tiny frame and placed her onto a pile of fabric beside the door. Blood trickled down her face from a small cut above her hairline and he searched his pockets in vain for a means to mop it up.

Noah intervened. He located a clean handkerchief and began wiping the droplets of blood away from the girl's face.

Tom perceived movement and her eyelids widened with realisation.

"What's going on?"

The young woman sprang from her makeshift bed, slapped Tom across the left side of his face and screamed.

"Don't touch me."

Tom dodged the next wild swing and moved a step to his right to avoid any further attempts.

Perspiration began to form on his brow.

"I ... Look ... I ..."

Tom's body temperature seemed to increase the moment he became aware of her; the sublime feminine quality of her super slim figure, her raven coloured hair and especially the vivid blue of her eyes.

Her unsolicited attack made him feel both blissful and angry; causing an uncomfortable longing, like experiencing joy and at the same time, being punched in the stomach.

"What are you staring at?"

Embarrassed, he blinked in rapid succession and looked away.

She struck out at him again. At that moment, Tom's fighting instinct may have been the only conscious machinery working. He allowed her to move in close, intercepting the attack by grabbing both of her wrists.

"Leave me alone. Get away from me."

Noah rushed over and shook Tom's shoulder.

"Tom ... Let her go."

Noah sighed, raised both of his hands and tried to smile.

"Isobel. Miss Kite. We're not here to hurt you."

"Who are you then? You attacked me."

Tom couldn't stop himself from staring at the girl once again; his heart pounding behind his ribs. He moved closer. Wanting the contact, he faked an attempt at placating her.

"Actually, we came through an open door and you ran into me."

"You still have no right just barging in here."

Noah stepped forward and moved between them.

"Isobel. My name is Noah and this is Tom Fox. I believe you've heard of him. We're not here for any reason, other than to meet you."

"You scared me."

"No. I don't think so. You seemed to be running for your life before you reached us. Is there someone else in this building?"

This is the famous Tom Fox. Her Tom Fox? No way.

She felt nothing but repugnance. He stared at her like most men did, like some kind of predator.

Isobel took in a deep breath and closed her eyes. She knew that her negative response to men acted as a means of defence; a shield created by a ravaged belief system, yet in the moment, it always felt like the truth.

"Miss Kite …"

Noah coughed and she realised that she stared back at the tall young man in front of her with equal intensity. She calmed her features, smoothing out her frown. With an effort, she removed her contact from his piercing blue eyes and concentrated on his companion.

"You still have no right …"

"Miss Kite, why are you so afraid?"

"I thought they'd come back."

"You thought *who* came back? You're expecting trouble?"

"Perhaps, I'm not sure."

Tom screwed his face into a scowl.

"This is serious, girl. We need to know."

Isobel felt the loathing come back and squeeze at her gut. Her facial muscles tightened and she returned Tom's glare with her own scornful look.

"I'm no girl. Anyway, why are we having this conversation? I don't even know you."

Isobel heard the buzzing. She noticed the black man removing a communicator from his pocket, before thrusting his palm into the air for silence.

"Isobel … There are men about to enter this building. Is there a reason the Special Religious Police are here, other than us? It's important that you tell me."

She nodded and pointed towards Tom.

"Yes. They're coming for me … because of him."

Chapter Sixteen

Frederick Vogel slumped in the back seat of the speeding Alfa Romeo sedan and watched the late afternoon sunlight recede from the hills of Lombardia. He viewed the shadows as a reflection of his darkening mood; long fingers of gloom reaching out to consume the light.

His annoyance escalated into sour anger on the way from Sydney to Japan. By the time he stepped from the Qantas jumbo and into the waiting lounge at Narita airport, his fury needed a target. He yelled at the first person who came near him. The confused Qantas steward took all of his insults before fleeing towards her departure gate.

The steward in charge of the British Airways flight to Rome's Ciampino Airport suffered a similar fate, as did the staff on the connecting Alitalia flight from Rome to Malpensa Airport in Milan. Even the easy one and a half hour drive to the city of Como did nothing to placate his anger.

The fools ...

They thought this meeting important enough to fly him across the world. Surely, nothing could be more vital than the Fox affair. Instead of controlling the priest and as a consequence, his own fortunes, his superiors deemed it necessary for him to waste his time trading banter with a pompous cardinal.

"Driver, go faster ... *Rapido.*"

Frederick needed sleep. He tried to close his eyes and induce slumber, but the negative ramifications of his absence kept him from relaxing.

The sound of stones striking metal brought him to alertness. His driver entered Villa Dal Santo, spinning the rear wheels of the vehicle, as he manoeuvred through a set of elaborate iron gates.

Frederick sensed danger. As his driver slowed, he searched the two eighteenth century buildings, once known as Villa Maria Taglioni and Villa Maria Serena, for any possible threat.

Nothing.

The two most beautifully elegant residences in the Como region seemed lifeless. He couldn't distinguish anything other than vague outlines.

It shouldn't be this dark.

The only illumination came from the vehicle's headlights.

Surely this can't be. My secretary organised this appointment in advance, yet the place's deserted.

"Driver, don't stop the car. Something stinks."

Damn it. It's too late.

The inside of Vogel's Alfa Romeo lit with brilliant light, as a Mercedes McLaren raced up from behind, cut them off and skidded to a stop in the gravel.

Frederick felt for his weapon.

A hit, but why? Why would a cardinal want to assassinate me?

He wrenched at his nine-millimetre Beretta, but he couldn't retrieve it fast enough.

As he struggled, a woman emerged from the driver's seat of the McLaren. She removed her cap, shook loose an abundance of curly auburn hair and putting her hands on her hips, looked directly at him.

The woman gave him a smile that he could only interpret as pure contempt, before strutting away towards the villa's entrance hall.

It's her. How could this be?

Vogel felt stunned. In the glare of the headlights, he saw the same slightly muscular shoulders and arms protruding from her body-hugging blue singlet. He recognised the movement of her perfect arse and the athletic legs beneath her white tights.

She's so much like Uta ... Surely not, it couldn't be her.

Uta hid with the PMSG in a terrace-house in the eastern suburbs of Sydney, half a world away.

He began to shiver involuntarily.

———————

The cardinal's eyes blazed with anger as he pulled the woman into a rough embrace.

"What do you think you are doing? You allowed yourself to be seen."

"It only added to his confusion."

"*Stupido, Idiota.* You presume too much."

"My timing shrunk his balls, my love."

The woman reached up and pulled the cardinal's head forward. She forced her mouth hard against his and cried out, as he bit her lower lip. She looked almost ecstatic as she sampled the salty taste of her own blood.

He pushed her away.

"How is our plaything?"

He needn't have bothered with his enquiry. He could see the lust in her expression.

"*Animale.* Control yourself. We shall have our fun later. When we won't be disturbed."

The cardinal watched her hips began to sway and gyrate to some unknown beat, causing his manliness to swell with sensation. He couldn't keep his gaze from her ultra-tight riding pants. They hid nothing and accentuated everything; the cleft between her legs clearly visible; threatening his composure.

He looked away and refocused his thoughts.

Vogel remained an unfortunate necessity; a means to an end. He smiled and warmth surged through his body. Enhancing the rest of the evening's activities, by taunting Vogel, provided a pleasing appetiser.

The thought of the main course exhilarated him.

A very fortunate boy ... Truly blessed.

Gratifying a cardinal's desire is the greatest of privileges. Every bit of pain experienced in the service of God and his ministry is a glorious sacrifice; an end hardly deserved by such uneducated peasants.

He sensed her eyes devouring him before she spoke.

"My love, I've done what you asked. All is in place. Fox believes he's the key. The game begins."

"Good. Very good."

He bent toward her, filling his senses with her natural perfume.

"Pour me a brandy, *per favore*. I think I'll keep our wretched little Vogel on edge for a while longer. The wait will do what violence cannot."

"Don't drink too much, Leonardi. I want you at your best, for our play ..."

He slapped her face.

"Insolent bitch."

She bit into her own lip and moaned.

"Go upstairs and make sure our little street urchin is ready the moment my business is concluded."

Frederick Vogel sat in the beautifully frescoed entrance hall and fumed. He hated this kind of treatment, even from the high and mighty Black Cardinal, Leonardi Dal Santo.

They're a bunch of hypocrites.

Vogel considered the man and his profession. How could such a corrupt bastard rise so high in any organisation, let alone the Holy Catholic Church? Only the Assembly board and a select few in the Curia, seemed aware of the Archbishop's passion for cruelty; the reason for the Black in his title.

Keep focused. Uta ... Only Uta The Raptor matters. Nothing else.

Her sudden arrival seemed staged; the cardinal trying to scare him perhaps. It worked. Her appearance terrified him. It created the very real possibility that his precious spy might be working for someone other than him; Uta or a woman so similar that they could be twins; an unthinkable state of affairs. Each scenario implied that the Black Cardinal secretly controlled the Fox operation.

For a second, he thought about his late father and his lame advice. 'Pull yourself together. Hide your fear. Never show the enemy your mind.'

He needed the advice. His longevity might depend on it.

Chapter Seventeen

As Noah communicated with the G11 placements around the building, Tom noticed the man's eyelids stretch open in surprise and his pupils dart from side to side.

He exhaled, lowered the phone and spoke to them with urgency.

"They're coming through both entrances. Isobel, get behind those drums and don't move. Tom, you come with me. We can squeeze behind the boxes at the far end of the room."

They raced to their allotted positions, with Tom the furthest away. He crouched behind a large cardboard box with: 'DANGER - Highly Inflammable Chemicals', stamped across each visible surface. He could see more of these cartons stored in a caged area behind him. In front on a metal bench, he noticed a range of glass testing apparatus, beakers and Bunsen burners.

He stiffened.

Men moved towards him in SRP uniforms and another man wearing a dark-brown suit.

Tom ducked down as far as he could and waited.

———————

Isobel heard the men enter through the rear door and move towards her position.

They're probably the same men who threatened to rape me.

She felt fear gush through her system.

Rape ... Stop thinking about it. Let it go ... Not now.

She quietened her breathing and held her knees to stop her hands from shaking.

Her thoughts raced; an idea coming to fruition in her mind; a notion previously suppressed; now unstoppable.

Rape ...?

The anatomy of rape. Rape not as an act of sexual intercourse, but the theft of her virginity. Control by another through violence; control ripped from her life. Control that she couldn't get back.

No. That's bullshit. That's the ultimate bullshit.

She could take it back ... If she chose. Without it, she felt that chaos and random events controlled her life.

No. No ... I can't. Look at me. I'm a little defenceless girl, hiding behind a drum with men coming to violate me; coming to take away any chance of control, ever again.

The footsteps grew closer. They could see her. She could hear the men's laughter.

She felt someone prod her with his boot.

"Well, look what we have here."

Isobel thought about capitulation; just sit there like a victim, accepting no choice, no control ... Even rape.

Alright ... Take a deep breath ... and do it girl.

Her tiny body shook as she rose; lifting the wooden three-legged stool above her head.

"Chief, look out ..."

As the suited man held out his arms, nodding and accepting the smiled applause from his men, he heard one of them call out and he stopped mid-movement.

He remained rooted to the spot; one hand staying aloft as the heavier seat section of the stool, struck him high on the left side of his head, grazed his ear and slammed into his shoulder; inflicting no serious injury.

"What the hell …? Grab the little whore and hold her."

Two SRP men ran forward and took hold of Isobel; one man for each arm.

She saw the suited man walk forward. With blood dribbling from his ear, he withdrew a knife from his belt and held it to her throat.

"You stupid, dumb bitch. Give me what I want or I'll feed you to my men, right here and now."

Tom understood fear; it acted as his greatest teacher. He also knew that it fooled most people, who often worried about fear rather than the reason for it; a misunderstanding resulting in stress and anxiety. He knew that terror helped him to survive; a natural phenomenon; an instinct that enabled the flight or fight in all of us.

He recalled his earliest and greatest dread.

Climbing to any significant height caused him gut sickening panic. He tried to avoid any scenario that required confronting this evil, making him a target for every crook and miscreant in the East End, including the SRP. Ground level doorways and windows provided little to no access, which left the roof highways as the best means of escaping an enemy.

One building frightened him the most and he whispered its name with reverence.

"The Red Citadel."

That's what the street kids called it. The old red brick building, once part of the West India docks, lay dormant and neglected since the nineteen eighties. The lifts and stairs to the top two floors collapsed years earlier, making it a secret haven for a few brave souls. Its climb guaranteed its exclusivity.

Tom couldn't get the Citadel out of his mind. Every time he thought about it, he imagined failing muscles, limp with fear, yet he kept mysteriously arriving at the docks to view it.

He climbed the building on his twelfth birthday, setting out in the half-light of early morning, alone and terrified. He ascended the crumbling brick walls, by following a network of pipes, window sills and missing bricks. He overcame the panic of vertigo and the difficulty of determining his way in a vertical environment, until somewhere above the third floor.

"Oh God …"

He couldn't find any handholds above him and his feet couldn't retrace his previous course. He told himself he needed to relax his mind and his body, but how could he? A loosening of his fingers meant certain death. Then he heard something, like a distant voice; a single word.

"Trust."

Tom's body hurt from the extra effort that panic required, yet in that moment, his courage returned. He did let go and he did find the next handhold, and the next, and every subsequent one, until he reached his goal.

Trust …

The voice he heard came from inside; from his own lips. A knowing, an inner knowledge that fear couldn't be defeated, without first accepting it as a friend.

Tom heard the man call out in anger and his memories dissolved; his mind racing back to the present.

"You stupid, dumb bitch. Give me what I want or I'll feed you to my men, right here and now."

Tom raised his head above the cartons and bales of cloth that acted as his sanctuary, just as the suited man raised his knife and pricked the girl's flesh.

"You cowardly …"

Anger strangled his words. He must do something. He couldn't just hide here while they hurt her.

His predicament didn't improve with his decision. He fought against nine enemies and he didn't have a gun. He began to search for some kind of weapon. He spotted the row of Bunsen burners on the bench and the cardboard boxes marked: 'DANGER - Highly Inflammable Chemicals'.

A plan started to form in his mind.

This just might work.

First, he needed to find an escape route. The SRP seemed focused on the girl. This gave him the time he needed to get to Noah's position without frying or getting hit by airborne debris.

Tom crawled around the fabric bales, past a row of stacked boxes and worked his way forward to the bench. He removed a four-litre plastic bottle from a cardboard box and poured its contents over the table and over the remaining containers, making sure that he opened as many lids as possible.

Come on, Tom. Think. What can I use?

He needed a wick and a means of igniting the chemicals. He crouched as low as he could, moving slowly forward towards a fabric sorting table. Raising his head to the height of the bench, he found a ruler and a pile of cloth scraps. He gathered them up, wrapping more than half of the ruler with the cloth. This left just enough room for his hand.

He crawled back to the first bench, sucked in a deep breath and doused the fabric with the remaining chemical. Turning on the gas for as many Bunsen burners as possible, he snatched up a lighter and crawled away to his launching site.

Tom lifted his head above the stack of cardboard packing boxes and spotted the girl. Two men dragged her towards the stairs.

Bloody cowards.

He lit the cloth and it flared up, affecting his sight. He rose, took a step for balance and launched the homemade wick as hard as he could towards the bench.

"Oh God. No ..."

He couldn't believe his misfortune. The cloth detached itself from the ruler and lay burning on the floor in front of him. He ran toward it, but only reached half of the distance, when he heard the sound of excited voices.

He raced on towards the failed missile; too late; the fire spread down a trail of previously dripped chemicals, towards the main storage cage and the naked gas.

With stealth no longer an issue, Tom turned and ran for his life. He dived for cover, just as the flames reached the first of the chemical deposits.

———————

Noah realised his error of judgment. To make amends, he required a feasible solution to repair the damage.

Think.

Three isolated placements with no way of exiting the area, and outer team locations that couldn't assist without a full-on assault, put them in a bad position.

He raised his head and looked over the drum in front of him. They held the girl. She fought against her captors as they dragged her towards the stairwell.

Come on, man. Do something.

He didn't have many options left. He checked his weapon, took in a deep breath and began to rise.

"Tom … What the hell …?"

A flash of light gained his attention; a flame. He watched Tom fling the object forward, but the burning cloth dislodged itself.

He heard the girl call out from the stairs as he rushed forward.

"Tom. No …"

He spotted the blur of movement and stopped his own charge, just in time to see Tom diving beneath a pile of boxes.

———————

Isobel stopped struggling with her captors. It only seemed to amuse them. She felt exhausted; the threat of rape destroying her resolve.

Something distracted her; a flash of light.

Her captors saw it and they reacted. In one motion, they dragged her up several more steps and dropped her. Her elbows struck the metal stairwell causing pain, then her body hit; producing even more pain. It brought her out of her apathy. With clarity, she heard one of the soldiers call out. She followed his pointing arm to where a flame hovered in the air. It seemed surreal; appearing to hang there, before slowly floating back to the floor.

Then she saw Tom Fox run and dive.

"Tom ... Look out."

Isobel pulled herself into a sitting position on the steps, as men ran towards him.

"Tom. They're coming."

Isobel didn't see what happened next. Her world exploded; her mind overwhelmed by violent noise and the force of the detonation.

Noah lay on his back, motionless under pieces of wood and cloth, and the remains of a chair. He fought hard to gain some measure of control, as he viewed the carnage of the laboratory with an unthinking mind.

His vision swirled and his ears thundered. He forced himself up onto his knees and tried to make sense of his surroundings. He could see no-one standing through the thick smoke. He shook his head several times, but his senses wouldn't clear.

A meaningful thought began to focus out beyond the confusion in his mind.

Tom ... Isobel.

Then he felt strong hands gripping his arms and he tried to resist.

"Noah. Are you alright?"

"Surat is that you? What happened? Tom and the girl, where are they?"

"No time. Come on old man, we have to move."

Surat dragged Noah into a stooped upright position.

"There could be a secondary explosion. We've got to get out. Stay low, under the smoke."

He heard groans behind them, as men began to wake. Once again, he remembered Tom and the girl. He tried to call to them, but he could only hear the ringing in his ears. His thoughts began to spin and the more he tried to reach out and grasp their meaning, the further he slipped into unconsciousness. He remembered the smoke. Thick, black, choking clouds that turned everything into darkness.

Chapter Eighteen

Frederick Vogel seethed; the opulence of the entrance hall unsettling him. He knew the building's history. In the early nineteenth century, the celebrated dancer Maria Taglioni bestowed the estate with her tasteful elegance and style. It reeked of wealth. There didn't seem to be another place in all of Italy where a commoner could feel less at home, than Villa Dal Santo.

Frederick tried to focus on his meeting with the cardinal, but he couldn't stop thinking about the woman. Why show her to him now? What would they have to gain?

It doesn't make any sense to me.

Time became a poison. He closed his eyes and listened to the constant tapping of insects as they bashed themselves against the windowpane. Despite his attempts to the contrary, the question of her appearance remained.

"Mr Vogel …"

Frederick jumped in surprise.

He recovered; following the cardinal through the near darkness to another room on the ground floor.

As they entered, light shone into the hallway, affecting his vision.

What the hell ...?

Frederick took a step backwards. A face stared at him from the wall. He relaxed; recognising the intensity in the figure's expression and the white Templar cross on his dark tunic; a Maltese Knight; a Caravaggio masterpiece worth more than his life's wages.

They entered the music room and Frederick looked down, forcing himself not to stare at the frescoed ceiling. He pretended not to see the majestic looking grand piano, or to look through the windows, out beyond the balcony, to where the lights surrounding Lake Como sparkled on the surface of the water. To notice proved his inferiority. Secretly, he strove for this; the power to make others sick with envy.

Frederick watched the cardinal sit down behind an ornately carved desk and flick on the reading lamp. He noticed the man's eyes staring out of the darkness at him with sullen malevolence, as if he saw Frederick as something foul on the sole of his shoe.

"I'll get directly to our dealings, Mr Vogel. Total secrecy is paramount to our mutual interests. What I require is for you to deliver my gift personally. It must be presented verbally and to the Assembly board alone."

Frederick could only nod his agreement.

My God ...

The shape in the darkness moved forward; the light from the lamp bringing his features into focus. Pompous, effeminate ... and truly beautiful. Frederick could only gape at the most striking human being he'd ever seen in his life. The man looked more like a Moorish princess than a cruel black-hearted cardinal.

"Are you listening, Vogel? It is most important that I meet with the board after they receive my gift."

"Yes. Yes, of course Your Eminence."

Frederick gave him a slight bow. Despite the man's beauty, the security chief's distrust grew with every smooth statement the cardinal uttered.

"What exactly are you offering?"

The cardinal smiled and Frederick couldn't stop himself from smiling back.

"Your superiors wish to be honoured by the Church. With all of their collective hearts, they desire what they've always desired. They wish to be bestowed with what they believe is rightfully theirs and I can make it so."

"Can you be a little more specific, Your Grace? I don't quite follow your meaning."

With a swirl of his robes, the cardinal rose and walked to the window.

"Out there is a world that is torn by opposing beliefs. It is in all of our interests, Mr Vogel, that 'God's True Ordained Order' be once again the structure for our earthly community. More specifically ... I am offering the Assembly families, the opportunity that they have secretly longed for."

With a subtle nod of his head, the cardinal motioned for Frederick to follow him. He headed towards the front courtyard entrance.

"It's been a pleasure, Mr Vogel."

Cardinal Dal Santo ushered him through the doorway with a condescending smirk.

"Don't look so perplexed, Frederick, my offer is this ..."

He grabbed Vogel by the collar and pulled him into an uncomfortable embrace. He smiled as he whispered into the security man's ear.

Frederick sucked in his next breath and exhaled loudly.

"My God ..."

"Yes, Mr Vogel. When you confirm my meeting with the board, I will deliver my terms in person."

The door closed and the light disappeared.

You black-hearted bastard.

His gut told him that the cardinal could pull it off. Now he knew for certain what the Assembly families wanted and because of this black-hearted Judas, nothing could stop them.

Chapter Nineteen

The G11's returned to their safe house the next morning. They searched the inner city terrace building for signs of intrusion and electronic monitoring devices; checking all outside vantage points for possible surveillance, before Tom re-entered the building with Isobel.

Tom sat on the dining room floor and rested his back against the wall. The remainder of the group lay scattered between the lounge and the dining room. No-one spoke. The occasional furtive glance became the group's only form of communication. The G11's brooded and he didn't like it.

Tom felt Isobel staring at him. He tried to make eye contact, but she looked away. In that brief moment of connection, he saw moisture in her eyes.

"Hey, are you alright?"

"What do you think?"

Her angry tone surprised him and gained everyone's attention.

"I don't know. That's why I asked."

"Just mind you own business."

"Why the attitude? We saved you didn't we?"

"Oh, don't be so modest. You deserve all of the credit."

Tom frowned; not understanding the direction of the conversation or her mocking tone.

"We all helped."

"Really, wasn't it you that burnt my laboratory to the ground?"

"That's brilliant. So you'd rather we left you to be murdered by the SRP?"

"No, but because of you, I've lost everything and I'm stuck here with this rag-tag lot. So leave me alone."

"She's right, Fox."

Uta cut in on the conversation and glared at Tom.

"We should kill you for your stupidity. Now the SRP knows we're here. We'll be lucky if we survive the week."

Noah moaned and everyone turned in his direction.

"Enough Uta. Keep your smart mouth to yourself."

He took a moment; making eye contact with every person in the room.

"Tom is the key to our endeavours. Without him, this mission is worthless. It's important that we stay focused. We need to find the start of this trail."

Noah turned and adjusted his trousers, tucking his shirttails neatly into his pants. He walked around Tom's sprawled figure and stood facing Isobel.

"Is there anything you can remember about your father and this business? Even the smallest memory might help us."

"Why should I help you?"

Isobel tilted her arm and unconsciously studied the old Seiko watch on her wrist.

"For goodness sake, Isobel. The people we're fighting against are the same people that murdered your father."

Isobel squirmed under the scrutiny of the group.

"Alright, alright ... There is something."

Tom watched her struggle to her feet and limp a step towards Noah; her arm outstretched. The other members of the G11's quietened to silence, as Isobel began to explain about the watch and its origins.

"Isobel."

Tom jumped to his feet and marched over to where the G11's surrounded her.

"Isobel."

His voice carried enough authority to part the group as he approached. When he stood face to face with her, his heart began to accelerate and thump in his chest.

"That belongs to me. I'd like it back."

Isobel returned his fierce expression with equal harshness. Without taking her eyes off his, she removed the watch from her wrist and placed it into his outstretched hand. Tom maintained the eye contact until he felt Noah's hand on his shoulder.

"Tom, can I see it please?"

"No."

"It's important, lad. It may be the clue we've been looking for."

"I said, no."

"You can't bring back a memory you don't have, lad. This watch may be the only means to destroy your father's enemies."

For reasons Tom couldn't explain, he looked back at Isobel and saw her approval. He nodded and handed the watch to Noah.

"I want it back."

Noah gestured for Petra to come over.

"Let's get this thing open."

Tension built amongst the group and Tom understood their feelings. Death appeared to be inevitable if they couldn't find the trail. Yet, another possibility existed: the watch could contain information more valuable than anything in existence.

He considered the excitement in their expressions. In just a few moments, they might possess the Prize, or face disaster; life and death precariously balanced.

Chapter Twenty

The chairman considered the security logistics in Vogel's report. Meetings of management for the Assembly of the True Faith, required lodgings for board members and their entourage, which meant taking over the entire eight floors of the Intercontinental De La Ville - Roma.

The plush surroundings of the penthouse suite acted as their boardroom and his personal office.

Good. Very good.

Enemies lurked in dark places. He couldn't afford to be lax. He ordered Vogel to close the hotel's doors, excluding the general public, while the seven inhabited the building.

Secure Assembly personnel replaced the hotel's staff, while trusted men guarded doors and secured the premises; searching the entire complex for concealed explosive devices and other covert equipment. Outside, Italian Special Religious Police closed the

Via Sistina to general traffic and security staff in plain clothes, monitored adjacent buildings.

The chairman nodded his approval. He could now focus on the other six men sitting around the ornate marble table.

Each member of the Assembly Council wore a black tailored suit, a white shirt and a red tie, with each having affixed a red rose and a small gold crucifix to their lapels. Like him, every man at the table owed his membership and position on the board, to a distant bloodline; an ancient connection that bonded the group.

With practised elegance, Antonio Costa raised his hand.

Silence replaced the general chatter in the room and all of the trusted assistants in the background come to attention; each knowing their master's will and after each imperceptible command, rushing to satisfy his requirements.

With an adept feel for ceremony, the chairman's assistant approached the table and rang a small brass bell, once for each member of the group. He bowed and announced his superior.

"The Assembly Chairman."

The other members of the board responded with the prescribed level of applause.

"Gentlemen. Worthy members. Thank you for your attendance."

The chairman lifted his bulk from the chair and proceeded to walk around the table, greeting and shaking the hand of each member.

"At sixteen, we of the bloodline received the secret words. We swore the sacred oath of the red rose. Do you still hold true to our beloved covenant?"

"Aye, we do."

The chairman looked into each of the six faces around the table.

"The recruitment of Tom Fox by the radicals has begun. The fact that this group is an unwitting conduit to our success is more than ironic. They are the vehicle that will drive Fox to our Prize; an act that will ultimately destroy them."

He paused, to heighten the anticipation.

"Brothers. Over time, our once mighty Angels have failed us and we are vulnerable, yet there is still great hope for our endeavours. Tom Fox will allow us the opportunity to rise up against all who oppose us."

He sighed and opened his arms; a saviour too heavy for any cross.

"This is a dangerous journey, my friends. If anyone used the Prize against us … You know what would happen."

The men at the table nodded in unison.

"Despite the benefits, foolish risks are not acceptable. Therefore, I propose that we continue with this endeavour, under very strict and tight controls. We must monitor our position at all times and if things turn against us, we can instigate a thorough clean-up, ridding ourselves of these un-godly dissenters at the same time."

He stopped and raised his face towards the heavens.

"It is time, my beloved brothers, to destroy once and for all, this satanic 'New World Order'. It is time for 'God's True Ordained Order' to take precedence over all.

Again he stopped. His face flushed with emotion.

"Christ is the King of all kings, and we are the bloodline; his earthly elect. The time will soon come my brothers when Tom Fox will give us the power of God. Let us say the words together."

"Christ is the King of kings and the pope is his spiritual ruler on earth. Under him shall be God's ordained kings to rule the world. Man by himself is inherently evil, we are evil born, only God is good, only Christ can redeem us. God help us, one and all. Amen."

The assistants withdrew from the meeting. Only the seven remained. They sat in silence around the carved marble table, awaiting the most important item of their agenda.

The chairman fidgeted with his gold crucifix and adjusted the red rose on his lapel. He took a moment to study the other six men before his assistant re-entered and rang the small brass bell.

The chairman coughed; clearing his throat before speaking.

"Bring in our guest."

The cardinal's vileness made him nervous, but even God's bishop wouldn't dare make such a request, unless he held some advantage.

Vogel noticed the chairman studying him, as he entered the Assembly penthouse suite.

Frederick refused to make eye contact. To maintain his perceived advantage, he avoided the official debriefing session and he could see that his boss knew it.

The chairman looked angry as he stood and addressed the Assembly.

"Your report please, Frederick."

Frederick Vogel sat back and smiled at the men who normally determined his fate. He did their bidding, but not for much longer. The moment Tom Fox appeared, everything changed. He risked his life on the outcome of this game; all or nothing.

He remained silent just long enough to create a little discomfort.

"Gentlemen, I'll get straight to the point. The cardinal only said one thing of importance. He offered you … a gift."

Vogel waited until the chairman coughed, clearing his throat.

"Mr Vogel …?"

"If you will allow me, I'll present it just as the cardinal presented it to me. Christ is the King of kings and the pope is his spiritual ruler on earth. Under him shall be seven kings to rule the world."

The chairman's face tightened in anger.

"Mr Vogel. What else?"

Frederick found it hard not to laugh.

"Gentlemen, the cardinal asked me, who I thought those kings might be."

He paused again; making them wait for his own enjoyment.

"He's offering them to you, the seven families of the Assembly."

After a general intake of air, several members of the board moaned.

Frederick smiled and nodded at the seven men. He felt like a rock star, performing in front of an adoring crowd.

The chairman raised his hand and all fidgeting ceased.

"Mr Vogel, normally I'd ask you to leave the room at this point, but, you know our business now. Please remain with us. We may need your expertise."

"Of course, Mr Chairman."

The Assembly board and the priest thought that they controlled this game; they thought that they controlled him, but only he knew the cardinal's secret; only he knew about the woman with the auburn hair.

Chapter Twenty One

The cardinal constricted the muscles around his throat, keeping his rising stomach acid at bay. After such a bout of prolonged pleasure, he felt nauseous and brittle.

He groaned and sucked in several deep breaths.

He suffered the after-effects of endorphin overdose as a sense of fragility and a horrible feeling of emptiness.

Filth ...

When the desire cooled, he hated his victims. Especially their horrid expressionless faces.

Dirty little vermin.

He took the life of an inept creature, a useless street urchin; a beast with no virtue; no different from taking the life of an insect. As a great cardinal, one of the elect, one of the true bloodline, he took the opportunity and delivered the boy's soul to God; bestowing a just form of purpose for his life. Hadn't kings and popes slaughtered thousands for lesser reasons?

"Heavenly Father, thank you for thy gifts."

Some mild penance would restore his serenity and rid his being of this unwanted burden; this unwarranted guilt.

"Forgive me this dalliance and refocus my energies. I am your son and accept your charge. I do your will on earth and will lead your Church to glory."

He sighed, feeling his own greatness coming to fruition.

On this earthly plain, God did not make his creatures equal; especially human beings. This foul satanic 'New World Order' assumed that all could share the same plate, that all should be kings, living in wealth.

What nonsense.

He knew the truth. The True Bloods required the labour of the many; the lesser. The world could not sustain delusional thoughts of grandeur for all.

He combed his fingers through his hair and without realising it, began rubbing the lobe of his right ear.

The seed I've planted is my assurance.

The Assembly meeting began minutes earlier, yet he felt only a small amount of anxiety; they would accept his offer.

But the traitors and the hypocrites won't support me.

His own people worried him. Politicised bureaucrats masquerading as cardinals never supported any endeavour unless assured of maintaining the ever-growing width of their arses. Even if most of the cardinals in the Curia felt compelled towards 'God's True Ordained Order', they would never show themselves without sustained pressure; the kind of insistence that the Assembly could easily employ, hence his need of them.

His thoughts shifted, as she started to wake.

Mesmerised, he held his breath as the powder-blue satin sheets slipped away from her body. As she rolled on to her back, he groaned; expelling the spent breath from his lungs.

Such a beauty.

Réz, named for the fire in her wild hair; a woman irresistible to men, yet the most adept weapon, for sending most of them to their graves.

"What are you looking at, my love?"

She turned over onto her stomach; offering him the sight and promise of her pleasures.

"Don't I please you?"

"Of course."

He responded honestly. He loved her beauty and fierce passion; a fantasy made manifest, but a contrast of absolutes: lean, yet curvaceous; a body as hard as a combat veteran, yet as languid as an overfed feline; the sweet little girl next door, who just happened to be God's instrument of death.

"Get up, Réz. Uta will be making contact soon. You must be ready."

"Sometimes I think you prefer her to me."

She teased him with her nakedness, but he knew she meant it. He laughed and patted her perfectly formed backside.

"*Si, amore mio.* Of course, you're my favourite."

He watched her strut towards the bathroom and wondered about the other sister. Uta seemed identical to Réz; the exact build and facial features, the same intense expression and the same black eyes that followed your every movement. Except for the texture and colour of their hair and a small height difference, they could be the same woman.

My famous half twins. My two little miracles.

Not many knew their secret; an enigma that always came to mind when he saw them together. In two separate Romanian villages, two different Hungarian mothers screamed in agony, as the two sisters silently forced their way into the world. This chiefly unnoticed phenomenon occurred on the same day and although he couldn't substantiate the precise time of their birth, he believed it happened at the same moment.

He called them the half twins, because the two women shared their resemblance and violent natures with the same Romanian father.

Only Réz grew up with him; accompanying her evil mentor on many of his murderous escapades, but at the age of twelve, everything changed. The SRP captured him, exacted revenge on behalf of the local Romanian community and publicly hanged him in the town square of Borsa, for crimes against humanity.

Réz watched the execution with fascination.

He smiled. He did prefer the other sister, but not for the reasons that Réz surmised. Her sister could deliver much more than physical pleasure. Uta The Raptor could ensure his rise to the supreme position of pope by presenting him with the greatest gift he could imagine; the Prize.

Chapter Twenty Two

Noah formed part of the scrimmage, jostling for position around Petra, as she began to remove the rear casing from the watch. He could see the pressure of their expectation building in her strained expression and hunched shoulders.

"Bloody hell."

Noah heard the casing clang as it bounced on to the floor. He also saw splashing droplets of blood, forming patterns on the surface of the table.

"Petra. What have you done?"

"I'm sorry, Noah."

"Everybody move back."

"I couldn't help it. I pushed a bit hard and the screwdriver went into the mechanism … then it slipped off the metal and into my hand."

"You'll live. Show me the casing, lass."

Her dripping fingers retrieved the jettisoned casing and placed it in Noah's hand without covering it with any of her blood.

"There are markings here. Petra, hand me the magnifying glass."

Noah hardly noticed the red stickiness coating the handle as he focused on the inner side of the casing.

"It's a row of numbers: 143, 12, ( ), 49."

Heads turned towards their neighbour, searching for the obvious answer, but no-one spoke. Noah stared at the numbers on his pad and tried to determine an explanation.

"It could be a phone number, or a safe's combination, or longitude and latitude coordinates, but without the missing numbers to decipher the code, it's just data with no meaning."

He closed his eyes, sighed and turned back towards Petra.

"Is there anything else, lass?"

"There might be more inside the mechanism."

"Alright, keep looking, but clean up first before you drown the damn watch."

It took fifteen minutes for the pained expression on Petra's face to change into a tight smile.

"Noah ... Noah. I've found a chip inside the watch's mechanism. A data storage chip."

"Alright, go off somewhere quiet. Let's see if we can extract some useful information without any more accidents."

Noah could feel the growing tension as he sat down next to Tom and squeezed the young man's shoulder.

"The waiting's always the hardest."

He felt a shiver of nervous anticipation. Even at Petra's pace, it might only be a short while before they found the location of the Prize.

———

Isobel caught sight of Noah, raising his hand, in an attempt to speak, but the clamour in the room seemed to frustrate his efforts.

"Alright everybody, a bit of quiet please."

She smiled. The noise level continued to thwart him.

"Everybody … Shut the hell up."

All noise ceased.

"Now, Petra, my clever lassie. What've we got?"

"I'm so sorry, Noah. There's a problem with the storage device."

"A problem …?"

"There's some corruption and loss of data."

"Because of the screwdriver?"

"Yes … I'm sorry."

The room hushed into another awkward silence. Isobel thought the atmosphere felt ominous. Only Noah appeared to remain calm.

"Just tell us what you do have."

Petra lifted the tiny chip and everyone bent forward.

"I managed to rescue the file heading. Just two words. It's a title, or a place perhaps."

"Yes, go on."

"That's all, just a name; Raptor Park."

Despite the rising sounds of disappointment around the room, Isobel noticed the excitement in Noah's expression. She didn't share his optimism. The name made her feel queasy.

"Has anybody heard of this place before?"

No-one responded.

"Petra, get on to the internet and find anything you can about Raptor Park. Don't forget that the enemy watch for particular words or phrases of interest, so use blocking software.

Noah turned towards Isobel; his expression severe.

"We need you to think hard, young lady. A bit of local knowledge might provide the answer."

She tried to respond, but Uta cut her off.

"I'm sick of this little bitch. She's a recipe for death. I vote we get rid of her. We can force the information out of the priest ourselves. Trust me; I'll make him squeal."

Isobel felt her heartbeat increase. She looked around the room for allies and held her breath. She only exhaled when Noah spun around to face the woman.

"Uta. Shut it. Now. Not another word."

Isobel squeezed her hands together to stop them from shaking. They felt clammy; this woman could scare the Devil. She made a quick decision to change the course of the conversation. Her soft voice immediately defusing the confrontation.

"Excuse me, Noah. Uta. What's this about a priest?"

Surat answered for both of them.

"He knew your father. They worked together. He's the one that led us to you."

Isobel's mouth turned down into an expression of loathing. Not even Uta's death threat caused such a look of revulsion, but only Noah seemed to recognise her distress.

"Are you alright, lass? You look like you're going to be sick."

Isobel didn't hear him. Her head throbbed with unwanted memories.

"What's his name … This priest?"

Noah rushed over, grabbing her by the shoulders.

"It's Dom. Father Dominico Rossi to be exact. Have you heard of him?"

Isobel didn't answer. She broke loose and staggered towards the window; her face stretching into a grotesque expression of loathing. She turned away from them before she spoke.

"Years ago, before my father died, he employed a technician called Mali. He always seemed nice, even though he felt ill most of the time. Before he died, he started to tell me about his friendship with my father. He told me about this Father Dom; the betrayer."

Isobel noticed Tom flinch and straighten in his chair. His eyes blinked in quick succession as he began to stand.

"So you're saying that the priest is involved in your father's death?"

"Yes."

Noah followed her to the window and again she felt his hands grab her shoulders.

"Don't … That hurts."

He didn't stop. Instead, he began to shake her with aggression.

"Stop it. Don't touch me. Leave me alone."

Noah let go of her and she backed away from him.

"Isobel, It's very important that we get this right. It's vital. The priest, Father Dominico Rossi. Are you sure it's him?"

Isobel felt aggrieved.

How dare he touch her.

"Isobel. Are you sure? Absolutely sure?"

Her eyes sought Tom's; they shared the same sadness.

"Yes. Yes. He's the deceiver. He's responsible for the murder of our families."

Frederick Vogel gave the cardinal his most condescending smile, yet it didn't appear to have any effect on the man's arrogance.

"I thought I made it perfectly clear, Mr Vogel. I chose to meet with the whole Assembly Council and not just with you. Perhaps you're not taking me seriously."

"Please, Your Grace, have a seat and some refreshment."

He offered the cardinal the very same chair in the eighth-floor parlour room of the Intercontinental De La Ville - Roma that previously harboured so much of his own suspense and worry.

"The chairman has agreed to meet you. He'll speak for the entire council."

The cardinal gave a grunt of disapproval. He fell into the proffered seat and turned his face away from Vogel.

"Regrettably, the chairman has been delayed. He offers his apologies. Please ring the bell if you require anything that will make your stay more comfortable."

Frederick hid his grin as he left the room. How pleasurable to be the one in the penthouse, while others perspired.

Vogel kept the cardinal waiting as long as possible, so he could utilise the time to study him, yet the man's body language and facial features did not change. He remained arrogant and superior, frustrating his planned analysis.

"Look at his airs and graces. He's not acting, he's confident."

The chairman nodded.

"He's sure we'll accept."

Frederick felt a moment of fear. The chairman's face remained expressionless, but his eyes bulged with anger.

"Before we bring in our pompous friend, tell me about these accusations concerning the priest."

Vogel handed the chairman his report.

"My spy inside the PMSG has confirmed this information directly to me. As you'll see in the report, the Kite girl has recognised the priest. She has already informed the PMSG members of his involvement with the Assembly and her father's subsequent murder."

The security chief smiled to himself. Destroying an enemy always felt good.

"This makes him an untrustworthy source. If he attempts in any way to continue, it will put my contact and all of our endeavours at risk."

The chairman gave a grunt of acquiescence.

"Given these circumstances, I authorise you to cease the priest's involvement with our enterprise. Remove him immediately, but do not terminate him. For the moment his knowledge may be useful."

Chapter Twenty Three

Tom sat at the kitchen bench and tried to remain calm, while most of the others paced and fidgeted. Isobel's identification of the priest seemed to smother their hope, adding suspicion to any information gathered from that source.

If the priest knew their movements, the SRP could take them at any time. So why hadn't they?

"Noah, can I have a word … In private? Just you, me, and Isobel."

Noah led them up the stairs to the far bedroom. As they entered, he checked that no-one else came behind, before closing the door.

"You know something?"

"Yes. I think I know what's happening here."

"Go on, lad."

"I think it's all been a setup. Our meeting. Isobel's rescue. Our trip here; it's contrived; controlled by the Assembly …"

Tom searched Noah's eyes for signs of accordance, but the man turned his face away before speaking.

"Yes ... Go on."

"If it all originates from them, then they're creating the timing. So why didn't they take us out?"

"I think you already know the answer, Tom.

Isobel joined the dialogue; her voice shrill with emotion.

"Those bastards could have killed me?"

Tom squeezed his lips together and shook his head.

"No. No way. They wanted us to be together. They wanted us in the PMSG and to have no way back."

"Yes ... And?"

"They're using us as pathfinders."

Tom felt Isobel's hand make contact with his wrist. He flinched, surprised by the soft touch. She jerked it away and he noticed her face begin to redden. To divert the awkward silence he sought her opinion.

"What do you think, Isobel?"

She took a moment to compose herself before answering.

"Yes, I agree, but I have a question for both of you."

"Go ahead, lass."

"If we lead them to the Prize, what happens to us?"

Noah's voice sounded harsh as he replied.

"They'll kill every one of us."

Tom banged his fist on the surface of the small coffee table between them. It made a cracking sound, but didn't break.

"Bastards."

"Tom, keep your voice down."

Noah stood, marched to the door and checked the hall, before returning to his seat.

"Brilliant deductions. Well done, Tom. But, have you worked out how they're doing it?"

"Yes."

Isobel looked baffled.

"What does he mean? Who's doing it, Tom?"

"We have a traitor amongst us. That's how they control our movements. That's how they monitor us."

"In our team? You're joking."

Noah laughed and Tom thought it sounded cruel. Their leader began to pace the room before he spoke.

"Brilliance. Utter brilliance. How did you work it out, lad?"

"Whoever placed that newspaper in the medical box is the spy. We would never have approached the priest otherwise. You know who I'm talking about?"

"Touché, Tom. Uta is the spy."

———————

Tom allowed himself a moment to ponder the man in front of him; the one person he felt he could trust. Once a family man with a beloved wife, now a hunted outlaw near the top of the most wanted list.

He focused on Noah's face, following the scar that ran a course down the inside of his right ear, over his jaw bone and all the way across the underside of his chin.

Tom knew how he received the wound. In June of 2029, Noah and his wife, Heather, took a flight to New York City, to participate in a rally for human rights. It got ugly, but that didn't stop them continuing on to Washington for another demonstration outside of the White House.

Noah returned to their motel that night, after a failed mission to locate a bottle of celebratory champagne, only to find his room full of security police; some bloodied and partially dressed.

His mind took some time to comprehend the rope that bound Heather's neck to the bed head. More cord secured her ankles to the smaller posts at the other end. Used prophylactics and the knife they utilised to torture her, rested on her stomach; a macabre setting created for him; a warning, a technique to control his actions.

Noah exploded with rage.

His allies found him fifteen minutes later, in a truck stop behind the motel; his throat cut and a bullet in his back. His beloved Heather, lay lifeless beside him. Tom wondered how any man could survive, or recover from such an emotional wound, yet the man in front of him seemed incapable of hatred.

The chairman disliked open displays of emotion. He hissed with distaste as his guest approached like a crown prince on the way to his coronation.

Haughty, self-important dandy.

He forced any signs of disgust from his expression as the cardinal entered the penthouse suite. With a grunt, he raised his bulk into a semi-erect stoop and embraced the cardinal in greeting, offering him a seat beside Vogel at the council table.

"Your Grace. The Dal Santo family is glorified by their son. It is a pleasure to have you as our most honoured guest."

"As I am sure the Costa family is honoured by your greatness, Antonio. It is indeed my pleasure to be here, not only to confirm such greatness, but to give it the power that God intended."

The chairman nodded, accepting the praise. The cardinal seemed in a hurry to deliver his terms.

"Mr Vogel presented your offer to our committee and I must say we found it most interesting, but difficult to achieve."

The chairman's expression remained stoic, giving the cardinal no hint of his intentions, but he almost baulked at the clergyman's display of arrogance.

"You surprise me, Antonio. I didn't think anything could faze you."

Vogel sat forward, raising his hand in an attempt to join the conversation.

"How do you propose to substantiate such an offer, Your Grace? Your very high standing aside, I just can't see how you could guarantee such an arrangement."

"Well you wouldn't, Mr Vogel. You're only privy to this information as Antonio's faithful servant. Please, do not interrupt me again."

"My apologies, Your Grace. It's my responsibility to ask such questions."

The chairman interjected with a grunt.

"I would be most interested to hear the terms of your offer. If this proposal is to be accepted, then we would need strong assurances of success."

The cardinal spent the next twenty minutes outlining his proposition. He remained confident throughout; his facial features giving no hint of negativity.

You soulless predator.

The chairman gave a convincing portrayal of indifference, yet he knew the cardinal could see through his mask. His proposal gifted the Assembly with its ultimate goal; vast dominion; power without constraint; the old world becoming the new, yet the man offering this miracle formed its greatest obstacle.

Don't test his powers of perception. Concentrate. The man is sharp.

The chairman changed direction, utilising all of his theatrical abilities. He needed to be convincing. Before him sat Caligula, the mad Roman Emperor reborn.

"Mr Chairman, like you, I am a firm believer in the old order of things. God awaits his sons, as they bring to fruition his will. Our old order is as He intended. As you know, the Kingdoms of Europe have turned to dust. Their fall from grace, is all part of the Creator's design."

He stood for emphasis, displaying his flamboyant presence.

"I own a hidden third of the will of Rome. Those cardinals will side with us, once given proof of ascent. You hold enough of the remaining vote to ensure our victory."

The chairman gave a slight nod.

"How long will it take for the pope's seat to become vacant?"

"Less than a year, I can assure you."

The cardinal compressed his lips. His long held hatred for the present pontiff, unmistakable. He guffawed and spittle wet his chin.

"He is cursed by God and his future is inoperable."

The chairman waited on the cardinal's vanity. He pretended not to notice as God's bishop turned away, using the sleeve of his robe to mop his indiscretion. Antonio put his repugnance aside and continued.

"Because of the timing issue, I will discuss your offer with the council, at their earliest convenience."

The chairman used his powerful forearms to rise, causing the heavy table to dip. With a convincing display of warmth, he placed his arm around the clergyman's shoulder and escorted him back to the parlour room.

"The Assembly Council will be in contact with you, as soon as possible. If all are in agreement, we will begin the plan immediately."

"Yes, Antonio. Together we will rid the world of this hideous new order. May God's rightful pontiff and his seven kings of the true bloodline reign together forever."

Tom's gaze shifted from Isobel and his expression hardened, as it centred on Noah.

"So, what do we do now? Pretend like nothing's happened."

"Yes. The advantage has come back to us. We can play them, but we must do nothing to alert our enemy. When the time comes, we can feed them misinformation and with luck, elude any traps."

Tom sat in silence for a moment, trying to digest the full meaning of this incredible revelation. They could control this situation if they could control her.

"We have to create a good story to keep Uta convinced. She can't learn the truth or it's over."

"Correct, Tom. Her treachery may be our saviour. Providing most of the truth is the best way of keeping her satisfied."

They heard movement. Noah lifted a finger to his lips for silence as Luther's heavy footfalls thudded towards them.

"Noah, you in there? Petra's found something."

"Good, bring her here. Don't let anyone follow you, then leave us alone."

Petra arrived in a matter of minutes. Her smile fixed on Noah the moment she entered the room.

"I've got something."

"Good girl. Out with it now."

"Tom's father owned an exploration company in the name of Raptor Park Enterprises. The article stated that the company existed as a sideline to his normal business. Apparently, it served as an excuse for his interest in palaeontology. They had some pretty good finds out there."

Noah's face creased into a frown.

"Where are we talking about, Petra? Where is out there?"

"Mostly locations spread over Northern Australia and Western Queensland."

"That's it …? That's all you found?"

Isobel jumped to her feet with excitement.

"No. It's more than that. The name. It kept bothering me. Mali, the old man who worked for my father told me about it. Tom, it's where you lived as a boy. Raptor Park is the name of your home."

Chapter Twenty Four

Uta relaxed her shoulders and continued on through the shadows, checking the perimeter of the safe house. She stopped and squatted in the darkness. The buzz in her left ear acute, yet it didn't alter her trained expression.

"My darling, Uta. What happened at Varful Pietrosu? What happened there that binds us with the curse of our blood?"

"They executed a killer."

"Yes, but who?"

"Our glorious father, Vladimir Remus Cel Rău."

"Yes, and …?"

"They put him to death in the shade of the Carpathians, amongst the piles of severed heads and the tortured bodies of his victims."

"Our Vladimir. Our Remus the Decapitator. The Assembly kill any threat in the name of their God; their ambition. Never forget this, my beloved. They're the ones that took him from us."

"Their time draws to a close, sweet Réz. Retribution is coming."

She raised herself and began rechecking the immediate area.

"Our last mission proved to be successful. Based on the clues we found in the broken watch, the PMSG travelled to Fox's childhood home in the mountains, west of Sydney. That's why I haven't been able to contact you. The mission proved to be a success. Fox remembered a secret hiding spot and we found a locked metal box with his name engraved on it.

"Did you find it? The location ..."

"No. They have to check the box for chemical traps and explosive devices before opening it. As soon as I know what's in it, you'll know."

"Good. As soon as possible."

The transmission ended.

Uta spat on the pavement as she crept through the darkness. She despised ordinary people and she detested pretending to be one. She belonged with her sister and the cardinal; amongst intellectual equals. After her communication with Réz, she felt intense anger tighten her body.

*I'm Uta Cel Ră*u *the best of the best.*

Uta remained the finest of the elite SRP commandos and the most experienced of their field agents; so clever that she operated her trade for three different organisations without any of them knowing about the other.

I'm The Raptor for a damn good reason. I'm the perfect instrument of death and soon I'm going to prove it.

Frederick Vogel gave her the nickname and she detested him for it at first. He told everyone that he derived the name from a species of dinosaur called an Utahraptor. The pronunciation of the two names sounded similar so the name stuck amongst her SRP comrades. This made her furious, until she discovered the Utahraptor's killing abilities. Their similarity intrigued her.

I'm reborn from the Cretaceous to kill.

She loved that the raptors ruled their world with violence. She began to love everything about them, especially their formidable killing weapons; the large, curving, single claws on each of their hind feet and the razor sharp teeth. They also possessed stealth and incredible speed, despite weighing up to a thousand kilograms.

Uta derived another reason for her growing attachment to the name. Utahraptor's similarity to the fabled *Dracul*, the dragon also filled her with pride. The infamous *Dracul*, known as Vlad Ţepeş, or sometimes Vlad the Impaler, or even Dracula in the West; her own kin; her own blood.

She hated the female line of her family, often feeling matricidal. Yet her mother died years before, denying her the opportunity.

Phlegm rose into her throat and it tasted foul. It made her sick thinking about the imbecile of a mother that squeezed her out. She never understood what brought them on, but her subconscious continued to drag disjointed recollections into her conscious mind.

Bitch ...

On the very day of her birth, the people of the village gathered in the town square, demanding her removal or worse. They considered her bloodline to be evil. She survived and as a tiny girl, acted like any other. Her differences emerged as a duality of traits. She could be sweet and alluring, yet in private, she loved to kill small animals and to play with their entrails. Despite this morbid behaviour, her true nature didn't fully reveal itself until she met the priest.

Uta spent her early years in the town of Borsa in the north of Romania, near the Ukrainian border. She considered the townsfolk there to be superstitious fools, but in the end, their folklore proved to be correct. She couldn't deny the evil in her nature.

When she reached ten years of age, the Church intervened and took her away from her mother; pretending to be afraid that the townspeople might kill her. They argued that many families still harboured revenge for her father's murderous deeds.

The Church placed her in an orphanage, which she viewed as a prison and sweatshop for slaves. The brothers made money out of her through the day and abused her in the evenings.

Sadists and rapists.

She detested her incarceration almost as much, as she despised the brothers. She could still feel the darkness and the cold damp walls. Each day her dreams of the world tempted her and in the end, she simply walked out.

Once free, she discovered the power of her body. The men acted like pigs and smelt worse, but at least they paid for their pleasure. Uta the dirty little angel, too young to bleed, yet every woodcutter and shopkeeper's desire.

Her mother disowned her when she reappeared in Borsa, forcing her to rely even more on her body for food and survival. She remembered making a lot of money; more than any enterprise in her village, which didn't endear her to the local female population.

No wonder the men wanted me.

Their disgusting wives wobbled with fat and tucked their ugly tits into their pants.

Uta laughed at the thought.

She mocked these women at every opportunity; attacking any courageous enough to return her barbs with her fists, or any other makeshift weapon at her disposal.

She remembered biting a piece out of one girl's ear; an action creating unwanted circumstances. The local policeman beat her close to death for injuring his daughter. When she recovered, he locked her in the back of a cattle truck and transported her to a foul smelling reformatory institution on the outskirts of Bucharest.

The fools couldn't break me.

Instead of reforming her, the place served as a steel-hardening furnace.

She inflicted her first bloody murder at the orphanage.

The violence of her incarceration grasped any remaining innocence and ripped it out. Uta knew what awaited her. Capitulate no matter the cost, or be prepared to fight the worst creatures imaginable.

Uta laughed as she remembered her first day. She killed the toughest of the girls before dinner.

Lovely Lucifer ... It felt so good.

She could still feel the rough handle of the knife and the power it granted her. She shivered with pleasure, just thinking about it.

Her older enemy hissed and cursed, as she attacked with her knife, but the heavier girl couldn't match Uta for strength or viciousness. She remembered the look of astonishment in the girl's eyes and the feeling of the knife, as it sliced into her stomach. The experience captivated her. She felt more excited than at any other time in her short life; an intoxicating taste of things to come.

Towards the end of that year, her vicious exploits came to the attention of a priest.

My beautiful man with the body of a boy and the rod of a god.

Her obsession still drove her after all of the years. This magnificent cultured male overwhelmed her with his ruthless and terrible power. He radiated a force that held her in wonderment and commanded her complete obedience; his fiery passion burning away any chance of redemption.

She trembled, remembering her education under the priest. It began the first night and she enjoyed the beating more than anything in her life. After this experience, she disappeared into his hedonistic world of pleasure, which become the very purpose of her existence. From that day on, she serviced his will, no matter its objective, or its cost.

Chapter Twenty Five

Tom dressed with a growing sense of excitement and bounded down the stairs.

Late the previous evening they opened the box he found at his parents old house, but after many hours of unyielding research, they gave up their attempts to decipher anything meaningful from the artefacts inside, until this morning.

When he arrived in the living room, he spotted Isobel sitting alone; staring at him with an intense expression that he found difficult to interpret. He thought it unusual that he couldn't comprehend her feelings towards him, as well as annoying. Women liked him naturally, even loved him. This phenomenon occurred without any extra effort on his part. Love's infatuations affected his partners, but not him; never him.

No damn way.

Tom winced at the lie. Every time he saw Isobel, he reacted; a feeling akin to a hand squeezing his heart.

I liked it better when it just pumped blood.

He cringed at the thought and skulked closer, sliding down the wall until he sat next to her on the floor. Neither spoke for some time.

"So, Isobel. What's going on?"

"The blond girl with the wide eyes …?"

"Petra?"

"Yes. She discovered something this morning, while you slept in."

"Hardly, I …"

"Do you want hear this or not?"

She paused until he nodded.

Tom felt his face flush and he looked away.

"The name on the key tag isn't a code. It's an alpine hut. Apparently, it belongs to a federation of walking clubs. Bushfires burnt it to the ground on several occasions, although it hasn't been destroyed since the 2030's."

"And, this is relevant, how …?"

Tom immediately regretted his sharp condescending tone.

"Because, smart mouth, after the last fire your father rebuilt it. Whatever you're looking for is probably up there in that hut."

"Hell …"

"Yeah, exactly."

"Something good. It's about time."

Tom felt a sudden flush of wellbeing. Without thinking, he put his arm around Isobel's shoulders and pulled her towards him.

"Don't."

He felt her body stiffen. She threw his arm over her head and tossed it away from her.

"Sorry."

"What the hell are you doing?"

Tom didn't know how to answer.

"Just keep your hands off me."

"Don't worry. It won't happen again."

"Good."

They stared at each other with fury; neither looking away.

Hey … What?

Tom tried to stand, but before he could, Isobel reached over and grasped his head with both hands. Her kiss felt soft and moist, and his body shivered.

She straddled him and he tried to wrap his arms around her, but she took hold of his wrists and forced them against the wall.

"No ... Don't hold me."

She kissed him again. Wider, harder, wetter; her hands and knees pinning him. Tom surrendered; letting go to her need.

"Hey? Where are you going?"

Isobel disentangled herself, stood and backed away from him.

"Isobel ...?"

She turned and kept walking, not responding or looking back.

Noah appeared and halted Isobel's retreat. His entire face beamed with amusement. He may have witnessed their intimacy, Tom couldn't be sure.

"Are you ready for a trip into the mountains, lass?"

"I'm not going anywhere."

Noah pulled back from her in surprise.

"We're all going, young lady. It's not much of a climb. We'll fly to an adjacent mountain and trek across a connecting ridgeline. Our march shouldn't take any more than five or six hours, depending on the weather."

Tom tried to concentrate on Noah's descriptions, but couldn't focus.

That kiss has put a spell on me.

He fought with his emotions. Could the others see his anguish?

Relax. Control your breathing.

Tom stood and thought about walking off, but something in Noah's expression stopped him; a warning of clenched teeth and deep creases of concern.

"Is there a problem, Noah?"

He leant forward, turning his face from Isobel and whispered to Tom.

"Aye, there's a problem. Even if things go well, we'll have to spend two days trekking across those mountains; exposed with no backup. Do you understand what I'm saying?"

Tom nodded; surprised. Noah rarely confided in him. He understood the man's anxiety. This could be a fatal journey. He tried to think of something meaningful to say until he felt Isobel brush past him, halting his thought processes.

"What are you two whispering about?"

Neither answered.

"Look, you can't be serious about this, Noah. I heard on the news that the mountains got weird early snow and wild storms. It'll be dreadful up there. I'm not going."

Noah relaxed and smiled at her.

"We've got no choice, lass. We have to go."

Isobel frowned and folded her arms, ending the conversation. Noah smiled at her and turned to leave, but Tom grabbed his arm and manoeuvred him into a quiet corner of the room.

"Tell me, Noah. Is this the end of it?"

"I don't know, Tom. I suppose we'll find out soon enough."

Tom turned to see if Isobel could hear them. She stared back at him with the same intense impenetrable expression that kept him baffled.

"Can you be honest with me, Noah?"

"That depends on what you're asking."

"What's going to happen to Isobel and me? Are we going to be killed?"

Tom maintained his eye contact with Noah, as the man struggled with his answer.

"Look, lad, I can't promise anything, but I'll do everything in my power to see us all through."

Noah's eyes dropped away and Tom thought he understood the underlying message.

Only a bloody miracle will save us.

Chapter Twenty Six

The G11 team landed ten minutes behind schedule at Mount Hotham Airport, due to low cloud and poor visibility. Tom fled the twin otter before the propellers ceased to spin.

He wandered into the car park sucking in the damp coldness of the mountain air. He felt annoyed that she followed him.

"Are you alright?"

"Yes."

"Are you sure? You look green."

"I'm fine … Just bugger off will you."

Oh God.

Could he never come up with the right words? Foolishness seemed to fall out of his mouth whenever he tried to speak to her.

"Please yourself then."

"Alright, I will."

"Good."

Great. Now I feel sick and stupid.

He began to focus on his new environment, not wanting to think about her or his stomach. For the first time, he managed a fleeting glimpse of the mountain. Clumps of vegetation appeared through the shifting fog, but little else.

He heard the clamour of raised voices. He turned back towards the arrivals area where an angry Luther shook a fist at one of the airport staff.

"Bloody incompetent imbeciles."

Luther rarely spoke and never loudly.

"These people ..."

Tom tugged on Noah's jacket as he attempted to ease past him in the narrow baggage claim area.

"What's going on Noah?"

"It's bad. The charter company lost two of our packs."

Noah's full lips stretched into a snarl, causing Tom's smile to slip from his face. Without consciously thinking about it, he altered the tone of his voice to fit in with Noah's mood.

"How bad?"

"We've lost a good deal of our light weaponry and ammunition, most of our rope, all of our crampons except one pair and all of the ice axes."

A prearranged taxi-bus arrived and Noah walked off to meet it before Tom could answer. Within minutes, all of the group and the remaining luggage, sped north-west towards Diamantina Hut; the starting point of the Razorback Track to Mount Feathertop.

Along the way, Tom marvelled at the natural ice sculptures clinging to the branches of the trees and the smooth wet bark that resembled human skin.

"This place's amazing, isn't it?"

No-one answered. No-one seemed interested.

He continued his study of the scenery, taking pleasure from the experience of seeing something unique. Outside of the heated van, the ice-trees seemed to be an impenetrable barrier to anyone seeking a way through. Squat trunks rose into a tangle of twisted branches with a thin canopy of leaves, allowing the ice to cling and hang in shards.

Noah bumped Tom with his shoulder and gave him a smile.

"We live on a strange planet, lad. This time last year, extreme heat and bushfires ravaged these mountains. This summer, we'll be lucky if it gets above freezing."

They reached the main resort village of Mount Hotham in just under thirty minutes and continued for several more kilometres down from the summit before pulling into a cutting, off the side of the road. Tom could just see the A-framed outline of the mountain hut through the fog; its snow covered roof extending all the way to the ground on each side.

As the taxi driver eased on the brakes and splashed to a stop in the mud, he turned to Noah and pointed in the opposite direction towards the west.

"The Razorback starts across the road."

The entire group turned in unison and searched the whiteness for any sign of a track. Tom could only see what appeared to be a very steep drop off.

Each member of the group alighted from the taxi and collected their gear. No-one spoke. Tom hurried across the road and down onto the track, where the rest of the group huddled together, waiting for Noah's final instructions.

"Isobel. Look."

Isobel turned in time to witness the thick cloud shift from the Razorback's narrow ridge; its long serrated rim jutting out above a lower layer of cloud. In the distance, it joined the sunlit peak of Mount Feathertop, before new weather submerged it from sight.

Tom felt a jolt of fear. Near the summit lay their goal and his destiny.

"Alright, pay attention."

Noah stood in the middle of a tight circle; using his index finger to emphasise his commands to each individual in the team.

"Uta and Julius will make up our vanguard, with Uta on point duty until they reach the Twin Knobs. The location is obvious."

Uta snorted, rolled her eyes and elbowed Julius.

"Two knobs are always better than one, hey?"

Tom studied Noah's face. All knew his aversion to crassness, yet his expression never wavered.

"Once we receive the all clear signal from the point, the rest of us will catch up. Luther and Surat will handle our rear guard. Is everyone clear on this?"

Noah gave each of his team a searching look.

"Good. Let's get on with it then."

Isobel strode up to Tom and for a moment, he didn't recognise her in the hooded wet-weather jacket and pants.

"How do I look?"

"Like a garden gnome."

"Nice. Thanks a lot."

"You asked."

"Look, I wanted to ask you if Noah's said anything further about the timing of this trek.'

"Yes. Why?"

"Well, the guidebook says it's a six-hour hike, but the taxi driver said something like four."

"Alright. I'll compromise and say five."

"Brilliant ... I'd say we have about five hours of daylight left, so if we don't get moving, we'll be walking in the dark."

Once they began, it only took eight hundred metres, before they reached a junction in the track. The left fork rose up along a snow pole line to the Bon Accord Spur track and down twelve hundred and fifty metres to the township of Harrietville. Noah led them to the right towards the main track, which sidled the eastern slope of the Razorback Spur, towards a deep saddle.

Here he stopped and pulled them into another tight group.

"We're heading down into the Big Dipper. It's icy and slippery, so be extra careful."

Noah fumbled with the scarf covering his nose and mouth. Tom thought he looked stern, even angry as he attempted to pull it free with heavy gloves.

"Listen carefully. Only Luther has crampons for his boots. This means, we'll have to rope ourselves together. With the weight of these packs, it'll be hard to stay on our feet. If someone falls, brace yourself. Jam your walking poles into the snow and hang on, to prevent yourself from going over the edge."

Frederick Vogel clung to the strap of his seat belt as his Assembly Learjet bucked and jerked in the dense cloud, on its final approach to Mount Hotham Airport.

He didn't notice his assistant arrive until he began to speak.

"Sir, as per your instructions, I've confirmed the status of the weather. Original forecasts proved to be inconclusive. The thick cloud around us is only a section of an approaching group of storms that'll start affecting us within fifteen minutes."

"And ...?"

"Sir?"

"That's not what I asked you to find out. We have two contracted helicopters at our disposal. One here at Hotham and one down in the valley, at Porepunkah Airport near Bright. I asked you to find out whether we're going to get them off the ground for this operation."

Vogel suffered the bumpy landing and watched his assistant return as the aircraft taxied towards the arrivals terminal. The man's face revealed his answer before he spoke.

Not good news. The fool looks nervous.

His operation required the speed and accuracy of air support. Walking in behind the PMSG meant plugging escape routes.

"Sir."

"Yes. What?"

"The contractors have informed us that they won't be going up until conditions are suitable. The storms will ground the helicopters until further notice."

With a flick of his hand Vogel dismissed his assistant.

To trap them, I need to keep thinking like them; I need to keep understanding their plans.

For this reason, he employed his backup tactics before boarding the aircraft in Sydney; requiring strategic placement of a small force of men at every major road and trail end.

I have to keep them in the net at all costs.

His backup team sealed off the northern end of the Razorback Spur walking track at the point where it became a four-wheel drive road down to the Ovens Valley. They also covered both the Bungalow Spur and the Northwest Spur walking tracks, leading down to the town of Harrietville.

Once the enemy moved through to the west of the Twin Knobs, he could secure the area and eliminate the Bon Accord and Diamantina Spurs to the east of that position.

If they managed to break free and elude their main advance, he could force them down one of the only escape routes and into a trap.

Not bad, but I need those helicopters and their infrared.

He nodded with certainty.

The backup strategy didn't change the rules of the game.

When Uta confirms the location of the Prize, they all die and I take my place at the head of the table.

Uta performed her tasks several hundred metres ahead of Julius. She left him to secure the Twin Knobs, while she began a reconnaissance further up the track past High Knob. Her route covered the start of the Diamantina track, which led east and descended to the base of Mount Jaithmathang.

She searched for specific points in the narrow terrain that could offer an advantage in defence, or be a likely area for possible ambush. On either side of the ridge, the land fell away steeply; five hundred metres on the eastern side and even further on the western slope.

Uta looked at her watch, hid herself from any possible surveillance and began the transmission.

"How did he kill them?"

Sometimes the routine identifying the caller and the correct frequency annoyed her, but it provided extra security around their communications.

"He ensnared them with a lance through the leg, my darling, leaving them defenceless against the knife; his true passion and the tool of their deliverance."

"I need to speak to him, Réz. It's important."

"The cardinal's not here my sweet. What's the matter?"

"That idiot, Vogel. Could he be more obvious? Like that old newspaper to bring Fox to the priest. So stupid."

"But, you're still operational ... Aren't you?"

"Noah's on to us, Réz. I've seen it in the way he looks at me. He's just biding his time."

"It's just a feeling though and nothing specific, maybe you're just imagining ..."

"No ... My instincts don't lie, Réz. If we lose the element of surprise, he could bring us down."

"Uta, listen my darling. If this man suspected you of treachery, he would never have allowed you to go on this mission. It'd be a fatal mistake. So stop worrying. Remember, we've almost won."

Frederick Vogel paced around in circles kicking at the snow. Being patient never appealed to him.

Where is the woman? I could kill her.

"Raptor. Why aren't you answering me?"

"Vogel, we're clear. Go ahead."

"Where the hell have you been? What's your status?"

"I'm on the ground at Hotham airport, with four to six hours to our destination. Where are you?"

"I'm still at our temporary headquarters in Sydney, waiting for your message. What's taking so long?"

He knew that Uta would be alert to every nuance in his tone; looking for any sign that he'd discovered her lie.

"You know I can't make contact, Vogel. Not unless I'm alone."

"Uta, it's imperative that you communicate information pertaining to the Prize and your movements. Make yourself alone. Is that clear?"

Vogel stretched his lips into a smirk. Out-deceiving the charlatan felt good. He couldn't wait to rid himself of these vermin.

"Listen up, Vogel. Noah has changed our plans. We won't be leaving Mount Hotham until the morning because of storms. This means I should have your confirmation by eighteen hundred hours tomorrow."

"Good. Out for now."

Frederick re-joined his SRP squad.

Lying bitch.

When the red headed devil-woman showed up at Villa Dal Santo, his instincts screamed betrayal. Now he knew for sure.

Uta has a twin.

Chapter Twenty Seven

Tom followed Isobel into a small depression, sheltered by an amphitheatre of rocky outcrops. He removed their packs and threw them onto the snow.

"Welcome to the Twin Knobs, Izzi."

"Izzi? Where did that come from?"

"I don't know … It suits you."

To discover her reaction, he searched under her rain jacket's hood for a face. Between darkened snow goggles and multiple layers of facial scarfs and beanies, he only found a tiny area of reddened skin on the top of her cheeks.

"Is this you trying to be nice, Tom?"

He noticed his reflection in her ski goggles and tried to picture her intense stare behind.

"Can you ever come up with a sentence that isn't a question?"

"No … It appears I can't."

He recognised the hurt feelings in her tone.

"Sorry, Iz. I didn't mean it to sound so bad."

"Yeah, well you can keep your Iz."

"Seriously, it comes out wrong every time. I meant it to be fun."

She stared at him for a long time, nodded, then walked to the far side of the depression.

Hell. Why am I so verbally incontinent?

Maybe he could keep his mouth closed and just nod, instead of embarrassing himself every time he spoke to her.

He saw movement, which distracted him from the melancholy of his thoughts. The remainder of the group began to appear out of the fog, forming a ring around their leader. Noah glanced over at Tom and smiled. In that instant, Tom perceived something furtive and mischievous in his expression.

"Everybody, move in tight."

Light snow began to fall on the huddle and their combined breath rose above like smoke from a chimney.

"Uta. You and Julius will stay here and set up a defensive position."

"No ... I'm the point. I go where the action is."

Tom could see Noah's hand resting on the handle of his automatic pistol.

"Yes. Exactly, Uta. Any action against us will come from behind. You're needed to secure this position. Both of you will take turns sweeping the area. I want a five hundred metre reconnaissance with regular communication and if the enemy engage, I want you to hold and retreat as slowly as possible until you receive other orders."

"Noah, I own the vanguard. I'm the best ..."

"I'm not asking, Uta. You will do what you're ordered to do."

Uta seethed. In the midst of the huddle, her anger felt palpable.

Tom forced his expression to remain neutral, when he really felt like flinging himself onto the snow and laughing with relief.

You're absolutely brilliant, Noah.

They knew her deception. She functioned as a scout to confirm the location of their goal and as a trigger to kill from within. This information allowed Tom to understand Noah's tactic. He made her impotent, by leaving her in the rear and eliminating her from the game.

Noah's actions compelled Vogel to assume that he still maintained control, yet rendered him powerless to act.

Brilliant. Hopefully he's given us the time we need.

Tom felt the wind intensify as they began to set out. He watched as Luther and Surat marched off to begin their forward reconnaissance; quickly disappearing into the denseness of the wind driven snow.

He knew that the ferocity of the weather aided them by shielding their activities. He also realised its fickle nature. The enemy remained blind to their endeavours, yet could utilise the same conditions to screen an approach.

The main group left five minutes after the vanguard. They roped up and began walking into a swirling world of white. Tom couldn't discern any difference between the path and the sky.

Concentrate ... Focus on your feet.

He couldn't see Noah at the head of their column, yet he understood the drop awaiting them on either side of the track. The group followed a narrow crest that wound around the western side of High Knob for seven hundred metres. After a short stop, they sidled left again and travelled a similar distance, before reaching a saddle that Noah called: 'The Cross'. He explained that a memorial cairn lay nearby, attesting to lives lost on this mountain.

Tom didn't need a warning. He walked with the very real possibility of falling, dying of exposure, or being murdered by Vogel.

He felt the rope go slack. Then he heard laughter and noticed a renewed enthusiasm in the voices ahead of him. He peered through the gloom and spotted Noah leaning against a thick, ice-covered tree with a sign reading: 'The Junction'.

The summit of Mount Feathertop lay two kilometres to the right and north of the junction. They set off immediately, turning left and travelling slightly down and south-west for another five hundred metres. They walked within metres of the high mountain hut before they saw it through the storm.

———

Uta gestured for Julius to come to her position with sharp tugs of her arm.

"Come on, I need you to help me with this shelter."

Together, they stretched lightweight tarps over a rough frame of eucalypt branches, hidden amongst the surrounding rocks. The blue material stood out initially, but within minutes, the falling snow hid the structure from any approaching force.

"Alright, give it a try, Jules. See if we'll both fit."

She noted his expression of suspicion.

"Come on, I haven't got all day."

"So you get first reconnaissance …?"

"Yeah, whatever."

Julius looked around. He still seemed wary.

Come on fool make a move.

He bent forward to enter the hide.

Yes.

Uta found time to pick a spot on the back of his head. She withdrew her side arm and in one easy movement, slammed the handle down onto the imagined target point on his skull.

Julius hung in the air, lunged forward, then slumped down into unconsciousness. She inflicted two more blows to make sure he stayed there.

"How's that feel, pretty boy?"

Uta removed one of the cords from the shelter, cut it into two pieces and tied his feet and hands. She knelt and tugged at his bloodied hair, until his face came level with hers.

"I'm going to make your last moments memorable, but for now …"

Time pressure intervened, deferring her gratification. She dragged his heavy unconscious frame into the shelter and sighed. Nothing beat a warm bleeder, with time to consider his death.

———

Tom lit a fire in the potbelly stove at the far end of the hut and waited to reload it with larger pieces of wood. He heard her behind him, rubbing her hands together to keep warm.

"It'll warm up in here soon, Iz."

"I hope so. I'm freezing."

Grinning, he turned and gathered her in his arms.

"No … Stop it, Tom. Leave me alone."

The swiftness of his actions seemed to frighten her and she resisted; her body stiffening and tugging against his grip, but he didn't let go.

"This is how the Eskimos keep warm, Izzi."

She began to relax and soften in his embrace.

"Bullshit, Tom. You just made that up."

He began to rub her back and shoulders, and she responded by wrapping her arms around his waist and nuzzling the side of her face against his chest.

The door burst open and they pulled away from each other as Noah approached.

"We've got no time for … mucking around. Prepare some food and a brew, while Surat and I start looking."

"I was just getting Isobel's circulation going."

"Get on with it, Tom."

The outer door creaked open and banged closed. Both Tom and Noah turned and faced the hut's inner door, just as Surat rushed through. He almost ran towards them; his eyes bulging as he gripped and shook Noah's shoulders.

"Noah. Uta's outside."

"No, she can't be."

"She's come back and without Julius. She says he slipped and fell and is probably dead."

Noah's placid expression expanded into a grotesque scowl of ferocity.

"Tell Uta to wait for me outside, then go and collect Luther. Get going and keep your wits about you."

Tom could see a nerve pulsing in Noah's neck. It took some time before he spoke.

"I fear our plans have turned against us. What the hell have I done, lad?"

"I think you did the right thing, Noah."

Tom hesitated before answering. He felt surprised. Noah never sought anyone's advice.

"I think that someone's desperate to be back in the game, but you can't let that happen."

Noah's mouth twisted into a bitter looking smile.

"Be prepared for anything, Tom. Keep Isobel close and be ready to leave if necessary."

He turned and marched out of the building.

The hut fell silent, as the remaining three occupants exchanged questioning glances. Petra tried to speak, but couldn't. She looked dumbfounded; her head tilted forward and her mouth fell open.

Tom's heart began to pound as he hurried out of the building with the two women following close behind. He spotted four people draped with snow; their faces aglow in the torch light.

As he approached he watched Noah's features transform themselves from fierceness into cool composure.

"Uta. What happened?"

"I did what you ordered; I completed a quick reconnaissance east towards Mount Hotham. When I came back, I thought I heard a call for help, so I went to investigate. I moved to a point only ten metres or so forward of our hide, but he'd already gone over the edge."

Tom couldn't believe Uta's sincerity. He considered her acting to be magnificent, but chilling, yet he didn't think any one of them believed her.

"He walked too close to the side and the tracks ended in a struggle to hold on. I found some yellow patches in the snow. He must have gone for a piss and without crampons ... Well, you can guess the rest."

"Did you call out to him?"

"Yes, but he didn't answer. The terrain's steep; more of a fall, than a slide. I couldn't get down there ... No way."

"Why didn't you call in?"

"My transmitter's dead. Check it yourself. The other one went over the side with Julius."

Tom could almost see Noah's mind working, as they stood there in the snow. They needed Uta to remain functional, but as far from the hut as possible. The original decision remained the correct one, even though it cost a life. Tom understood Noah's guilt, but they couldn't deviate from their plan, despite his feelings.

"Luther. Take Uta and gather the remainder of our rope. Petra, I know it's not your job, but I want you to go as well. You'll handle communications and help Luther with whatever he needs."

Petra's eyes widened. Tom understood her solemn expression as she nodded. She knew the danger and accepted it.

"I need you to find him. If he's dead, leave the body and get back here. All except you Uta. I want our best person out there covering our retreat. You're to stay there, until we move out. Alright ... Get going."

None of the remaining party thought to move, until Uta's torchlight disappeared into the night.

Chapter Twenty Eight

Tom couldn't stop thinking about Uta; the monster lurking in the shadows; the ever-present threat to the mortality of every member of the group.

Just saying her name implied fear. She killed in the darkness, forcing all of them to wonder about the unsuspecting thrust of the knife. For the sake of sleep, denial replaced any need for bravery.

"God ... You evil bitch of a woman."

His whispered profanity gained Noah's attention; the man's cheeks bunching over his clamped jaw, while his lips peeled back in anger.

"I don't like that language, Tom. We're bigger than that. It's cheap talk, nothing else."

Tom noticed the anguish in Noah's expression. His leader stretched forward, banged his fist against the wall of the hut and cried out in grief. Tom knew he felt responsible for Julius, his friend and colleague, but such displays from Noah ... Unthinkable.

He turned and stared at Tom; his moist eyes reflecting the flames from the open stove.

"I may have sent Luther and Petra to their deaths, lad."

Surat coughed before Tom had a chance to reply. His eyes and face, empty of expression.

"Perhaps we should be getting on with business. It's all for nothing, if we don't find this thing."

Tom watched Noah rise above his suffering. The man refocused, creating structure in their search.

"Surat. Break through the corrugated iron and lining timber on the outside of the verandah and crawl under the building. Search for any markings, or any soil that isn't rock hard. Also, check the underside of the floor-timbers for any sign of activity."

Noah swung his arm in a wide arc, encompassing all aspects of the room.

"I want the rest of you to delve into every conceivable hiding spot. Alright, let's get going."

After fifteen minutes, they found nothing. Tom felt his disappointment as a knot in his stomach. They couldn't have missed anything in this shoebox of a place.

The hut consisted of a small entrance and storeroom, and one other larger room, with a combined wood fire and stove. On the outside, corrugated iron on both the walls and roof, covered a strong hardwood frame. A tough layer of plywood lined the inside walls and ceiling with only two inbuilt cupboards created for storage. Bench seating ran along two walls of the main room with an old table beside the stove; none of which concealed their Prize.

After having no luck under the hut, Surat widened his search to the closest of the snow gums, but with no results. All four searchers regathered in the hut. No-one spoke for several minutes, until Surat began to pace the room.

"You'll have to make a decision soon, Noah. This storm is covering us for the moment, but if we wait here much longer, we could well be taken."

"How we handle Uta will determine our immediate fate. It's a perilous situation. If the woman overreacts, then we'll cop hell.

Let's ready ourselves. When Luther and Petra return, we'll keep up the pretence with Uta and move out."

"No."

Tom felt devastated. How could they give in so easily? He sucked in a ragged breath and began jabbing his index finger at both Noah and Surat.

"No. No. No. We've come all this way. There could be other things we've missed. I think we should all grow some balls and start again."

Tom noticed the lines on Noah's face begin to change. They creased into a tight frown around his eyes and then his entire face slowly widened into a smile.

"Well said, Tom."

He gave a slight nod. Tom thought he recognised the man's approval.

"Alright, back to work everyone."

They searched everything again, covering all of their previous territory, but they found nothing but the same frustration.

Tom and Isobel continued checking the last patchwork of carved graffiti covering the walls. Tom felt overwhelmed with tiredness. He gazed over at Isobel. She appeared to have no such heaviness, seemingly buoyant in her meticulous study of each marking.

"Stop slacking off, Tom. Look for anything with an RP or an AF."

"An AF...?"

Tom felt his face redden with embarrassment. Sometimes his memory couldn't retrieve the obvious. A psychiatrist once described it as aphasia. A description he loathed. He hated feeling stupid, particularly in front of her.

"Alexander Fox; your father's initials."

The tone of her voice stung him.

Annoyed, he looked away to see how the others fared, but at the same time he heard her subtle expulsion of breath.

"Iz ...?"

He twisted back around and saw her pointing. He followed the direction of her finger to a chaotic bunch of scribble carved into the ply.

Her eyes bore into his.

"This could be it, Tom."

She looked away from him and engaged the others.

"Hey. Noah. Surat. We've found something."

She seemed to wait for their full attention before continuing.

"There's initials and an engraved figure here, but someone's carved over them. That's why we didn't notice anything before. Look, an RP and the figure looks like a tiny dinosaur."

Tom recognised the condescension in Isobel's smile and the shake of her head.

"Hello. Is somebody going to do something about this?"

Surat took up his camp axe and attacked the plywood with enthusiasm. It took some time for an opening to appear.

Tom thought the hole looked like a crown of thorns, but it didn't stop him from approaching it first. He edged his hand forward and searched the narrow space. Sharp pieces of plywood dug into his arm the further he delved. He pushed in harder and a splinter pierced the skin on the inside of his elbow.

"Ow ... Not fun."

He withdrew his arm in one involuntary movement.

"Not so nice. I'll try that again."

This time he eased his arm in more slowly, but a dagger of plywood still managed to puncture his bicep. He withdrew it, closed his eyes and took a deep breath; pushing his arm in to its fullest extent. She watched, so he closed his eyes to disguise the pain. He could feel blood trickling down his arm and dripping off his fingers.

"I've ... got it."

His hand felt a box-shaped metal object, but he couldn't grasp it fully with slippery, bloodied fingers.

"I just have to ease it out."

The fingernail on Tom's middle finger found and held behind a tiny hinge. He increased the tension and the box gave up all resistance and came free.

"It's a book ... bound in metal."

He placed the bloodied book-like object on the table and they all stared at it in confusion.

"Is this it?"

Tom and every other member of the group stared at the person opposite, imploring them for an answer.

Tom beseeched Noah for his.

"Is this the Prize, Noah?"

"I don't know. It's not what I expected, but I've a good idea how we'll open it. Do you remember what we found in Katoomba?"

Noah reached over and squeezed Tom's shoulder.

"The key has the same initials marked on the tag."

"You're right. Let's get it opened."

To Tom's surprise, Noah raised his hand, pushing the palm at his face.

"No, wait ... Surat?"

Tom looked around in confusion. He found Surat stepping up on the far bench, peering through the window. Then he pulled back and jumped down; his expression more ominous than usual.

"Turn off your torches, I just saw something."

Noah replaced the stove's lid, concealing its illumination. Simultaneously, the glow from four head-torches went out.

Surat stepped back up onto the bench and spent several more seconds staring through the window.

"We've got trouble. We're receiving a continual SOS signal from somewhere under Molly Hill. It's intermittent; probably torchlight between moving clouds."

He turned away from the window and spoke to Noah with urgency.

"I don't trust this. It stinks. Our people use communicators."

The renewed light from Noah's head torch lit up the room. He leant forward and placed both hands on Surat's shoulders.

"Yes. That's where you come in, old friend. I need you to find out what's happening out there with as much stealth as possible.

"Should I kill her if I get the chance?"

"No. Don't engage her, unless it's your only chance of retreat. Even as our worst enemy, keeping the woman out there remains our greatest hope. Now go."

Chapter Twenty Nine

Every time Noah looked at her, Uta could see the disdain in his expression. She felt his distrust as a burning sensation in her chest.

The bastard knows and he thinks he's won a victory, well he's about to find out how wrong he is.

The group marched in single file with Petra leading and Luther in the rear. This confirmed her suspicions. If they trusted her, Petra would not be on point duty and looking for their trail.

The stupid bitch couldn't find the toilet in the middle of the day.

Uta could feel the storm easing. Between moving clouds, she could see the light from the hut in the distance, which meant that she needed to utilise the weather to disguise her covert activities.

Noah must be made to assume that they're alive. Even when they found the Prize, they wouldn't move without Luther and the Russian.

The group maintained a steady pace along the side of Molly Hill, before moving up onto the crest of the ridge towards High Knob; the place where Julius tumbled off the rim.

She saw her mark in the snow; a small protruding branch placed to prompt her; time to begin.

"Luther, stop. We've gone too far. It's back twenty metres behind us."

He made a fatal error. Uta counted on him turning and looking back down the trail.

"I'll see you in hell, Luther."

The nine-millimetre slug drilled its way through the big man's back and exploded into his stomach. It splintered on impact, sending shrapnel ripping through the body like hundreds of tiny knives.

Luther fell forward onto the track. His head struck first and the weight of his body drove it deep into the snow. With a kick, Uta made sure he didn't move.

Saliva flew from her mouth, as she turned and sneered at the bewildered Petra.

"Now it's your turn, peasant."

The blond Russian appeared unresponsive; subdued by shock. Uta laughed and aimed the gun at her stomach.

"Get your clothes off, bitch. Do it now."

She felt a gush of pleasure at Petra's fear, sending shivers through her body.

"You pathetic piece of shit. I wouldn't waste vomit on you. Get naked or die."

Petra moved in stiff jerky spasms, her functions overwhelmed by fear. She sobbed as she began to undress.

The sight of the Russian stripping flushed Uta's limbic system. Dopamine blasted her libido; causing a storm of lust to thunder through her body. She ached for the terror in the girl's eyes, the panic, the horror; the darker the mental taboo the greater the physical gratification. She craved the forbidden; she craved murder.

She began to perspire, delighted by the wet presence between her legs.

"Get ready, bitch. No guns. No knives. Just hands and teeth, baby."

Uta noticed the Russian stop undressing. She saw the girl's eyes staring; connecting. She felt movement and then the tingle of erect hairs on her neck.

Luther ...?

She spun around and spotted him searching for his weapon. A hulk of a man; his head and shoulders drooped over his wounded core. He looked spent, but Uta knew the man's strength.

He attacked as she reached for her sidearm; his lunge driving Uta backwards, causing her weapon to discharge and fall from her grasp. In her peripheral vision, she saw the bullet strike Petra in the elbow and witnessed a spray of blood splatter against the whiteness of her body.

Uta forced Luther's hands from her neck to avoid strangulation. She disentangled herself from his grasp and rolled away from him. As she jumped to her feet, she heard him call out to Petra, beseeching her to move, as he raised himself from the snow.

"Don't just stand there. Get going girl. Run and keep running."

Uta frowned. Her weapon lay at Luther's feet.

She smashed into his body as he tried to retrieve it. They grappled, twisting and turning, trying for an advantage. Uta couldn't allow him to free his hand and utilise her weapon.

In the midst of the battle, she smiled at his consistent calls for the Russian to flee.

Some people just can't accept their fate.

"It's time for you to die, Luther."

Uta maintained her grip on the big man with practised techniques, striking him repeatedly with her elbows. In the heat of the contest, she couldn't stop herself from laughing. The big oaf waged war with desperation, but she fought for another reason; the joy of inflicting death.

Red-hot neural impulses exploded into the cortex of the Russian's brain and tore her from her stupor. She screamed, as more pulses of pain, reached her brain through the limbic system.

A concoction of neurochemicals raised her awareness and she started to run; fear and adrenalin forcing her to gain momentum and accelerate down the track. The madness didn't stop for several minutes until the pain of her injury and the biting cold on her bare feet dragged some sanity back into her mind.

"Oh God …"

A new panic beset her; the absence of any light. How could she have run so far without falling off the edge? Oblivion could be a few steps in any direction. Even the smallest miscalculation meant death.

Petra, you idiot.

When the fight broke out, she stood on the eastern side of the combatants.

I've run the wrong way. Away from any chance of help.

After a quick estimation, she determined her position to be somewhere near the entrance to the Diamantina Spur.

Uta's between me and the hut.

Once more, fear began to rise as acid in her throat. If she moved in this darkness, she might fall, but if she didn't …?

––––––––––––

Uta feigned, pretending to pull away from Luther's grip. She knew he wanted to utilise his strength in order to land at least one telling blow, so she twisted and rolled him. Never allowing him the possibility of leverage.

She enjoyed his agony and understood that he couldn't continue this level of intensity with such extensive injuries.

"Come on, you big ape. You're not trying hard enough."

Uta employed a simple ruse; dropping her hands in search of her weapon.

He'll try for it now; one last effort.

He came at her hard, striking out with elbows and fists. Several punches grazed her face and she absorbed two more fierce blows; one to the body and one in the mouth before he withered towards impotence.

She smiled at him through bloodied lips.

"Come on. Get it over with."

Uta anticipated his next move. He pulled back from her and tried to lunge for her legs.

"Nice try."

She struck out with her boot. It smashed into the damaged area of his stomach and his knees swayed and buckled.

Uta savoured his pain.

"Yes, you big self-righteous ape. You're about to die."

She needed to locate her weapon, but she kept him in her peripheral vision as she searched. Once retrieved, she began circling, taunting him about the upcoming death of his lover.

"I know about you and your peasant girlfriend. It's a shame you're not going to see me cut her up."

Luther raised himself from his knees and stood; his entire body shuddering in spasmodic jerks.

"She's gone. You won't catch her now."

"Rubbish. She's dead and you know it."

She laughed when he switched off his headlamp.

"What are you doing, you fool?"

She could see him clearly; just a big ugly piece of meat, awaiting the knife. She moved to her discarded pack, reached in and removed a bone-handled dagger; eight inches of killing blade.

"Luther?"

When she turned back, she couldn't see him.

Uta raced to the spot where she saw him last.

"Where are you, Luther? You pig."

She could see no footsteps heading away in any direction. She walked closer to the edge and spotted the slip marks disappearing into the abyss.

"No ..."

The bastard took his own life to deny her. She tried to look down after him, but the clouds raced by and the beam of her headlamp turned all vision into a dense whiteness.

Alright. Change of plans.

She needed to despatch the Russian with only a brief period for her enjoyment; not quite the ecstasy of slow torture, just a moment of pleasure.

She searched the snow for tracks.

"You stupid foolish girl."

Uta examined the trail. Deep extended footprints marked the track.

She laughed into the storm.

The Russian ran for her life, but the wrong way.

The stupid cow's running close to the damn edge.

"Don't go and die on me, bitch. I want my fun."

Chapter Thirty

Luther propelled himself off the edge in one fluid motion. He spun around in midair, using his hands to slow his progress as he plummeted down the steep ice-encrusted slope.

His plan didn't work. His fingers lost traction and he continued to fall.

This is it; death.

He hit an object and pain exploded through his upper body; his fall suspended, as a branch smashed through the soft tissue of his armpit and speared its way out through the front of his shoulder.

Not death. Agony.

Big Luther they called him, as tough as a bear; a man who respected his calling, who respected himself. Thirty years of training, service and belief, grasped at the pain and stifled his scream.

Fight. Pull yourself up ... Come on.

Luther used the elbow on his non-injured side to prop himself up on the trunk of the tree and alleviate some of his pain. After a brief assessment of his situation, he realised he hung from the fire-hardened branches of a dead snow gum. It captured his bulk and prevented any further slide down the mountain.

I'm lucky. It could've gutted me.

He wanted to live, he couldn't deny his instincts, but his frantic attempts at survival seemed futile.

I haven't got much time left for life.

He felt he didn't have the strength for a further climb, even if he could escape the branch protruding from his shoulder.

Then he saw a light searching from above and kept as still as possible.

Uta ...

She wanted to finish him off.

I can't just hang here. I either wait for death, or have a go.

Attempting a climb back to the top of the ridge meant suffering, but waiting for death held the same reward.

Alright ... I know what I have to do.

He thought about Noah. The man taught him everything and made him part of a special family. He tended his emotional wounds and helped him recover from the loss of his birth family. The man gave him purpose and the will to live. He gave him back his life.

This is for you old mate.

Luther wasted no further time on reflection. He raised his right arm and grasped the highest branch he could find. Arching his back, he lifted his knees as high as possible, driving the metal teeth on the front of his crampons into the ice. He rested, taking a moment to build up his courage. As a means of coping with the pain to come, he tensed his body and gritted his teeth.

It's time ... Go, now.

With all of his strength, he pushed with his legs, using his right arm to pull from above. In one rapid movement, he drew himself off the twisted stake.

It's meant to hurt. If the pain stops, I'm dead.

His entire being throbbed with excruciating agony. He stiffened, as another involuntary scream built momentum in his chest and tore into his throat; an unstoppable force that threatened to explode from his mouth, but Luther didn't utter the slightest sound. With all of his will, he choked it down and silently held his position.

He sat unencumbered in the branches; a leg dangling on either side of the trunk.

Just a few moments to recover. Not too long.

He utilised the hand on his uninjured side to search the branches in the darkness. He selected two limbs with sharpened ends. The wind helped him. It rose in swirling gusts as a new storm approached. Its roar diffused the loud crack as each wooden spike broke free.

Luther knelt up on the tangled trunk and used his good arm to punch the wooden spike into the ice.

No. It won't work.

The other spike fell from his grasp the moment he attempted to use it. He couldn't raise his injured arm above chest height.

It's useless.

Blood poured from the wound in his shoulder; his left arm flopped back and hung by his side, but he didn't stop to think about it. He pushed up with his legs, using the remaining spike and his crampons to hold himself in an arched position, before extending his reach and punching the wooden skewer higher into the slope. In the same motion, he drove his crampons higher into the ice, taking two small steps up at a time.

He repeated this process, inching his way towards the top of the ridge.

Acids began to seep into Luther's stomach cavity and he suffered like never before. The blood loss from multiple injuries and the hurt gnawing at his flesh turned his short climb into an Everest.

Damn it ... Hang on.

He almost fell; his spike bouncing off hard wet rock. To compensate, he threw his knees and chest against the slope. He wavered; legs trembling; his life limited to the length of his crampon's steel teeth; the only purchase holding him to the edge.

Punch lower. Get the spike in and move.

He crabbed around the protruding rock and continued his upward momentum.

Don't think ... Just focus on each movement ... One step at a time.

The darkness saved him from the distance to his objective; he couldn't see far enough to feel dissuaded. When his spike found the snow over the top of the ridge, he felt a moment of surprise, then an overflowing of elation.

Luther forced himself onto his knees and searched the immediate area for his lost communicator. Without it, there seemed no way of achieving his goal.

My torch. Yes. I can use the light.

In the distance, between fast-moving clouds, he saw a faint glow coming from the hut's window. He controlled his pain, pushed himself into a standing position and steadied himself. He aimed his headlamp towards the hut, sending a continuous SOS signal in that direction.

He repeated this process as he staggered down the track towards the hut. He realised the pointlessness; he understood his situation, but having a purpose provided him with a mechanism to control his pain.

It's too late. I'm not going to make it.

He faltered, weak and exhausted from blood loss and pain. Through his growing delirium, he realised that death waited for him at the end of his walk.

Petra searched the path ahead with each outstretched step. She understood the reality of her situation and she felt frightened and angry.

I betrayed him. My beautiful Luther. If only I hadn't looked ...

She needed clarity. If she remained at this place, Uta could use her torchlight and catch her. She considered several of the other serious problems facing her: falling, blood loss and the problem foremost in her mind, the pain of exposure. She wore only brief underwear with nothing on her feet; allowing the cold, free access to her body.

Oh God ... If she catches me, she'll gut me.

Petra began to sob; wondering if she possessed the courage to throw herself over the side and choose her own end.

No. Not yet ... Maybe ... If it's necessary.

By staying and not moving, she created at least one of two certainties; either she froze to death or died under Uta's blade, yet if she continued both certainties became only possibilities.

As she considered her situation, she saw movement; flashes of light that she couldn't comprehend. Over time, she possessed a library of expectations and experience developed for most situations, yet this Jedi-like display, didn't fit into any scenario she could imagine.

"Luther ...?"

She felt buoyed by hope. That's it, she understood. Luther continued to fight with Uta. The duelling light from their headlamps proved he lived.

"Oh no."

One of the lights went out.

"Luther?"

The remaining light bobbed towards her position. It came fast; at a run and panic seized her more tightly than the cold.

It's not him. With those wounds he couldn't run like that.

"He's dead ... It's Uta."

A positive thought occurred to her. If she ran far enough away from the hut, Uta might give up the chase, preferring to re-join the hunt for the Prize.

No. She won't want an enemy at her back either. She'll come.

Petra knew she required the kind of speed that put her in danger of falling.

For God's sake, get moving. Go.

With long probing steps, she moved off along the Razorback in the direction of Mount Hotham. After ten frightening minutes she stopped, spotting a light moving in front of her to the east.

No ... It can't be. It's coming from the wrong direction. From Mount Hotham.

She felt numb; for a moment not heeding the cold's sting on her body, nor the pain from her wound. She tried to focus her failing senses towards an understanding of her current situation.

No-one's crazy enough to travel on this ridge in a snow storm, especially at night. No way. This couldn't be a group of innocent trekkers.

"Bloody hell."

Whoever it is, they're coming straight towards me.

———————

Uta didn't need to check the edges. The deep sliding impressions in the snow made trailing her easy. She considered the gap in her tracks.

The mad bitch.

The Russian raced ahead, often stopping for no reason and wandering around in tight circles. Uta laughed at her uncertainty. Her next movements seemed slow and precise, her feet feeling ahead in perfect arcs.

Then the tracks grew longer and deeper; accelerating.

She knows I'm after her.

Uta kept the torch pointing down, as she approached a small crest. Petra couldn't escape, but might go over the side if she sensed immediate danger.

Stay with me you bony cow.

Uta switched off her light and crept quietly over the crest. With the easing of the wind, she could hear the girl's panting and the occasional panicked sob. She estimated that she stood within fifteen or twenty metres.

Just a little closer and I'll flick the light on.

If necessary, she could blow a hole in the girl's leg to prevent any nonsense. She stood, readying herself to switch on and focus the beam of light.

Damn it ... Moving lights ... Vogel.

Uta fell to the ground, crabbing backwards behind the safety of the small crest. She raised her head above the snow to determine her enemies' movements. The light came from behind the next small crest, thirty metres in front of her.

Uta slid across the snow to her left. Once out of sight, she raised herself high enough to see through a clump of snow gum saplings, as the erratic beams descended into the depression.

Petra stood alone in the clearing; milky white and bloodied. Her entire body shook in wild spasms.

You bastard, Vogel. You've stolen my kill.

Uta needed to quickly determine her next move. She couldn't call out and identify herself.

No. If I show myself, they'll kill me.

The timing of the soldier's arrival provided her with two absolutes: that Vogel knew of her treachery and that he lied about his own movements.

I can't get caught between Vogel and Noah that's for sure.

She required noise to muffle her escape. She needed the storm to intensify, or the girl to start screaming. She decided to wait for the screams.

At least make it entertaining.

She reset the safety switch on her weapon as the two-man SRP forward reconnaissance jerked to a stop at the sight of the girl.

"You ... Halt. Don't move."

Uta smiled as she considered the soldiers' bewilderment at finding a bloodied and nearly naked girl alone in a snow storm.

"Get your hands up where we can see them. Do it now or we'll shoot."

Petra tried to raise both of her hands, but her wound prevented her from complying.

"Don't … Don't shoot. I'm hurt."

The two men stepped forward, one scanning the area for ambush and the other forcing Petra to kneel on hands and knees in the snow.

"If you want to live, answer quickly. Are you alone?"

"Yes."

"Who are you?"

"Marilyn. My name's Marilyn."

"Why are you here? Who did this?"

Petra didn't answer. She understood her plight. She could only hope that her fear wouldn't betray any of the others.

"Sir. We've captured a woman just forward of the High Knob. She's nearly naked and she's been shot in the arm by an unknown."

"Who the hell is she? Quickly, find out what's going on."

The soldier gave Petra a prod with the barrel of his gun and asked an assortment of questions, but she didn't speak.

"She's in a bad way sir. She's not talking."

"Alright. Hold her until we arrive. This woman's about to discover the meaning of pain."

Chapter Thirty One

Tom sat against the wall and stared across the room at Isobel and Noah; two different faces, one etched with experience, the other smooth, yet both producing the same expression of worry.

He stood and paced the room.

"No. I can't go without opening it, Noah. We might never get another chance."

"Alright. Enough. Unlock it, but if I say we have to go … then we have to go. Understood?"

Tom nodded several times, before turning his head torch to the lowest setting. He removed the key from his pocket and began unlocking the diary; opening the three locks built into the metal surface of the binding, from top to bottom.

As he eased opened the cover, he noticed the electronic device.

"Tom. Stop … Don't move. That's an explosive mechanism."

Noah identified the miniature bomb and checked its workings for any variations from the factory version. He glanced at the others, before removing it from the binding.

"You're a lucky, young man. The three locks disarmed the mechanism. If you undid it in the wrong order ... Boom."

"My father's stupid precautions could've killed us."

"No. I'm sure he provided us with the instructions. Petra would have wiped them when she damaged the chip."

Thoughts of metal shards tearing his face off, drifted through Tom's mind, but nothing could deter him from reading his father's diary. He leafed through several of the first pages.

"This is hard to understand. It isn't a conventional diary; more like a scientific journal."

Tom continued his search for something he could understand; a connection to his father.

"Hey. What's this?"

A folded piece of paper fell from between the pages and into his lap.

He read several sentences and stopped. He felt a tear licking his cheek and sensed Isobel staring at him. Embarrassed, he attempted to say something, but it came out as an unintelligible stammer.

Isobel reached over and grabbed him by the arm.

"Tom. We're dying here. Can you read it aloud?"

"No, I ... You read it for me, Iz."

He searched her eyes for any sign of ridicule. Her expression seemed harsh.

"Sometimes I ... have trouble reading aloud. Just sometimes."

"Sure."

Did she mock him with her barely concealed smile? No. He noticed the moisture in her eyes and his ribs and stomach contracted into tremors of sensation.

"Of course I will, Tom."

She reached over, took the letter from his hand and began to read it aloud.

"Mr Chairman,

All current experiments regarding the Angels' deterioration have proved fruitless. The suits have undergone every test possible and the only conclusion is that this alien technology is too advanced for us to fathom.

As you are aware, the seven suits initially supported their inhabitants, not only creating ultra-human performance, but also heightening the experience of life for the wearer to levels akin to ecstasy.

We do know that the suits altered human flesh, changing the DNA of the occupant's tissue. This alien biology took over every system in the body. Firstly, the autonomous and reflex systems and then the endocrine system, with specific glands including the hypothalamus, secreting a range of hormones that we haven't been able to identify or understand.

We have also been unsuccessful in determining why each of the seven men grew more than one hundred percent larger. This includes all of the organs and especially the brain. The electrical impulses from each brain have increased even more than the growth of the tissue and the signals to other parts of the body have grown accordingly.

Unfortunately, we have been unable to identify most of the neurochemicals concerned. Each brain is working at nearly full capacity, which has previously been impossible for a human being.

The suits are living organisms with their own intelligence that have lain dormant for millions of years without any kind of nutrition, or means of sustainability. Yet they have survived.

If we are to draw any conclusions from our current dilemma, it is to make comment that human beings were never meant to be the recipients of such technology. They were created for beings with vastly different physiology and mental development.

As a consequence, we have been unable to open the suits, or to stop any of their processes. There is also no current way of inflicting any kind of injury to this technology.

I am sorry, Antonio, but it is my duty to inform you of this tragedy. It is my guess that the suits will eventually expel the men once they have perished.

In the meantime, I will work tirelessly to develop a method of making the suits more habitable for the wearers. There has to be some way of gaining control and moulding them to our purpose."

The crackling of the fire and the gusting wind outside became the only sound permeating the room.

Tom's voice rose in anger as he ended their silence.

"I can't believe what I'm hearing. This is total bullshit. Everything I've ever been taught about the Angels is a damn lie."

Tom's scripture teachers taught him this garbage, that the entire Christian world rejoiced at the coming of the Seven Angels; that they came from heaven to defeat the enemies of Christ and to bring the world back to true Christian principles.

"Total nonsense. Why, Noah?"

"It just proves that Angels don't wear alien suits, Tom."

"That's not funny."

"Listen, lad. It's just a grab for power. Men have used religion for this purpose for thousands of years. They've become quite proficient at recreating God in their own image."

"Man can't create God."

"Can't we? Look at history. We've created thousands of Gods so that we can control the masses. It's cheaper than military force. That's what it's always been about; power and control."

Isobel shifted her attention to Tom.

"Are you alright? You look like you're going to be sick."

"My father ... he helped them with this fraud. He's ..."

Tom flinched. Noah's communicator beeped fear into the room.

"Tom, Isobel. Get your packs and be ready to move."

Noah stood and began striding around the room as he answered the call.

"Surat. Go ahead."

"Noah. I've found Luther. He's badly wounded. I've dragged him back past the junction, about two hundred metres from your position. If you want to see him before he passes, come now."

"Did you find any sign of Julius?"

"He's most likely dead."

"And Petra?"

"She left a blood trail heading east along the Razorback. She's as good as dead, Noah. She ran the wrong way in the dark. I found her headlamp lying in the snow beside her cloths. Uta's prints follow hers. You can guess the rest."

"But you can't confirm?"

"No, but it gets worse ..."

Tom reached out and took Isobel's hand. They could both see the pain etched in Noah's face.

"I saw lights coming west along the ridge from High Knob. The SRP are coming across the Razorback. No-one else would attempt it in these conditions. We have to get going. We have to move out as soon as possible."

176

Chapter Thirty Two

Uta watched Vogel and the rest of his SRP troop march into the hollow near High Knob. He seemed angry. He strode forward, ignoring the men from his forward reconnaissance and slapped Petra across the face.

"Who are you? I want your name and your position in the G11's."

"My name's Marilyn. Marilyn Munro."

"Alright, sergeant. Convince her we're serious."

Petra whimpered, but she continued to resist Vogel's attempts at getting information from her.

"Look at me you stupid woman. This is your last chance."

"I told you. I'm Marilyn."

"Sergeant. Make it hurt."

Uta maintained her vigil, fascinated as the SRP sergeant attacked Petra's body with a knife.

Don't die too quickly, bitch.

Uta trembled with want, as she witnessed the agonizing expression on Petra's face. The girl looked frightened by Vogel's rants, yet she still defied him.

"Cut her again, Sergeant. If she doesn't spill her guts, you spill them for her."

The Russian arched over backwards and tried to scream, yet only managed a choking gurgle. Even from her position, Uta could see liquid trickling down the Russian's legs, colouring the snow yellow.

Go girl.

Uta knew this scenario from countless sessions of torture. Once you piss yourself in front of a group of men, there's nothing you could ever do to restore your dignity.

She smiled as she continued her vigil; enjoying the men's brutality.

They propped Petra up to stop her from falling; forcing her to confront the man who cut away pieces from her flesh. Around the interrogator's boots, Uta could see sprays of red blood blending with the yellow patches of snow.

The critical moment arrived and Uta recognised Vogel's growing desperation. If he didn't get information from her soon, she might die.

"Do I have your attention, girl? Or do we need another demonstration?"

Petra raised herself and shook off her attendants. Her legs trembled and almost gave way, but she managed to take several steps towards Vogel before she answered.

"I've spent my life fighting bastards like you and dying here won't be so bad."

Several of the men broke into stifled laughter, but Vogel silenced them with a wave of his arm.

"Spare me the theatrics, you stupid bitch. Tell me what I want, or the pain gets worse."

SRP torches lit Petra's face; deepening her shadowed lines of anguish. She looked done for, but Uta realised the bony Russian would not beg for her life.

"As I said, my name's Marilyn."

Petra covered the three metres to the northern edge of the ridge without any reaction from the men around her. Without hindrance, she turned and faced her tormentors.

"You're all cowards and you'll never beat us."

Uta gasped and Vogel yelled, but the Russian only laughed.

"No … Stop her …"

Petra dived over the edge as five bullets exploded into her flesh.

What a show … Almost better than doing it myself.

Uta shook her head in wonderment, amazed by Petra's courage.

She noticed movement amongst the SRP.

Vogel readied his men, which meant she couldn't delay leaving any longer; the SRP could follow and identify her tracks. She needed to reach the mish-mash of traffic further up the trail.

I've stayed too long. Wait for a wind gust and then go.

She needed to utilise the storm to cover her retreat. The exposed space between High Knob and Molly Hill provided no concealment. She knew it created a death zone without the cloud for cover.

Uta slid backwards, turned and ran headlong into the gloom; disappearing into the swirling snow. Once far enough away, she deemed it safe to switch on her own torch and search the eucalyptus scrub for her marker. Instead of following the track along the western side of Molly Hill, she climbed through the foliage and over the top, coming out and crossing the track leading to the summit of Mount Feathertop.

I still have the element of surprise. When the time comes, they won't know what hit them.

As she jogged west above the tree line, she tried to determine which track the G11 team might choose for a successful escape. This far north and west along the Razorback, they could only reasonably consider three choices, two of which meant travelling past the junction.

No way … Noah's not that stupid.

That only left the Bungalow Spur, which began at Federation Hut.

———————

Noah handed Tom an automatic machine pistol and he hesitated before taking it.

"We're running out of people, Tom. You're to use this if the enemy try to cut off our retreat."

Tom massaged the grip of the Serbian Plaskovic automatic pistol. It felt heavy, yet balanced, even with the weight of the added silencer. Just holding the weapon made him feel powerful. With this he inspired fear; having the power to take life.

They trudged on through the snow in a tight group, the sleet stinging Tom's face. They travelled as quickly as the conditions allowed and came to within metres of Luther before they saw him.

Surat gestured for Noah to come close.

"He's still alive, but not for long."

"Luther, it's Noah, can you hear me?"

"Noah … Noah …"

Luther began to gurgle, as blood filled his throat.

"You're a hero, my friend. You'll make it through this."

"Uta … She's the killer."

Noah called to Tom.

"I need you to hold his head up, so it's not so hard for him to speak."

"Noah, I'm sorry. I couldn't help Petra … I let her down."

Surat and Noah took hold of Luther's arm and together they lifted him into a shaky standing position.

"You lived your life protecting others, Luther. You let no-one down."

The men bore Luther's weight, as he drifted in and out of consciousness. Tom followed close behind with Isobel. He could see her bottom lip quivering; everyone liked Luther.

They plodded along, heads down, solemn in their procession; each awaiting the inevitable outcome. It still shocked Tom when it happened. The big man stiffened and called out to Noah; his body shaking into violent spasms; his dead weight almost pulling Noah and Surat to the ground.

Surat bent down and closed Luther's eyes.

"What'll we do with him, Noah?"

Noah sighed, his expulsion of breath sounding rough and irregular. He knelt down and ran his hand through Luther's hair.

"Goodbye old chum."

"Noah, Look."

Isobel tugged at Noah's coat and pointed towards the north.

"They're coming."

Through the swirling cloud, the group could see a faint light to the north. It moved faster than several similar lights following behind. The leading light changed direction, moving upwards towards the summit of Molly Hill, before it disappeared from sight.

"She switched her light off to evade capture. She's escaped Vogel. We have to move, there's not much time left. The enemy are almost here."

Surat nodded towards Tom and Isobel.

"We can't outrun the SRP. Not with them."

Tom swung around and glared at Surat; their faces almost touching.

"We can take care of ourselves, despite what you think."

He turned back towards Noah, his face throbbing with anger.

"I've got an idea. If it's time we need, then I think this might work."

Noah gestured to Surat and they hefted Luther up the steps to the hut.

"Alright lad, what's your plan?"

"To stay alive."

Tom handed the gun back to Noah.

"And I don't need this."

After witnessing the death of such a brave man, his previous enchantment with the weapon, disintegrated into the horror of a wasted life.

Chapter Thirty Three

The failure of his SRP commandos to perform their duty filled Vogel with anger. He might never understand the *what* and the *why* as a result of their incompetence.

"You. Come here."

He jammed the barrel of his pistol into the side of the man's head.

"You were the closest to the girl. Get on your knees."

"Sir. We didn't expect … I didn't have a chance."

"Idiot. I ask you to hold her and what do you do? A dead woman doesn't help our cause, does it?"

The man slumped, bowing for his life.

"There's no room for this kind of mistake. This man is nothing more than faeces to me. The next soldier that doesn't obey me will not survive this journey. Is that clear?"

"Sir. Yes sir."

The man remained prostrate, as Vogel strode away. He needed to think about how these events affected their mission. He needed clarity.

It could be a form of punishment. It could be a G11 mutiny, or Uta playing for another team. Taking all of these possible factors into consideration, he came to a realisation.

It doesn't matter. I still hold the advantage.

He felt sure that the G11's remained at Federation Hut and even if they didn't, he held the three possible escape routes with a small force of men; enough to keep them in place and enforce his trap.

But I can't have that woman at my back.

Uta created his biggest problem. He needed to kill her as a priority. Because of her deceit, he didn't have any further intelligence on the G11's. Did they have the Prize already? Could they be running at this very moment? Only a visual on the hut could give him these answers.

Uta took no chances; heading quickly away from the action; away from the net she knew Vogel intended to create.

You can't outwit me, Vogel. I know how you tie your shoelaces.

She headed around the northern side of Little Mount Feathertop, skirting west, using the thick cover and steep slope to shield her approach. She planned to be in position to strike, before the SRP deployed their men around the hut.

The weasel will follow textbook tactics. He won't expect an attack from this point.

Uta knew every trick the SRP could utilise against the G11's and herself, especially the placement of their troops. She needed to kill off at least two of these positions on either the western or the north-western perimeter of the hut.

You're about to be played, Vogel.

Uta laughed, as she moved away through the snow gums. With this weather on her side, nothing could stop her.

————————

Tom stood in front of Federation Hut and addressed the others.

"Surat, we have to get Isobel out of here. We'll follow you down the Bungalow Spur when we're finished our business."

Surat's facial expression twisted with anger.

"Piss off, Fox."

He turned towards Noah, but the big man only nodded his support for Tom.

"Do what he asks. Take her up the hill behind the hut and cut across to the Bungalow Spur. No tracks. We don't want to be too obvious."

Noah hurried to help his young protégé. Together they dragged a heavy log from a summer camping area; their hands uncertain on the wet slippery trunk. They placed it strategically, just inside the door.

Tom organised Noah and together they hung strips of paper and torn cloth above the fireplace; the heat making them sway creating a show of moving shadows. When viewed from outside, it created the illusion that people strolled about within.

"We have to get the fire burning as brightly as we can. The log will keep the hut door slightly ajar, so the light flickers out onto the verandah."

Tom thought he understood Vogel's dilemma.

"He can't just rush in without securing the area. He's committed to waiting. He wants to believe in the reality we're going to provide."

Tom turned and looked towards the north; checking the Feathertop trail for any sign of the enemy.

"They've switched off their lights. It's time to get going, Noah. We're done here."

"It's a nice deception, Tom. I hope for our sake that it works."

Chapter Thirty Four

Vogel studied the muddle of bloody tracks between Molly Hill and the Twin Knobs; searching the detail for understanding. He could see that they travelled in both directions along the ridge and he wondered about what the implications might hold for his mission.

It's a combat zone, but for what purpose?

He didn't mind if they slaughtered each other; casualties helped his cause. His only goal required capturing the Prize, or keeping Fox alive until he did.

He ordered his men forward; keeping them in a tight formation as they set off towards Federation Hut. Employing no lights and no sound, they moved off to secure the junction, which eliminated several escape options for the G11's.

After several hundred metres, they discovered yet another depression in the snow, with a profusion of tracks.

There's more blood, yet it seems to be a different scenario.

Frederick needed no tracker's translation to understand this story.

"I get it now."

A large wounded man with huge deep footprints met with several others. They dragged him back towards the hut.

Vogel called to his sergeant and jabbed his forefinger at the evidence.

"Good. I've got them trapped and they don't know we're coming."

"Sir ...?"

"Look. Someone assisted our wounded big foot to this location and you killed the blond woman."

The sergeant groaned.

"There's a lot of tracks, sir. There could be others."

"No. If a perpetrator still existed after the fight, they'd have gone after them, wouldn't they? These tracks aren't rushed, sergeant and they sent no-one to guard their backs."

"Yes, sir, but ..."

The sergeant's strained expression portrayed a different opinion.

"You disagree?"

"There could be other possibilities here. Apart from surprise, we have no advantage at all. If the enemy got behind us ...?"

"Rubbish."

Vogel walked away, shaking his head.

No. This is my opportunity; my chance to hold power beyond any man's reckoning.

He imagined himself face to face with Noah after they stormed the hut; making him kneel in front of him, like a slave; begging for his life.

Before I kill you, I'll make you admit that your stupid cause is nothing but a joke.

He refocused on business; considering the benefits of the weather.

This is good. We'll be right up close and they won't see us.

The track between the junction and the hut wound down five hundred metres to the south-west and reached a position due south of Little Mount Feathertop. He sent four men to skirt the area. They set up checkpoints covering the exits behind the hut and any departure point leading down the Bungalow Spur. The rest of the party secured the main track.

"Sergeant. Once your men are in position, report back to me and we'll attack without delay."

He knew his team could be inside the building before the enemy found time to react.

He couldn't contain his smile.

In a few moments, I'll have the Prize.

Uta stepped higher, propelling herself through the deep snow, but the trees hampered her progress. Snow gum saplings grew from the butt of burnt parent stock and offered what appeared to be a soft passage, but the branches beneath created a trickery; claws that ripped at her clothing and tore at her flesh.

This isn't good. To get there in time, I'll have no face left.

She could feel her oozing blood begin to freeze as she traversed across the steep slope in the darkness. With no light, every metre gained caused damage. She wasn't afraid of death, but her looks mattered.

She knew Vogel's kill squad already surrounded the hut and possessed the advantage, but she held the benefit of surprise considering the invisibility created by the growing blizzard.

She spotted her first target.

He's standing out in the open.

It could seem beneficial in the conditions. A potential foe couldn't exploit the scrub and get too close, but in these conditions it seemed foolhardy.

She utilised the cover of fallen logs and eucalypt saplings, and waited for the wind to drive in the cloud and blot out her approach.

The soldier let out a strangled wheeze, as his last breath escaped from the slit in his throat.

"Ah. Ah. Ah ..."

She stabbed him a further three times for pleasure, as she struggled to control her bloodlust.

Maintain your focus ... Think about the next target.

She searched the body and took the soldier's SRP communicator. Uta knew that Vogel required a check from each position before he proceeded with the attack, which caused a major predicament for him. She realised that he couldn't afford to waste time, yet couldn't begin with a lost man and a possibly compromised position in his net.

This left Vogel with two options.

A blind attack or dig in.

If they decided to wait, they could hold the G11's inside the hut, until reinforcements arrived. It all depended on what Vogel wanted. She knew that if he didn't get the Prize he needed to take Fox alive.

He won't wait. He'll attack, but only when he's certain of success.

She considered her own strategic requirements. She needed to eliminate the next closest position; cutting off any chance of escape to the west of the track. The perfect positioning for her next assault, required good cover, a view of the hut and most importantly, that she keep the ridge at her back. If the G11 team broke free, she could retreat down the Bungalow Spur and welcome them in some lonely glade, further down the mountain.

Uta took a moment's rest. She removed the glove from her right hand and used her fingers to trace the deep lesions that ran along her face.

Damn it ... Damn it to hell.

The sensitive tips of her fingers explored her face, feeling the damage; determining the extent of the wounds and with this understanding, she felt beset with panic.

He won't look at me the same way ... If I'm scarred.

Uta knew the Black Cardinal didn't consider sympathy a virtue. She loved his ruthless approach to life, but she never considered its impact on her.

And right now, he's with my perfect sister ...

She began to shake, feeling the cold for the first time.

Her face didn't matter; nothing could ever matter, if she delivered the Prize.

Chapter Thirty Five

$\mathbf{T}$om followed Noah along the pathway leading to the latrine. At the halfway point, they jumped from the slush of muddy tracks and into the nearest clumping of burnt snow gum forest.

Tom protected his face with glove-covered hands, as he fought his way through the dead wood and profusion of saplings, but it compromised his balance and he fell several times into the tangle of branches.

Keep on your feet. Keep dry.

He felt Noah's hand grasp his arm and lift him to his feet.

"We've made it to the track."

He reached over and pulled Tom close.

"We're quite some way below the hut and the storm's blowing pretty hard, so I think we can risk some light. It's going to be slippery, but we need to run from here on. Are you ready?"

"Does it matter, Noah? Does anything matter? Even if we get off this mountain we'll die."

Noah started to push Tom down the hill.

"We all die, Tom. Sometimes it's just smarter not to be smart."

"So I have to lower my intelligence … Unsmart myself?"

"Yes. If your mind's full of fear, you'll fall into a cycle of hopelessness and you'll begin reacting in accordance with your belief."

"How do you stop thinking about the inevitable?"

"By employing something I call mindless confidence. When the fear comes, don't think, just act."

Tom concentrated on following the dark loping shape in front of him; his lack of thought becoming a meditation, which altered his perception of time until it disappeared entirely.

He existed in a vacuum, somehow separated from reality, yet not from the weirdness of his surroundings.

Steady rain replaced the snow and sleet, and instead of the squat, frozen snow gums, pillars of rough eucalypt boles rose high above a thick understorey of bush. Tom dodged long moving strips of bark as he jogged down the track. They swayed and creaked from the upper branches in unison with the wind.

"Tom."

Noah spoke for the first time since the beginning of their run.

"We're at least half way down. We should have caught up with the others by now. They must be moving faster than I thought."

Tom discerned movement. A dark shape in the undergrowth.

"What the hell … Isobel?"

She smiled and he flushed; his skin beginning to tingle and his heartbeat accelerating beyond the rate of his run. For a tense moment, he felt an overwhelming desire to run over and take her in his arms. He teetered there, holding his breath until she spoke.

"I'm glad you made it, Tom."

His shoulders slumped out of their tension and he stuttered an almost unintelligible welcome.

"Yeah … Likewise."

She seemed tired and drawn, and vulnerable.

"You look like shit, Iz. Are you alright?"

"Oh, thanks so much, Tom."

"I didn't mean you look bad. I meant ... are you ... uninjured?"

"I'm just fine. Thankyou."

For God's sake, say something that isn't garbage.

"Iz. I ... You look great."

"What?"

"Look. Can I just start this conversation again?"

"Tom. I'm tired and I'm freezing, and I'm scared ... and ... I don't give a damn how I look."

"Right."

Oh God. I just can't keep being this stupid. We're in danger and I'm acting like a complete dick.

Surat materialised from the scrub, saving Tom from further embarrassment.

"What do we do now, Noah? They'll be hard at us soon."

"Yes. From behind and in front. There'll be SRP guarding the bottom of this track."

Tom entered the conversation as a means of diversion.

"How could they have known which way we'd go?"

"They didn't. They'll be a small force; one or two at the most. Vogel will have them stationed at the most likely exit points."

Tom thought Isobel's voice sounded shrill as she asked the obvious question.

"How the hell are we going to get past them?"

He noticed her flinch and try to pull away as Noah gripped her shoulder.

"Let's get down first, Isobel. We'll worry about the bottom when we get there. Surat, take the rear. Tom and Isobel, you're in the middle. I'll lead. No more talking."

Isobel's question brought Tom back to his previous unwanted reality. Surviving their current dilemma would not be the end of their predicament.

Vogel crouched in the snow, hidden amongst a clump of frozen eucalypt saplings. Beside him, his sergeant searched the area around Federation Hut with infrared field glasses.

"Yes, sir. I can just see him through the blizzard."

For brief moments between the swirling clouds, the hut became visible.

"He's guarding the hut from the shelter of the verandah. I can see an automatic weapon resting on his lap."

"I can see people, sergeant. Please confirm."

"Yes, sir. I can see moving shadows through the window."

Frederick considered only one option. As soon as he received confirmation of troop placements, they could start the gas attack. With such an effective weapon and in such a tight space, it could bring a man to unconsciousness, as fast as a bullet.

"What's the hold up, sergeant? How many confirmations do we have?"

He felt frustrated; troop placements didn't normally take this long unless a difficulty existed.

"We're still waiting on two positions. There could be a problem."

"Like what?"

"They're the second and third placements in a ring around our objective; the positions covering access to the Bungalow Spur and the northern area of the hut. They should've been the first men with confirmations."

"The G11's don't seem to have left the hut. It must be Uta."

She doesn't know that we found her tracks and saw her light over Molly Hill.

"There are so many tracks, sir. It's near impossible to know if she returned to the hut or is still out there."

"What about our rear defences?"

"Still intact. Nobody's broken through and nobody's left the hut."

Frederick felt like throwing up. His forefinger shook as he aimed it at the sergeant.

"We need a new tactic. Do something."

"Yes, sir. Our net may already be compromised. Under these circumstances, I'd advise a lightning, one-man reconnaissance. If the positions are vacant, our man reports and retreats without taking any further action."

"There won't be any retreat, sergeant."

"No, sir. He pulls back only enough, so we can either tighten the net, or attack at once."

Vogel gave the order and within minutes, their scout made contact.

"Sir. Our man's missing and there's blood on the floor. I repeat there's blood on the floor at position three."

The sergeant shifted the formation of his team; moving each man in the circle in a clockwise direction. He tightened the ring, until the closest man reached the first of the vacant positions.

"Sergeant, signal the attack. When the hut's secured, send more men to strengthen our defence. Let's go."

Gas bombs exploded through the hut's small windows and a barrage of bullets struck the guard by the door. Within fifteen seconds, the SRP secured their objective.

Vogel raced towards the hut. By the time he reached it, three of their men moved to fortify their northern defences.

He felt anxious and his gloved fingers fumbled as he tried to fit his mask. Once on, he burst into the small room; his eyes attempting to adjust to the smoky environment.

"What's going on here?"

People shuffled about in tight circles. Each wore a helmet and the uniform of the elite Australian SRP commando unit.

"Sir, they're gone."

Frederick ran from the building and flung his mask at the storm.

"You bastard, Noah. This isn't over. It's not nearly over."

In his rage he didn't hear his sergeant walk up behind him.

"Sir. They propped a dead man up as a ruse and used the firelight to create the illusion of movement."

"I don't care, sergeant. Leave one man to cover our northern perimeter and call the rest back here at once. Find their tracks and make no assumptions."

Vogel felt so angry, he struggled for breath.

"And, sergeant, if any one of them get away, I'm going to make you eat your own testicles. Is that clear?"

Vogel waited until his sergeant ran off shouting orders to his men. He walked a short way from the cabin and into the storm. He couldn't let these men see his anxiety.

No ... No way.

Frederick shook with hatred and under his Gortex jacket, his inner woollen layers felt wet with sweat.

I don't lose. Not ever. This is just a setback. They can't escape.

No matter what track the G11's and Uta attempt, he'll have them in his net.

People are going to die and that's a promise.

Chapter Thirty Six

Uta spotted the two men hiding near the track that zigzagged down from Feathertop junction. In disbelief, she watched Vogel's sergeant raising his head above the cover.

If she could see the idiot from her position, then so could the man sitting on the verandah.

You're blinded by your own greed, Vogel.

Noah would never have a roaring fire going and leave the door open, on such a delicate mission and the man on the verandah …?

It's a poor ruse, but a clever distraction. Vogel can't afford to be wrong.

Uta wrenched the glove off her right hand and dabbed at the grizzled mess of wounds on her face. Her skin felt clenched and taut, like a permanent scowl.

She tried once more to convince herself that it didn't matter.

Will he still want me?

Her cardinal's opinion meant everything. It also mattered operationally. She couldn't see herself as a clandestine agent, with a multitude of scars on her face.

You're The Raptor ... Focus.

She needed a clear mind to determine her next move. Taking the Prize meant everything, including the heart of her cardinal.

I need flexible tactics to suit a range of differing scenarios. A mistake and they'll kill me on sight.

She hurried into position and assessed her target. This soldier seemed wary. He gave the area a brief check, reported in and backed off to a defensive position.

This guy's way better than the others.

A close kill didn't seem possible, which forced her to change strategy.

Uta knew she could utilise three different strategies. The first of these involved the elimination of Vogel and his force, which created the greatest danger. She couldn't hope to keep the element of surprise until she completed the job. Once in full attack, these SRP soldiers could be lethal.

No.

Possibility two meant applying a scavenger's tactic: get behind them and follow at a distance, allowing Vogel to do her work and hope for maximum casualties. Then she could finish the job. This scenario required the weather to remain foul. If the SRP got the chance to reinforce, or employ helicopters with infrared, her chances became ruinous.

No.

Uta marched into the wind and it battered her senses; hampering her thought processes. It swirled and gusted and fired ice projectiles into her facial wounds.

Keep on track. Don't waiver.

She slapped her own face, causing fresh blood to dribble off her chin. She must decide. Each scenario required a different timing.

The sound of breaking glass and gunfire solved her moment of indecision.

Alright ... Option three.

Within seconds of her surety, fresh troops arrived to reinforce the SRP's western perimeter; covering the entrance to the Bungalow Spur. As she expected, they stayed put and didn't advance.

It's time for The Raptor to hunt.

She crept forward and waited for movement. It didn't take long. The soldier died before his face hit the snow. The other two soldiers in the vicinity reacted; spraying bullets into the storm.

Uta smiled, returned fire for three seconds and retreated.

Suckers ... Part one completed.

Because of her actions, the enemy behind her could not proceed with pace. They could move only after their forward party secured each section. Her plan required operating this tactic until she located a site that posed the most danger for their advance; hold them there and begin the second part of her plan.

———————

Panic overtook Frederick Vogel's ability to rationalise. He couldn't stop the chaos bombarding his mind. It felt to him as if his stress levels escalated out of control, like an over-revving engine that he couldn't switch off.

"Bastards ... I'll kill you ... I'll kill you all."

A tiny part of his consciousness began to communicate a danger: if he didn't turn it off he might blow a piston through the side of his brain.

He became aware of his sergeant. The man marched toward him, switched on his torch and came into view.

"Sir. We're under attack. We need to respond at once. We need your orders."

He could see the confusion in the man's expression, yet he couldn't answer him.

They stared at each other. No-one moved.

"Sir ... Is everything alright?"

"No."

His hatred boiled in his mind and needed to spill out; needed a target. He withdrew his handgun and pointed it at the bewildered soldier.

"Get down on your knees. Down. Now."

The sergeant continued to stand; his head jerking from side to side.

"You're all alone, sergeant. No-one's going to help you."

"Sir. Our team's under attack. We've got to turn this around, or …?"

Frederick's smile felt ugly.

He didn't need this imbecile to explain their vulnerability. Of course they needed a counter strategy. Their underbelly remained dangerously exposed.

"Get on your knees, soldier. I won't tell you again."

The sergeant lowered himself into a kneeling position and continued to plead with his superior.

"Sir. We're letting the enemy take control. The longer we leave it the harder it'll become …"

Vogel stepped forward and placed the barrel against the soldier's head.

The man's a brave one.

The sergeant didn't sag or show weakness. He returned Vogel's angry expression with equal menace.

"Sir. You've got to listen to me."

He pushed his face against the gun and rose back to his full height.

"Stay where you are, sergeant."

"No. If I'm going to die, it won't be on my knees."

Vogel started to laugh. It sounded hysterical even to him. He removed the gun from the soldier's head and holstered it.

"Alright … Your courage has earned you a chance to live. But, you have to prove your loyalty."

"I took the oath already."

"Shut up soldier and listen. When this mission is over, apart from Fox and myself, there will only be one other left alive; it could be you."

"The others … Why?"

"The Assembly marked you all for death, but you're a fortunate soldier. My covert SRP soldier is dead; killed only moments ago."

"Yes, but why?"

"Don't look so dumbfounded, sergeant. The Assembly utilise the clean-up when they have to keep a secret hidden. Witnesses have to be taken care of."

"You're asking me to kill my own men?"

"No. I'm *ordering* you to kill them. If you refuse, you die here and now."

Vogel removed his weapon and for a second time, forced the barrel into the side of the sergeant's head.

"Take note, soldier. If you accept and betray me, the Assembly will hunt you down no matter where you go. No traitor has ever escaped their wrath."

"This is murder. Most of these men are friends."

The heady power of determining whether this man lived or died alleviated some of Frederick's anxiety.

"Sergeant. I want your answer."

"And what about me? Am I expendable when this is done?"

"Good question. The Assembly never take out the clean-up man. Your survival is guaranteed. You'll live and you'll be promoted well above your current station."

Vogel nodded and smiled with satisfaction. For the first time, the man before him began to wilt.

He'll kill to save his own miserable life. I can see it in his eyes.

"So what's it to be, sergeant. Their blood or yours?"

"You already know the answer."

"Yes, but I want to hear it from you."

"Theirs … I'll take their blood."

The sergeant couldn't live with such a betrayal without smothering his guilt with hatred. Frederick knew from experience that to finish the job, the sergeant needed to loathe his men from this point on.

Good.

"Sergeant. You're forthwith promoted to captain."

The security chief removed the gun from the man's head and turned his back on him. This human being belonged to him now. He owned his soul.

Chapter Thirty Seven

They reached their first destination and Isobel considered it unremarkable. Wombat Gap didn't appear to differ from any other turn in the track; just more sodden trees and another bracken covered clearing.

She sat with her back against a log, feeling a little nervous.

Tom, where are you? Come back ... This might be my only chance to tell you ...

With Noah and Surat resting around a bend below her, she sat alone waiting for Tom to come back. She assumed he went into the bush to relieve himself, but because of the wind, she couldn't hear any movement.

She smiled when he returned and lowered himself onto the ground beside her. In a brief moment of torchlight, she noticed his breath rising in vapours as he spoke.

"How do you feel, Iz?"

"Great. I've run out of adrenalin and everything hurts."

"But, no injuries?"

"No. Just sore around my knees."

She turned just enough so that she could make out his faint profile.

"Tom, can I ask you something?"

"Sure."

"Do you like me?"

"Ah … Yeah, sure."

"I mean more than just a friend?"

"I … Is it that obvious?"

"You don't have to try so hard, you know. I feel the same way."

He didn't respond for some time and she stiffened with anticipation.

"But, Iz … you're always pushing me away?"

"Yeah, well, I'm a complicated woman."

She tried to make out his expression, but the darkness defeated her. How could she hope to explain how she felt without the truth?

"How complicated?"

"I … Alright, here goes. I hope you don't hate me for telling you this. Years ago, I went to a party and …"

Damn it, Noah. Great timing.

Noah appeared out of the darkness. His facial features illuminated by the lowest setting on his torch.

"How's it going you two?"

Neither answered.

"Don't allow yourselves to get cold. If your muscles cool down, you won't be able to walk. We'll head off in five minutes."

As he strode off in Surat's direction, she sighed and stretched out onto her back. She looked up at the sky. Between fast moving clouds and a little intermittent drizzle, she caught a brief glimpse of the stars. The view didn't last.

"These raindrops actually feel good."

She opened her mouth and tried to catch some of the moisture, but there wasn't enough to swallow. She sat up; hugging her knees for balance and watched as the clouds raced by.

"Does it bother you being thought of as a criminal, Izzi?"

"No. I'm already a criminal. I earned that status before we met."

"What are you talking about?"

"As I said. I'm a complicated woman."

"You're also full of surprises."

She flinched as he leant over and tried to kiss her. His lips initially felt rough and cold and she fought against the need to pull away.

Oh God ... No ...

He rolled towards her; his body covering hers.

"Get off ... Get off, Tom."

She felt sickened. Panicked. She thrashed her head from side to side and pushed at him until he rolled away.

They both lay on their backs without speaking; her ears throbbing and her ribs expanding with pain as she tried to regain some control.

Oh God ... Oh God ... What have I done?

She could hear his heavy ragged breath. He groaned as he got to his feet and stood over her.

"Alright, I think we're done here."

"You shouldn't have touched me, Tom."

"Why the hell not. We're adults who apparently like each other."

"I need to explain something to you."

"No ... Enough."

She heard him shuffle away in the darkness. She shivered. Her body feeling stiff with cold.

I'm so sorry, Tom ... So, so sorry.

She started to sob.

Tom felt the heat of embarrassment on his cheeks as he eased his way through the darkness towards Noah and Surat. He also recognised the feeling in his chest.

How does she do it? I actually feel ashamed for kissing her.

Women seemed to like kissing him; all of them except the one he really wanted. He didn't understand her.

She throws herself on me one minute and pushes me away the next.

He clenched his teeth in anger and slowly shook his head. He felt wet and cold, and an almost constant sense of alarm, yet his feelings for her created more anguish than anything else. He felt distracted to the point of debilitation, which he knew equated to extreme danger in this environment.

No matter how it feels ... Don't go there. Focus. Take control. Be strong.

He heard Noah breathing heavily and to his surprise, the sound of gunfire coming from higher up the mountain.

Tom leant closer and whispered to Noah.

"I don't understand. Who are they shooting at?"

Even in the shadowy light, Noah's concern seemed evident.

"The odds aren't good that it's Petra. That leaves Uta. She's fighting her way down the track. There's no other explanation I can think of."

"She's following us? She can't come back."

"No. She doesn't want to."

"Then why would she put herself in danger's way?"

"You can't compare her to other human beings, Tom. She doesn't feel fear like us. She doesn't know if we have the Prize, but she'll attack now nonetheless. If she doesn't get it, she'll take the next best thing ... You."

Tom felt a lump in his throat.

"This must be what paranoia feels like; everyone's out to get me."

"I'm afraid so, Tom. If she gets past Vogel, we'll have to kill her to stop her."

"Looks like we're in for a pleasant evening."

Great conversation. Who wants a truth like that?

His truth created fear in all of its forms. The future seemed impossible. To get off this mountain, they needed to outrun Vogel, keep Uta at bay and break through the Assembly SRP defences at the base of the mountain. If they achieved this, they still required a disappearing act to evade capture and a miracle to find the Prize.

Tom closed his eyes and attempted to focus on Noah's mindless confidence technique; tricking his brain into believing that he could exist amongst so much chaos.

He heard Noah groan as he raised himself from the ground.

"Alright team, this is it. From here on, we're in danger of running into their forward placements. Tom, you and Isobel, are to stay at least ten metres behind and use whatever natural light to watch me for directions. Absolutely no speaking from here on."

Without another word, the group moved into formation; Surat controlling the rear, Tom and Isobel the middle and Noah further forward, taking the point.

They reached Tobias Gap, their next rest stop, without incident.

Tom considered the cutting just as indistinct as the previous rest stop, or any other part of this difficult terrain. He sat down just as Noah began to rise.

"Alright. Time to go. Same formation. No talking."

Tom didn't even have time to normalise his breathing. He moved forward and passed Isobel; making sure he gained the front position so he didn't have to keep seeing the faint shape of her body.

Don't think, just act. Focus on Noah and nothing else.

His empty mind technique failed. Moments seemed exaggerated into hours. Thoughts kept creeping in; her kiss, the feel of her body and strangely, his father's broken watch. In time it became the dominant thought. Something about it troubled him.

This doesn't make sense ... Unless?

It occurred to him that the remaining hand might be a clue. His father performed tasks in a precise and measured way; a man that didn't do anything without a specific reason.

Why would he leave it to me in such poor shape? There must be more to this than the storage chip we found in the mechanism, yet the missing hand seems far too obvious.

He heard a low and urgent voice.

Noah?

"Stop. Wait."

In the few moments of their stoppage, Tom felt his sweat turn cold and he started to shiver. As he rubbed himself for warmth, he perceived movement in the forest beside him.

"Noah. Quick. To your left."

A blood-soaked creature sprang out from the fern scrub; her movements so fast that nobody in the G11's found time to react.

Uta.

No-one moved. Uta held the group within the sweeping arc of her weapon's rapid side to side movement. The barrel communicating her threat, far better than any words.

"Fox. You. Here. Now."

She pointed the weapon at Surat and her facial expression twisted into a bloodied scowl.

"Sir … Rat. You self-important prick. Say goodbye to your friends."

Surat dived headlong for cover, but the force of the bullets tore him apart and destroyed his life. With a thump, he tumbled amongst the bracken beyond their view.

"I always wanted to kill that idiot."

Tom grabbed Isobel by the arm and pulled her behind him. He glanced back at Uta. Her grin looked like it belonged to a blooded skull.

"Time to wave bye-bye, Noah. You're about to become a corpse."

Chapter Thirty Eight

The chairman scrutinised the other six dapper men sitting around the table. They appeared grotesque, with old stone-hard faces, beak like noses and enormous jowls. Their horrible expressions amused him. They reminded him of a sentry of gargoyles, employed by the Church to scare away the devil and all of his imps.

I know your collective mind.

Their eyes and lower jaws appeared to be the only part of their anatomy to move; each making use of a stiff demeanour and a formal set of manners, as a well-constructed facade.

You can't hide your black hearts from me.

Their stoic faces disguised all thought from those that didn't know better; concealing any hint of emotion.

Good. They honour their true Gods; money, power and title.

He felt relieved. The group cast their vote and to a man, they agreed, but the chairman knew that none felt happy with the decision.

None could refuse such an offer, but the cost ...?

The price meant granting a monster the power to rule the spiritual world. In return, they elevated themselves to the summit of Mount Olympus; he like Zeus and six other man-made Gods to rule the physical world as they liked, yet each man suffered his decision with anxious unease, like smelling wood-smoke deep within a forest.

With a slight tilt of his head, Antonio Costa, Chairman of the Assembly of the True Faith, motioned for his assistant to attend him.

"Keep the cardinal waiting. A little stress might minimise the cost of our negotiations."

Antonio turned and concentrated on the other six members of the Assembly. Breaking a long-standing protocol, he revealed his palpable distaste for the cardinal to every member of the gathering.

He smiled at their astonished expressions.

"You see my feelings on this matter, gentlemen, as I clearly know yours."

He spat the words at them, like unwanted phlegm.

"I have no doubt that the man can deliver his promise, but we will need to perform miracles to keep him in line. If we give our power to this black-hearted cardinal, we will no longer be behind the scenes. Instead, we'll be exposed in our holy quest, for all to see."

Antonio held back his smile, as the small balding man rose to address the board. Secretly he considered him the antagonist of the group; the one bringing hostility to the table at every opportunity.

"This is a perilous situation. What do you propose, Mr Chairman?"

"I propose nothing. I am just stating the obvious. When this endeavour begins, we will have to control the environment like never before. This means eliminating any opposing us. We must take every measure to win our rightful place in God's plan for humanity, despite the probable toll. Remember gentleman, men have fought many wars for God. Body counts don't matter, only victory does."

"And how will we control the cardinal?"

"With all of our means. He can't pass wind unless we have caused it to happen."

"Mr Chairman, is this feasible? Once he holds the high ground, it will be much more difficult to apply our influence."

"We have the man-power inside the Vatican. We will monitor his every movement, his every word; day and night. I am more than confident that we can control him."

"And, what of the Prize, Mr Chairman. In the wrong hands …?"

"Yes. Even from the holiest of positions, the Black Cardinal will answer to us, unless he gets his hands on the Prize. If that occurred, we would become unnecessary and you know what that would mean."

After a long silence, the balding man rose once again to speak.

"This Fox situation requires permanent closure, Mr Chairman. It's time to remove the threat."

"Yes. I have given this a lot of thought and I agree. It's time."

The chairman swallowed down his repugnance. He didn't agree, but what choice did he have?

"The Fox situation is dangerous, given our involvement with the cardinal. If you are all in agreement, I will order a thorough clean-up operation. We'll simply remove all of the other parties, including Vogel. I have reason to believe that duplicity already exists as far as he is concerned."

"And, the priest …?"

The chairman suppressed a need to groan.

"Everyone involved in an operational sense will have to be eliminated, including Fox and the priest."

He struggled to hold back his feelings regarding the priest, the man he once knew like a son. Yet, hadn't God given his Son for the greater good?

"If the Prize isn't recovered, there is always going to be the danger that it will resurface at a later and more inappropriate moment. Once the order is made, both the players and the Prize are mere rumour."

"And how soon can this be achieved, Mr Chairman?"

The bald man continued to test him.

Stay focused. Stay strong.

"Ah, clever. Very clever. You have scratched the surface and discovered our new dilemma. We've lost contact with Vogel … For the moment."

"We've lost contact? Surely this is dangerous?"

"We've lost contact, not control. This situation presents little danger to our endeavours."

A dangerous lie. Divert their attention. Focus on their success.

"I suggest that we wait for a renewed connection and then send in our clean-up crew without alerting him."

Antonio took a deep breath and tried to let go of some of his tension.

"I have already taken the liberty of finding a replacement for our head of security. I'll present him as soon as possible. Are we agreed so far, gentleman?"

The Assembly board cast their vote without betraying the slightest trace of emotion. Seven expressionless nods confirmed Vogel's fate. The same warrant included the termination notice for Tom Fox, Isobel Kite and all of the G11 team.

"Gentlemen, it's time to bring in our black-hearted cardinal. We're about to make him God's holiest living man and His leader on earth."

Chapter Thirty Nine

Vogel watched his captain jog down the Bungalow Spur track, berating his men at every opportunity.

Good. Enough hatred and he'll kill without hesitation.

Frederick stiffened at the sound of gunfire. It came from the track below them; two loud reports and several rounds of return fire.

The main group of SRP stopped and took cover, while the captain and another soldier moved forward. Frederick saw them encounter their returning scout.

He interrupted their discourse, beckoning the officer with a wave of his arm.

"What's happening, captain?"

"We've got one down wounded, sir. They've employed a moving rear guard action to slow us down."

"So, what are we going to do about it? We're not going to be held up by a few stray shots are we, captain?"

"If we keep losing our soldiers, we'll become vulnerable … Sir."

"As long as we drive the enemy hard into our men at the bottom, it doesn't matter how many of ours we lose. It'll save you the trouble later."

"There's another way to counter their rear guard without further damage to our force of men."

"Yes?"

"We redistribute our force, utilising a forward position to move ahead of the group, firing timed sprays of bullets."

"And, if they lay in wait?"

"They can't afford to be trapped on the mountain. Our forward team will run and hold until the second group catches up. Then the second group will continue the attack. We'll force them out of cover into the men below."

"Good."

The captain's proving his worth. If he continues to perform at this level, I might have to consider letting him live.

"Bring me Tom Fox alive and your worth will rise ten-fold."

Frederick felt relieved. Intermittent showers replaced sleet and snow, and as the temperature rose, the visibility improved.

He removed his communicator and punched the keypad with his forefinger.

What the hell is going on? Where are they?

He couldn't contact the soldiers guarding the bottom of the spur. He reasoned that it could just be a technical problem, yet his assumption required failure from both of their communicators. That scenario didn't seem likely.

"Captain. Stop. Rein in your men."

Perspiration soaked his undergarments and the cold began to creep in and chill his body.

"Captain …"

We have to change tactics. Don't push the enemy. We have to catch them now, or all could be lost.

Tom chanced a look in Noah's direction and noticed his surreptitious nod.

I have to act or we're going to die.

He felt a sudden rise in body temperature and his ears began to throb. His breathing becoming rapid and shallow and his vision blurred.

Alright, this is it.

He increased the pressure of his grip on Isobel's arm and in one slinging motion, threw her crashing face-first into the bracken.

"Now."

Tom charged.

As he leapt forward a spray of droplets erupted from the ferns where Isobel entered.

Dive. Dive at her legs.

He saw the barrel of The Raptor's gun swing towards him. He also caught sight of a dark blur moving to his left.

Noah.

They charged at her together and in that instant, Tom realised the unescapable truth.

We're not going to make it.

Uta backed away from the onrushing threat.

Kill Noah. Smash Fox.

Even under the pressure of this attack, she found time enough to raise the gun to her line of sight before firing.

The Spitter, her beloved Croatian automatic pistol, spat at its victims like a cobra. She felt almost no vibration, as it delivered its toxic spray of bullets at the blur of flesh racing towards her.

The captain worked his way into the fern covered depression and began reporting as he crouched down beside Vogel.

"They're keeping to the shadows, sir. We can't pinpoint the exact location of their shooters."

"I don't give a damn. Stop what you're doing, captain. There's been a change of plan. I want them caught here and not any further down the track. Is that understood?"

"We're not driving them into a trap …?"

"No. Things change. Give me a new plan of attack. I want this to end here and now."

"Sir. What about Fox?"

"What about him?"

"He might be killed."

"You're not listening. I want this done without endangering Fox."

"Sir … To stop them retreating we'll have to go in heavy. That means there'll be a lot of lead in the air."

"No. Tom Fox can't be harmed under any circumstances."

Vogel thought the captain looked like a man on his way to the gallows.

"Pull yourself together, man. Our entire mission depends on Fox."

"Then we'll have to use the gas."

"No again, captain. I saw the remaining canisters. That gas is as deadly as any bullet."

Frederick's throat felt so dry he could hardly speak. He took a deep breath to calm his growing anxiety and used his sleeve to wipe the sweat from his face.

"What the hell are you thinking, captain?"

"Sir, let me explain. We can utilise non-lethal gas."

"And the danger to Fox is minimal?"

"Yes, the target will be unconscious for a short time only, but it's still a combat zone. There's always some risk involved."

Vogel felt like punching the man.

Solutions. That's what I want, not complications.

"Sir. The wind's stopped. This's good for us. This type of gas is less efficient in a windy environment."

Frederick started to calm down. The plan appeared to be workable.

"Alright, let's get it done."

If all went well, it could all be over in a matter of minutes.

The weather's good, but I'll hold off on the Porepunkah team.

The backup helicopter crew awaited his orders, thirty kilometres to the west, near the town of Bright. Calling them now created more bodies. His captain needed no more to deal with in the clean-up. He could make contact with the helicopter crew after their success.

There can't be any witnesses.

When the captain dispatched and buried the SRP commando team he needed to finish the job.

I'll bury you in the same hole as the men you murdered ... No-one will find the graves, but it hardly mattered if they did. Soon, I'll be unassailable; I'll own every soul on this planet.

—————

As the object smashed into Tom's face, flashes of light burst into his mind and explosions of pain reverberated around his skull; the force of the object, driving him headfirst into the waiting mud.

All went black.

Chapter Forty

Tom heard the question and understood its urgency, but the words seemed to be for someone else.

"Tom. Are you alright?"

He felt a hand grasp his shoulder and shake him; the action rousing him from his stupor.

"Noah?"

A face started to take shape, like a reflection in the dying ripples of a pond.

"What the hell happened?"

"You got yourself knocked out, Tom. You had a run-in with my elbow."

"Tom … Tom …?"

Isobel ran and fell to her knees beside him and Noah moved away.

"You're alive."

Tom felt her take his hand and squeeze it. She leant forward and kissed him. Her lips wet with rain, saliva and tears.

"You scared me. I thought you were gone. I don't want you to be gone."

Tom sat up and she helped him rest his back against the trunk of a tree. He felt dazed, fearful and elated all at the same time.

She knelt beside him, her hand still in his; her intense gaze still beyond his understanding.

"What are you doing, Izzi? I thought ..."

"Don't."

She put her forefinger to his lips.

"Please. Don't say anything."

She began to stroke his face with the tips of her fingers.

"Just so you know, Tom; if you die, I'll be really pissed off."

Tom stretched out his arm and pulled her closer to him. He felt her tiny body stiffen and then relax. He tried to return the softness of her kiss, but their lips came together with passion.

What now ...?

Isobel broke away and glared at him without any semblance of a smile.

"I mean it, Tom."

"Yeah ... Alright. I won't die; for a while at any rate. I promise."

In the faint light he saw the truth in her expression; she believed in the inevitability of their death.

"Tom. You're wanted."

He spotted a dark shape waving at him from amongst the shadows.

He patted Isobel on the shoulder and moved towards Noah on his hands and knees. Dizziness forced him to stop, but after a few seconds of stillness, he set off again.

As he approached the spot where Noah stooped, he began to recognise the limp and bloodied figure lying beside him.

Uta ...? The gun ... I remember.

"We should be dead."

Noah screwed up his face and brought a finger to his lips.

"Not so loud, Tom. We've been under attack. While you were out of it, the SRP hit our position from higher up the trail."

Tom flinched. He couldn't believe it. The corpse began to shudder and cough.

"Don't gawk at me, Fox. It should be you lying here."

Tom started to rise.

"No, Tom."

Noah pulled him back to the ground.

"That's how she copped it. She backed into the moonlight and the SRP shot her. So keep your head down and stay in the shadows."

The contrast between the moonlit, open ground and the deep shadows made it difficult for the enemy to see them. As Noah crawled away towards Isobel, Tom looked back at Uta; he could feel her staring at him.

You're a pitiless murderer.

He could see dark blotches on her clothing and more bloodied gashes on her face. It looked fatal.

"Your wound, it hurts?"

"Of course it hurts."

Tom wondered about the hurt that Julius, Petra and Luther must have endured.

"Good."

He could gather no sympathy in his heart for this woman; his feelings of pity gone.

"It's the devil for me, Fox."

"You're a murderer. That's where you belong. You deserve hell."

"And you don't? What do you think you're going to do with me? Carry me down the mountain and nurse me back to health."

"We'll have to leave you here. There's no other choice."

"In about two minutes your precious Noah, is going to come back and blow my brains all over the place and you'll get to watch."

Tom didn't know what to say. The thought of such a thing made him feel ill, even if the hideous cow deserved it.

He heard a scraping sound behind him. Right on cue, Noah began crawling back towards them.

"Tom, get ready. We're moving out fast. We'll have to leave her, I'm afraid."

Tom let out a long, slow sigh.

"It doesn't matter. Vogel will do what you haven't got the stomach for."

"Save your crap for him then."

Tom felt Noah pull on his arm.

"Leave her now, Tom. We have to go."

Noah led the few remaining members of the G11 troop from the clearing. They bent low, staying in the shadows.

"No."

Tom stopped and Isobel jerked at the end of his arm; his thought so consuming that he forgot to let go of her.

"Noah, stop. I've got to go back."

He held out his hand.

"Give me Uta's weapon. It needs to be fired one last time."

"No, Tom. Ending it quickly is a noble gesture, but she doesn't deserve it. If you go back, it might cost you your life."

Tom nodded towards the weapon with determination.

"I have to go back. That's all there is about it."

Isobel grabbed at his coat and pulled him towards her.

"Tom. No. It's murder."

Tom kept his eye contact with Noah. The big man shook his head and sighed, but he handed over the weapon. Without another word, Tom turned and hurried back to Uta's side.

"Hey, what's this? You suddenly grown balls, Fox?"

"Shut it, Uta."

"Come on brave boy, get on with it."

"Just shut up and listen. If we leave now, Vogel will kill you, but if I left you this gun …?"

"You want me to watch your back. Ha. That's funny. What do I get for saving your scrawny backside?"

"Revenge. I know you hate Vogel."

"What makes you think I won't kill you, when you hand me that spitter?"

"Maybe it's because you like me."

Tom smiled and nodded at a spot on the ground, not far from her.

"Or, because I'm going to put it just out of your reach and Noah will blow your head off, if you try to retrieve it too quickly."

Chapter Forty One

Tom heard voices and looked away from Uta towards the source of the sound. SRP commandos hid higher up the track and he could hear their whispers floating in on the wind.

They're close. It's time to go.

He took one last look over his shoulder at Uta's silhouette and stopped short.

No ... How did she retrieve it so quickly?

Uta held the spitter in her hands; its barrel aimed in his direction. She could kill him any time she wanted.

Tom didn't dare move. You never knew what this woman might do.

"Piss off, Fox. I'll keep to my end of the bargain."

He saw her turn the gun away and he exhaled in relief.

The G11 group moved off, walking as quickly as the conditions allowed. Noah led them, but instead of silence, he fed them a constant brew of positive encouragement. Tom felt warmer as a result of the man's courage. No matter how unreasonable, he could see the possibility of a life forming beyond the abyss and it focused his spirit, forcing him on.

They heard the clamour of gunfire, several minutes into their march. After a constant barrage, the firing became sporadic and eventually stopped.

It's over ... She's probably dead by now.

Tom wondered if he should feel sorry for her. Could redemption be possible for someone like Uta?

He shook his head.

No. Probably not, but she did give them a chance to escape. That must be worth something.

They continued their march for another ten minutes before halting and taking a brief rest. Noah pulled them in close and spoke in low tones.

"We're nearly at the bottom. It'll begin soon."

He sighed in the middle of his speech. His breath forming a deep resonate note that Tom associated with grief.

"Listen you two. We can't allow ourselves to be caught in the middle of their forces, so we'll have to shoot our way out. It's our only chance."

Tom hardly recognised Isobel's voice when she spoke. It quivered from cold and fear.

"Noah, won't they hear us coming and be ready?"

"There's no other way, Isobel. We can't get around them. The blackberries are too dense near the bottom. The only way is through and we can't waste time either. Vogel's coming. He'll be hard at us now."

Noah reached over and grabbed Tom by the shoulders; the action so violent that his head flew backwards.

"Before we do this, there's something I have to tell you."

Tom stiffened. Even the low light couldn't hide the anger in Noah's expression.

"I'm sorry. This isn't easy to say. If things get bad down there and we're going to be caught, I'll have to take action."

"What does that mean exactly?"

"There's only one way to say this. I can't let them take you alive. Do you understand me, lad?"

Tom's stomach contracted as the statement became clearer in his mind. The man he trusted most, needed to end his life while his enemy needed to keep him alive.

"No. No way."

Isobel flung herself at Noah; her bony fists striking his upper body.

"You bastard, Noah. You leave him alone."

Tom pulled her to him, restraining her in his arms. He felt the fight in her soften and her breathing return to normal.

"Iz, Noah's right. These people killed our parents and God-only-knows what they'll do, if they get this Prize; if they get me."

"No. That's bullshit, Tom."

"No it's not, Iz. Once they've got what they want, they'll kill me anyway. If it's necessary ... He has to do this."

Noah gently prised them apart and tilted his head towards the track.

"When I start firing, you run and you keep running until I tell you to stop. Alright?"

Noah grasped Tom's hand and shook it with passion.

"Good luck, Tom. Godspeed."

He reached over and pulled Isobel into a hug.

"Good luck to you too, lass. You'll be alright. We'll all be alright."

Tom turned towards Isobel and tried to smile. He felt vulnerable and hesitant. This could be their last moment together and he might never get another chance to tell her how he really felt.

"Izzi ... I ..."

"No ... Just hold me."

Tom's arms enveloped her and he could feel her tiny body trembling. She reached up and pushed her cold lips against his.

"Tom, Isobel. I'm sorry, it's time."

They set out with caution, slipping and sliding around a sharp turn to the west.

"Noah."

Just as Tom noticed the track beginning to flatten, he saw movement to his left and his heart pounded with a rush of adrenalin.

"Noah, behind you."

A dark figure sprang from the scrub and before anyone could react, he jammed a gun into the small of Noah's back.

The man turned and Tom glimpsed his features in the moonlight.

"My God, it's you."

Chapter Forty Two

Uta lay in the bracken; so close to Vogel's advancing troops that she could hear their breathing as they approached. She sat back against a log and utilised the cover to make an assessment of her situation.

Damn crappy luck.

She felt empty. Dying a useless death on this mountain so far from her cardinal and her sister, didn't feel glorious. Even the pain couldn't stop the sensation of feeling hollow.

"What are you doing? Get up. Get going."

Uta slapped away her self-pity; the blow from her open hand stinging the wounds on her face. She rolled onto one elbow and made herself a promise.

I'll never heed pain again. I'm Uta Cel Rău. I'm the master of death and I'll kill anyone who gets in my way.

Uta moved back towards the Bungalow Spur trail in time to see Vogel's troops creeping forward for what looked like a front on assault; their positioning implied gas.

Why and why here? Why stop pushing them towards the bottom? And why no air support?

She didn't understand his tactics, but he must be worried. If the G11's got too far ahead, he may not be able to contain them at the trail's end. Noah could fight his way through without the worry of attack from behind.

She considered Vogel's other major dilemma. If the G11's didn't have the Prize, he needed Fox alive.

Yes. Gas. They won't risk any hurt to Fox.

This suited her purpose. She crawled into the area between Vogel's men and the targeted gas zone and waited.

————————

The captain gave the signal and Vogel watched the small group of masked men ease their way forward. Ten seconds later he heard a hissing sound as the gas canisters flew over his head towards the enemy.

Good. No breeze, they'll be unconscious in seconds.

Muffled explosions erupted in the surrounding forest, but instead of the silence of his perceived victory, gunfire filled the air. Several flares lit the area like daylight and for the first time he viewed the target area.

Frederick recognised the captain as he rushed forward with the backup team, but they stopped well short of their goal.

What the hell's going on?

The captain retreated, shouting orders as he came.

"Fall back. Everybody back. Now."

Frederick knew that an attack like this depended on surprise, the wind effectiveness of the gas and a good knowledge of the enemy's position, but the unmistakable sound of the spitter amongst his forward placements told him that they held none of these elements.

Damn it, Uta.

Frederick thought it strange how people reacted when death raced at them. He raised his head above the protection of a fallen tree as wraith-like figures crashed through the smoking scrub; projectiles zinging around him. In this dream-state, he felt no fear. Nothing seemed real.

He felt strong hands grab his shoulders and push him back below the level of the tree trunk. The shaking action cleared his state of mind and life raced back; the volume on high.

"Captain. What's happening?"

"Someone got inside our forward perimeter. That's what's happening. The gas went right over them. When our men went forward they got slammed."

"There's not that many of them. How could you get this wrong?"

"There's no time for this now. Uta did this alone. The G11's are gone. They left before the attack even started."

"For God's sake do something. They're getting away."

Frederick felt anger thump in his temples. Instead of bringing the men to order, his captain rolled onto his back and stared at the moon.

"What are you doing?"

"These people are good, very good. There's no way in hell, I would count on the two men you have below."

Vogel's bowels clenched at the mention of his missing men.

"I'll ask you again, captain. What-the-hell are you doing? What's your plan?"

"We need air support and we need it now. There's not a cloud in the sky down here. So, for God's sake, call in your damn helicopter."

Chapter Forty Three

Tom tried to maintain his hold on Isobel's hand, but sweat ran down his arm and into their intertwined fingers. When the two of them became extended by the terrain, they slipped apart.

After each fall he tried to contain his frustration.

That's the reality. We've only got a lunatic's hope of survival.

His existence seemed like a ridiculous topsy-turvy ride to oblivion. He looked over at the dark shape beside him. She probably felt the same sense of exasperation.

She must be scared.

In the last few minutes he heard Isobel moan with each step on the steeper terrain. He supposed the muscles around her knees hurt as much as his.

"Iz. Try to stay strong."

He felt the need to comfort her, even though his words sounded stupid and demeaning.

He heard the dreaded priest call for them to stop and he let go of her hand.

"We're almost at the bottom. From here on, I want you to run."

Tom felt confused. The clergyman's order didn't make sense.

Why would they need to run from the Assembly, when they'd just been captured by them?

They started off at a trot and almost immediately Tom began to slip and slide; the characteristics of the track changing from rocky and firm to mud. As he sloshed along he noticed the lower-altitude eucalypts towering above him. About one in every twenty having a massive white trunk, which seemed to glow in the moonlight in comparison to its darker, shadowy cousins.

The priest's bellowed commands tore him from his thoughts.

"Pick up your speed, we need to go faster."

They rounded a sharp turn in the track and the township of Harrietville became visible below them; its lights twinkling with what should have been a measure of relief, but instead it represented a depressing reminder of what awaited them.

The priest raised his hand, signalling another stop. In one motion he utilised the same hand to usher them into a small grove beside a swiftly running creek.

"I have a vehicle not far from here. We can rest for a few moments. Then we'll make a run for the car."

Tom sucked in a deep breath and exhaled. It made a noise like a snarling dog.

"No … If you're going to kill us, do it here."

The priest turned and Tom could see his teeth in the moonlight. It looked like a smile.

"Who said anything about killing you?"

"You're the Assembly. You're the enemy."

The clergyman began to chuckle.

"Here then. You take it."

The priest thrust the butt of the gun forward in offering.

"I hope you're a little more experienced with it than I am. I've never actually fired one."

"What …? Why? I could kill you."

"This is no place for lengthy explanations. Kill me and Vogel's men will definitely do the same to you. Take a chance and you might just make it out of here alive."

Tom reached forward and took the weapon from the priest.

"Where are Vogel's men? The one's placed below us. You must have come up that way, so you have to know."

"Come. I'll show you."

The priest left the track and pushed his way through damp bracken before entering a tight clump of tree ferns. At his feet, two men sat, gagged and tied to a branch.

"I suggest we make a run for it. We have to get to my vehicle before their helicopter arrives. I'm surprised it's not here already."

They began to run with renewed vigour. The kind that is fuelled by hope. Tom felt almost joyous, as he raced towards the end of the forest. In only a few more minutes they could be out, but then he heard the whirling of spinning rotors approaching from the west.

Noah stopped and threw out his arms as a barrier to the others.

"Everybody get down. Into the bush. Hide yourselves."

Tom ignored him and remained on his feet. He felt the weight of the gun in his hand and this time it didn't feel out of place.

"No ... I've had enough of this rubbish."

At that moment, he felt he would rather die than be dragged another inch.

"I'm the one you all want. So ... from now on, I'm in charge. You either agree, or Isobel and I are gone."

Chapter Forty Four

The captain stood over the soldier, watching him die; the man's abdomen torn beyond assistance. He tried to lessen the tension in his own stomach by controlling and slowing the rate of his breathing.

You're the lucky one. You'll soon be dead and gone from this hell.

As his heartbeat began to regulate, he considered his own situation. Could survival be worth this betrayal? Death might be a better option than having this shame on his conscience.

Vogel interrupted his thoughts.

"Have you found Uta's tracks, captain?"

"Yes. She left a blood trail that a drunk could follow."

"Leave her for the dingos then. She'll bleed to death anyway. We have to stay on Fox."

He didn't agree with Vogel's logic. If left alive, Uta The Raptor remained a significant threat, but he couldn't afford to divide and deplete his small force of men any further in an attempt to find her.

"Do we have an estimate on our helicopter, sir? Fox must be close to the bottom by now."

"Yes. The timing's perfect. They'll have to make a run for it, knowing that we're close behind. With infrared, they'll be out in the open with no cover and visible from the air. There's no escape. I've got them."

The captain shook his head; a lot of things could go wrong. He looked over at his boss. Vogel's excitement made him nervous. He appeared unstable; mentally.

How do I deal with this? If I help him, my men die and if I kill him, we die as well.

Uta let her blood spill purposely onto several false trails. She knew the SRP didn't want to follow her, but she added this further motivation to help with their decision. Vogel needed all of his dwindling force to chase after Fox and the remnants of the G11's.

They must also know I'd kill whoever they sent. It's a shame ... I owe these bastards a little hurt, but they won't waste men now.

She continued to crawl through the wet bracken and despite her waterproof outer layers some of the moisture found its way underneath. Combined with her sweat, the dampness made her inner layers sodden, freezing her skin.

"Keep focused. Concentrate."

The trunk of a huge fallen eucalypt acted as cover; providing her a place to assess the extent of her wounds without being harassed.

They've only managed to hit me twice.

The first strike creating the most damage; the projectile entering her back and shaving the top of her hip, before exiting. As she lay wounded on the ground another projectile punctured the left side of her upper chest, carving a passage up and through the top of her shoulder. Neither bullet seemed to fracture any bone or damage any vital organs, or arteries, but any movement in either area, felt excruciating.

The pain didn't stop her from smiling.

"I might actually survive this."

Blood loss and distance to an evacuation point created her most immediate concerns. Once she stemmed all of her leakages, she still needed to negotiate the steep and difficult terrain to a possible pickup area below. Such escape routes existed, but from her current location, they required a bush-bash over two separate ridgelines, to the west branch of the Kiewa River and finally down to the Dungey Track.

No, that's out of the question ... I won't make it.

The only other choice remaining, meant following well behind the SRP, down the Bungalow Spur. From here she could make contact and be picked up by one of the cardinal's men.

Despite her positive determinations, she realised that she could just as easily die here from her wounds.

Like a giant bird of prey, the helicopter hovered overhead; its catch caught in the beam of its search lights.

"I've got them covered, Mr Vogel."

"How many are there?"

"I have three adults, two male and one female. What're your orders, sir?"

"Land and send your guard in to contain them until we arrive. Do not take the light off them for any reason and don't kill anyone. Wound, if you have to shoot. Is that understood?"

"Yes sir. They've already surrendered their weapons and they're horizontal and immobilised."

"Have you seen any SRP personnel in the vicinity? Anyone other than the three you described."

"No, sir. I haven't seen anyone else."

Frederick felt a shiver move up his spine and spread across his back. He shuddered and pulled his shoulder blades together to counter the sensation. He couldn't come up with any viable reason for their disappearance.

I'm going to make you pay, Noah. You're going to spill your guts, literally.

Why show them any mercy? He shook with power; trembling at the thought of butchering all of them, except Fox.

He rubbed his hands together with delight. He risked everything on his plan succeeding and for several horrible hours, his doom seemed the more likely outcome.

He rushed over and shook his captain's shoulders with an enthusiasm that the man didn't return.

"We found Surat's body and we know Uta's behind us. That only leaves Noah, Fox and the girl; two male and one female. We've won, captain. From here on you need to concentrate on your strategy for the clean-up operation. Is that understood?"

Vogel didn't wait for a response. He ran out in front of his team without any apprehension, or concern.

"I can't wait to kill you, Noah. It's going to be a pleasure."

The thrill of capturing your enemies and knowing that you are going to dispatch them, begging and screaming into oblivion, is the right of all truly powerful men.

He felt dominant and superior. He could see himself at the head of the Assembly table. He could see them kneeling at his feet, kissing his hand.

"I've done it. I've won."

Chapter Forty Five

The roar of the helicopter's rotors assailed the clearing as it descended on the captives beneath.

Tom's eyes hurt from the force of its search lights. He tried to look back at the others in the clearing, but couldn't see them through the dense foliage.

Sharp sticks and small jagged rocks dug into his hands and knees as he crawled through the gully.

Maybe this isn't such a good idea.

He earned every metre he gained, once the tangle of blackberry vines took hold of his clothing and skin. They lacerated his legs, arms and a good proportion of his torso, with crisscross patterns of stinging, superficial cuts.

Through the vines he spotted a soldier jumping from the helicopter. The man backed out into the light and moved cautiously towards Isobel and the others.

Now ... Go.

Tom took a deep breath, freed himself from the vines and ran to where the man exited the helicopter. He didn't need to be quiet; the whirl of the slowing rotors covered the sound of his footfalls.

He pushed the top half of his body into the cockpit, produced his weapon and confronted the pilot.

"You. Stop. Don't move. Don't give me a reason to kill you. Do you hear me?"

The pilot nodded his understanding; his fear obvious, which lifted Tom's confidence.

He pressed his advantage.

"I'm going to back out of the cockpit and you're going to follow me. Move very slowly. If you try to warn your friend, I'll blow a hole through the back of your head."

Tom manoeuvred himself and the pilot out of the aircraft. His plan depended on the SRP shooter not being able to look back directly into the glare of the search lights.

He whispered an instruction to the pilot and pushed the barrel of his weapon into the man's back for emphasis.

The pilot obeyed and called out to the soldier.

"I've found some rope to tie them up with. I'm coming over to give you a hand."

Tom continued to shield himself behind the pilot, by utilising the man's shadow. He gambled on the fact that the pilot didn't get paid enough to die for other people's causes.

"Down. On your stomach. Now."

With a prod from the barrel of Tom's gun, the pilot went to ground.

Too late … The soldier turned and spotted him.

He struck out at the SRP trooper with the butt of his weapon, but the man moved quickly. He flung out his arm and deflected the blow; Tom's gun striking him on the wrist and discharging. Both weapons fell to the ground.

The soldier recovered and took the initiative. From a crouched position, he flung mud into Tom's face and launched a kick towards his stomach. Tom backed away from his strike, as pain burst into his head; the blow coming from behind, propelling him forward into the full force of another kick from the soldier. It struck him in the upper stomach region and he doubled over and fell; the air driven from his lungs.

Tom attempted to roll away and rise to his feet, as the two men kicked and punched his torso and legs. He fell onto his back and tried to cover his mid-section by pulling his knees up and continuing to roll.

"No ... No you don't."

Tom reacted as the soldier reached for his weapon. He couldn't allow him to reach it. He struck out at him with his right leg.

The man tripped, stumbled and fell over.

Tom forced himself to his knees and his lungs filled with oxygen. He tried to stand, but the pilot took him in a headlock, using his strength to roll him onto his stomach. The man grunted with effort, as he twisted Tom's head towards the light.

As Tom gasped for breath, he saw a dark silhouette in the blinding glare in front of him; the man carried the unmistakable shape of a gun in his hand and pointed it towards him.

Chapter Forty Six

Vogel saw a glow from the town of Harrietville and the brilliance of the helicopter's searchlights through the trees ahead of him.

He panted for breath.

"Just five or six more minutes … and you're mine, Fox."

If the G11's didn't have the Prize, he could easily take control of Fox's mind with the right concoction of drugs and find it that way. Once they took effect, Fox could not deny him.

"I'm close … So damn close."

A powerful feeling of exhilaration flooded through him. The feeling of escaping a probable death at the hands of the Assembly made his success all the sweeter. As he raced on towards his destiny, he couldn't feel the pain in the muscles around his knees and he no longer felt tired.

"Hurry up, you imbeciles."

He laughed aloud as his imagination created a glorious visualisation: He reclined at the head of the marble boardroom table, confronting the Assembly board. He smiled at their faces, rigid with shock, but each expression turned to respect; each succumbing to his wishes without compromise. Every man stood and raised his glass to the *new* chairman.

"Sir ... Vogel ... Look."

The captain's warning took several seconds to break through his fantasy and gain his awareness.

"Look ... The helicopter, it's moving."

———————

Tom gasped for breath as the pilot choked off his oxygen supply with a forearm across his throat. He squinted and tried to focus on the shape in front of him. It appeared as a ghostly apparition; a black nothingness, only granted form by the fierceness of the light enveloping it.

Could this be the end? The grim reaper coming for my soul.

He heard the evil entity begin to speak and felt surprised that he recognised its voice.

"Let him go. Now, or you're a dead man."

The man let go.

"Now roll onto your stomach and pull your hands up behind your back."

Tom filled his lungs with precious oxygen and allowed himself a moment to recover.

"Noah. Thank God."

"Get up, Tom. Hurry."

Isobel rushed over and embraced him. She felt wet and cold and her body shivered beneath his arms.

"Well done, Tom. Noah slipped and took ages to find his weapon. I thought ..."

He touched her lips with his forefinger and smiled.

"We're all alright. We're safe, Iz."

Isobel frowned and pointed towards Noah as he tied the pilot's hands behind his back.

"Don't we need him? If we're going up in that thing, won't we have to take him with us?"

Noah herded both Tom and Isobel toward the aircraft.

"No. We don't need the pilot, lass. I trained in one of these old Shikra strike helicopters. This beauty's called a Black Baza, like the Asian hawk. It's famous for its attack manoeuvrability. This little Indian will do back-flips if you want it to."

Tom tried to talk back over his shoulder, as Noah pushed him on.

"Where on earth did you learn to fly an Indian helicopter?"

"In the RAAF before I moved camp and joined the old SAS, but that's a long story. Right now we've got to get into the air and get out of here."

The captain continued to call to his superior as he ran.

"Sir. Can you hear that? The engine. They've fired up the engine."

"So? What does that matter?"

"You ordered the pilot to land and contain. To stay there until you arrived. Well, he's just increased the speed of the rotors."

"For God's sake, be clear captain. What does that mean?"

"It means that either your pilot is disobeying a direct order, or our enemies are about to escape."

What? No. This can't be happening.

"Run captain. We have to stop them."

Frederick didn't hear the noisy creek beside him as he tried to keep up with his men. His whole being lost its sense of exhilaration and he struggled with sudden exhaustion. With each stride, his knees began to hammer; his legs feeling more like blocks of concrete than flesh.

As his panic began to rise, his voice became a piercing shrill.

"Captain, do something. For God's sake, do something."

The captain didn't answer. Vogel watched him run on towards the clearing.

"Shoot the pilot. Kill him before they can take off."

He could see the glare of the helicopter's searchlights and he began to realise the difficulty of hitting a target through the trees whilst on the run.

"Captain. Look out."

As he ran, he began to make out two dark shapes emerging from the glare; both figures charging towards his captain.

Noah removed all weapons from the hostages and gave them an ultimatum.

"Run up the Bungalow Spur track as fast as you can and don't deviate, or I'll blow your heads off. Got it?"

The men seemed eager to please and Tom smiled at their speed, then he saw Noah waving at him ahead.

"Tom, hurry up and get back in. This is going to be a close thing. I've got to get this beauty off the ground before Vogel arrives."

Tom sat in the front with Noah and wondered how he could make any sense out of the montage of gauges and switches.

I hope he knows what he's doing.

As he thought this, the helicopter began to shudder and buck as it lifted into the air, causing Tom to grab the sides of his seat. He winced, again wondering about Noah's dubious skills as a pilot. Based on his performance so far, he thought them either delusional, or worse still, suicidal.

He attempted to counter his heaving stomach by following the progress of the escapees. They ran in the bright glow of the spotlights, but the erratic movements of their ascent made the view difficult to sustain.

Between jolts, he managed to spot several different men running straight at the fleeing pair; one with his weapon extended, ready to fire.

"Noah, look. Over there. The SRP are here and the men …"

Before Tom could finish his statement, gunfire erupted on the track above in the clearing and the pilot went down. The other man fell to his knees and raised his hands in surrender. Another burst of gunfire struck him and he fell back over the pilot's body.

Tom felt like throwing up. He shouted at Noah and grabbed at his arm.

"Noah. They've just killed them. Look … Look."

Because of Tom's pulling motion, the helicopter lurched to one side, narrowly missing a clump of tall stringy-bark eucalyptus trees. Tom twisted round in his seat trying to see Isobel.

"Iz, are you alright?"

Isobel's hands grasped her knees; pulling them up in front of a face, bloodless with terror.

"Hang on. We're nearly away. We're going to make it."

Tom hoped he sounded more convincing than he felt.

Vogel fell further behind his captain; the man sprinting far ahead of him. He appeared as a dark moving blur against the glare of the light. Frederick attempted to use a hand to shade his eyes, but it remained difficult to ascertain anything occurring ahead of him.

Shoot the pilot … Shoot the damn pilot.

He heard gunfire and saw a man tumble to the ground.

No …

The helicopter began rising into the air. Its lights flashed across the clearing, as it jerked from side to side.

Frederick started to scream, desperate to gain the captain's attention.

"The helicopter. Quickly, it's nearly up."

Again the captain didn't answer, so he ran on until he drew level with a body, then another; one wearing an SRP uniform.

We've been duped.

"Captain. Shoot at the helicopter. Shoot … Shoot … Shoot."

Chapter Forty Seven

The Assembly board studied Bruno Wolf on seven separate monitors and the chairman nodded. His candidate oozed confidence, which appeared to have an immediate effect on most of the board.

The Darkman sat back in his chair and smiled with an ease both reassuring and at the same time disturbing. Wolf exhibited a ruthless intelligence and his record backed this assessment. The man got the job done.

He's my choice, so why do I feel so anxious?

He removed a secret dossier compiled on Wolf, from a locked draw. It matched the file that the rest of the board scrutinised, apart from several omitted references; an overwhelming body count, a long list of sexual misadventures and an obsession for power.

This man has the potential to be a tyrant.

The chairman never decided anything without caution, but timing required him to be expedient. Despite his spectacular credentials, the man's ambition remained a worry.

If he starts to become a threat, I can have him eliminated in due course.

He began to tap his fingers on a second file which also concerned him; a portfolio containing other reasons why he needed to handle this situation with care.

The first item on the list provided a growing amount of evidence that Vogel acted against them, for his own benefit.

I can't just have him killed.

He needed to know if Vogel worked alone or in league with another. He needed to determine the identity of his competitors, before he could strike.

You won't be a thorn in my side for long, Vogel. That I promise.

Antonio sat back in his chair and took a moment to survey the men around him. They exuded power. Each member of the group headed their own family's vast interests. Between them, the seven board members of the Assembly owned and controlled the entire world of banking, with every country on earth sick with the debt they owed them.

He knew that if this group judged his leadership less than satisfactory, they could be unforgiving. He chose the man in the monitor for this very reason; to take back the advantage, but he needed the entire board to ratify his decision.

"Any questions, gentlemen?"

One of the Assembly brothers stood and addressed the board.

Antonio could see the advanced cancer in the grey pallor of his complexion and his deep sunken cheeks. He wondered how anyone could exist in such a paltry frame.

This living corpse will try to bring me down.

He viewed the man's ancient sagging skin, with distaste. It hung lank and lifeless, over protruding, meatless bones.

He wears his mortality like a badge of honour and flings it in our faces.

Antonio considered his appearance incongruous to their proceedings. Even though he dressed according to protocol, his suit fell away from his wide fleshless shoulders, further accentuating his skeletal appearance.

"Mr Chairman, it seems that this Fox situation may be almost out of our control. Perhaps we need to clarify what has gone wrong, before we rush into employing this new man."

The chairman nodded, pretending to agree. With the question of his competence before them, he took a moment to answer.

"You have all been fully advised on our current predicament. I have kept nothing from you. There seems to be little doubt that Vogel has crossed over. Why this is so, and for whom, is still unclear."

The thin man continued to stand. He seemed unwilling to accept anything less than an admission of poor judgement from their leader.

"Your man has placed us in a very vulnerable position, Mr Chairman."

"Gentlemen. Let us at least conclude this business before we start assessing performances. We have always taken the hard road in defence of our Mother Church, have we not? We can't allow ourselves to ..."

"Mr Chairman ..."

"Gentlemen. You must understand that our business is often difficult and we must always show courage. This is a great quest ..."

"Mr Chairman ..."

Antonio raised his voice in rebuke, as if he addressed an insolent child. He wanted no further interruptions.

"Enough. Let me finish. We all know that we have suffered a setback, but let me emphasise a point. It is not a defeat. Battles sometimes sway to and fro, but we will win and win convincingly."

Another aging man stood before the gathering. He needed the weight of the marble table to support his frame. As he leant forward, his large balding dome shone with perspiration.

"How can you be so sure of this? We would all like to share in your confidence, Mr Chairman."

"Because we have the power, my friends. We can throw unlimited assets against our enemy. Like the house against a lone gambler, we keep raising the stakes until the enemy has nothing left. He becomes defenceless … Defeated."

The chairman stopped and lifted his hand for silence. Breathless and red-faced, he needed several gulps of air before he could continue.

"Acts of terrorism are the only actions that the weak can employ against the strong. They are nothing but a thorn in a giant's foot. Behold gentleman. On the other side of that monitor sits a Godly man, who is uniquely qualified to remove that thorn for good."

Antonio Costa felt his body sag with relief. Winning this small battle gave him the time to put vast amounts of resources into place to find the Prize, but the unknown factors bothered him.

Vogel … Would he risk such an enterprise on his own?

If he won the Prize alone, he could name his price; he could take the chairman's position; his position. That made him a personal enemy.

The other possibility created an equally dangerous scenario. Vogel could only be seduced by an adversary as great or greater than the Assembly.

You've stolen my eyes, Vogel. I'm a blind man in the middle of a battlefield.

At that moment, even surrounded by all of his power, the chairman felt vulnerable. All of his hopes now lay with The Darkman.

Chapter Forty Eight

Tom grasped the bottom of his seat with both hands as the helicopter bucked and jerked its way towards the tree tops. He managed a sideways glance towards Noah. Sweat dripped off his forehead as he attempted to manoeuvre their craft.

Tom could see the raised and corded muscles in his friend's forearms as he gripped the cyclic stick between his legs with strong hands. At the same time he managed to control the collective lever to his left, while maintaining the throttle and working the pedals with his feet.

"Noah … Everybody. We're under attack."

They heard the sound of gunfire and the metallic thuds as projectiles struck the frame of the helicopter.

Tom attempted to twist around in his seat so that he could see Isobel.

"We're nearly up, Iz. Hang on."

The Baza tilted and Isobel screamed. Tom's window became the floor and he stared straight at the ground as it rose towards him.

"Oh, hell. Tom ..."

He tried to call back to her, but Noah's shout exceeded his in volume, as they rolled, straightened and rose.

"We did it. We're away."

It took Tom a moment to recover and make sense of Noah's words.

The sound of enemy gunfire seemed further off and then ceased altogether. A period of heavy breathing followed, with all of the occupants staring straight ahead, oblivious to all else except the circumstances of their escape. Even the engine and propeller noise appeared to recede within the cabin.

Between exhausted breaths, Noah quashed the suppressed atmosphere with staggered bouts of laughter.

"A close one ... but ... we did it."

Isobel reached forward and touched Noah on the shoulder; shattering his moment of relief with a rush of questions.

"What do we do now? Where are you taking us?"

Noah remained focused on the horizon; his bland expression and awkward, silent avoidance, answering the question for all of them; danger existed in every direction with only a slim chance of survival.

Tom's jaw tightened in anger.

Petra, Julius, Luther, Surat, even Uta; all dead.

Why?

To win a Prize that supposedly saved men from slavery. Once won, what do brainwashed people do with their freedom? How many wars are won so that men are free to stupidly enslave themselves to the same people, over and over again?

At that moment, Tom felt like a beast on his way to the slaughter-house.

What's the point?

He withdrew his weapon, swung around between the front two seats and aimed it at the man behind him.

"I've had enough, priest. Start talking."

"Perhaps now isn't the time for exhausting explanations, Tom."

"Tell that to our parents … Start talking."

"Yes, alright. It's important that both of you know everything, but there are other questions that should take precedence."

Isobel's face flushed with redness the moment the clergyman spoke.

"Like how you arranged the murder of our families?"

Tom glared at the man, but even with the gun pointed at his face he remained calm.

"The most important question is where we're going from here."

Isobel snarled; her teeth showing through tightly drawn lips.

"We? There's no *we*. How does a murderer think he fits into our plans?"

"Yes. This's an unpleasant business, but if we don't focus right now on our current predicament, we'll all be dead."

———————

Tom sat back in his seat and ignored the chatter in the cockpit. He needed to consider his next move carefully, but he couldn't make a decision based on little to no knowledge.

Forget the priest for now … I need help … I need good advice.

When it came to running from the International Special Religious Police, the Assembly of the True Faith and the Australian authorities, Tom understood his lack of experience. When it came to developing a plan to win against such impossible odds, he felt like an amateur.

"Noah. Does this flight have an actual destination?"

"No. Sorry, Tom. It doesn't. We trekked to the hut as a risk-it-all operation with no actual backup strategy for this side of the mountain. We just didn't have enough manpower or time to arrange anything else."

Noah turned in his seat and nodded towards the priest.

"I think you should ask him, Tom. He wouldn't endanger himself without some sort of backup plan."

"Is that right, priest? You have a plan in place?"

"Yes. I have some resources at my disposal."

Isobel raised her voice above the others.

"No, Tom. He's a killer."

"We have to make it out of here, Iz."

"No. No way. He's the enemy. How could you trust him? You know what he did to our families."

The helicopter shuddered and jerked as Noah struggled to manoeuvre his seating position in order to face Isobel.

"Lassie, we have to survive. That's our first priority and this man may be the key. We've no choice but to trust him. He's already saved us once."

"He's a snake."

The priest turned away from Isobel; his expression showing anger for the first time.

"Do you want my help or not?"

"Just tell us your strategy, then we'll decide."

The priest stared at Tom, searching his expression for several seconds.

"I have a business jet and a flight crew waiting for me. Will that do?"

"To go where?"

"To find the Prize. You have no other choice. The moment your father started this business ..."

Tom felt his face flush with anger. He tried to stand, but his seat belt pulled him back into his seat.

"What the hell do you mean by that?"

"The enemy will hunt you forever, Tom. No-one will survive this. Not unless we get to the Prize."

"So why help us? Why change sides now? Surely, they'll kill you too."

"But I haven't changed sides."

Isobel punched the back of the seat several times before she spoke.

"Don't listen to him. He's a liar."

Tom nodded his agreement before turning his attention away from Isobel and back to the priest.

"You haven't changed sides ... I don't believe you."

The priest's smile turned into a sigh. He waited some time before continuing.

"Alright, Tom. By now you'll have the watch, the box and the diary, or we wouldn't be here. It should have gone a bit smoother, but we didn't expect Vogel to break from the Assembly and go it alone."

"How do you know this ... Through the Assembly?"

"No. Not at all. The Assembly didn't know the road to the Prize. No-one knew this information except your father, Professor Kite and myself. However, they did receive some information from Professor Kite, when ..."

Isobel's face glowered with hatred.

"Before you murdered him."

The priest couldn't hold Isobel's sullen stare. He turned away and focused on the back of Tom's seat.

"Yes, a terrible waste, but for the Assembly a godsend. Because of his information, they knew they controlled the key; meaning you, Tom. Because of this, our plans changed. You know this because you have the diary. You know what he found and what he developed."

He knows my father's secrets. Maybe he is telling the truth.

"So, you say my father planned this from the beginning?"

"Yes. The three of us initially. I knew everything, except the true and final location of the Prize, but you must know that by now, Tom. You have the watch."

I knew it. The broken hand.

Eerie figures began to gather in the clearing; men with sullen and bitter expressions surrounding him.

Don't show fear ... Ignore them.

Frederick closed his eyes, sucked in some oxygen and tried to focus on his ruinous venture. He realised with absolute clarity that his career, his dreams and even his mortality became subject to the outcome of his next decision.

I have only one undeniable truth to consider: If I can't follow Fox, I'm finished.

He opened his eyes and noticed the captain striding towards him. In the moonlight, his expression looked menacing and his weapon hung from a tightly squeezed fist.

"Vogel. Get here."

"What's this, captain? You're planning a mutiny?"

"Get over here, or I'll have great pleasure making you."

Vogel grit his teeth. Even in this situation, he hated being ordered to do anything. Begrudgingly, he followed the captain to the far side of the clearing.

I can't let him take control, or I'm dead.

"Because of your stupid decisions, Vogel, we're all going to die."

"So what do you propose, captain? You didn't drag me over here to kill me. You could've done that in front of your men."

"What do I propose? That's beautiful, considering you've stuffed up this entire operation. There's also the small fact that my men and I are marked for death on your orders."

"You're going to make me cry. Just get on with it. What do you want?"

"I'm going to walk back over to my men and wait. You've got five minutes to come up with a plan that guarantees every man's safety, or you won't leave this clearing."

"What about our deal, captain?"

"You've got five minutes, Vogel, and it'd better be good."

The captain made a point of checking his watch, before he marched back to his waiting men.

Vogel looked back across the clearing at the ghoulish figures standing in the moonlight. If he failed to convince them, he died. He needed to think, but his mind didn't want to respond. He looked at his own watch.

Time's up.

The captain approached.

Chapter Forty Nine

Tom snuck a look over his shoulder at their makeshift pilot. Despite the smooth ride, Noah concentrated on the Baza's controls as if he expected an imminent disaster.

"Where are we heading, Noah?"

"For the moment, north-west away from the mountains."

There didn't seem to be any purpose in his choice of location, other than a panicked escape from Vogel, but despite his worry over their lack of direction, Tom's thoughts kept returning to the watch.

Before I say anything about this, I have to be sure.

He felt famished as he looked down at his old timepiece. He considered the missing hand the answer to their mystery, but couldn't concentrate.

"Does anyone have anything to eat, I'm starving?"

He watched the priest's hand disappear into an inner coat pocket and when it reappeared, he held up a chocolate bar, which he handed to Tom.

"Hey, thanks."

As he stretched forward to accept it, Isobel slapped his hand away from the priest's. With an anguished moan, she sat back in her seat; her face white and drawn and her darting eyes wide-open with anger.

"Don't thank him, Tom. I don't know how you could accept anything from that man. You're unbelievable."

Even in the cabin's low light, he could see her despondency. He could feel her need to strike out at someone for the loss of her family and he didn't mind that she chose him.

"I don't know what to think, Iz. He might be the enemy, but I don't want to make a decision on this. Not until I'm sure one way or the other."

"Tom. He killed our parents. How could you side with him?"

"Iz …"

"No. Just leave me alone. You're as bad as he is."

Tom felt flabbergasted. Even if he wanted to, he couldn't have come up with anything coherent to say.

"Yeah, whatever."

Their conversation trailed off to silence. No-one spoke and no-one connected. Tom felt the sensation of time slowing down, creating a vacuum that accentuated all feeling, particularly the negative kind.

I hate this … When she's like this she makes me feel …

He struggled to find the word, then it came.

Exasperated … She's excruciating.

Despite the strained tension in the cockpit and his annoyance, a thought occurred to him.

How does anyone's perception alter the experience of time?

His thought brought on another; an epiphany.

Altered time … Time standing still … The watch … The hand … The direction.

"That's it. I've got it. I'm sure."

He felt annoyed when Isobel ignored him, but Noah stirred from his thoughts.

"You've got what, Tom?"

"I understand. It's the watch. Quick, I need pen and paper. This is it. I'm sure of it."

Sometimes trying to remember even the obvious, created difficulties for him, but today, the numbers they found from the inside of the watch, re-entered his consciousness on demand. He wrote them down on his piece of paper and sat back, admiring his creation.

My father left this information for me. Thank God I didn't let him down.

He smiled and looked into each face before he spoke.

"I've discovered the missing set of numbers from the watch."

Noah's eyes widened in an expression of disbelief.

"How, Tom? What did we miss?"

"I found the answer on the outside of the watch."

He held out his arm so they could all see the old timepiece.

"Look at where the one remaining hand points. It's fixed on the number twenty-two."

Again he felt annoyance. No-one moved, or uttered a sound.

"Look, I'll prove it to you. Noah, I need a map of Australia with longitude and latitude coordinates."

"Try the pilot's case, Tom. It's the black leather bag between our seats."

Tom began to fumble with the bag's catch, but he couldn't open it.

The priest reached forward to assist.

"Allow me. I know how to read these things."

The clergyman sorted through a variety of maps. He raised one from the bag and spread it out over his knees.

"Tom. The full set of numbers please."

"They're 143, 12, the 22 we just found and 49."

To Tom's great dismay, he noticed the priest's enthusiastic expression fall away; his head slowly shaking from side to side.

"Latitude 22. 49 and Longitude 143. 12. No … These coordinates don't work, Tom. They pinpoint a spot in the middle of the Pacific Ocean, somewhere north of Micronesia. I've tried them several times now. I'm sorry."

Tom felt numb; devastated. After having his final hopes destroyed, his emotions felt like flotsam and jetsam washed out to sea.

"Damn it to hell and back."

Once again, Tom endured the silence. He felt it fill the empty spaces produced by the absence of his hope.

He closed his eyes and considered another bleak thought.

No ... Silence is a sound. It's the noise nothing makes; the nothingness of a ridiculous journey going nowhere.

Noah turned in his seat and the helicopter bucked its displeasure.

"Tom. I think it's time we made a decision about our destination. Perhaps the priest's jet ...?

Tom nodded his agreement.

"Where's it parked, priest?"

The clergyman grinned, displaying ultra-white teeth between bushy layers of black beard. He didn't seem affected by Tom's disrespect.

"You're already heading directly for it. It's parked in front of the Air-Facilities terminal at Albury Airport."

"So what do you propose?"

Before she could interrupt, he turned to Isobel and curled his lips into an awkward looking smile.

"Let him speak now, Iz. This is important."

She made another unpleasant face and looked away.

"Don't call the tower, that's for sure. They'll be listening; they'll trace it. There's some parkland by the river with no housing nearby. We can land there and walk to the aircraft. It's not that far."

Tom interjected.

"How do we get aboard? By force?"

"No. No. I'll talk us in."

Isobel reached over and grabbed him. He could feel her arm shaking.

"Hey ... I've got something to say about this."

"Now isn't the time for an argument, Iz."

The priest tried to pat her on the shoulder, but she stiffened and pulled away. He removed his hand and spoke gently.

"You have something to tell us, young lady?"

Isobel sat forward and focused her attention on the other occupants of the cabin, ignoring the priest.

"Tom's right. The missing number is twenty two. It didn't work because it's the nothing that's missing."

They all looked equally puzzled.

"Tom. I know."

Chapter Fifty

The chairman scrutinised the man on the screen with a great deal of trepidation. Wolf radiated confidence and something far darker, yet he felt he didn't have a choice when it came to hiring him.

He clamped his jaw as he considered the ramifications of his decision and the man himself. Somehow God made a terrible mistake when he fashioned him. The beautiful olive skin of Italian youth created a facade that covered a heart and frame, more robotic-metal, than flesh, cartilage and bone.

His thoughts drifted away from Wolf and back to the members of the Assembly board.

By the time they find out I'll have won and all will be forgiven.

He justified his deception by believing that their success vindicated his actions and also because of a need for expediency.

They'll eventually find out the truth and they'll applaud the outcome.

As the televised interview of Wolf continued, Antonio counted on the man's powerful presence to prevent any questioning until the right moment.

He smiled as each member of the board appeared to succumb to The Darkman's charm. They concentrated on the strong angular jaw and the black wavy hair, but his most prominent feature created the greatest effect on his comrades. Wolf stared back at the board members with the black and expressionless eyes of a shark. Antonio wondered just how many men have searched those dark mirthless orbs and in their reflection, witnessed their own demise.

The chairman felt relieved as he counted his comrade's subtle hand gestures; each signifying their acquiescence.

Good ... It's done.

No-one doubted Wolf's heritage. His dark looks may have come from a Napolitano-Calabrese beauty, but the powerful frame and legendry fierceness came from his father; a pink faced English assassin with a penchant for excessive violence.

"Gentlemen, I give you our new head of security, Mr Bruno Wolf."

The members of the board applauded their newest appointment, displaying no emotion and four precise claps.

I got what I wanted, yet ...

He looked at the other members of the Assembly board and couldn't help noticing just how easily this man dominated them from across the world.

It's too late to question my decision. I just have to live with the consequences.

———————

It remained a shadowy twilight in the glade. The dawn needed several more hours before it could clear the steep slopes of heavily forested mountainside. Frederick took refuge in the gloom, wishing that he could disappear entirely.

No. I have to clear my mind of fear ... I have to think.

He needed not only to survive, but to change this situation to his advantage.

He strode into the middle of the clearing.

"Captain. We have an appointment."

The captain removed his sidearm. He meant to carry out his threat.

"Alright, Vogel, get on with it."

"Captain, you stand there threatening my life, but without me, everyone in this clearing is going to die. Do you understand? Without me we can't win this game."

"Win what game? Don't play with me, Vogel."

Frederick nodded towards the waiting SRP soldiers.

"I'll tell only you, captain. This story's not for your men. That's my deal."

"You're in no position to make deals, but I'll agree for the time being. Now, start talking and don't get boring, or you won't get the chance to finish."

"Alright, but let me call in the other helicopter from Mount Hotham. You can talk to the pilot yourself, so there'll be no danger to you, or your men. Whatever happens, we can't let Fox get too far away. Our lives depend on it."

After arranging the helicopter, the captain listened as Vogel explained the meaning of the Prize; his story of Angels and wars, and ultimate power never becoming boring.

I'm back in control; back in the game. With the helicopter I can still win.

He insisted that his position remained paramount, but agreed that the captain could take control of all operational military concerns. By the time the helicopter arrived, he owned a small, private and very motivated force of men.

———————

The Darkman smiled into his mobile monitor. The most powerful men in the world applauded him, confirming his rise to the heights of the organisation, but his face remained passive, his smile demure.

Show no emotion. I'll celebrate in private.

He saw the chairman nod, followed by the rest of the board; his cue to address the committee. He intended to display his serious intent to the men of the Assembly.

"After lengthy studies of Vogel's file and psychology, I am forced to respectfully disagree with the board's assessment."

He stopped and smiled, but it contained nothing but venom; daring anyone to disagree. His lips curled back into a savage looking smile, when the lion of the group took up the challenge.

The chairman smiled back with equal malice.

"How so, Mr Wolf? And before you answer, please bear in mind that we are only interested in facts, not personal assumptions."

"Vogel's psychological report indicates that there are no circumstances which could drive him to change to a weaker side. If he aspires, he will do so for his own power, either going it alone or with an organisation he judges to be greater than the Assembly. I have checked every possible source and every conceivable organisation powerful enough to take on the Assembly, yet in the end, only one name stood out; the Black Cardinal."

He stopped speaking so that the name could gain emphasis.

"Gentlemen. I have people in place who will be able to substantiate our suspicions, but even if there is another entity involved, we haven't got time to waste. We can't allow Vogel or any other to win the day. He must be put down at once, like the dog he is."

Chapter Fifty One

Isobel couldn't remember having to deal with so many conflicting emotions all at once. She felt frustrated that these men didn't always take her seriously. She felt hot anger towards the priest and Tom's passive acceptance of him. She also felt powerless when it came to the events controlling her life and in the midst of all of these feelings and emotions she felt aroused.

Damn it. I hate you Tom Fox.

At times he made her so furious … but she couldn't deny the truth to herself forever. Even when the projectiles zizzed around her, she could only think of Tom.

Why am I so attracted to him? Maybe it's those damn amazing eyes …

He seemed to sense her feelings and she stiffened in surprise when he turned and looked back at her.

Oh God.

He stared at her in that special particular way of his, with his slightly crooked smile and raised eyebrow, and she shivered with intense sensation; surprised by the warmth and wetness between her legs.

I haven't felt like this since ...

She felt amazed that she couldn't recall the last time she thought about the rape.

Maybe I've got you to thank for that Tom, or maybe like you, I've grown.

War hardened men accepted Tom as their leader, despite his lack of experience. She realised that he accepted his potential and his confidence reflected his growth into manhood.

It's not just the sexiness ... I trust him ... With everything.

She felt tears come to her eyes.

Even if he reciprocated, could she do this? Could she let him ...?

When she sat close and concentrated on the sensual movement of his lips, she thought she could abandon all of her fears, but ... time to think brought them back in abundance.

Isobel felt his eyes on her once again and looked up from her thoughts.

Sweet Lord. How long have you been staring at me?

She felt embarrassed. Could he see her mind ... Read her thoughts? Then she realised with some dismay that all three men stared at her with equally expectant expressions. She also noticed that Noah took in a long slow breath before addressing her.

"Isobel, you have everyone's attention."

"Oh, yeah. Well ... as I said, it didn't work because it's the nothing that's missing."

Tom turned to her and she laughed as his smile grew.

"Izzi, you're a bloody genius."

Noah's voice sounded gruff when he questioned her. He seemed annoyed that he didn't understand.

"Isobel. What nothing is missing?'

"Tom. Tell him what's missing from the watch?"

"It's the hand, Noah. It's minus the hand."

Isobel flinched as the priest moved forward in his seat. He began searching through the pilot's case; rustling through a stack of maps, until he withdrew one and held it out for Tom.

"Tom's right. You're a genius, young lady. That's why Professor Fox removed the other hand. The number 22 has to be a minus. Minus the hand."

She searched Tom's eyes for his approval and got it. He looked like he might explode with excitement.

"It's been staring at us the entire time."

Tom handed the map back to the priest who spread it across his lap; his expression of concentration to the point of ferociousness.

"Tom. I recognise the location. It's a place called Raptor Park."

"Raptor Park. No ... We checked the old house already."

"No. No. Not the house."

Isobel could almost feel Tom's frustration. His confusion bordered on anger.

The priest also seemed aware of Tom's annoyance.

"I'm sorry, I'll explain. These new coordinates represent a place on the map that has significant meaning. It's a place that doesn't officially exist. You'll find no reference to the name on any map. Tom. It's just your father's name for a particular dig site."

"So this is the location of the Prize?"

"Yes. The coordinates pinpoint it exactly. Only a few people know of its existence other than us."

Isobel felt her face flush with redness.

"Us? There's no *us*. You're not one of us."

The depth of her anger made her shake and the priest's attempted smile broke her resolve. She lost control.

"No, Iz ... No. That's not the way."

Several of her blows struck the clergyman and he didn't resist or even attempt to protect himself. She felt Tom's hand grasp her right wrist and hold it tight and slowly her senses returned.

"Alright. Alright. I'm sorry."

She pressed her lips together and tried to look at the priest though tear-blurred eyes. He didn't respond or even see her. She noticed that his head bent forward almost to his lap, with a hand covering and pressing hard against his gouged eye.

Noah turned in his seat. This time the helicopter didn't buck as he focused on Isobel.

"Alright everybody. Settle down. We're getting close to Albury and I need a place to land."

Without looking up, the priest directed Noah to fly east of the city and come in south of the airport.

"Follow the Murray River. Over there."

He pointed at a sparkling serpentine shape towards the north-west.

"There's just enough light to see our way. Our destination is a park called Mungabareena, on the other side of that hill. Follow the river. It's one of the local swimming holes and not a bad spot to put the Baza down."

They landed the helicopter without incident and proceeded towards the airport, walking as quickly as possible. Tom utilised the rest of the journey, asking questions and going over their plan to take control of the jet.

Despite a determination to be civil, he felt annoyed with the priest. The clergyman's ideas seemed calculated and dangerous. He didn't trust him.

"Tom. You and Noah are wanted men and highly recognisable targets amongst Assembly personnel. I'll have to go alone. I'll signal when I've taken care of the crew."

Tom returned the priest's smile. It felt as bitter as his looked.

"No way. That's not going to happen. I don't trust you enough to be totally in your hands. How do you know that the crew will even be there at this hour of the morning?"

"Because they're employed by the Assembly as my crew and I've put them on standby."

"Alright, but I'm not letting you go over there alone."

The priest looked back over his shoulder towards Isobel.

"That just leaves one person and it might get a little rough."

Tom winced hearing Isobel's angry response.

"If there's anyone you should be afraid of, it's me, priest. I'd gladly kill you."

Tom felt he needed more time to consider the priest's proposal, particularly considering Isobel's hatred of him, but their predicament required immediate action.

"Alright. She goes."

Noah's expression seemed grim as he strode over towards Isobel. In the dim light, Tom watched him search her eyes for signs of weakness, but she didn't falter. He removed a silencer from inside the folds of his jacket, attached it to the barrel of a Browning thirty-two calibre automatic pistol and handed it to her.

"Have you ever fired a weapon, lass?"

"No, but I won't hesitate if I need to. If we're all going to die, then at least I'll avenge my father."

Wolf felt duped. The ultra-sensitive information transmitted to him by the chairman made him cringe.

This's a bloody death sentence.

After skimming through the documentation he realised that only total success could save him and even then …?

Now that I've read this I can't turn back … I'll be executed for sure.

He began to delve through a history that few people knew existed.

Whoever has this thing … My God, what power?

He quickly realised the significance of owning it. Even the Assembly's ascendency could wane; history overflowed with fallen empires, but possessing the Prize infinitely altered that eventuality.

Financial dominance and military might could ultimately be defeated, but not the Prize. It afforded a much greater power; an irrefutable ideology, which meant they could control the world's population, bending the will of any government or financial power to their own.

And, what a weapon.

They could wield it against anyone who opposed them, domestic or otherwise. He remembered that the Church once utilised a different weapon. The fear of hell maintained their supreme power for centuries, but without the Prize, fear eventually failed.

Now they can bring back the fear of hell and no-one can refute them.

No longer will they require faith and a gullible flock. No-one could disclaim the Angels. If the Assembly controlled the Prize, then they wielded the power of God. Literally.

———————

Vogel sat in the front next to the pilot. The captain and the remainder of the SRP commando team sat in the troop compartment behind him in the rear.

Frederick liked this Shikra helicopter. He knew a good deal about its specifications. It came from the same Indian factory as the Black Baza that the G11's stole, but where theirs excelled in manoeuvrability, the Shikra won out in its weight bearing ability and sheer speed.

You're an ugly bird, but just what I need.

This craft could carry his entire team and gear and gain time on the enemy.

And, I know where you're going, Fox.

The G11 team headed towards Albury; the closest major centre to their current position. The city maintained a range of domestic transport alternatives, but he doubted that anything could have been prearranged.

No. I pushed them down that mountain trail. Nothing's organised.

He felt flustered. The G11's escape bothered him. Luck could not have intervened in these circumstances.

"How could they take the Baza so easily? Maybe, just maybe, someone assisted them ... Another member of their team, or outside help. It's the only way they could have achieved it."

Even though the captain warned against it, Vogel made contact with the tower at Albury Airport. From the flight controller he determined that the Black Baza didn't land there and that their logbook contained only one new unscheduled arrival in the last forty eight hours; a private jet owned by the Assembly, parked at the terminal overnight.

Is this our unknown player?

He wondered whether the board authorised this as a means of checking up on him, but scrapped the thought immediately.

"No. There's something else happening here."

Who could play at that level and utilise company assets. Jets didn't get assigned lightly, especially for trips to Australia. Outside of the board, only one person came to mind.

"The priest."

Clear and precise actions defined Bruno Wolf. Meticulous preparation rather than rashness created his legend. He always got the job done, utilising effectiveness and efficiency in every task. It didn't produce the sure thing, but as close as it got.

I know the colour of your shit, Vogel.

His predecessor hunted Fox, following him and the G11 squad to Mount Hotham. They knew that much. They also knew he pursued them across the Razorback towards Mount Feathertop and began an attack.

But then, who knows ...?

With the death of their inside man, they received no further confirmed information. For Vogel to have taken control at that particular point, meant that he held all mountain exits and believed that the G11's controlled the Prize. He could then trap his foe somewhere that provided him with an easy exit.

You won't use a fixed wing aeroplane, Vogel. That's for sure.

Getting to any potential airport created all sorts of logistical problems, mostly around distance, speed and vulnerability. The same rationale applied to road vehicles of any kind. The possibilities began to narrow.

You've got yourself a helicopter.

His first destination remained the easy part. He could effortlessly track any aircraft coming out of this region, but needed to cover any other possibilities, no matter how remote.

He looked up as his secretary rushed in.

"Sir, the target has contacted the Albury tower."

"What? No."

You're no fool, Vogel. Why do that?

To give up his intended destination that easily, seemed beyond foolish.

It seems too easy. It must be a ruse.

With Vogel's position and aircraft confirmed he could be tracked to hell and back.

At 0750 Eastern Standard Time, an ultra-wide-bodied Qantas 949 – 500 landed at Melbourne's Tullamarine International Airport, en route from Rome. At almost the same time, a vehicle carrying two men and a doctor, made its way towards the bottom of the Bungalow Spur, near the township of Harrietville in northern Victoria.

The driver; an old SRP soldier with real fighting experience, gasped and pulled back in his seat, when the gore-covered creature limped out onto the track in front of them.

—————

At 0810 the beautiful, auburn-haired woman left her commercial Qantas flight and entered the customs area of the airport.

She strutted and smiled; all style and elegance, accepting her preferential treatment as a matter of course. Within minutes of her turning on her communicator, she began receiving information from a source inside Australian Air-force flight-control. By the time a smitten assistant ushered her through customs, she already knew details of an Assembly company jet landing at Albury Airport with no further flight plan.

Her own chartered aircraft waited for her, not far from where she stood, as did the small force of loyal, fanatical men awaiting her command. Like her, they belonged to an extremely determined cardinal.

Chapter Fifty Two

Even from his hiding place behind the aircraft maintenance shed, Tom could see Isobel shaking; her earlier bravado completely gone. If the need arose, he doubted her ability to aim and hit something as large as the jet, even from point blank range.

Tom understood her predicament. She needed to harass the priest, but for this assignment, she depended on him. Tom could almost feel her tension as they shuffled towards the jet; exposed under tarmac security lighting.

He could hear the strain in her heavy breathing thanks to a communicator they left switched on, in her coat pocket. He could also clearly hear all conversation, particularly the deep confidant voice of the priest. For a clergyman, Tom felt surprised that he seemed so relaxed.

"Are you alright, young lady?"

Isobel didn't look at the priest when she spoke. Tom thought her voice sounded harsh and bitter.

"I'm perfectly fine ... Thank you."

"Except for the shaking?"

"I'm just cold. Not that it's any of your business."

"We don't know what information they've received since I've been gone, so rub yourself. Show them you're cold and not nervous. Remember, no eye contact with the crew and get your chin in the air. You want them to think you're important. So nasty up. Look arrogant."

The priest banged his fist on the airframe and called out until he woke the captain. He pretended to be upset with the man and kept up the charade, so the pilot remained off balance.

"Get my friend here a blanket will you? And wake up the co-pilot. I want to be underway as soon as possible."

"Yes, sir ... Father, but the co-pilot isn't here, he's ... There's a woman he met in town ..."

"There will be two others joining us. Ah, here they are now."

Tom stepped up into the aircraft, followed by Noah.

"Hello. My name is Tom Fox. I need a jet ... so I'm taking yours."

"Don't be ridiculous. You can't do that."

The priest smiled at the pilot and put his index finger up to his lips for silence.

"I think you'll find he already has. Now, please remain calm and forget about the Assembly's secret alarm. Having to shoot you this early into our journey would be quite a waste, don't you think?"

Father Dom escorted the surprised pilot to the secret compartments in the rear of the jet, which housed the aircraft's extensive range of weaponry. Most countries forbade such equipment, so they remained well hidden. Once the priest received all of the keys, he marched the pilot back to where the others waited.

"This is Noah. He'll be your commander for this flight and will fill in for your missing co-pilot. Depart from his instructions even a little and you'll die. He's an experienced air-force pilot, so your death won't affect us in any way. I don't want a situation where I have to shoot you. Are you clear on this so far?"

"Yes."

"If you do the right thing, you'll be treated with courtesy and you'll be left unharmed. At worst, it'll be a great story for the grandkids."

The captain shrugged his shoulders.

"I've seen what happens to heroes in this organisation. I'll do exactly, as you say."

"Good, now if we could be airborne as quickly as possible. Don't provide a flight plan or speak to the tower. Fly us directly north and avoid the main flight paths. Our destination will be revealed to you later."

The remainder of the G11's made themselves as comfortable as possible. Noah instructed the pilot from the co-pilot's seat, while the priest chose a place in the lounge area of the fuselage, in the row directly opposite Tom and Isobel.

"You did well, young lady. You're very brave, I think."

"Say what you want, I still don't trust you."

"Alright, it seems I owe you an explanation. I would ask you both to put aside your former judgements and listen to what I have to say. I assure you that everything will be made known to you."

Tom listened to the priest, but also maintained a secondary focus on the sound of the engines, as the aircraft began to move away towards the main runway. The powerful thrusting roar felt like pure relief, even though they taxied slowly.

He decided to give the priest one chance to tell the truth.

"If anything you say deviates even a tiny bit from what we already know, then you'll be treated as a prisoner from then on. Do you understand?"

"Yes, fair enough. Before I get started I must be clear here and now about our current position. From the moment we enter the air, we will be tracked and hunted. If it seemed bad before, then it's about to get even worse. This is a one-way ticket, I'm afraid. Only the Prize will save us and perhaps not even that. I'm sorry."

Tom shivered. He looked over at Isobel and she stared back with an expression he couldn't interpret. It became very quiet, but the strange tension drained away the moment the priest began to chuckle.

"Tom, did you know that you received your name from Isobel's father, Tom Kite?"

Tom couldn't answer. The priest's happiness defied the dread of the previous moments.

"My idea actually. I hope you like it."

Despite Vogel's best attempts at intimidation, the pilot could not make the helicopter gain any further speed. Frederick found it difficult to remain calm. He couldn't afford any more setbacks. They needed to catch up with Fox as quickly as possible.

Assess ...Think ... Find the way.

He had no men stationed at Albury and using the local authorities provided too much risk. He needed to take Fox at the airport and if possible, capture the Assembly's aircraft, which he could utilise to go after the Prize with his captive.

Vogel clasped his hands together with renewed hope. He could see the border twin-city ahead. He wiped his window with his sleeve and peered out into the morning light.

He couldn't see anything, initially. The glare and lack of sleep affected his eyes, flooding his vision with tears. His eyelids rasped with grit. He rubbed away some of the moisture and caked rheum and ventured another look.

Laid out below he could see the city of Wodonga, which spread its suburbia over most of the river basin and into the surrounding foothills.

Frederick began jabbing his index finger in the direction he wished to go.

"Ignore the damn flight path and take the fastest route. Go straight over the city towards the airport."

They crossed the border into New South Wales and the pilot banked their craft steeply to the east, directly over the city of Albury. Below them, Frederick identified the Murray River slithering its way into the west, dividing the two states and cutting the cities in two.

"The airport's dead ahead, sir. What do you want me to do when we get there?"

"I want you to make sure that the jet doesn't take off. Use your initiative. Land in front of it, so they can't get going, if you have to."

The captain pulled hard on Vogel's shoulder.

"Sir … Look. There's a jet taxiing onto the runway."

———————

Noah's voice crackled out over the aircraft's intercom and the priest stopped talking.

"Father Dom, to the cockpit now. Everyone else buckle up. We have visitors."

Noah turned and pointed, as the priest arrived.

"We've got a helicopter approaching at high speed and he's ignoring the flight-control tower. It's got to be Vogel."

The priest didn't believe they could take off in time. He fumbled with his seatbelt as the pilot swung the jet around onto the main runway. Half way through their turn the engines started to scream with thrust and the Cessna accelerated; the airframe rocking and twisting as they straightened.

Dominico could only just hear Noah call out to the pilot.

"Get her up. Quickly. Vogel will try to shoot out our tyres. If we're already in the air, he has no choice. He'll let us go."

"No. No. I know that man. He'll bring us down. We'll be killed."

"Do as you're told and pull her up. This cargo's precious to him. He won't risk anything once we're airborne."

———————

Vogel turned in his seat so he could make eye contact with the captain; his menacing facial expression conveying an implied threat: don't fail or else …

"Get your men ready. We have to take out their tyres. We'll only get one chance, so don't mess it up."

Frederick attempted to urge the pilot and the helicopter forward with sheer willpower. He felt sure they could make it in time.

Faster. Go faster. We have to cut them off.

The helicopter flew in low and at high speed. They came at the jet from the rear and at the last moment, the pilot jerked the helicopter hard to starboard.

"Now, captain. Make the shot."

Only metres above the sleek wing of the Cessna Peregrine 8000, an SRP soldier slid back the helicopter's side door, while another prepared to fire.

"No. What're you doing …? What's wrong?"

Vogel couldn't believe it. The soldier put down his weapon and waved back into the cabin as he spoke to the pilot through the intercom.

"I haven't got a shot. I can't see the wheels. They're under the damn wing."

Vogel began waving both of his arms in agitation as he yelled instructions to the pilot.

"Go further forward. Quickly, man. They're nearly up. We need a shot at the front wheel."

The pilot threw the helicopter further to starboard, as he tried to judge the jet's increasing speed. He made it past the aircraft's nose and pulled in very close; allowing a clear strike at the tyre.

Vogel turned in his seat and looked back through the fuselage. One soldier stood strapped to the open door, while another squatted behind a machine gun on a tripod. Each man took careful aim and waited.

This isn't working.

They still didn't have a shot and they faced the danger of being struck by the wing of the accelerating Cessna.

"Shoot. For God's sake start firing."

No ... Damn it. It's too late.

The nose of the Cessna rose from the tarmac and the helicopter swerved away to avoid being hit.

"No. No. No. Stop. Don't shoot ... Not now."

Vogel unbuckled himself, jumped from his seat and rushed back towards the gunmen.

"No."

As he ran, a blast of gunfire echoed through the helicopter's fuselage and he saw pieces of the jet's front tyre explode into the air.

Chapter Fifty Three

The secretary knocked once and entered the aircraft's makeshift office unbidden. He stood at attention, while Wolf ignored him.

"Yes, what is it?"

Bruno Wolf required constant information, which he insisted the man carried to him personally, but he also hated to be interrupted, with his entire being focused on the hunt.

"The Albury police have located the helicopter, sir. They found it in a public reserve near the airport."

"And the occupants?"

"They found no-one, sir, but ..."

"Yes ... what?"

"An Assembly jet just flew out of Albury airport."

"You're sure of this?"

"Yes, sir. The pilot didn't provide a flight plan and refused all communication with the tower, but there's more ...'

"For goodness sake, get on with it man. Give me the full report, damn you."

"Yes, sir. A helicopter attacked the aircraft, a helicopter chartered by Frederick Vogel. The police have called in the Royal Australian Air Force for assistance and they're tracking each of the aircraft."

The Darkman ordered his secretary back to the cockpit to personally monitor every bit of incoming information.

Damn it. What the hell are you doing, Vogel?

The chairman received the same data as he did. He knew it wouldn't be long until he received a call from Rome.

———————

Vogel carried a mobile state-of-the-art frequency scanner that revealed his enemies' movements.

Thankyou heaven, thankyou hell. I'd be flying blind without this thing.

He could listen to the chatter between the Australian Federal and State Police forces as well as the Royal Australian Air force, simultaneously, on separate band widths. With only a little more difficulty, he could pry into the International Special Religious Police Command Centre and listen to most of their dealings.

The more secret communications between the Assembly hierarchy and their vassals, required weighing known actions against commands to ascertain any differences in their strategies.

They must think I've lost after the escape of the jet ... They'll think I've made a run for it.

Utilising his extensive field experience and his intimate knowledge of Assembly and SRP tactics, he could create his own strategies around each changing enemy scenario.

The fools. They'll think that I'm isolated and desperate ... Good.

He could use this to his advantage; allowing them to gauge his moves, based on their assumptions regarding his past performances and tactics.

They'll assume on this basis, which leaves me plenty of room to manoeuvre.

He felt much stronger now and in control. He wondered how he could have allowed his nerves to overwhelm him. He couldn't remember ever being fearful. He lived a life of danger. Killing meant nothing to him.

I made it to the top because I did what sickened everybody else.

Body counts didn't matter. Even having to dispatch women and children didn't bother him.

The truth is that only one life matters and that's mine.

His experiences in the field made him question whether a supreme being ever existed and after many years of slaughter and killing for a living, the hideousness of life answered the question for him.

It's a load of rubbish. I'm the only God in my world.

He ruled his own universe; esteeming himself based on his record of successful achievement and attained positions, and the ruthless cunning he utilised to hold on to them.

I want real power ... I want them to bow down to me.

The Assembly provided the perfect staircase for the realisation of his dream, but with each achievement he wanted more.

I want absolute power; God-like power.

And with the Prize, he could have it. Once begun, he knew he couldn't turn back. The very moment he threw himself into this Fox affair, two ultimate possibilities presented themselves: total success over the Assembly and with it control over everybody's world, or oblivion in the form of a nasty death.

"Take this thing down as low as it'll go and set a course west of Wagga Wagga. I have an officer at the barracks there. He'll be waiting for us."

"What do we do about the police?"

"You have a lot to learn, captain. The Assembly won't directly employ any local authorities. There are too many negative possibilities."

"Yes, I agree, Mr Wolf. It's imperative that we call down the Australian authorities; especially their air force. We don't want any interference. We have to contain this situation and work it to our own advantage."

"And the woman, Mr Chairman?"

"It can't be a coincidence. Do we know who she is?"

"No. She presented a false passport. We're working on it."

"Watch this situation closely, Bruno. I don't like not knowing my enemies. Your plan appears to be seamless, which is just as well. I will accept only success. No mistakes, is that clear?"

"I have men in all of the major airports and there's only so many places that they can land. Our net is closing."

Chapter Fifty Four

Tom heard two cracking reports above the noise of the jet's engines; gunfire that didn't seem to hit their craft.

He attempted to follow the helicopter's movements, by squashing his face against the starboard window, but its jerky movement made it difficult to distinguish. Then another head started competing for some of his viewing space.

"No, Iz. They're shooting at us."

"Then why are you watching?"

"I ..."

Another loud burst of gunfire erupted, followed by an even louder bang, causing their aircraft to rock on its axis. Tom felt pinned to his seat as the jet ascended with what seemed an almost vertical trajectory.

Once again, he tried to spot the helicopter from his window, but it disappeared from view and the shooting ceased.

"I think it's over, Iz. I think we're away."

Tom looked up as Noah burst through the cabin door and into the aisle.

"Tom. Isobel. Is everyone alright?"

Tom noticed the strained look on his face. He appeared anxious despite their escape.

"Yeah, everything's fine."

"Good. Good. We should be able to relax for the next few hours. I don't think anyone will attack us for the moment. Tom, could you come up to the cockpit for a minute. I need to discuss the flight plan with you."

Tom stood, climbed over Isobel and began to move forward, but she grabbed him by the arm and pulled him to a stop.

"Why do they exclude me, Tom? Because I'm a girl?"

"No. He respects you. I know he does. Maybe it's just a fatherly thing … He thinks he's protecting you, by keeping you away from the uglier side of our business."

Isobel let go of Tom's arm and turned her face from him.

"Yeah, whatever."

As Tom entered the cockpit, Noah offered the co-pilot's seat to his young protégé.

"I'll get straight to the point, Tom. We have a problem."

"Something too bad to tell Isobel?"

"They shot out our front tyre and some of the mechanism."

Tom's eyes lost focus, as he attempted to process this information.

"We're going to crash then?"

The priest answered for Noah.

"We'll have to make some sort of crash landing, yes. How bad it is, will depend on the skill of our pilot."

The pilot turned and frowned at the three men. Tom didn't think his expression conveyed a great deal of confidence.

An anxious silence lingered in the cockpit, before the priest continued.

"We have just enough fuel and a good bit of time to make our decisions. The immediate problem is our course. I have instructed the pilot to fly west and …"

Tom silenced the priest by thrusting his palm towards him and slowly shaking his head.

"Let me see the map."

The clergyman spread the chart out over Tom's lap and pointed to both their current position and their desired destination.

"Longreach is certainly the closest airport to the site. I think we should ..."

"No. No way. You don't make any decisions for us. Is that clear?"

He gave the priest a hard look.

"But, you're welcome to offer advice. Your knowledge of our enemy could be helpful. For instance, will the Assembly have a presence at Longreach airport?"

"I don't know ... Perhaps."

The priest closed his eyes and nodded several times. Without a word, he turned and left the cockpit.

Tom felt livid, as much with himself as with the priest. Their circumstances remained dire with no room for error. He needed to know the difference between the good guys and the bad. The solution came quickly to mind. He felt for the gun in his coat pocket and followed the priest out of the cabin.

He raised the weapon as he approached the priest. The man stood half way down the aisle, staring at his feet. As he shuffled forward, Tom noticed Isobel's eyes widen with understanding as she spotted the gun.

"We need to clear a few things up, priest."

The clergyman raised his head and nodded. Without being bidden, he moved to a seat directly across the aisle from Isobel.

"Alright. You want the truth ... I'll give you the truth, but it won't be pleasant."

The priest took in a long, quivering breath and began fingering his beard.

"Firstly, it must be said that in joining you, I have left a great deal of people in peril. One of which is my soul mate. If we fail, they will most certainly die, which I think gives me a rather large reason to succeed."

Tom looked intently at the priest.

"Not good enough. If you can't verify it, don't say it."

"Very well."

Isobel joined the conversation.

"She's your wife?"

"Unofficially ... Secretly. Catholic priests can't have wives."

Tom wasn't sure if he felt annoyed, or just confused by the gentle tone in Isobel's voice, but the priest continued talking, before he could express his bewilderment.

"Perhaps I should start at the beginning. At seven years of age, I found my parents hanging in our living room; both murdered. Not long after, a prominent Italian family took me in, treating me as one of their own. They provided my religious education and eventually brought me into the priesthood."

Tom still held the gun, but it rested on his knee.

"For many years I performed my priestly duties with due diligence, unconcerned about most earthly endeavours, until the day I discovered who killed my parents."

The priest stopped speaking and lowered his head into his hands. His chest expanded with oxygen before slowly expelling it as a ragged sigh.

Isobel spoke to him, gently prompting him to continue.

"Who did it? Who killed them?"

"Even after all of these years, I still find it difficult to talk about. You see, for most of my childhood I gave my affections to a high ranking Assembly family; the same family who carried out the murder of my mother and father. You can't imagine my guilt ... It ate away at my soul and overwhelmed me with grief."

He stopped talking and Tom noticed his pained expression. He seemed to be searching the back of the fuselage for some hidden past that only he could see.

"I suppose I've changed somewhat since then. Over the years I've tried to justify it, but in the end, guilt becomes hate and hate needs its revenge."

Chapter Fifty Five

The Shikra landed in a small valley to the west of Kapooka Military Barracks, eight kilometres from the city of Wagga Wagga.

Vogel jumped from the helicopter, rushing bent over, until he ran out of range of the still-spinning rotors. An out of season frost covered the landscape, which crunched under the soles of his men's feet, as they followed their captain to join him.

Vogel spotted his contact slouching against a waiting troop carrier and his body stiffened at the sight.

Don't overreact. Be nice to the man. You need him.

He considered him a stereotype; a big, exceptionally tough squadron leader in the Royal Australian Air Force. Frederick hated the way he swaggered, the way he tossed his fringe from his face and the gravelled mix of guttural and cultured speech; each aspect creating the archetypical impression of the heroic officer in uniform.

I can see right through you ... You bastard.

Frederick knew him as an unpleasant and arrogant man with no scruples at all; a man to fear on every level and a total displeasure to know.

"I hear your worth has changed, Vogel."

"Why's that?"

"Don't play with me. Our boys just got a hands-off, on an Assembly jet and here you are in the Shikra that attacked it. I could sell that pelt on your head to the Assembly for a fortune."

"You owe me."

"Yeah ... One phone call to Rome and I could retire."

He laughed and withdrew a knife from his belt, testing its sharpness with the edge of his thumb.

"Don't threaten me. There are quite a lot of us."

"Don't sweat it, Vogel. I pay my debts. Get this rag-tag lot in the back of the troop carrier ... Weapons unloaded and stored before we leave."

Vogel's captain strode forward.

"The guns stay loaded. We don't answer to you."

The squadron leader laughed and it held such menace that both Vogel and his captain backed away several paces.

"Vogel. Do what I bloody-well-tell-you, or piss off. Got it?"

———————

Wolf's aircraft banked to the north on its approach to Darwin, turning south between Nightcliff and East Point.

He felt relaxed as he watched the dark objects swimming below the surface, as they came in low over the clear aqua water off Coconut Grove.

Hammerheads by the hundreds. Not a good place for a swim.

He hated sharks, especially the human variety, like Vogel and the mystery woman.

For the moment, his current schedule appeared to be achievable. The timing depended on how quickly he could determine the enemies' route and ultimate destination. Once known, the net closed to a secondary point, until Fox recovered the Prize. Then it closed completely, capturing their quarry.

He selected Darwin as his first stop, mostly because it sat on the top of the jet's north-south axis point of escape. Three attack helicopters awaited his orders at Richmond Airbase, west of Sydney, covering all southern regions and three more at Rockhampton, covered the north.

The enemy could only land in so many places, with no realistic way of escape; the air remained their only sanctuary, but only as long as their fuel supplies lasted.

It's a fail-safe mission.

Barring an intervention from God himself, he could conclude this mission without delay. His only real concern remained the two miscreants following Fox.

─────────────

As they approached the RAAF airfield on the eastern side of Wagga Wagga, Frederick noted the surrounding paddocks and the grazing sheep; there appeared to be no other activity at the base.

As they neared the security check-point, he could see that the boom-gates stood up and open; the entire area, including their hangar unoccupied.

"My debt's paid, Vogel. If there's ever a next time, I'll mount your precious anatomy above my bar, without you attached. Don't hurry back."

Frederick forced his lips together and nodded. He could feel a flush of anger heat up his cheeks, but he gave no retort.

Handle it. Don't react. He might be arrogant, but he delivered the goods.

The transition from truck to aircraft occurred swiftly and uneventfully thanks to the squadron leader. No-one came near or seemed to notice their endeavours.

"Get going, Vogel. Before I change my mind."

Frederick wanted to shoot the man. It irked him not having the last word. Normally, he let no-one get away with such insolence.

Keep your mouth shut ... Control yourself.

Without the squadron leader's contribution, he could never have continued his pursuit of Fox. The man just supplied him with a fully fuelled Royal Australian Air Force G39 Landsborough troop carrier, with a range of new weaponry and an abundance of extra ammunition.

I'm back and in a better position than before.

He tried to laugh, but he felt too tired to sustain his mirth.

The squadron leader's contribution also included a lovely charade. The outgoing tower log-books listed an RAAF aircraft leaving Wagga Wagga on a secret in-house undercover operation, requisitioned by the highest authority; the orders routed through RAAF headquarters in Canberra.

No-one can interfere with our progress.

In the air he remained untouchable. He could follow Fox to the Prize with no resistance.

"Look at their new coordinates, captain. Fox has turned to the north-west. That only leaves a few possibilities, but I'd be willing to bet your life on Longreach as their destination."

Chapter Fifty Six

Noah groaned, stumbling from the cockpit, as the jet dipped through a pocket of turbulence.

"I've lost my air legs."

Isobel smiled at him, but quickly turned her attention back to the priest.

"You mentioned earlier that the Assembly killed your parents?"

"Yes. I discovered their bodies as a boy, yet didn't discover the truth until adulthood."

"So what did you do?"

"I changed. I began to question my place in the scheme of things and to pursue answers."

Tom felt his anger rising as he listened to the priest's narrative. It's similarities to his own story creating an ache in his chest.

"I don't understand. How could you live with the people who supposedly murdered your family?"

"Live with them. What does that mean?"

"You cohabitated with the killers."

"Yes, Tom. I understand that you mean revenge, but for me the need for revenge grew into the need for justice. And, despite what you might think, revenge and justice are very different. I couldn't just wipe out an entire family and then another and another. No. I needed to beat them at their own game … For a better cause."

"This is your reason for working with them; with the Angels?"

"No. I had no choice in the matter, but something good came out of it."

Isobel looked over at Tom and raised her brow.

"Something good; I don't get it?"

"In my search for truth I found a group who shared my beliefs. They became my real family, even though they were being persecuted by the Church and the Assembly. Amongst this group, I could be myself. I could be a man, as well as a servant of God. So naturally, I helped them."

Isobel nodded and smiled.

"Ah, so this is where you met her; the soul mate you mentioned earlier?"

"Yes. Very perceptive, young lady. She's the other reason I worked for them. The Assembly discovered my participation in this … unlawful gathering. I helped them with the Angels to spare the group; to save her."

Tom's voice sounded harsh, even to him.

"What went wrong? I mean, you've risked those people to be with us?"

"When the Angels began to decline, the Assembly started threatening me with the murder of the group to make me comply. I pretended to obey until we could safely hide them and bring you into this awful game. You, ultimately changed everything."

"Me? How?"

"You provided me with an opportunity to defeat them, which became paramount. Their threats became beatings and then disappearances. How long do you think I could wait, before these monsters came for her?"

The priest seemed to be lost for a moment in his own private world. Tom didn't trust this man for many reasons, mostly because he needed someone, an actual person, to blame.

Perhaps he's telling the truth. No-one could fake the look in his eyes.

"What should I call you?"

The priest looked up at Tom and searched his eyes.

"My full title is Father Dominico Rossi. You can call me Nico if you like."

"Well Nico, if what you say is true, then it seems you're part of our pathetic little family."

"Our family ...?"

Isobel gave Tom a questioning look, but the priest answered for him.

"You, Tom and I, have all been orphaned by the same people and for the same purpose. That makes us connected."

The priest turned and pointed towards Noah.

"As for substantiation of my story, perhaps you should be asking him. Noah has been my closest friend for over three decades."

Tom looked over at Noah and then at Isobel. She looked totally bewildered.

"What do you mean friends? How could that be, Noah?"

Chapter Fifty Seven

Tom pushed Noah's hand off his shoulder in anger. He felt confused and betrayed. How could he possibly make sense out of this subversive world?

He began to stammer; his words barely coherent.

"You lied to us, Noah?"

"Tom, please. Let me explain …"

"No … No I won't. Go, before I get really angry."

Tom waited for Noah to retreat several paces down the aisle, before raising his weapon and aiming it at the priest.

"Tell me everything and no more lies. Make me believe, priest."

"Alright, Tom. Alright."

The clergyman closed his eyes and pulled back his lips as he spoke. Tom thought he looked as angry as he felt.

"One very rare, hot English summer, we all found one another. I met my Emma at the same garden party as your father met your mother. I already knew Noah and when Alexander, your father, introduced me to Tom Kite, we all became ridiculously idealistic and naive friends. Despite our hideous predicament we stuck together until the end."

"Hideous predicament … You mean the Prize?"

"No, no, long before that. It began when our group of gullible friends first beheld the Angels. Before we could even grasp at the truth of our situation, we become submerged in a very ugly lie. The truth of which, didn't set us free. Rather it enslaved us. People got killed who didn't go along with the Assembly's fraudulent activities."

Isobel cut in, her voice no more than a whisper.

"Yes. Your happy little club cost me my father."

"No. No. No. The Assembly took both of your parents. Noah and I are the only ones from that group to survive."

He stopped talking for a moment and Tom almost retreated from the intensity of his gaze.

"Noah feels guilt over our deception, but I won't apologise for either of us. We've lived a life of secrets just to survive. You must understand; Noah not only lost his wife, but his closest friends. Your people."

Isobel shook her head.

"Our people …?"

"Noah and your parents became inseparable, Isobel, like family. That's why he tries to act like your guardian."

Tom noticed Isobel's shoulders droop. Her strength seemed to die away and she began to tremble.

"I can't handle this. It's too much."

"I know, my dear. We've all suffered at the hands of the Assembly. Tom didn't even get to know his parents."

He smiled and Tom thought it held genuine warmth.

"I can't change the past, young man, but this might help."

The clergyman's hand delved into the inside of his jacket and returned with two photographs between his thumb and forefinger. Tom's heart began to beat faster as he realised what the priest offered him.

"These are for you, Tom."

Because of his own features, he expected his mother to have long, wavy, blond hair, but instead, she chose to have it cut short, like a boys.

His hands began to shake as he examined irises as black and appealing as the raven colouring of her hair.

Oh my God. She's so beautiful. Perfect. Even better than I imagined.

His mother stood next to her husband; her mouth open in the midst of laughter; perhaps amused by her exaggerated attempt at an elegant pose. Tom smiled as he searched his father's features. He wore a dinner-suit over a tall lean frame, crowned with a mop of unruly blond hair. It felt like looking into a mirror and viewing a future version of himself.

He looked over at Isobel. Her smile conveyed empathy, and he began to feel a warm longing in his chest … until he noticed the similarities.

Mum … Isobel …?

Apart from the colour of their eyes and his mother's height, they looked almost identical.

What does that mean? Is that the reason I'm so attracted to her?

He felt nausea constrict his throat as he tried to come to terms with his mother's appearance. His hands continued to shake, as he began to examine the second photograph of his mother. She stood alone in a ridiculous looking yellow swimsuit.

Her body's the same as … as Isobel's.

Katherine Fox stood with legs apart and hands on her hips; her long, slightly muscular limbs, adding to the elegance of her super slim torso and hips.

God … They could almost be twins.

A sweet voice brought him momentarily out of his thoughts.

"Tom, can I see?"

"Ah … sure, but in a moment. I just want to look at her for a while longer."

"Yeah, alright, Tom."

He became aware of Isobel's expression. She seemed to be reading his thoughts? What would she think if she saw the picture?

He felt like throwing up.

His attempted grin felt out of place as he moved off towards the rear of the plane. After several steps he stopped and listened. He could hear Noah calling for the priest from the open cockpit door.

"Nico, I need you here ASAP."

Tom returned to where Isobel sat. She smiled at him and he tried to hold her gaze, but couldn't. He felt troubled as he turned away.

Is it sick to desire someone identical to your mother?

Then another thought occurred to him.

Oh God. They could be mother and daughter ...

How could he possibly find the awareness he needed to sort this out, with the SRP and the Assembly on his tail?

He turned towards Isobel and once again tried to hold her gaze. Her eyes seemed to smile at him by themselves; bright and blue.

No. No. When I look at that tiny body and get aroused, it's ... my mother's.

Once again her voice broke through; ending his thoughts. This time it sounded strained.

"Tom ... Tom, you're wanted."

Isobel pointed towards the cockpit door, where he could see Noah gesturing for him to come.

No-one looked up as Tom entered the cockpit. Noah and the priest stood behind the pilot, looking intently at a map spread over the man's knees.

Noah didn't look at him when he spoke.

"We have a situation, Tom."

"Well, that's a surprise. What is it this time?"

"We have an unknown private jet and an RAAF aircraft following us from the south. We also have an Assembly P34 jet approaching, even faster from the north. All of these are unscheduled flights heading in the Longreach direction."

Chapter Fifty Eight

Tom tried to discern the lay of the land, as they began their descent towards the red earth of Longreach.

It looks too small; no bigger than a village.

The problem of determining any real perception of size from this height, especially in such a vast landscape seemed deceptive.

"I can't see any vehicles. The airport looks deserted, Noah."

"We're fortunate. There's no scheduled flights at this hour."

Tom could feel the tension amongst the men in the cockpit.

The pilot coughed in an attempt to be heard.

"Gentlemen. I can't be sure if the front wheel mechanism activated. Do you understand what this means?"

No-one answered.

"Even if the tyre is blown, the wheel mechanism can potentially stop the nose from hitting the tarmac. Either way a crash landing remains inevitable."

Tom left the cockpit and returned to his seat. He sought Isobel's eyes and tried to reassure her with a smile.

"It's going to be a little rough, but we'll be alright."

In that moment of crisis, he remembered reading somewhere that you needed to assume the correct crash position.

Come on, pull yourself together.

He checked his posture: his feet pushed hard into the floor and his body remained stiff with dread anticipation. He raised his head and looked out the window to check their height. The ground looked close.

"This is it, Iz. Learn forward and place your hands and forehead on the seat in front. I read that it helps to stop whiplash and cushions the impact."

"I don't want to die, Tom. Let's live, alright?"

"Yeah sure. Of course we will."

Above the roaring of the engines, Tom thought he heard Noah's voice.

"Tom. Nico. Get up here. Quick."

Tom began to ply Isobel's fingers from his arm and he felt her shudder.

"It's just something minor. I'll be back in a minute."

"Bullshit, Tom."

He squeezed her hand and rose to follow the clergyman, just as the aircraft lifted with full power. The thrust threw him backwards and he bounced off a seat in the opposite aisle, crashing to the floor and landing on his back.

He felt pinned by the jet's forward momentum. It took a great deal of strength to rise and climb up towards the cockpit. Half way there the aircraft started to level off. He adjusted by letting go of the nearest seat, before pushing himself to a more upright position.

What the hell's going on?

He tried to take a step forward, but at that moment, the aircraft banked sharply to the south, wedging him sideways between two rows of seats. He braced himself and used the chair's frame to regain his feet. He managed enough forward speed to enter the cockpit on the run.

"What's this all about, Noah?"

Tom followed Noah's glance, out beyond the aircraft.

"We have another situation. We spotted several police cars in the big aircraft hangar on the near side of the terminal."

Once again the pilot cut into their conversation. Even in the confines of the cabin, he needed to raise his voice to be heard.

"We've got no choice, we have to land. We haven't got enough fuel to go anywhere else. We have to go in now."

Tom grabbed at Noah's shoulders and shook him in frustration.

"We can't give up this easily, Noah. It'll all be for nothing."

"I agree. So, what do you suggest?"

Tom's voice sounded chilling, even to him.

"If we survive the landing, I have a plan for handling the police."

Tom returned to his seat as the aircraft came around and lined up for another attempted landing.

"I think it'll be easier the second time around, Iz."

He lied to comfort her and himself. He couldn't stop thinking about their possible demise. Passing away in bed, age ninety-something, seemed far more appealing than plummeting from the sky.

Some deaths seem a lot worse than others.

"Here we go again. Hang on, Iz."

The aircraft came in bum first. Tom thought the cabin pointed ridiculously upright. Everything seemed to be moving slowly, as if time warped with fear. As the rear wheels struck the tarmac Tom's world became a place where everything held worth; even boredom mattered.

He braced himself for the crash, but the rear wheels didn't smack down, as he anticipated. Instead, they eased onto the tarmac.

"Stay in the brace position, Iz. It's not over."

His fingers dug into the seat, as the front of the cabin began to drop.

This is it. Hang on.

He heard the engines squeal in protest, at being thrown into reverse thrust. Would the front mechanism hold under the weight of the aircraft?

I'm about to find out.

Chapter Fifty Nine

The chairman raised his enormous bulk into a standing position and employed an old, well utilised technique. He opened and spread his arms wide; raising his face towards the heavens with an anguished expression, like the Saviour beseeching his Father for guidance.

Stupid theatrics, but they'll fall for it. They always do. I'm going into battle against a pack of hunting dogs. I need every trick in my arsenal.

The expressionless faces around the marble table confirmed his need for any tactic that worked.

This is their opportunity to replace me, but I'm ready.

"Gentlemen, we are the elect of God's Church and we've been given many privileges. We have become exalted through His greatness."

He stopped and searched each face.

"Never forget that our cause is greater than each of us. It is this responsibility that binds us together and I congratulate you all, for your years of courage and fortitude."

The men at the marble table stood and clapped.

Ah ... Deception ... The beautiful lie ... Always appropriate.

Even after so many years he felt amused by the committee's mock spontaneous protocol. He felt compelled to smile back at them with the same feigned appreciation.

What kind of world would it be, if men became openly honest? Wouldn't the blackness in each man's heart, be exposed for all to see? Wouldn't religion and government and even culture, struggle as a means of control for the world's masters if they told the truth about their wealth? Without such cultured lying, all men descended into chaos and became animals.

He felt it his duty to manipulate and lie, like all good hierarchy did as a matter of course. His position and its dark machinations created no guilt, rather he felt esteemed by the responsibility of providing such structure to the world.

He raised his right hand for quiet.

"Gentlemen, thank you. I am now in a position to tell you that we are close to achieving our goal. Soon the Prize will be ours."

He let them absorb this information before continuing.

"This boon will grant us the right and the means, to bring about true order."

The chairman nodded his acquiescence to a challenger who slowly stood and faced him; the man's sloth like exertions causing his ancient bald scalp to shine with perspiration.

"What of Wolf, Mr Chairman? Can we be sure of our success this time, given the antics of his predecessor?"

The chairman understood his comrade's words as an obvious and calculated measure to test the strength of his leadership.

"Yes, a very good question. As usual your candour strips away the unimportant and brings us straight to the point. It is because of our new appointment that we know the location of the Prize. Wolf and the enemy are headed towards the Raptor Park dig site as we speak."

"No. That can't be, Mr Chairman. We searched that area with absolute thoroughness and ..."

"Well it appears that you didn't search well enough, my friend."

"Yes, Mr Chairman, but the area ..."

"Of course, no-one is blaming you."

Antonio felt both relieved and amused, as his most likely opponent fell into his own trap.

Good. Because of his stupidity, the others will be inclined to hold back and support the stronger man.

"Gentlemen. Wolf has helicopters and ground support, so there won't be any mistakes. Not this time. He will surround the area and hold off until the Prize is fully revealed. Then we will take back what is ours."

The bald man remained standing, but already his body language held much less menace and authority.

"Mr Chairman, if my calculations are correct, Wolf will never make the site in time? Won't this allow the enemy to use the Prize against us, or even destroy it?"

"No. No. No. It cannot be destroyed. We will safely secure it and eliminate God's enemies."

Ignore the question ... Wait for the precise moment.

The day already belonged to him. Once again he held off the predators, but he realised that the jackals in the group grew bolder. Only the Prize could keep the pack from devouring him. This is how men are meant to behave and how he took power so long ago.

"Gentlemen, I am duty bound, not only to weed out disloyalty, but to protect us against its outcomes. For this reason, I have taken a liberty on behalf of the board. Wolf is already half way to Australia."

An elderly man rose from his seat with the help of his assistant; his physique so gaunt and wasted of flesh that he resembled a corpse.

"This is a terrible breech of your position, Mr Chairman. We are of equal authority and are to be consulted in all important matters, yet you predetermined the entire voting process."

"Yes. The reasons should be clear to you all. Circumstances forced me to act in a decisive way for the benefit of expediency. For this reason, I have also dispatched another aircraft, which will arrive shortly after Wolf … To, as you say, eliminate any antics. On board, is the seventh and last remaining Angel. He will ensure our victory."

"Mr Chairman, this is too risky. He is extremely unstable and has lost much of his power. We don't know what might happen if he is directly exposed to the Prize."

"The Angel will act as a deterrent only. Agreed?"

The six other members of the Assembly yielded to the stronger man.

"Gentlemen, I have acted for the good of all. If I didn't act, it could be us kneeling before another victor. Is that what you want? No. I will not allow our enemies to impose terms upon us. Our obligation is holy."

He stopped and sipped some water.

"Don't worry, my friends. I do not envisage that the Angel will be actively involved. He is our insurance. What man or technology could stand against him, even in his current state? No, gentlemen, we will not be dictated to. There will be no compromise. We will win and we will destroy our enemies."

Bruno Wolf made a fist in annoyance. He lived in the shadows where he could watch others in the light, yet others shared his darkness.

It has to be his predecessor, but who is the woman?

Two unknowns and more. By accident, his assistant discovered that two jets flew from Rome, on this same quest.

So, the chairman employs another to keep me in line, or possibly remove me once the job is done. How quickly the hunter becomes the quarry.

The facts: an RAAF troop carrier followed Fox, as did a Fokker T950 business jet and an Assembly Cessna Peregrine 8000 followed him. An educated guess suggested that Vogel, a representative of the Black Cardinal and an Assembly heavy; probably someone closely associated with the chairman, like his son Roberto, completed the list of watchers in the shadows.

First, some insurance.

He punched a number into his communicator.

I must deal with the tangible and gain leverage, then work on my growing competition.

A surprised and cultured voice answered his call.

"Yes, who's speaking?"

"We've never met priest, but we have heard of each other."

"You have this number, so I know you're the Assembly."

"My name is Bruno Wolf. I've been sent to hunt you down."

"Yes, The Darkman. I've heard of you, but really why the call? We've moved quite a bit past silly threats, don't you think?"

"No. Not at all. You see I have a proposition for you, priest. One that will change your life."

Vogel knew that his whereabouts could be easily determined if he made contact with any local authority, yet, if he could utilise the state police effectively and maintain secrecy at least for the short term, he could steal an eventual victory.

My troop carrier won't be a concern to the Australians or the Assembly. They're convinced that the aircraft is on a mission concerning top-secret covert activities.

Vogel maintained many contacts around Australia, which included high ranking members of the Queensland State Police Force. He could gain the assistance of the Longreach constabulary with one call.

The Assembly won't involve the Australians ... No way.

They won't allow local participation. He felt no such qualms. With everything to gain if the G11 group got caught, the police became an asset. Even if this didn't occur, he could monitor and control their pace and movements.

"Captain. You are about to receive an important transmission from the senior sergeant in charge of police in Longreach. Please inform him that their objective is to bring Tom Fox into custody and contain him until we arrive. Under no circumstances is he to be harmed. Also inform him that all of the others on board the aircraft are expendable."

If these police yokels pull this off, nothing can stop me.

"And captain, please inform the officer that this is a top-secret endeavour. No paperwork and no communication."

He groaned involuntarily at the thought of Fox's capture.

Fox, you may be the most precious commodity in the world, but once I get the information I need, I'm going to slit your worthless throat.

Wolf presented his proposal to the clergyman and nodded when he heard the expected expulsion of breath. Silence followed.

"I take it that your lack of response indicates a yes, priest?"

"I have no real choice ... Yes."

Bruno Wolf fell back into his leather chair and laughed.

Now that's genius. I've won this battle with a single call.

The priest fell back to earth like a shot bird; how easily he capitulated.

"Ah. Winning always feels so good. No matter how easily it occurs."

The assistant looked bewildered as he entered the fuselage and heard his superior talking. Wolf continued the private conversation for his own amusement.

"The priest will do whatever I ask. He belongs to me ... He's mine."

Chapter Sixty

Tom's fingers grasped the seat in front of him, as the nose of the aircraft dropped towards the front wheel. He heard a strange noise, which he recognised as the front tyre ripping from the wheel frame.

"I don't think it's over, Iz."

He heard a loud, cracking bang and the aircraft shuddered.

Damn ... The wheel mechanism's collapsed.

The nose squealed as it struck the airstrip and Tom flew forward, propelled against the extent of his seatbelt.

"Iz ... We'll make it. Hang on.

The aircraft's nose ground into the tarmac and the jet bucked and swayed; the rear wheels beginning to bounce.

Well bloody done. You're a miracle maker.

Tom marvelled at the pilot's skill. Through the jolting confusion and blinding shower of sparks, he somehow maintained his composure and kept them in a straight line.

At last the aircraft screeched to a stop. Its nose cone a smoking, twisted wreck.

Alright, we made it ... It's time to act.

Outside of his cabin window, Tom noticed movement. Three police vehicles raced towards the wreckage; parking directly adjacent to the aircraft's main exit.

Tom wondered at their lack of caution.

"They seem rather nonchalant, don't you think?"

The priest's voice sounded hoarse as he responded to Tom's question.

"Yes. Yes. Odd behaviour given the circumstances. This can't be the Assembly. They wouldn't risk apprehending Tom at this stage. Not without the exact location of the Prize."

Tom frowned.

"You're suggesting another party's involved other than the Assembly?"

"Yes. The Assembly won't allow the Australians to be involved."

"So who?"

"Someone powerful, with their own motives. Someone who could organise a local police force from the air."

"Vogel?"

Noah broke into the conversation. Tom thought he detected excitement in his tone, despite the presence of the police.

"Now we can understand the hands off on Vogel's helicopter and the RAAF aircraft. It's him and he's acting without the Assembly's authority."

Tom suspected as much.

"This doesn't change our tactics. We stick to the plan."

Father Dom forced his shoulder against the door and it gave way and opened. He stood still for a moment and allowed his eyes to adjust to the light.

He spotted the highest ranking policeman and waved for him to come forward.

"Almost everybody on board is injured. We could do with some help here."

Good. The plan's working. They're already off balance.

He noticed the police looking from one to the other in confusion. Medical assistance didn't seem to fit in with their expectations. There didn't appear to be any ambulance or emergency crews on site.

He could see no stairs from which to descend onto the tarmac, but he soon realised that it didn't matter. Because of the aircraft's twisted frame, the concrete runway lay less than a metre from where he stood.

I must look the feeble and pathetic priest. They seem to think I'm harmless.

His smile broke into a chuckle.

"Excuse me, Sergeant. If you could surrender your weapons peacefully, the men behind me with the automatic weapons, won't kill you. On the other hand, if you refuse, you'll be shot."

The five police officers looked from the priest to the wreckage, where two men held automatic weapons pointed in their direction. He saw each of the five uniformed bodies stiffen, as they considered their options.

"If you don't comply, sergeant, these men will not hesitate. Please, lay down your arms."

To the priest's surprise, the sergeant burst into a routinely used spiel that seemed comic, given the circumstances.

"It would appear that you are in no position of arrest good fellow. Now shut up and lower your damn weapons."

Four of the officers threw down their service handguns. In unison they raised their arms and looked over at their sergeant. Instead of releasing his service weapon, he raised and pointed it at the priest, continuing to demand their surrender.

Tom missed his cue; his thoughts about Isobel and his mother consuming him.

Great. It's my plan and I'm not even in place to execute it.

A huge frame filled the doorway as he hurried towards the exit.

"Noah, I'm coming through."

With a grunt, he forced his head through a gap under Noah's arm and the strong light assaulted his vision. He tried to push past him, but his foot slipped out of the door and he almost fell.

"Damn it."

Noise and chaos erupted around him. In his battle to stay on his feet, he squeezed the trigger and a terrifying burst of gunfire exploded out onto the tarmac.

Oh, God. What have I done?

When Tom regained his composure, he spotted the sergeant dropping his handgun and backing away towards the remainder of his men; his hands held aloft.

Then he spotted the priest giving him a thumbs up, as if the discharging of his firearm happened intentionally.

"Tom, it might be best if we rope these men together and confine them to the hangar. We can take one of their vehicles and disable the others."

Tom slowly nodded his consent.

With the pilot and their hostages, and two of the police cars still hidden in the aircraft maintenance hangar, it seemed safe to leave.

Tom activated the satellite navigation system in their vehicle to determine directions, while Noah and the priest acquired police jackets and caps from their captives, so as not to raise suspicion on their drive.

They negotiated their way through Longreach, utilising a patchwork of seldom-used dirt roads, creating a plume of red dust behind them.

Tom sat in the back with Isobel and tried to take in the unusually sparse, out-sprawl of the town.

"It's so flat here, Iz. Except for the dust, you could see forever."

"Flat and stinking hot … And the flies …"

Noah turned his head searching for Tom. His smile gone.

"They'll know soon enough that we don't have the Prize, so the Assembly will back off and watch for the moment. They won't attack us until we've led them to the site at least. The other interested parties, may not allow us that much latitude, so we'll have to be extremely cautious. We may be attacked at any time."

Chapter Sixty One

The cardinal noticed a flurry of movement, as Assembly staff hurried to leave the area. Several seconds later a bell rang and the chairman entered the parlour room.

The cardinal smiled.

The man might be a fat pig, but at least he has a sense of occasion.

"Cardinal Dal Santo. Thank you for coming so soon."

"Bless you, Antonio. I'm at your disposal."

He knew the chairman loathed him, as did the other members of the board, but that mattered little. Once committed to his plan, they couldn't turn back, which made him irreplaceable.

They're afraid. They need me, but I'll soon be the most powerful ruler the world has ever known and that scares them.

He moved into an intimate closeness, before addressing the chairman.

"I've come at your insistence, Antonio. Is there a problem?"

"Yes. The timing's changed. Our affairs have begun to accelerate."

The cardinal felt like laughing as he searched the chairman's face. The man before him hid his emotions; he hid everything unless he wished to use it as a tool, yet today, his expression betrayed a subtle hint of stress. He understood men of this nature. Rather than succeed as a team, they preferred to work against their neighbour to gain personal advantage. Men like Antonio, lived their lives in a perpetual struggle for power. The idea of a peaceful endeavour never entered their minds

"I've done precisely what you have asked of me, Mr Chairman. I have sown the holy seed amongst those who will support me, but I can't openly promote our objective. You know this. Not until you bring the others over to our holy cause."

"There are a lot of cardinals as you know ..."

"Antonio. If the seedlings aren't watered they will die, no matter how fertile the soil is."

The chairman struggled from his seat; panting as he dragged his heavy frame to the closest window. Before him stretched a magnificent vista of terracotta roof tops and church domes, all contrasted in the brilliant blue of a typical Roman day.

He required just a moment to refocus his thinking. He needed to win this battle of wills, here and now. This disgusting little Satan presumed too much. Openly displaying his amusement of Assembly protocol amounted to imprudent rudeness.

It's about time I created a little tension, for the benefit of future, cordial relations.

"Your Grace has done well so far and we will dutifully hold to our end of the bargain, but the timing is important. We are sure of our numbers, but these are egos that require constant petting."

"I am well aware of this already, but ..."

"I will get to the point then. Some of our brethren wondered about your ability to perform such tasks. The decision to have you as our spiritual leader, wasn't shall we say … unanimous."

Already he could see a dark recognition in the other man's eyes. He held the silence for a brief moment, so his strength could fill the space between them.

"I will break a rule and be frank with you. After all, this is a dangerous business for both of us. If either of us fail in this endeavour … As chairman or pope, then I'm afraid the others will rid themselves of the problem. You see, they don't seem to share our high opinion of each other."

"Are you threatening me, Antonio?"

"No. I am giving you an opportunity, Your Grace. We cannot change what we have started. There can be no back-peddling. The doors behind us have long closed. Whether you like it or not, we have become bonded together by necessity."

"If one goes, we both go."

"Indeed."

The chairman felt satisfied. In a matter of minutes, he managed to transform this enemy into a trustworthy accomplice.

The cardinal understood the penalty for failure; a quick departure from this world and, given their antics, heaven could not be guaranteed.

"I understand the need for our privacy, Antonio."

The Black Cardinal used a sweeping motion with his arm to indicate the lack of humanity in the room.

"But this isn't the only reason for you bringing me here is it? My invitation came from the whole board, so this matter of urgency is something else."

"Yes. You are very perceptive. God often changes the plans of mere men, even those who work for Him. With or without the Prize, we must now act."

"Something has happened?"

"Without any assistance from us, our holy father has become gravely ill. My informants suggest that he won't see out the month."

Chapter Sixty Two

The G11's sped along the Landsborough Matilda Highway, travelling north-west away from Longreach, towards the township of Winton.

I wish he wouldn't do that.

Tom felt his own stress levels increasing as he suffered the priest's anger. In the last ten minutes he watched the man's irritation grow from impatient finger tapping on the dashboard, into fist thumping agitation. Despite their predicament his actions seemed out of character.

"This is far too dangerous, Noah. This highway leaves us dangerously exposed."

"I agree, Nico, but what choice do we have? The side road off Maneroo Station that you keep suggesting, is no more than a goat track. We don't have forever to achieve this."

"Alright, I'll grant you that. It could well be slower, but surely it would provide us some cover. We could use Tom and Isobel as spotters and get down into the creek bed, if trouble presents itself."

"The planet's most talented killers are following us and you're worried about surveillance aircraft. They could obliterate us whenever they like."

Isobel threw her head back against the seat and let out a groan.

"Look, you're both right, but surely this's Tom's decision."

Tom's face remained impassive as he listened to their squabble. The priest's arguments didn't make sense and he felt a moment of concern.

"The way I see it, we have to get there first."

Over time and without conscious acknowledgment, the two old warriors in the front seat accepted Tom's formal leadership of the G11 group. They both remained respectfully silent as he decided their path.

"The enemy must have a rough idea where we're heading. I think we should stay on the highway."

Noah grunted and the priest sighed, shaking his head.

"There's one other thing that's been bothering me about this situation. How do we use the Prize to hold off these jackals, when no-one seems to have any idea what it is, or how to use it?"

Noah and the priest exchanged furtive glances and a heavy silence pressed down around them.

Oh God. This's madness.

Their continued reticence confirmed his thoughts. Their entire enterprise rested on a crazy hope.

"Damn you both to hell."

The priest turned away from him before he spoke.

"We didn't have a choice, Tom."

"So we've come here to be butchered?"

"They pulled the trap closed the moment we began. We could never go back. With every step we took forward, they erased our past. We've been forced here."

The anger in Isobel's voice silenced the others.

"Why are we being so predictable then? We need to change the rules. We don't have to be puppets."

Noah twisted around in his seat and sought Isobel's eyes.

"We've been fighting them for a long time, Isobel. They have all of the resources. It's their game and we don't …"

"They don't have this."

Isobel held up the forgotten diary.

"Tom's father went to a lot of trouble to hide it from the Assembly and we have no real understanding of its contents."

Tom could see Noah's scar. It appeared to throb with redness as he spoke.

"I propose that we do as Tom suggests. We follow the highway until we turn west on the Evesham Station Road and then off into the bush between Maneroo and Bull Creek. Isobel and Tom can decipher the diary as we go."

Three nods confirmed their agreement.

They needed to travel another thirty minutes on the highway before they could leave the tar for the dirt road. Raptor Park lay just another fifty kilometres through the scrub.

We have to get there first or we won't have a chance.

Tom studied a map that he spread across his knees. Further north he could see an easier route, but it created a longer journey both in length and in time. If they went that way, they might not get to the area before the enemy arrived.

The day lived up to its predicted forecast of temperatures above forty degrees Celsius. Tom could feel sweat trickling down his spine, causing his shirt to stick to his back. He found it difficult inhaling the hot dry air as he refolded the map and turned his attention to the diary.

"Have you found anything, Iz?"

"That depends. Most of the entries are scientific notations to do with testing the suits."

She attempted to relate sections of the formal text to the men, but only got more frustrated with her inability to provide something useful that they could understand.

Noah cut off her complaints with an idea.

"Isobel, I've been thinking about that diary. We may have missed something. Given that we destroyed the instructions for its usage when we damaged the chip, there may be hidden elements that we're unaware of."

Isobel began to check the diary's casing for any possible clue. There didn't seem to be anything obviously different. Then Tom noticed Isobel's smile. He knew it betrayed what her fingers felt beneath the leather and his heart began to thump in his chest.

"Iz …?"

"I need a knife, then I can show you."

Noah reached into his jacket, removed his Swiss Army Knife and passed it over to her. She plied the blade open with a fingernail, then delicately sliced through the top section of the leather, before peering into the hidden pouch.

"You're a smart man, Noah. There's definitely something in here."

She couldn't remove it on the first attempt, so she utilised the knife to cut away more of the leather before the object came free.

Tom held his breath.

Come on … Please. We need a miracle.

Their lack of time felt like sand seeping through their fingers. They needed to come up with something before it ran out completely.

"It's a document … A letter … Addressed to you. It's from your father."

Tom didn't understand. Rather than feel excitement, his brain wanted to shut down. He couldn't think and for a moment, struggled for breath.

Isobel held the letter with reverence.

"Should I read it for you, Tom? Out loud I mean."

Tom began to shake and his mouth filled with a bitter tasting bile. Weren't the people in this vehicle part of what killed his father; part of his misery? He turned and glared at each of them and felt surprised at the genuine warmth he discovered in each expression. His anger began to fade.

Tom nodded his consent and Isobel began to read.

"Dear Tom,

How inadequate this letter must seem to you. The very fact that you are reading it means that I have long departed this world and you have endured a hard lie for a life. I know that saying sorry is nowhere near enough. I can only hope that you will one day understand that this isn't what your mother and I wanted for you.

By now, you must know either Dominico the priest, Tom Kite or Noah, for they are the only way you could have made it to this letter. You can trust these men with your life. They are true friends and are committed to our cause and your wellbeing.

You will also have understood the fraud that has been perpetrated on the Catholic Church and the world by the Assembly. No matter what happens, do not trust them, or be a part of any compromise. They have only one agenda and they will kill you unless the Prize can be used against them.

On page 38 of this diary, you will discover a list of numbers pertaining to a group of test findings. At first glance they appear to be results regarding the suit's ability to withstand heat. On the twelfth line from the top, there are several numbers that can be used to locate the Prize. The first number is the distance travelled due east from the old memorial cairn, to the hidden entrance of the cavern. The other two numbers are distances from specific reference points. The first reference is a rocky outcrop to the west, which you will discover, has a small dinosaur carved into its face. The second is the concrete remains of an old shed, which is north-west from the desired spot. The distances and references described will lead you directly to the entrance, but you will have to dig down through a metre of loose dirt to expose it. This is where we originally drilled through the rock. There is now a round steel hatch and a ladder leading down into the cavern.

The Prize is your legacy, Tom. So, you must go in by yourself. Once you have entered the cavern, you will find that it is about the size of a country hall. It is roughly rectangular and very dark, so you will need a good torch. The cavern narrows to a tunnel at the back of the hall and the ceiling drops down to less than two metres. Here you will encounter a small, secondary cavern, which contains two sealed metal containers. One of them holds the Prize, which I returned to the site after the Assembly conducted several thorough searches of the area. I then covered the entrance and destroyed all notes pertaining to it, except this letter.

For a time I argued with the others over your destiny, Tom, for they don't know the full truth. They were right about one thing, your life could only be saved by a sick bargain and a lie. I know this has cost you dearly my son, but no other options could be pursued. The first priority required saving your life and the second our cause. The others clearly know that you are that cause.

You are a long time into a future that I cannot know, but I have to assume that the Assembly have followed you along this pathway. For this reason, I have written another letter, which is hidden behind where this one is placed.

THIS LETTER IS FOR YOUR EYES ONLY, TOM. Under no circumstances are you to show it to anybody else and that includes my good friends.

Tom, even as I write this letter, I know with both sadness and triumph that you will succeed, for you are my son. Whether you like it or not, this heritage has become yours. I know you have been dragged into this mess, but you have no alternative now other than to rise up and be its outcome. You will understand this when the time comes.

I love you,

Dad."

No-one spoke for a long time, which suited Tom. He need time to absorb his father's message and his own emotions.

His mind seemed to split into two parts while he listened to Isobel read; one excited and emotional, the other cold and detached. An analytical question arose in the parietal lobe in the left hemisphere of Tom's brain. Disconnected from his emotive self he discovered an underlying meaning in the letter, which he found perplexing and worrisome: 'Rise up and be its outcome' and 'trust these men with your life', but don't trust them with the hidden letter. These conundrums, his father instructed, could only be understood when the time came, but what time did he have?

Why don't I understand? Why don't I see ...? Perhaps the second letter will fill in the gaps for me.

The whole affair felt strange and disturbing. His father purposely crafted a journey for his son that existed on the sharp edge between life and death, but his father didn't explain how he could survive the coming hours? How could he win when there seemed no hope?

Tom turned to Isobel and nodded towards the diary and she handed him the second letter.

Chapter Sixty Three

The passenger door opened and a gust of inrushing air stung Vogel's face. Within seconds the moisture lubricating his eyes seemed to evaporate making their movement feel scratchy and sore.

I'm breathing hot sand instead of air. How can anyone stand to live here?

As he descended the steps to the tarmac he could see his man waiting for him.

"Captain, your report."

"They survived the crash, sir. The local police confirmed that four people left the aircraft. The descriptions fit Fox, the girl, Noah and also the priest."

"What happened to the Pilot?"

"He's tied up in the hangar with the police."

"And our fugitives have transport?"

"They took one of the police four-wheel drive vehicles, but none of the men saw what direction they took."

Vogel looked on in amusement as the small group of policemen left the hangar.

Useless ... They deserve a bullet. How could they stuff this up?

Their anger and frustration seemed like a fitting reward for their stupidity.

"Captain. Tell our sergeant of police that this is over. They are to forget that this ever happened. Let it be known that they'll be well compensated for their misadventure."

"And the pilot?"

"Leave him as he is. I have questions and I'm going to make sure I get answers."

Apart from the pilot and his own team of men, the airport remained deserted. Several regular scheduled flights to Longreach flew out of Brisbane, but not for several hours, leaving him free to begin interrogations without having to be worried about civilians. He entered the largest of the maintenance hangars and approached the pilot.

"Do you know who I am?"

The flight captain nodded.

"You have knowledge that I require. So, I'm going to arrange a small demonstration to save time."

Vogel gestured towards his own captain.

"Shoot him in the leg."

Vogel enjoyed the man's fear. The pilot's eyes bulged, as he began to beg for an unlikely deliverance.

"No. No ... Please ..."

The blast sounded thunderous in the confines of the hangar. It reverberated around the tin walls of the shed where it merged with the high-pitched screams of a totally convinced pilot.

"Stop moaning and shut up. I'm going to ask you a couple of questions. If I don't like the answer, you get another bullet. Understand?"

The pilot tried to respond between gasps for breath. His nod of ascent so vigorous it caused Vogel to laugh.

"Alright ... Alright. I'll tell you whatever you want."

―――――――――

The secretary saluted his superior and stiffened to attention.

"Vogel's military aircraft is on the tarmac, sir. What should I tell our pilot?"

Wolf concentrated on a map of the Raptor Park site and didn't look at the private as he spoke.

"Are you in contact with the local sergeant of police?"

"It appears that Vogel used him, sir."

"I'll have the full report later. For now, just fill in the dots."

The secretary explained Vogel's tactics and how he manipulated the police.

"He commandeered a fully fuelled police four-wheel drive from their headquarters. It has a police scanner, so he can monitor their activity. They headed north-west on the highway towards Winton."

Wolf nodded without taking his attention away from the map.

"Instruct the pilot to land immediately. After drop off, he's to fly east to Rockhampton and await further orders. I also want our helicopters here ASAP."

"There's one more thing, sir. We have confirmation that the mystery woman landed briefly in Albury and took on two passengers. A man and what the flight controller assumed to be an injured woman."

"And their destination?"

"It looks like they're on this course."

"Well get going. I want updated reports of her progress. I also want estimated arrival times for our helicopters, updated every five minutes. It's imperative that we tighten our net. No-one gets in and no-one slips through. No-one."

Chapter Sixty Four

The fugitive G11 team continued to speed north-west along the Landsborough Matilda Highway, travelling parallel to the rail line. Tom counted six railway stations since leaving Longreach, all with dull yellow one-room buildings and minimal platform space.

The station names: Darr, Payne, Morella, Rimbanda, McMaster and Chorregon, hung above the door frame of each building.

"This's Chorregon Station. Go left here."

Noah turned off the main highway and headed west onto a dirt road towards Maneroo Creek and their final destination.

In places their vehicle's suspension jolted and vibrated over the rough corrugated track and between bumps, Tom managed to look over at Isobel. Somehow she read from the diary and relayed a steady flow of unhelpful information, as if she sat in her home on a comfortable couch. The current story related the failure of the professor's last expedition, which attempted to find an elusive carnivore.

"Apparently this thing lived in the late Cretaceous, about ninety-five million years ago; a Tyrannosauropus species, which he thought to name Manerooasaurus."

Tom didn't feel enthused by Isobel's scientific fervour. It might have taken his mind off their inevitable confrontation, but any budding interest in palaeontology required them surviving the next couple of hours.

Despite the bumpy ride, their new road proved to be serviceable. They made good time, shaking and bouncing their way past the remnants of Clyde Cattle Station and on through the dry beds of Alice and Maneroo Creeks. They couldn't have been more obvious, trailing long clouds of dust as they went.

In the middle of the Maneroo Flood Plain, they turned south towards the junction of Spring and Sancho Creeks. Here they left the road and headed further east on a rougher track towards Raptor Park.

Tom studied the area. To the north and west, he identified the sparsely wooded Forsyth Range. It rose with just enough elevation to funnel what little precious rain they received; redistributing it into the mostly-dry creek beds that flowed south into larger and more permanent water supplies.

"Hey, Iz. Look at that."

Isobel ignored him; continuing to relay segments of the diary, but Tom's attention focused elsewhere as he scanned the road ahead.

"Iz … Look. It's a mob of red kangaroos. They're bounding across the road up in front."

"That's great, Tom. Now listen, this's important and relevant. Millions of years ago, this place became a swamp. Apparently, herbivores got caught in the mud here. This whole place became a trap for big dinosaurs."

"This's relevant …?"

He saw her pursed lips and the subtle shake of her head and decided to concentrate.

"The trapped animals attracted the carnivores, who followed the smell of decaying flesh, but here's the catch. The killers got caught in the mud when they tried to feed on them. That's why your father named the area, specifically around the dig site, the Raptor Trap."

Tom knew her tone implied a question, but he chose to remain silent. The scenario seemed a little too poignant and horribly ominous.

"We're like the herbivores, Tom. We're in the trap surrounded by the raptors."

"Thanks, Isobel. I'll slit my wrists now and save them the trouble."

His attention shifted as he looked out the window, scrutinising the baked earth of present day, outback Queensland.

She's right. Wetland or not, the raptors are coming and we're just as stuck.

An image of them all, hip-deep in mud flashed into his mind, with Vogel and the SRP circling; readying themselves for the kill.

Once more he became aware of Isobel's monotone ramblings.

"Alright, Tom. Here's something. The hidden chamber where your father first discovered the suits eventually became sealed by time."

"So?"

"So … It proves the suits came here millions of years before we even existed, and because we've found no evidence of any interim culture, it's more than probable that this technology got transported here by an alien people. The diary also states that the cavern walls are crusted with up to five hundred centimetres of a blackened substance, not found anywhere else on Earth. It does however, infer a crash site."

"Alright, you've definitely got my attention."

He looked into her eyes and attempted to smile an apology.

How could he be so obsessed with such a tiny being? Everything about her made him ache and burn and swell; the shape of her slim hips, the tiny white hairs on her otherwise smooth skin, the sound of joy in her laugh; each a wonder.

She makes me shiver just looking at her. Does it really matter if she looks like my mother; a beautiful woman I never met?

He understood that God instilled beauty in all of creation. He also realised that discernment played a big part in its realisation. With Isobel's beauty, it felt like he journeyed across space and time, just so he could watch her lips move. In finding her, he understood that a great love coloured perception with the ultimate beauty.

Yeah, but ... she could be my sister.

How could he find out without making a dick of himself? Noah and the priest knew his parents. They must know something.

Her look jolted his focus away from the form and curve of her eyebrows, back to a reality, where men destroyed women like her without the slightest bit of compassion.

"I thought you said you're all ears? Tom?"

"I'm listening ... What happened to these aliens? Did they find any remains after the crash?"

"Oh yes. It appears they stored their equipment and your father found several bodies laid out in a neat row, so at least one must have survived the crash. That's the only clue."

"So the Prize is definitely alien?"

"Alien, yes. These creatures looked like humans in basic appearance, yet huge and with an intelligence that we can't begin to understand."

The priest turned in his seat and joined the conversation; his smile appearing sour and a little frightening.

"Your father discovered that the suits they wore remained alive after the crash and managed to stay that way for millions of years, without any means of sustenance. He also discovered that each suit exhibited a high level of intelligence, which he presumed, reflected the intellect of each alien individual."

He stopped and took a breath before continuing.

"This is why fitting them to humans, created problems. Once on, the suits took over the wearer's consciousness. They literally regrew the new inhabitant's tissue, towards predetermined alien dimensions, including a massive expansion of brain capacity."

Tom felt a jolt of fear as he listened to the priest's explanations.

No. No. No ... I'm leading all of these people to their deaths.

Tom's mouth hung open, as he considered the priest's words. He well remembered his encounter with the Angel. His chest still burnt from the ordeal.

I can't do this. I can't do this to Isobel.

How could he risk her life so recklessly? How could he ever hope to win against such an indestructible monstrosity?

Chapter Sixty Five

Réz Cel Rău knew that the pilots watched her undress from the cockpit. Nakedness never bothered her and she couldn't care less about the staff.

In truth, she loved life stripped bare; the place where true savagery lived without need for concealment.

Once someone finds that truth deep within them, naked violence becomes their reality ... Their true nature ... My nature.

The thought made her pulse increase as she strolled into the cockpit in her cotton sports underwear; her face smeared green and black with camouflage paint and her curly auburn hair pulled into a tight ponytail, all of which made her appearance seem severe.

Now for a little fun.

She knew her tight underwear accentuated her long, muscled body. She also knew that the leanness of her frame, more than emphasised the perky fullness of her breasts. She liked them to want her, but more so to fear her. She loved to see it in their eyes; raw desire and naked terror.

"Give me our estimated time of arrival."

Both pilots looked nervous.

"Fifteen minutes only. You'd best get ready."

"Don't presume to tell me my business. Just do as you're told."

Réz smiled; recognising their apprehension. Both men stared straight ahead and avoided any eye contact; having worked for Cardinal Dal Santo, they would well know her reputation.

"Madam. What you're asking is illegal and very dangerous, we …"

"You will do what I ask. You will land on the highway at Chorregon Station, just long enough to unload our equipment. Then you'll fly to Mount Isa, refuel and wait to be contacted. Is that understood?"

"Yes, but there might be traffic."

"Are you defying me?"

"No, certainly not, but …"

"There will be little traffic on the road at this hour and you'll have a visual in both directions."

"Yes. I suppose I …"

"Good. This is not a matter for argument. It will be done and it will be done perfectly."

Bruno Wolf possessed a well-practised smile which he used to hide the darkness of his inner being.

The good people of the world don't need to know what I do for a living.

For years he fought against his inclination for brutality. Its violent urges became his personal hell. Then an idea occurred to him. Why fight it? Why not put his abilities to good use. Organisations existed that honoured his kind of skill set, legitimising them behind a business-like facade.

His idea became his life. The Assembly's SRP program turned him from villain to valuable company asset. Surrounded by other like-minded people, he soon learnt he didn't need to justify his actions or show the slightest remorse.

His ferocity gave rise to another aspect of his nature, which he thought of as raw cunning. His ability to think under pressure and act ruthlessly made for a dramatic rise within SRP ranks.

Twelve years of meticulous planning and a lot of bodies is all it took, but he knew if he didn't get this mission right, it could all end here.

"No mistakes ... No tears."

As part of his strategy he made contact with all of his pilots, insisting that each captain recite the plan back to him for confirmation. He also spoke to all of the leaders of his elite SRP squad, keeping them informed and motivated.

I'm ready.

His team waited, all in perfect position. He also knew both Vogel's and the G11's current locations. The unknown woman caused him a minor concern, so he left two men at Longreach airport with orders to disable the aircraft and to kill all on board.

"Excuse me, sir."

Wolf waved the man away.

"Not now, I'm busy."

"Sir, it's the woman. She's overtaken us."

"What ...? Impossible. How?"

Droplets of sweat appeared on the secretary's forehead as he attempted to answer.

"They didn't land at Longreach, sir. They changed course and passed us to the south after we landed. They're heading straight at the target area, but surely they can't land. It's a business jet and there are no airports."

"There's more than fifty kilometres of straight highway you idiot. Go back to the cockpit and follow their movements. Report everything, don't assume. Now get out."

They're doing a drop. She's going to suffer for her audacity.

Réz Cel Rău strode out of the cockpit and entered a compartment at the far end of the aircraft. On a makeshift bed lay the lithe, naked body of a severely bruised and lacerated woman.

As she approached, she watched the doctor apply ointments to the cuts on the woman's cheeks. Réz studied the raked gashes on her sister's face. Her flesh looked torn and swollen.

"Am I that hideous, Réz?"

"The bullets caused only flesh wounds, my sweet. You'll heal well enough."

"I'm going with you. I'm still strong."

Réz left the room with the doctor. She knew her sister's determination and needed confirmation before she made a decision.

"Your assessment, Doctor?"

"Apart from the wound stitching, I've filled the remaining lesions with a special, new kind of ointment. It's a jelly-like substance which seals the affected area and acts like a second skin, preventing further bleeding and hopefully any reopening. It will also minimise the chance of infection. I have prescribed a non-drowsy high dosage form of pain control, so that Uta will remain sharp and motivated if required."

Réz heard Uta call out from behind her.

"I told you, my love. I'm just fine; battle hard and ready."

"You're sure?"

"I'm not staying here. I'm going. The SRP are about to get a lesson in guerrilla warfare."

Chapter Sixty Six

Tom turned in a full circle; evaluating the terrain of Raptor Park. His first appraisal brought only disappointment. No features distinguished the red parched earth, except for a fallen down shed and several piles of excavated dirt.

He squeezed his eyes shut and clawed at the tiny black flies that searched for moisture around the lids of his eyes. When he reopened them, he spotted Noah strolling towards him, kicking the dirt as he came.

"It's not my idea of paradise, Tom."

"Maybe not, but the big sky is awesome. It makes you realise how small you are in the scheme of things."

Tom didn't notice the priest walk up until he joined in the conversation.

"What's our next move, young man? This's your show and they'll be about us soon enough."

"First, I need you both to find a way of defending this place, while Isobel and I use the diary to locate the entrance."

Tom pointed to a spot on higher ground and Noah bowed his head in agreement.

"You'll have a view of the entire area and it keeps you out of the enemy's sight."

He spotted Isobel in his peripheral vision, striding out with the diary held out in front or her.

She's lucked out ... She didn't want any of this.

No matter how much he felt like it, reality came and pushed away his need to flee. The feeling lingered there in his subconscious; take Isobel by the hand and go to safety, but what safety could ever be found?

Isobel probably felt the same way, but he knew she acted with courage, especially for someone so unaccustomed to such a life.

She began reading aloud from the diary as Tom came near.

"The first number is the distance travelled due east, from the old memorial cairn, to the hidden entrance of the cavern. Walk that out and when you get there, I'll give you the next numbers."

Tom paced out the distance, unsure of his feet placement and the length of his stride.

"Alright I'm here."

"There's a rocky outcrop ahead to your left and an old shed foundation to your right. You have to reach a point where all the three reference points are exactly the same distance from each other."

Tom felt a sudden urge to run towards this invisible spot, but he held himself back and maintained his self-control.

"Alright I'm here, but I can't see a damn thing."

"First, we have to re-step it out and make sure it's the right spot. Then we dig."

When the shovel hit metal, the shock of it reverberated up Tom's arm. He fell to his knees and Isobel joined him. Together they cleaned away the last traces of dirt with their hands.

"This is it, Iz."

They strained at the weight of the old steel hatch. It took the leverage of their shovel to open it.

Tom could see the metal ladder, leading down. The diary didn't describe the depth of the chamber and the dark hole gave no indication. It looked to Tom like it went down forever … Into some evil void.

Alright, it's time.

He called out to Noah and the priest and eventually gained their attention by waving.

The two men drove back from the hill and jogged towards the entrance. Noah arrived first.

"Well done, Tom. You found it."

"Yes."

When the priest arrived, the group positioned themselves around the cavern's entrance. Tom stood in front of both men. He reached out and placed a hand on each man's shoulder.

"It's time. I need you to leave the cavern and find cover on the hill."

Noah stared back at Tom with the same intensity.

"You and Isobel can't stay here alone. You'll be killed."

"Yeah. You're right. That's why I wanted you to come back from your position. She's not staying either. You have to take her with you."

"Wait. What's that noise?"

They all turned to the north.

"It's a jet aircraft and it's close."

Tom let go of the men's shoulders and turned towards Isobel.

"Time to go, Iz. You'll be fine. We're all going to make it."

"No. I'm not going to leave you here alone. We have to stay together."

Tom saw Noah shaking his head. None of them wanted to leave. He needed to be stronger.

"My father made it plain in his letter that only I could enter the cavern. It makes sense that everyone else is away from here and hidden, especially you Isobel. So don't waste any more time. Get going."

Tom saw the expression change on the priest's face. He looked ill and about to throw up, but instead, he stepped back several paces from the group and removed a weapon from his pocket.

"I'm sorry, Tom. I can't do that. I'll be coming in and we'll be taking Isobel for insurance."

Tom looked over at Noah and Isobel. They appeared to be just as shocked; all rendered impotent by the impossibility of the situation. He turned back towards the priest in an attempt to discover some kind of explanation.

"What's this about? Are you betraying us?"

"Tom, you and Isobel down the hole."

He turned and faced his long-time friend and associate.

"Noah, I'm sorry, I have no alternative. I have to shoot you … I have to take your life."

Chapter Sixty Seven

Uta carried out a thorough inventory of each piece of gear, the pilot and co-pilot removed from the aircraft.

She checked off two black 500cc BMW Motocross trail bikes, a variety of hand-held weaponry and munitions, and two tight-fitting daypacks that clung to the body for hard running. The daypacks contained medical kits, grenades, handguns and a variety of explosives, as well as high protein bars and water.

With her sister's help, Uta stowed their firearms into specially made racks on both sides of each bike that could be reached when needed.

"Good. Let's make haste, Réz. We need to get to Fox before the jackals arrive."

Once on their bikes, neither women noticed the aircraft speeding north up the highway towards Winton. Both sisters focused on Raptor Park, obliterating the scene behind them in clouds of red dust.

They rode fast, on corrugated gravel roads and over loose rocky terrain; the rushing wind and the crunch of their tyres blotting out all other sound. Between bumps and slides, Uta snuck a glance at her sister.

She knows. She always does when I lie to her.

It didn't matter. Réz accepted, knowing all the while that Uta's injuries hurt her continually and affected her movement.

She knows she couldn't stop me, but she doesn't want to. This's our day.

She adored her sister in a way that ordinary people could never understand. In all of existence, only the cardinal stood higher in her esteem than her twin, but that created a growing problem. They lived as a happy threesome, but lately …

Something's changed. I know it. I can feel it.

If she could put her uneasiness into words …

One day he might choose one of us over the other and I couldn't live without either of them.

———————

Vogel searched a topographical map of the area around Raptor Park, to determine their point of entry.

We're nearly there. Soon we make our turn … West towards our final destination.

"Sir … Can you hear that?"

"What? Yes … What kind of devilry is this, captain? Jets don't fly out here. This is a flight path to nowhere."

Within seconds it appeared, rising out of a mirage of shimmering, windswept lakes to the north-west of their position.

"Sir, it's just taken off. It's got to have been from the highway up ahead of us."

Vogel felt as if strong hands grasped his throat; cutting off his oxygen supply.

Come on, breathe … Get a grip … Think.

"Captain. The jet …?"

"It's a Fokker T950 business jet, which the Assembly don't normally use. Their entire fleet are Falcons."

"You're sure of this?"

"Yes. The Assembly don't take these kind of chances. It's madness, risking a mid-sized jet on a highway, when they could more easily employ any number of attack helicopters; their military resources are endless."

"Alright, this isn't the Assembly, but definitely another competitor with enough resources and pluck to get at Fox first. For the moment, who they are doesn't matter. If we don't overtake them, we become targets when we arrive at the site."

"Yes sir, but it might not be as bad as we think. They probably won't have that much of an advantage."

"Go on, captain."

"A small jet landing on the highway leaves them with a very small force, which means, their only hope is speed; a smash and grab, but it's a poor tactic. They won't have the man-power and they'll get caught with no backup, between the G11's and us."

"And we deploy, how?"

"They have an immediate logistical problem. How could they make it from the turn-off, to Raptor Park? Fokker T950s have a relatively small fuselage and weight capacity and no sizable cargo doors. That only leaves one possibility: a motorbike off-load."

"A team on motorbikes. They can't have too many men."

"Two or three at best, sir."

Vogel's body began to tense as he considered the captain's assessment of their situation. They needed to fight their way into the contest, which could be ruinous to their overall chances of success.

"Wake the men, captain. From here on, it's full alert."

Chapter Sixty Eight

Tom thought he understood the desperation on the priest's face, but it didn't make this strange moment any more real.

I have to do something ... We're dead ... All of us, if I don't.

"Nico, I have a gun and I'm going to take it out and use it if I have to."

"Keep your hands up, Tom. I mean it. You move and I'll kill you."

"You can't win. If you shoot me, the Prize is lost to you. So, drop the gun and we'll work this out."

The priest raised his weapon and jabbed it towards Tom's face, as a steady stream of tears ran down his cheeks and into his beard.

Oh God ... He's going to do it.

Just when he felt the clergyman might shoot, he heard the softest of voices beside him.

"Are you going to kill me too, Nico?"

The priest spun round and glared at Isobel. He looked into that beautiful, innocent face. Could he shoot her? No. Tom didn't think so.

Father Dominico Rossi wailed as he dropped to his knees; the gun falling from his hand as his forehead sank forward into the dirt.

"I've killed her, Noah ... Em and all of my brethren. The Assembly found the safe-house and used them against me. Now they're all dead."

You poor, poor man ... What kind of devil forces a man to make a decision like that. If these bastards held Isobel, would I make the same choice?

Tom watched Noah lower himself and kneel beside his comrade. As he patted his back, the priest's chest started to heave and he threw up.

"Bring it all up, old friend. This kind of foulness has to come out."

———————

Isobel rushed in and the others helped her to raise the fallen priest. She understood his predicament; forced into an impossible choice by monsters.

The priest turned towards her and their eyes met.

"I'm so sorry, Isobel ... My beautiful Emma. I thought ..."

"You thought you could save her. Nobody should be made to do that. Hell can't be worse than this."

"I've been a fool. I so much wanted to believe ... But the truth is, they're doomed and have been since they found her."

"We need to bring this Assembly down. They need to pay for what they've done."

It seemed unreal that she felt so compelled to hug and stroke the man who just threatened their lives. She studied the faces around him. Noah looked traumatised and Tom, plain angry. As she considered this, she noticed him nod as if making up his mind

346

about something. He put his hand on Noah's shoulder and pointed towards a distant group of hills.

"Noah, do you see that ridge and clump of trees over there, to the south-west?"

"Tom, no. After what's just happened I think we should stick together."

"Did you trust my father's judgement, Noah?"

"Yes."

"Then trust me."

Noah seemed reluctant to move. He looked up at the ridge, shook his head slowly and turned back towards the others.

"Only to the ridge, Tom. That's as far as I'm prepared to go. We can cover you from there and I can protect Isobel ... For a time at least."

Isobel looked back at the priest. He appeared to have recovered some of his resolve. Noah gave him Tom's orders and he also nodded his agreement. She didn't feel as inclined.

If I leave. I might never see him again.

The word *love*, flashed through her mind and she shivered.

I felt love before my parent's died, but not since ... Until he came.

"I'm not going. I'm staying here with Tom."

"You're going, Iz. Noah will carry you if he has to. It's too dangerous here."

"Exactly, I ..."

What could she say?

I'll die with you ... because I think I'm falling for you.

A strange thought appeared in her conscious mind, so natural that it felt as if it always dwelled there. In that moment it seemed perfectly normal to be thinking about her sex life. She wanted him to touch her and it didn't feel awful, it felt liberating.

Wow. I want to and it's alright.

She wanted to be esteemed by him as well as herself, but with this last thought, came panic.

"Alright, I'll go if I have to, but you have to promise that you'll stay alive."

His smile brought pangs to her chest and for a second or two, her legs felt like jelly and her knees wobbled.

"Stay alive ... For you?"

"Yes, for me."

"Good ... Then I'll do my best, Iz."

———————

The air shimmered with heat, making it difficult for Tom to discern any actual movement up on the ridge. At forty-five degrees Celsius the temperature played tricks with his vision and threatened to empty his eyes of all moisture.

He shaded them with his hand and once again, attempted to follow the progress of his retreating friends.

I hope this isn't the last time I see them.

His heart began to pound.

I have to survive. I have to see her again.

He searched the horizon once more, but couldn't see them through the shifting mirage.

They're gone.

He took one last look at the sky.

This it ... I have to do this for everyone's sake.

He climbed down through the steel entrance and disappeared into the darkness.

Chapter Sixty Nine

Noah tried to avoid them, but the wheels of their vehicle continued to smash into potholes and gullies. With each violent jolt, Isobel's brain felt detached, as it bounced and sloshed inside her skull.

"Hell, Noah. Slow down. You're giving me whiplash."

They bush-bashed their way from the site, racing towards an elevated area to the south.

"Sorry, Isobel. I know it's rocky and uneven, but we need to get there fast. We have to get out of sight so we can give Tom covering fire, if he needs it."

Isobel twisted in her seat, searching for Tom, but she couldn't see him. Then, not for the first time on this awful journey, she wondered what life might be like without him.

"How will he survive, Noah?"

"He's a brave lad, Isobel."

Isobel heard the priest's grunt. She thought it sounded angry. Judging the vehicle's wild jerks she leant forward and searched his tear-streaked face.

"You don't think he's brave, Nico?"

When he turned and looked at her, she felt scared. His wide eyes searched backwards and forwards with a look of desperation, like a wild animal cornered by a mortal enemy.

"He's on a fool's journey. Tell her the truth, Noah."

"He's a strong lad, he'll be fine."

The priest began to shout at Noah and Isobel recoiled in her seat. She didn't like what he said.

"That's simplistic rubbish, Noah. The truth is … we don't know what'll happen and there are extra risks."

Isobel raised her voice and screamed just to be heard.

"What does he mean, Noah? What extra risks?"

Noah ended his furious eye contact with the priest and turned towards Isobel. He hesitated for a few moments before he began.

"Tom's father didn't get the chance to finish his research on the Prize before they killed him. It could be unstable for a human to …"

"What if Tom uses this thing?"

The priest cut back into the conversation, his voice snarling with anger.

"Tell her, Noah. It's a dangerous substance. Anything could happen."

Isobel attempted to stand upright in the jerking vehicle, but the seatbelt held her back. She fumbled with the latch and once free, she began to yell.

"Stop. Stop the car. Stop."

Noah slammed on the brakes without thinking, which gave Isobel the time she needed. She fled the vehicle before either man could react.

Alright, I've got to run … Hard. I've got to get back to Tom, before the Assembly get here.

She took one last look over her shoulder before she left. The priest sat very still with his face in his hands, while Noah waved his arm, gesturing for her to return.

She smiled at him and he stopped waving.

Goodbye, boys. I hope I get to see you again.

She turned towards the cavern's entrance and started to run.

Chapter Seventy

As Tom climbed down the metal ladder into the darkness, he counted forty-seven steps, before his feet came in contact with the cavern's floor. He took several more tentative steps away from the stairs, before the oppressiveness of the cavern enveloped him.

Panic set in and the muscles stiffened along his spine.

Keep calm ... Turn on the light.

He fumbled with the torch, as he tried to find the on-off switch and when he turned it in his hand, he saw its faint glow.

Bloody hell. It's already on. What kind of dark magic is this?

Then he remembered his father's warning. His words seemed like an understatement. The black emptiness of the cavern felt like it sucked the light from his torch. In this dark abyss, he lost all ability to determine direction.

"Come on ... Relax ... Breathe."

He stilled his mind, then slowed the intake of oxygen until his attack of anxiety subsided.

More black magic.

He began to feel a strange elevation of thought, as if this new awareness somehow compensated for the lack of light.

Am I imagining this?

He could hear the long vertical leaves of distant eucalyptus trees rustling in the hot breeze. He could hear motorbike engines revving in the distance. He could also determine female voices from faraway and the sound of feet pounding the ground in a panicked run.

I've heard those voices before.

"Uta ..."

He tried to remember the sound and tone of the other women's voice: 'I'll find you no matter where you go.'

It's the auburn-haired monster who chased me in London ... Speaking with Uta. Oh my God, they're here together.

He shook his head in the darkness.

I get it.

They looked and acted the same and rode together towards Raptor Park; hardly a coincidence.

"That's just great. They're twins and they're working together, against us."

The heightening of his thought continued and he began to see his life with remarkable clarity. Every event in his world seemed connected, like a multitude of individual strings, skilfully woven into a perfect rope.

The word *destiny* appeared in his mind, but its association with the death of his parents made his chest tighten with anger.

It can only get better. It's been crappy so far.

With an effort, Tom dragged his mind back to his present circumstances. Having no sense of direction inside the cavern, he needed a way to start his search. He began by walking in the opposite direction from the stairs. On his twenty-first step he collided with a hard surface. He took a step back and aimed the torch at the wall.

I'm less than a metre away and it's invisible.

He decided to turn off the torch and save the batteries, but in his fumbled attempts to find the switch, he dropped it.

It didn't make any sound.

He kicked the ground and slapped his thigh, but the sound that normally accompanied the action, didn't occur. Even yelling, made little difference. The noise seemed to vanish the moment it left his mouth. He could only determine resonance as an internal reverberation or a strange knowing of sound outside of the cavern.

I need help ... I need the letter.

He squatted down and fumbled around until he found the torch. Balancing his weight on the balls of his feet, he rested the paper on his right knee, flicked on the torch, placed it as close as possible to the script and began to read.

Dear Tom,

I must again stress that the letter you are reading is only for you. Even our special friends are to be excluded from its contents. My reasons will become obvious as you read on.

I am very proud of you, my son. Your journey must have been terrible and your previous living arrangements equally unbearable, but I do believe necessary in avoiding disaster.

Tom, you know now that the cavern contains the Prize. Only a select group from the Assembly board know the meaning of the Prize. It is now time for you to understand your destiny, which you share inexorably with this Prize.

As you are already aware of the basic truths concerning the Angels and their suits, I will skip most of the history.

The discovery of these alien suits allowed the Assembly to create the fraudulent Seven Angels, yet the same suits started to bring them undone. Once the Assembly's first born sons put them on, they became trapped and although they lived an elevated life, they experienced it as a brief existence compared to our standards. They lived the experience of the ages, for each of our years, but to our eyes, they grew old quickly. I estimate that only one or two could possibly survive into your time.

When the Assembly sons began dying horribly, they hired me to find a means to reverse their decline. That's when I found the Prize in the cavern; the place where it all started.

Over time, I discovered that the alien blood-like substance contained only a small similarity to the DNA structure of the suits, which we assume the original owners hid to counter possible blood loss.

I began experimenting with the alien DNA strands using gene sequencers and vastly better computers than are available at present. I managed to come up with a modified DNA, which I believed enabled humans some compatibility with the suits.

This now brings us to the difficult part, Tom. Back then, I didn't want to test my findings on another human being until I personally proved its safety. The Assembly didn't agree and, after a lot of argument, their heavies injected me with the compound.

I suffered at first, but after only a short time, I began to feel healthy and experience heightened senses, such as sight, hearing, smell and awareness. I didn't, however, gain the super powers of the Angels nor the immortality of their suits.

When your mother started to show signs of her pregnancy, I became worried about how this alien DNA might affect you, but apart from a super IQ, you didn't present with any other observable indicators in your early years.

In subsequent tests on live human organs, I determined that the Prize, in its purest, unaltered form, dramatically changed human flesh, yet the same tests created different results when applied to your blood work.

Tom, I have worked hard to make sure that you are the one who finds the Prize; you are the only person I could ever trust with this paranormal Excalibur.

By now, you will fully understand the danger involved. If the Prize is correctly harnessed, it has the power to resurrect the Angels and we can never allow that to happen. Any wearer, who has the benefit of an alien DNA, might live almost indefinitely; consider the life span of the suits for instance.

This is not a situation that we can tolerate. At their prime, the Angels became an unstoppable force and their alien nature made them objects of worship, even without the Angelic disguise.

Tom, it is my shame to send you on this terrible journey, knowing that every possible outcome has undesirable consequences. Unfortunately, you have no choice and must follow through, no matter what.

The Assembly are frightened of you; frightened that they may not be able to control you if you're the one to administer the Prize, so they will hunt you and try to end your life.

Once you find the Prize, you should inject, into a vein, all of the liquid that can be found in the second and adjoining chamber of the cavern. Once the liquid has started to take effect, there is no return. If you are under pressure you may swallow the substance, but it will be a far slower and more painful undertaking.

Leave absolutely none of the material, for it only takes a small amount to regrow and for some unknown reason it has a need to recreate itself. Strangely, this process ceases, once seven of these creatures have been created. If the Assembly gain even the tiniest portion, they could create another six of these powerful beings and they have the suits, which add to their strength and range of capabilities.

As I write this my beautiful son, I am sitting here imagining you sleeping and it is not that hard to envisage the man in the boy. Go to your destiny now Tom, with our love. It will be difficult, but always remember, we will be with you in spirit.

Dad.

P.S. The back of this letter contains a small map of the separate caverns, where in one, you will find the Prize.

Tom tried to picture his father sitting by his side, but his concentration became saturated by an unwanted understanding of his heritage.

I'm part alien. God knows what will happen once I take the stuff?

His entire expectations came down to either a horrible death at the hands of his enemies, or the possibility of suffering a supernatural nightmare that could turn him into something horrific and even more alien.

Chapter Seventy One

The two black-clad riders raced their BMW trail bikes along the main track before reaching the end of the Maneroo Creek Flood Plain.

Uta noticed the offshoot, which she didn't need to relay to her twin. In unison they turned south, travelling through the dry watercourse to where it joined the junction of Spring and Sancho Creeks.

As they approached the dry creek bed they slowed their pace creating no obvious dust trails.

We've almost made it to Raptor Park and it doesn't seem like anyone spotted us.

Without any signal, they both eased to a stop and Uta pointed into the distance.

"Réz, do you see their dust. It looks like the G11's are moving up towards that ridge."

"It's a good position, except for helicopters. They must be trying to cover Fox from there."

They preceded west up Spring Creek, encountering a continuous quantity of tree fall, sink holes and exposed tree roots and their progress slowed even further. Uta could see that the watercourse suffered from infrequent, but damaging storms, where a sudden deluge could tear the landscape, sending trees and debris tumbling down the gully.

It took longer than their original estimates, but eventually they found the smaller tributary that joined them from the south. One hundred metres further along, they hid the bikes and entered the plain.

They proceeded with caution. The dig site sat near the middle of an open and exposed area.

"I'm glad we got here before Vogel and Wolf, Réz. We couldn't cover any of this ground without being noticed."

"The G11's haven't made it to the top of the ridge yet. We should get a clear passage. Let's make haste my love."

In the flat surrounds, both women spotted the open metal-hatch and the fresh piles of earth lying nearby. They proceeded at a run, keeping as low as possible. Then Uta stopped and took hold of her sister's arm.

"Réz. You hear that? Quick. Get down behind that pile of dirt on the left. I'll take the other pile to the right."

"It looks like Vogel's made good time, Uta, but we'll only have to wait for a moment. The fool's taken the longest route and gone up the far tributary. It gives us plenty of time to get the job done."

"It also gives us a safe line of retreat to the bikes and good cover when the killing starts."

Uta stopped talking. She spotted movement further out on the plain.

"Réz. Look."

A girl emerged from the creek bed directly south of their position and ran across the open plain towards them.

Uta smiled in wonderment.

How opportune. Little girl, you've made my day.

"Time for a new plan, Réz my love. Stay here and cover me. Only fire if it's necessary. I'll stay hidden until the girl is close. Fox must be in the cavern. I'll capture her and take her down. He'll give us whatever we want for her."

"Don't waste time, Uta. I won't be able to hold this position if things get too hot."

Between bandages Uta's mouth stretched into a smirk.

"Vogel won't wait long before he approaches the cavern. When the shooting starts, he's the target. The others will fall away and run once he's dead. They have no cover and no choice. Then we can make our exit just as we planned."

Isobel's throat felt like fire; she could hardly swallow as she ran. She felt on the verge of passing out.

Oh God. I hope this isn't the most stupid thing I've ever done.

She knew she needed to stay positive. Her foolish act could compromise Tom's position and both of the men she left behind.

It's too bloody late to worry about it now. I have to keep going.

Nothing mattered, other than the entrance to that cavern.

She started to stagger only metres from the hatch and didn't notice the physical presence directly in front of her.

Isobel screamed.

"My God … No … You're supposed to be dead."

"The devil spat me back out, so I could come back for you."

Uta forced the barrel of her spitter into the side of Isobel's head.

"Get down that hole. We're going to see your boyfriend."

Chapter Seventy Two

Noah attempted to gain some control over his emotions, yet his chest heaved and his heart continued to race, he felt so furious.

"Nico. My God. Look what your idiotic truth has done. Put her right out in the open."

"I'm so sorry, Noah. It's my fault. I just couldn't hold the anger in."

"We'll have to go back for her."

"No. I'm not sure that's a good idea."

"Look, I know you're hurting, Nico, but we can't just let her run straight at our enemies."

"The only way we can protect her now, is from up here. You know I'm right, Noah. She's far safer in that hole with Tom."

Noah's face tightened into an angry grimace. He felt annoyed with his friend, despite the pain he must be feeling.

"Nico. I loved Emma too, but now we have to take care of the living."

Noah tried to wrestle their vehicle over an outcrop of rocky ground and at the same time follow Isobel's progress across the plain. With each of her ungainly loping strides, he silently urged her forward, but with a thud, they dropped down into the dry bed of Sancho Creek and his stomach clenched in fear as he lost sight of her.

Run, Isobel. Get down that hole as fast as you can girl.

They slid and bounced across the creek and headed directly south towards the wooded ridge. Noah knew it provided a view of the entire area and created cover for their vehicle and themselves.

As he approached, he made a quick assessment of their intended position.

"You're right, Nico. From here, our spitters will cut down anyone who approaches Tom's position. This's the right place for us."

Noah drove through the loose sand and up the bank, but he still couldn't see the girl. Once they made the ridge, he jumped from the vehicle to get a clearer view of the events occurring back at the site.

"There's a lot of dust to the north of us, Nico. The enemy are moving in fast."

"Forget the dust, Noah. Look … Look at the entrance."

"I can't see … Wait … Oh no."

Noah let out an anguished gasp.

"Isobel …?"

He could just distinguish her tiny frame contrasted against a taller and more powerful figure. Even from this distance, Noah could discern the woman's cat like movements.

"Uta."

───────────────

Tom attempted to consult his father's map, but it made little sense to him in this directionless void. He could determine down and up, but little else.

I'll have to use my hands and slide them along the wall to see if I can find an opening into the next chamber.

He fumbled along, stepping first, then reaching with out-stretched fingers along the black, absorbent wall. He counted twenty-one as he stretched again along the chalky surface, but it vanished and he fell with arms flailing, into complete nothingness.

He attempted to twist and throw a leg out for balance, but he spun too far and his back smacked onto the ground, followed by his heels and the back of his head.

Keep calm ... Breathe evenly and wait for a moment.

He stayed on his back for several minutes, in a bid to reorientate his senses.

Is everything different down here, or is it just my perception?

His senses seemed magnified in this strange cavern, especially the feeling of being lost.

He took a deep breath and raised himself up onto his right elbow. He could feel his composure returning. Then he noticed the glow.

"There's light."

I've landed in the hidden chamber. That must be it ... The Prize.

Tom could see two rectangular objects, each roughly the size of a small toolbox, no more than ten metres from where he lay. Moments after he fell into the chamber, one of the containers began to glow an eerie green.

That's weird. It must somehow be aware of my presence.

Uta raged, her strategy faltering before it got a chance to begin; her plan requiring the light from Fox's torch to manoeuvre in the darkness. She didn't see a light, only claustrophobic darkness.

Damn it. I could've sneaked up close to him before he saw me.

Uta grabbed Isobel by the hair; yanking it until she cried out in pain.

"Scream, bitch."

She saw her scream, but heard nothing.

"Hey, Fox. I've got your girlfriend hostage. I'll kill her if you don't show."

She roared her statement into the blackness, with little result. The sound of her voice seemed to vanish into the silence; sucked directly from her mouth.

"You hearing this Fox? Come save your girlie, before I slit her throat."

Uta clicked her tongue in annoyance.

She growled in anger and gave Isobel's hair another tug. Then she saw it.

"My God. It glows."

Without thinking, Tom stepped out fifteen metres towards the middle of the cavern, which, when he thought about it, seemed like a fatalistic positioning, as if he intended to sacrifice himself on some unseen central altar.

Once there, he lifted the lid of the luminous container and looked inside. It contained only one item: a glowing metal canister, the size of a large test tube. He reached out and touched the object and immediately removed his hand. Instead of being hot, it felt cold and wet with condensation. Tom opened the remaining container and discovered an empty vial and a large syringe.

Just what I need to send me to hell.

Chapter Seventy Three

V ogel entered Raptor Park via a small and very rough tributary. He came in from the north-west to avoid open conflict; not wanting to fight any battles in gaining the field. Only the Prize mattered. He needed the easiest, protected access to that goal.

It took another ten minutes of travel up the tributary before they entered the larger, dry bed of Spring Creek. Here the captain stopped and pointed.

"We can take up a defensive position along the bank beside that fallen tree, sir."

"Why here?"

"Because of the cover. It serves our needs for the moment, until I can find the best possible entry point for our team to cross the plain."

"As far away from our competitors as possible?"

"Yes. I'm sure they'll take the more direct route."

Vogel followed him up the steep embankment and watched as his man surveyed the area.

"I can't see any sign of the G11's, or the motorcycle team. If there are any vehicles here, they're not moving at the moment."

Vogel snatched the glasses and studied the area for himself.

"If they're not on the plain, then where are they?"

"On the far ridge or the adjacent creek bed, is my bet. They're the best vantage points and the easiest places to defend."

"How do we get to Fox, captain?"

"I saw fresh piles of earth out there, right next to an open metal-hatch. I'd bet it's where Fox is. To get there we need the shortest approach. We're too late to control the ridge, we'll just have to take our chances utilising as much speed as possible, but we need to go now, before more forces arrive."

The captain ran his men hard, before deploying them briefly along the banks of Spring Creek, some two hundred metres to the west. From here, they moved onto the plain, with one of the men remaining at the fallen tree and a second, scouting west to cover their advance.

No-one considered setting a serious rear guard. If they didn't get there first, they could never fight their way out.

Wolf's mouth twisted into a scowl as he tightened and bunched the pterygoid muscles controlling his jaw. He set standards and he expected compliance; nothing less, yet the cohesive communications needed to complete his planned encircling of two different enemies, lacked the precision he required.

"Sergeant. What in heaven is going on? I need you to confirm that our men are in place."

"Yes sir. Group one has arrived from the east, through Hartree Station and are in place. Group two are coming up from the south along Vergemont Creek and through Highfields. They'll be in position within ten minutes. From here we'll hold the high ground, as you ordered."

"Good. Keep me informed of every movement. Ours and theirs."

Wolf felt relieved. The completion of his first goal set a trap that effectively out-manoeuvred Fox's G11 squad, the mystery woman and Vogel's team, simultaneously creating a crucible that couldn't be escaped.

I have to keep my team focused on the plan. The key is to force the other competitors into tactically vulnerable positions, as far away from the Prize as possible and destroy them; quick and clean, leaving Fox isolated and helpless.

A beep from his communicator announced the arrival of a message from Rome. One name stood out in a page containing several hundred words.

"Uta."

Reports from Albury airport indicated that Uta Cel Rău, the former SRP operative, may have boarded the aircraft containing the mystery woman. Amongst a ream of other information, he also discovered that the other woman resembled Uta in appearance.

Interesting. A coincidence? I don't think so.

Rome didn't seem aware of this anomaly and he decided to keep it that way.

I think I know who our mystery woman is; information that may prove useful. I might need some leverage with the Assembly before this's over. Whoever these women are, they're bold and confident.

He knew from experience that non-fanatical soldiers, displaying this kind of persona, usually felt assured of a victory.

What's the trick?

All of his projections indicated that only a surprise pulled from a magician's bag of tricks, could save anyone once his trap closed.

So what do they have that I'm not seeing?

As he considered the possible threats posed by these women, he absentmindedly rubbed at his neck; his fingers massaging stiffening muscles.

And what should I make of this Assembly aircraft following us from Rome?

It smelt like a setup. He did the dirty work and another team cleaned up. He didn't fancy being dead this early in his career. Only a fool played with snakes without some sort of antivenin.

His face expanded into a smile.

Owning the Prize should do the job for me.

Crouched behind her pile of dumped earth, Réz took note of the forces gathering around her.

"Damn it, Uta. Answer me."

Nothing.

This can only be a communicator malfunction, or ... Uta's unable to answer because she's dead or injured.

A sigh rasped from her lungs.

Surely I'd know.

Either scenario presented her with several blind choices: hold, make a run for it, or get into the hole and finish the job herself, but one big problem presented itself. If Uta remained operational, any advance by her sister compromised their entire plan.

She spotted the dust. As predicted, Vogel approached the site and Wolf couldn't be far from making his entrance.

This isn't going to be good.

The piles of red earth protected her from both groups, but she began to detect additional movement as another group of soldiers advanced along the southern ridges, leaving her exposed.

If I stay here I'm going to be target practice for someone.

Waiting meant death, which only left her two options. She could either make a run for the cavern, or pull back to the bikes and try to cover Uta's retreat.

It's an easy decision. I'll never make it to the hole.

Réz ran, stooping as much as possible, as she covered the last twenty metres. Here she became visible to possible snipers at the western end of Spring Creek. She saw movement and increased her pace to a sprint; diving and rolling over the edge to safety.

She recovered quickly and attempted to stand, but flinched when something hard jammed into the back of her neck. She didn't need to see it.

Damn it ... It's a gun.

Chapter Seventy Four

Tom jumped backwards in surprise, as two ghoulish phantoms moved out of the darkness towards him; one with a face like a striped hyena, hideous in her triumph, the other its victim, terrified in her plight.

Misery grew large in Tom's mind. A scarred Uta stood in front of him; one of her hands gripping Isobel's neck and pushing her forward.

"Izzi ...?"

How could this be possible?

He focused on Isobel's pained expression, trying hard to connect. He understood her fear. Death seemed imminent.

Tom didn't notice Uta closing in on him until he suffered her tugging his hair. Then another pain shot through his temple, as the barrel of her spitter collided with the side of his head.

He felt her breath on his cheek as she leaned in close; yelling directly into his ear.

"If you want your bitch to live, Fox, then start walking. We're getting out of this hole, so I'm going to let go of you. Don't do anything stupid, or I'll kill her."

For protection Vogel placed a ring of men around himself, with their captive, the auburn-haired vixen from Villa Dal Santo, acting as his shield against Uta and her spitter.

Ten metres from their destination, Vogel stopped the group with a raised hand and whispered to his captain.

"I want silence. Order them all to keep quiet."

As they approached the entrance to the cavern, Frederick stiffened and pulled back in surprise. He could see a head emerging from its depths; a female, but not Uta and because they crossed the field from a different direction, she didn't see them.

Vogel concentrated on the small, soot-covered feminine frame. It took him a moment to recognise her.

The Kite girl.

When she saw him, she backed away. He noticed that she seemed stunned, but complied with his wishes as he raised his weapon and placed a finger to his lips for silence. Then another head began to appear.

Fox ... And he's got it with him.

The skin on Vogel's neck began to prickle. Fox carried the glowing object in front of him, with reverence.

The Prize.

Vogel started forward, but stopped when he spotted the barrel of a spitter extending upwards from the black hole.

Uta.

The barrel of every other gun moved from Fox to the rising woman, as she took the last step up the ladder.

No. Don't move. Don't give us away, Fox.

The young man stood as stiff as a corpse, but Vogel saw his eyes move and so did Uta. Before they could react, she bounded

372

off the ladder and pulled Tom and the Prize, in front of her for protection. No-one fired; her instant change of speed defeating them.

Despite the tension, Frederick almost laughed at the woman's stupidity. She began to yell, once out of the cavern.

"Don't move, Vogel. Fox is the only one who knows what to do with this thing. I'll kill him if you do. Tell your dogs to back away."

"You're in no position to give me orders, Uta. I've got five guns aimed at you."

"You won't shoot, Vogel. Not if it means damaging the Prize. Move your men back and we can make a deal."

"How ...? There's only one Prize and only one outcome."

Vogel quickly realised his predicament. A stand-off wasted valuable time, which brought Wolf into play.

He feigned interest, giving her a slight bow of agreement. At the same time he adjusted his position and winked at the captain. He saw understanding in his man's expression. If a clear shot presented itself ... Take her down.

"Alright, you've got a few seconds. Convince me."

"I've seen the Prize, Vogel. There's a syringe. We can share it."

"How's that possible?"

"There's enough of this stuff for both of us. We can both win."

"I don't believe you."

She shoved Tom's head forward with the palm of her hand.

"Ask him, if you don't believe me."

Vogel prided himself on his ability to differentiate between the truth and a lie. Even trained subtlety rarely escaped him and he knew she told at least some of the truth.

Could he trust her? No way, but I still can't take the shot.

While they negotiated, Uta placed Isobel in front of Tom, so she could protect both herself and the Prize.

Frederick felt frustrated and a moment of panic.

Damn it. I can't risk open conflict.

He couldn't allow it to be damaged, not unless their time ran out.

"Alright, how do you propose we do this?"

"We split the Prize and we trade. You can have Fox and his bitch and I'll have my sister."

"I'm not liking what I'm hearing, Uta. With only one canister and one syringe, how can we realistically share this thing? Come on now, your time's up."

"That's easy. I'll go first."

Without waiting for an answer, Uta reached into the box and removed the canister, while continuing to maintain Fox and the girl as her shield.

Vogel could see her dilemma.

This's our chance ... Be ready.

Carrying the spitter left her only one hand to work with and she couldn't trade security for efficiency; her gun remained pointed at him. With her free hand, she placed the canister between her legs and grasped it with her inner thighs. This allowed her to retrieve the syringe, but at the critical moment, she dropped it.

"Fox. Pick it up and hand it to me. Hurry."

Vogel tensed. Fox didn't move. He started to put pressure on the trigger, then he heard him speak.

"You can just drink it. It works the same. You only need a few drops."

Uta looked like she didn't believe him, but didn't hesitate. She flicked off the canister's latch and took a small sip of the Prize.

In that moment, Frederick noticed the slightest change in the wind's direction and with it a warning that they all heard.

"Helicopters."

Vogel took a firm grip of his weapon.

No matter the risk, I have to shoot her now ... My time's up.

He saw the sister move, but too late. In that precise instant, Réz jerked backwards into his body, recovered quickly and dived to her left. At the same time, Uta sprayed them with bullets. Without taking aim, he returned her fire.

Damn it, Wolf's arrived ... He risks killing Fox and damaging the Prize ... Why?

The field around him erupted with noise, as projectiles from an Assembly helicopter cut through his men. With the wild swirling dust, the shooting seemed to be coming from points all around him.

Find cover ... Get down.

He dived for the ground, landing hard on his stomach, as bullets whizzed around him. Through the clouds of dust, he attempted to search for a means of escape. In that moment, he spotted Fox falling to his knees with a look of shock on his face.

No. Not yet. I need you alive.

Fox stared down at a weeping green wound that frothed and bubbled where, moments before, a bullet exploded into his stomach.

Chapter Seventy Five

Noah and the priest lay stretched out, face-first on the ground, covered by handfuls of tossed red dirt for camouflage.

Noah felt taut with stress. His finger quivered; trembling, as it rested with only the slightest feathery pressure on the trigger. He didn't know how long he could hold on without firing, when only five hundred metres away, out on the bare plain, two groups of enemies threatened the lives of their comrades.

"We've got to do something, Nico. If we allow this to go any further …"

"No, wait … Don't shoot. They're too tightly grouped. We don't want to hit Tom, or Isobel."

"Shh … Enemy … Lay still."

Only metres away he could hear the crunch of boots on gravel.

Damn it to hell.

Noah felt his stomach heave with fear as the men approached them. With each step their precarious advantage slipped away.

Gently, he nudged the priest with his elbow and whispered.

"Do you hear that, Nico? Helicopters … They're approaching us from different directions."

"Yes. I can see one over in the Spring Creek direction, near where we entered the area, but he's holding back; staying at the edge of the plain."

"I count five and not all of them are staying put. Look. One's heading for the cavern."

As gunfire erupted out on the field, Noah twisted and stretched his neck to take in the view. He saw bodies falling near the entrance to the cavern, then a new series of gunfire began along the creek beds to the north of their position.

"Nico. Keep down. They're coming."

As the enemy behind them ran forward to join the battle, the two dirt-covered men regained their freedom to act.

Noah raised his weapon to fire, but stopped when a hand grasped his wrist.

"Look, old friend … Look at the entrance."

Noah tried to focus his vision through his high-definition telescopic viewfinder. Through clouds of billowing dust he caught a glimpse of Isobel clinging to a wounded man.

"Tom."

His protégé knelt in a puddle of dark blood, his head and shoulders stooped, as he clutched at a green stain around his mutilated stomach. He looked about to fall; only Isobel's frantic efforts held him upright.

The swirling of the helicopter's rotors seemed to suck the oxygen right out of Tom's mouth.

They're firing at us. I've got to get Isobel down that hole.

He grabbed for her, but in doing so, Uta's weapon caught in the crook of his elbow and the hot barrel seared his skin.

"Get out of my way, Fox."

She swore and reefed it out, spinning Tom around, and they collided as she tried to push past him. A cold object bounced off his shoulder and without thinking, he caught it and grasped it against his stomach.

Oh, God.

Before he could move, a new pain assaulted his mind. He cried out, as burning hot metal ripped into his stomach and exploded his insides to mush.

Tom grabbed at his belly and fell to his knees, as the madness around him continued to intensify. He could see Uta running with the red-headed killer he recognised from the cul-de-sac in England, and he spotted Vogel lying flat on the ground, yelling something to his men.

He also saw Vogel's captain suffering in his attempts to return fire. Bullets bombarded the ground all around him. The man raised himself up on one knee and began to flap his arms about. Tom saw blood pouring from his mouth, as he bucked in jerky spasms. Then the dust swallowed him and everybody else.

It's over ... I've lost.

———————

Uta dived to the ground, rolling and firing before the others. Like any exceptional soldier, she knew that thinking became the ultimate distraction in any critical moment. She defeated her enemies because they wasted time to reason. Action meant life, reaction ... death.

Her first volley killed one of Vogel's men, but she avoided firing wide groupings of bullets at the man himself because of his proximity to Réz.

I have to give up that canister to the Assembly. I can't get back to get it.

She tried to discern her enemy's movements, but the dust obscured everything.

What's this fool of a pilot doing?

It did have some benefits. The storm of dirt covered her retreat, gifting her the opportunity to escape. In a blur of movement, she jumped to her feet, grabbed Réz and ran low across the open plain towards Spring Creek and their waiting motorcycles.

Once clear of the dust, she could see that Vogel and his remaining forces lay pinned down out in the open and that only fifty metres south of the bikes, Vogel's one remaining scout, fired west up the ridge at Wolf's men.

We've got away with it ... We're out.

They lifted their pace, running hard towards a clump of eucalypt trees that lined the dry river bed.

No ... They've seen us.

With their sanctuary in sight, a group of soldiers from the Sancho Creek area began shooting in their direction and a projectile zinged close to Uta's face.

"Get down, Réz."

She looked for any possible cover, as a deadly stream of bullets began filling the air.

Damn it.

Together they dived to the ground and slid into a shallow depression, as lead and copper slugs smacked into the earth all around them.

For several precious moments, the last of Vogel's scouts opened fire on the group that kept them pinned down. Then the barrage aimed at them, ceased. Uta didn't wait. She grabbed Réz and tried to crawl forward, but the weight of her sister pulled her back.

"Réz, get up."

Réz's hands remained tied behind her back and with each thrust of her legs, Uta dragged her sister's face into the earth.

She smiled to herself as she grunted with the effort it took to haul her forward.

I should keep this up. A few more minutes and we'll share the same scars.

"Réz. Stop struggling and open your mouth."

Uta rolled her over onto her back and spat liquid down her throat.

"Enjoy."

Despite being under fire, Uta thought to retain the tiniest amount of green liquid, which she held in the pockets of her cheeks. Even this miniscule amount caused Réz to gag, as the freezing cold liquid hit her throat.

She stared up at Uta in disbelief.

"You did it?"

"Just for you my love."

Uta sprang back into action. She cut the bonds around Réz's wrists and they both rushed towards the relative safety of the creek bed. Just before they jumped over the side, Uta took one last look at the carnage behind them.

That pilot's a first-class tool.

She watched the helicopter move off towards the south-east, creating columns of dust as it went. Between the swirling clouds, she managed to get a glimpse of the field. She saw bodies scattered everywhere, but she couldn't determine whether Vogel lay with his men.

Uta roared with delight, as she plunged over the bank to join her half-sister. Even knowing the risk of swallowing the Prize, she felt elated.

For good or bad, it's inside of us now. Either it kills us, or we're invincible.

Chapter Seventy Six

Pain exploded through Tom's body and he heard himself cry out. At that moment, despite his blurred vision, he caught sight of Isobel and realised what he must do.

"Izzi … No. Stop."

He saw her attempt to rise up into the field of slaughter.

I can't let her die. I have to get her out of here.

His mind felt groggy and he couldn't think.

Where … Where should I take her?

Then he remembered that Noah and the priest hid up on the ridge. He felt a surge of joy, but when he focused on the distance they needed to cover, his elation vanished.

I've got no strength left. I'll never make it.

He couldn't even be sure if he could get to his feet.

"Izzi … Help."

He looked over at her. She seemed lethargic with shock; her eyes unfocused and vacant.

"I need you. Quick. Help me up."

She responded to the tone of urgency in his voice, helping him struggle to his feet, as random groupings of projectiles pierced the dust cloud and thumped into the ground around them. He looked up through the swirling brown and red vortex and realised the helicopter hovered directly overhead.

He yelled so Isobel could hear him.

"Iz. Where are you?"

"On my knees behind you. Stopping you from falling."

"Please. Help me up. We have to get out of here and the dust from this helicopter is our best chance."

She tried to lift him, but a clump of flying debris struck her in the face. She squealed, let him loose and covered her eyes with her hands.

The sound of her distress brought him further out of his stupor; she needed him. He didn't know how he achieved it, but he stood and lifted her into an unsteady embrace.

Then he noticed a dark shape amongst the churning dust. He brought his hand up as a shield and tried to look between his fingers.

The man's face twisted into a hateful expression.

"Vogel ..."

The wind from the helicopter's rotating blades pushed the flying dirt aside, just enough to see him raising his weapon and aiming.

"Vogel ... No."

The helicopter spun around in an arc and the dust returned. Just as the dense cloud enveloped him, he saw a flash from close by and felt a violent jolt, as something smacked hard into his body. As the sound of the report registered in his mind, the pain arrived as an explosion, then in waves that made him cry out.

A sudden understanding consumed him.

The bastard's shot me.

Vogel's bullet ripped through the joint of his left shoulder shattering bone and cartilage as it went. Once this understanding hit home, Tom couldn't believe that he remained on his feet.

I bounced off someone ... Isobel?

He turned to look for her and pain assaulted his senses. He found her staggering and out of balance; trying to stop herself from falling. She grabbed at him and dragged him towards her.

"Iz. Hold on."

He reached out, but she vanished from his grasp, as if the vast dirt plains of Queensland opened up and swallowed her. Then he felt her grasp his hips as she fell into the hole.

Tom attempted to correct the weight imbalance by throwing his right leg back, which only dislodged her grip.

"Tom. I can't hang on."

She slid all the way down his leg and in one last desperate effort, closed her fingers around his ankle.

He staggered with the weight of her momentum shift and his feet slid forward and gave way. He tried to grab at the entrance as he fell, but as his elbow made contact with the rim of the metal entrance, pain ripped down his arm and he slid off; disappearing into the darkness of the void.

Wolf ground his teeth in anger. The battle for Raptor Park may have been over, with Vogel's captain and most of his small force of men dead, but he didn't have any knowledge regarding the whereabouts of any of the other participants.

He struggled to control his temper.

How dare they interfere with my operation.

He gave strict orders to his flight crew, but an unauthorised Assembly helicopter did not obey. They entered the plain and shot anything that moved and their dust obscured the outcome of the battle, allowing the Prize and its bearer to disappear.

I know their mind. These jackals plan to collect the Prize before it gets to me.

His shoulders and neck stiffened as a thought occurred to him.

It may have been their intention all along, to include me in their clean-up operation. Dead, I'm no threat to them.

As he watched, a slight breeze drifted in and the spiralled column of dust began to move away to the east. Wolf couldn't see any movement out on the plain. Bodies lay where they fell.

The dead are all in uniform; no Vogel, no crazy women and no Fox. Where the hell are they?

It didn't seem safe to move his men onto the plain, but he needed to act.

He strode with confidence into the glare, despite the unwanted presence of this new Assembly intrusion; his soldiers forming a queue behind him to be utilised later as an inner perimeter around the site.

My men will be loyal, even if the Assembly hierarchy mean to betray me.

He claimed this victory and with it the spoils. The Prize belonged to him; its possession his only insurance against termination.

What new devilry is this?

Bruno Wolf could focus in any situation and in any given environment. Distraction meant a short career and usually death, but the sudden piercing screech from behind, brought him to a confused halt. At the edge of his peripheral vision, he saw the flickering light and his skin began to prickle.

No ... I'm so close.

He stood only metres from the greatest prize he could possibly imagine, yet in the midst of his glory, the last of the dreaded Angels appeared and he could feel his private victory slipping away.

Tom sat up, but it cost him; even the slightest movement brought excruciating pain. As his mind started to clear, he thought of Isobel. He looked into the darkness, but he couldn't see her.

"Iz ... Isobel. Where are you?"

A beautiful face appeared before him. She moved so close to him that her nose brushed his cheek.

"Iz?"

The apparition began to change. With each movement of the torch, her face became angry and distorted; each expression appearing to him as a nightmarish projection.

"Tom … Tom. Wake up."

She grabbed his shoulders and shook him.

"Iz, stop. You're hurting me."

She let go and pulled away.

"No, don't let go."

Tom could feel himself starting to slump, but she raced back and caught him, before he fell.

"Oh, Tom."

"It's alright, Iz."

Tom's brain throbbed in his skull, yet despite the pain, his mind began functioning more effectively than ever. Something tangible formed from the inflow of confused information and he felt a foul presence above, in the outside world.

I've got to move. He's here.

He tried to twist around in Isobel's arms, but fell back and almost fainted with pain. He felt a shower of dirt spill in on them from the entrance above and with a sudden boost of adrenalin, his system responded.

"Iz, quick. I need your help. He's coming in. I need you to drag me away from these stairs."

Chapter Seventy Seven

Bruno Wolf raised his right hand and his men gathered around him.

I don't have a choice ... They've got an Angel in tow.

He stopped and waited for his new enemy to approach. Only one group of men could betray him and bring him undone, but if he needed to fight his employer ...

I'll do it. Alright. Think fast.

He clamped his teeth and considered the nature of their duplicity. In one clever move, the chairman assumed total control of the Raptor Park operation and made sure that his security chief didn't become another potential enemy. An invisible gun at his head, guaranteed acquiescence.

Whilst he tried to come to terms with the Assembly's treachery, he spotted a figure striding out onto the field towards him. He recognised the man's arrogant swagger; an attitude born of self-indulgence and a lifetime of false adulation.

Why would the chairman send his son? And why the Angel, when the thing is so unstable?

He thought it reeked of desperation on the chairman's part; something he might be able to use if things got rough.

Bruno sized up his competitor as he drew near. He knew that Roberto Costa lived by the same rules as his father, that's why people referred to him as the Cobra. As the youngest and only remaining son of Antonio, the Assembly chairman, he held the rank of second in command in the world's biggest private corporation. Despite being small in stature and physically unimpressive, together with his father, he held power greater than most countries.

Their position and connections within the Assembly, give these two more personal clout than any individuals on the planet.

He looked farther back over Roberto's left shoulder, to where an enormous angelic creature hovered; the last of the Seven Angels.

He holds back and I think I know why.

The Angels inspired fear and terror. They killed without remorse and nobody could stop them, yet at the height of their power they diminished and ultimately died.

That's why this one's unstable. His time's almost up.

He noticed the body language of the one remaining colossus. He no longer seemed as invincible and he suspected that the Prize pertained to this situation. The Assembly sought power and the Angels in their prime represented the greatest force of power to ever exist.

The Prize must allow the Assembly to keep the Angels healthy; keep their power.

He looked back at the shimmering creature. He could be mistaken, but he seemed almost timid in this environment, like an elephant afraid of a mouse.

Wolf turned back and faced the interloper.

"Roberto. What in God's name are you doing here?"

"I'm here to collect our due, Wolf. We've had enough of rogue employees."

"Good. I'm glad you're here. You can save me some trouble. Just climb down into that death-pit and the Prize is yours."

Wolf realised he wasted the banter; the man couldn't be intimidated easily. The Cobra demonstrated the same mettle as his father.

Roberto smiled and walked past him towards the cavern.

"That's my intention, Wolf. Even if it's what we pay you for. Perhaps we'll have to review your salary arrangements, when this is done."

Bruno nodded with understanding; his suspicions proving to be correct.

Once he has it ... I'm dead.

He knew the deal. In such instances, mentioning an impending employee downgrade implied having a future; a type of ruse for the purpose of distracting and pacifying a victim, until they could be dispatched.

He quickened his pace; he wasn't going to be second down that hole. Securing the Prize first remained his best hope.

What now?

As he swang around to follow Costa, a group of soldiers approaching from the Spring Creek area diverted his attention.

They've left their posts without my direct orders.

His men herded two people towards him; one with flaming auburn hair and the other with her face partially covered in bandages.

Tom caught sight of a man's silhouette entering the circle of light above him. He watched him clamber down the initial section of the metal ladder and just before he disappeared into the blackness, Tom recognised the stiff jerky movements of his body.

"Vogel."

Oh God. I'm not sure I can handle this.

The pain in Tom's body kept escalating; fast approaching a point beyond his ability to manage. He wanted to cry out, but he held the scream and gulped it back down his throat.

I'm dying.

He could feel death's cold hands creeping over his body.

It's coming ... Not long now ... It's close.

It felt strange that he didn't fear it; the thought actually soothed him, yet the idea of Isobel dying alone made up for his own lack of distress. He could feel her behind, propping him up and he prayed for the strength to help her when the end came.

Ever since she appeared and became a part of his life, he agonised and exulted because of her.

If only we could have been given a little more time.

Their predicament never allowed him the opportunity to fully investigate his feelings towards her.

I never understood. How could I? I've never felt anything like this before.

His emotions seemed alien. How could he form an understanding of this strange phenomenon without time to absorb the experience of her?

Should I tell her how I feel, or would it make it worse for her?

It felt selfish, but he really needed to say something, yet even as his life ebbed, he didn't know how to begin.

Chapter Seventy Eight

Vogel felt the immediate relief of escaping death as he came down the ladder, but his liberation from fear turned from alarm to outright panic, the further he descended into the cavern.

I think I'm going to throw up.

As he lowered himself, one agonising foot after the other, he remembered deeply buried images of a young tormented face.

No ... I don't want to think about that little trouble maker.

Years earlier, he wrapped the eight-year old in a rug, before murdering her mother.

Why do I remember killing her, after disposing of so many?

He could still hear her muffled screaming, her excruciating cries for help, mixed with his laughter.

No ... Get out of my head.

He saw her face in his mind, morph from terror into mirth, but nothing about his current situation seemed at all humorous. He couldn't see the irony, just the darkness that engulfed him; a suffocating horror beyond anything he could imagine.

Pull yourself together ... You're losing control.

He closed his eyes and slowed his breathing; imagining his rise to the heights of the Assembly and beyond, and he regained a small sense of calm. He opened his eyes, flicked on his headlamp and tried to determine something of his environment.

His stance became rigid. He didn't dare make a sound. Without consciously thinking about his actions, he very slowly raised his arm and pointed.

There ... It glows and flickers, like the Angels.

After the initial shock, Vogel not only realised that he could see the light, but also that the sound of his voice reverberated off the walls.

He heard another noise and stopped moving.

Someone's behind me.

He imagined the gun; anticipating the imminent indignity of a bullet entering his back, but nothing happened. He inched his right hand downwards until he felt the smooth handle of his gun. He sucked in a nervous breath and spun around to face his enemy.

"You."

He couldn't see any guns, only a dirty young woman and a dying man.

"A little sick are we, Fox?"

"Can't you see he's dying? Leave him alone, Vogel."

Tom raised his head and Vogel could see the truth of her statement.

The girl's right. He's as good as gone.

This didn't thrill him. He needed Fox for his own salvation. He found the Prize, so he must know how to use it.

He looked from Fox back towards the centre of the cavern, to where his Prize lay waiting. Even wrapped in Fox's discarded shirt, it pulsed with a growing intensity.

He strode over and scooped it up; holding it aloft to demonstrate his victory.

"You've kept this for long enough, Fox. It now belongs to me."

With impatience, he ripped at the shirt until he held the bare metal casing; almost dropping it when his touch created an instant response from the contents. It started to flicker and intensify until the dynamics of the cavern changed. Instead of the light being lost in the black, porous walls, it lit the cave-like hall with waves of iridescent green.

He knelt on the sooty floor and continued to stare at the damaged canister.

Men are being slaughtered outside for this thing and I have it.

His thoughts sobered when he considered that he held no clue on how to use it.

Uta swallowed the stuff, but what happened to her? If I do the same, I might die a hideous death.

He turned back and glared at Tom.

I need Fox.

Frederick didn't waste a moment making up his mind. Very carefully, he laid the canister on the ground and started walking towards the girl; running the last few steps to catch her unawares. Once he gripped her arm, he spun her around and took her in a headlock, dropping to his knees and forcing her to do likewise. His free hand found his weapon and he jammed the end of the barrel into the side of her head.

"Listen very carefully, Fox. I want to know how to use the Prize. I want its secrets, or I'll kill her."

Without Isobel's support, Tom fell back; his head thumping onto the floor. Vogel heard him grunt with pain, then moan as he struggled to rise into a sitting position and face him.

"No sane person would trust you, Vogel. I want a guarantee first."

"Don't be ridiculous. There's no guarantee. I'll kill you both, if you don't do what I want."

"I don't think so. Without me, you're powerless."

"I mean it. I'll kill you, Fox."

"Bullshit. We both know what they'll do to you, if you can't use the Prize, Vogel."

He hesitated. Fox understood his predicament. He couldn't bully him.

"Alright, what guarantee?"

"That you share it with Isobel."

"No. That's impossible."

"No it's not. She goes first, then you. That's the deal."

"I'm not sharing with anybody …"

"Didn't you hear me, Vogel? You do it or you die. Make your decision."

Vogel pushed Isobel aside and stumbled to recover the canister. He noticed his hands trembling, as he handed the precious object over to Tom.

———————

Uta seethed with the frustration and humiliation of capture.

It's Réz's fault, but I won't openly blame her.

She looked over and gave her sister a knowing glance. They must keep their partaking of the Prize secret.

Uta turned her face away from Réz and the gawking of Wolf's men. Excruciating pain ravaged her insides and she didn't want them to see her distress.

In the beginning it just burnt a little and tasted bad, like sweetened petroleum running down her neck, but in the last ten minutes, her situation began to change. With intermittent surges of agony, the feeling inside her body alternated; a frozen wasteland one moment and the heat of a firestorm, the next. She also kept regurgitating a metallic tasting bile that made her gasp and gag.

Maybe I should have waited, but it's too late now.

Her stomach and bowel area felt as if she carried a womb full of vipers; their movement made her feel like throwing up.

I can't stop it now … No matter the outcome.

Chapter Seventy Nine

Tom thought about re-checking the contents of his father's letter, but he couldn't retrieve it in Vogel's presence without ending their bargain. With the absence of a syringe, he needed to remember if a process existed for safely drinking from the canister, before Isobel took her turn.

I have to get this right.

If he made a mistake, it could be disastrous. His decision could cause her to die, but without it … her death rated a certainty.

He forced himself to look at Vogel, despite his anger at the man.

"The Prize is alien blood. It's what the suits are made from and it has its own consciousness."

"You're telling me this ooze can think?"

"Yes. Do you want to hear this or not."

Vogel pursed his lips and nodded

"My father found it and studied it. You can't swallow any more than a lid full and even that might kill you."

"Will it give me the same power as the Angels?"

Tom gave Vogel made up answers, but he seemed happy enough to accept them.

"It will either kill you or change you utterly. No-one knows for sure, but to have the same power as the Angels ... you need their suits."

Tom felt Isobel's breath on the back of his neck as she spoke.

"Am I going to die, Tom?"

"I ... I think the Prize will allow a piece of you to die, so that another part can grow."

Tom tried to concentrate. He needed to pour the green substance into the canister's lid, but he felt aghast at Isobel's morbid statements and his fever caused his hands to shake.

"I can't do it, Tom. I can't take this stuff."

Vogel grunted with impatience.

"Don't be stupid, girl. Hurry up, or none of us will make it."

"No. I won't do it. I won't become a monster, like the people who took my father. These Angels are controlled by someone and they killed people. They killed thousands."

"Come on, Iz. Please ..."

"No Tom, I've made up my mind. You're dying and I want to go there with you. I'm not going to stay here alone and become one of them."

Vogel reached forward, took Tom by the foot and shook him.

"You made a bargain, Fox. You gave me your word."

Isobel struck out at Vogel and slapped his hand away.

"You'll have to finish us, Vogel. It's the only thing you're good at."

Tom tried to speak, but no words could portray the confusion impeding his decision making processes.

No matter what she says, I can't just let her die. This liquid is all I can do for her now. I have to follow through.

"Vogel put your gun away, or I'll spray this stuff all over the floor."

Tom's stomach burned with inflammation and his shoulder throbbed with pain, but he still found the strength to maintain his newly found authority. He turned and smiled an apology to Isobel and her eyes narrowed with suspicion.

"Nothing's changed, Vogel. The bargain still stands. Grab her and open her mouth. Then you'll get your own dose."

Vogel didn't hesitate. He grabbed her before she could move and held her easily, despite her screams and feeble attempts to pull away.

"No, Tom ... Please. I don't want to live like this."

Her cries for help accused him. Overriding her decision filled him with guilt, but he couldn't let her go, despite whatever consequences arose from his decision.

Once she swallowed the liquid, Vogel let go of her, allowing Tom to reach for her hand, but she pushed him away.

"Izzi ...?"

He tried to meet her eyes, but a bolt of pain caused him to clutch at his chest and he doubled over.

Something's eating my insides ... God it hurts.

Tom rolled over onto his side and tried not to yell, but some of the grunts and moans he tried to hold in, escaped from his throat.

Through the agony he glimpsed Isobel's expression; her eyes seemed to widen in panic and disbelief.

Tom's body began to jerk and bounce causing even more pain. He experienced an almost overwhelming feeling of relief when Isobel crawled back to him and tried to hold him still.

"Vogel. I'll help you with your dose, but first you have to help Tom."

With a nod of annoyance, Vogel straddled Tom's body and sat on his legs. In the same action, he pinned both of his arms to the floor.

"Look at him. Everything's moving."

Tom heard Isobel scream.

He lifted his head so he could see his upper torso and his mouth flew open in surprise. Something alien moved under his skin; an infestation of some kind; Finger-long creatures that raised the skin as they slithered inside his body.

Tom slowly lifted his arm and eased the palm on his right hand onto his chest, but the movement underneath felt sickening and he instantly withdrew it; the momentum causing him to fall backwards off his elbows. He remembered feeling the back of his head hit the ground, then all went blank.

"Come back, Tom. Please."

Tom responded to Isobel's cry and woke fully to a stab of pain. He smiled at her, but continued to lay still even though the strange phenomenon appeared to be over.

"Tom?"

He noticed Isobel's eyes widen and her expression seemed all the more frightening, when he realised she stared at him. Once again he rose up on his elbows and strained his neck as he tried to see his mid and upper torso.

Oh God. Not again.

He could see two of his wounds; both swollen into egg-sized volcanos. One after another they began to erupt; spitting green frothing muck into the air and onto his stomach.

Chapter Eighty

Wolf found it difficult to believe the half-sisters legend, but here they stood, roped together in front of him. Everyone in his business knew of Uta Cel Ră024, the infamous SRP commando, but not many knew a twin existed. He didn't believe the rumours, until now.

"What are you looking at, Wolf?"

"At your beautiful smooth face, Uta."

She snarled at him and struggled against her captors.

He looked from Uta and began appraising the other sister. Droplets of blood dripped off a recently marked face, but unlike Uta, they appeared to be superficial.

These are impressive looking females; as lithe and as violent as wildcats.

"Ladies, do you know what happens to people who kill SRP soldiers?"

Uta strained forward against her bonds, coughed up a globule of blood and spat it towards his feet.

"Drink that, Wolf."

"I want to know who you work for and just so you know, I can execute both of you on the spot, if I don't like your answers."

"You haven't got the balls."

Wolf didn't have time to respond. His peripheral vision captured movement; a man marched past him and grabbed Uta by the throat.

The Cobra ... What's he doing?

"Wolf, look at her you fool."

"I'm in charge here, Roberto. You have no authority in this theatre."

"That's where you're wrong. I've officially taken over and that comes from the top. Any man who defies me will be dealt with accordingly. Even you, Wolf."

He let go of Uta and moved back towards the agitated Angel.

"Get these women away from him. The scarred one has taken some of the Prize. Look at her body. The process has already begun."

Isobel shoved her personal feelings and emotions aside and focused on Tom.

He's become my best friend and my family and I want more.

She looked down at his sweaty soot-covered face and tried to deny the truth of what she saw.

I couldn't bear it if he ... left me.

Every now and then he opened his eyes and seemed to look at her, which she interpreted as wakefulness, but his eyes seemed dull and vacant.

Isobel sat beside him and stroked his hair, while Vogel poured a measured amount of the Prize for his own deliverance. She could see that only about a third of the substance remained in the canister, yet it continued to glow and flicker.

I can't remember ever feeling this lost. Perhaps God's misplaced us down here and we're too lowly for Him to help us out.

She heard a gurgle coming from Tom's throat, so she sat behind him and propped his head in her lap. The gurgling quickly became a cough, followed by a gush of green liquid that splattered his chest.

"Vogel, help me."

Isobel watched in horror, as Tom began to convulse; the wound in his stomach swelling into a fist-sized pyramid that stretched the skin, turning it a deep purple.

She heard Vogel call out and turned to investigate.

"What?"

He looked frightened and shocked and his mouth hung open. He started yelling at her and jabbing his forefinger in Tom's direction.

"Look. Look at his wound."

A dark object appeared at the extent of the swollen wound and Tom's entire body began to vibrate and jerk. Then the object popped out, followed by a wash of green pussy liquid.

She heard Vogel gasp.

"Look … It's starting over."

Isobel hung to Tom as tightly as she could, as the process began again. This time the bullet could be seen squeezing from the swollen wound in his shoulder.

Isobel couldn't stop her tears as the wound shot out the slug and a small piece of jagged bone.

Oh my … Tom, what's happening?

Within seconds, both of the swollen pyramids began to recede and lose their purple discolouration and within a matter of minutes, she could hardly see the original wound.

She winced when she saw Vogel crawling towards her. When he covered the distance, he grabbed her shoulder and shook her.

"How could this be? He didn't swallow any of the liquid."

Isobel didn't listen. She pulled away from Vogel and looked into Tom's eyes with excitement, as he began to wake up.

Bruno Wolf never disregarded his instincts, which continued to deliver the same message.

If I relinquish my authority now ... I'm a dead man.

He studied the body language of his new foes, as he considered his next move.

That's got to be relevant. The Angel calmed down the moment the women moved back.

His wild flickering light receded into a glowing green, yet the look of worry on Costa's face didn't alter, suggesting the Angel became agitated and even frightened by the women.

"Costa. Come closer and take care to understand what I'm going to tell you. Your father charged me with succeeding here and that's what I intend to do. You have no real authority in this place, other than that damn Angel and he doesn't seem all that happy to be here."

"That's betrayal, Wolf. They'll hunt you down. There's no way you can succeed on your own."

"You talk easily enough of betrayal, but we both know who's been shafted here."

"So?"

"You can stay, but I deliver the goods and we all win."

"What if I refuse?"

"Then I'll do my duty and shoot you. I'll even throw those devil women at your glowing friend over there and with a bit of luck, he might start working for me. It's a good plan, don't you think?"

Chapter Eighty One

Tom lay on his back floating just above the ground. He drifted slowly through the grassy fields, ablaze with black and yellow daisies, but as his head began to clear, he realised that he still sat in a black hole surrounded by enemies.

"Tom, you're awake."

He smiled back at her, a little amused by her announcement.

"Are you alright?"

"Yeah. I think so. Sort of anyway."

He noticed Vogel bending forward for a closer look. Without his usual hat, Tom could see the man's bizarre scalp of reddish orange hair, with its prominent patches of black and grey.

"What do you mean, sort of? What I just witnessed is impossible."

Tom didn't wish to have this conversation with Vogel. He could never trust a man like him; a man who killed without remorse.

The bastard's perceptive ... I'm different now, although I'm not sure how exactly. I can feel people, even remotely. I can feel and see what they're thinking. I can also see images ... I can see Uta and her auburn-haired sister bound together and I can tell they've taken the Prize. I shouldn't be able to do that. How am I able to do that?

"Fox. Are you listening? What about your wounds? Is there pain?"

"They're fine. I don't feel any different than I did before. That is before you shot me."

"Rubbish, Fox ... Projectiles hit us from all directions. You just caught a stray shot."

"Liar."

Tom remembered perceiving Vogel's hatred through the swirling dust and now because of his strange new sense, he could see something far more disturbing.

"You. You did it."

Vogel turned away from Tom towards the entrance. He could hear people approaching and someone calling Tom's name.

"Look at me, Vogel. I saw you kill them."

"What are you talking about? We're about to be attacked."

"I can forgive you doing your job, Vogel, no matter how sick it is, but you laughed. Even when my mother's beautiful innocent face begged you not to kill her, you laughed."

Tom's words tore away Vogel's facade and stripped him bare.

Yes. You enjoyed it, you bastard.

He confessed to his crimes with a twisted hateful expression; seemingly delighted with his achievement. At least he didn't need to continue his loathsome charade.

"You're so clever, aren't you, Fox?"

Vogel backed away and drew his gun.

"She begged me to spare you."

He stopped moving and Tom cringed at his evil looking grin.

"Before I shot her, I explained in detail how I intended to murder you. You should have heard her scream."

Oh God ... Oh God.

Tom could feel and empathise with his mother's terror. The weight of his sadness bore down on him and he bowed his head and cried.

"Don't worry, Fox. Crying runs in the family. I also made her watch while I killed your father and you should have seen her howl. Now you get to bawl, watching me kill your skinny little girlfriend. Then you're going to share her fate."

Wolf caught up with the Cobra and both arrived at the cavern's entrance at the same moment.

Once there, Wolf hesitated, as did his companion. Instead of a dark opening in the ground, they found a vortex of shimmering green light. This seemed enough to extinguish any need to be the first inside.

"Call a warning, Wolf?"

"And if they don't surrender?"

"Then we send in the Angel."

They agreed without once taking their eyes from the hole. Wolf only took one tentative step forward, before shouting his demands down through the entrance.

"Fox. If you want to live, come out now and bring the Prize."

He waited several seconds for a reply and when it didn't arrive he repeated the message.

Nothing. He's either refusing to heed us, or he's dead.

Roberto Costa gestured to his Angel and Wolf stiffened with expectation. His mind not wanting to accept an encounter with something so alien. He focused on its movement and his mind continued to reel. The creature didn't walk like other living things, it hovered and travelled so quickly that he couldn't discern its movement.

It's either here, or it's there, with not even a blur in between.

It occurred to Wolf that the Angel itself didn't bother him as much as its reason for being here.

How could something so powerful be made subservient to any agency, other than God; especially an organisation as morally corrupt as the Assembly?

Then an explosion of light tore him from his thoughts. The Angel hovered between him and the cavern's entrance. Its pulsing flashes of light stung his eyes and he retreated several steps.

So far, things haven't gone so well for me, but at least I'm not having to face what Fox is about to experience.

Noah lived with the possibility of violent death in every waking moment, which he handled by disciplining and controlling his emotions, yet having to watch while Tom and Isobel waited to die …

I can't do this.

The priest employed no such discipline. Every time things worsened, he gave a tortured groan and turned away. Noah felt for him.

The bastard's forced him into a choice that no man should ever have to make.

It didn't matter that he displayed his grief. He condemned his own soul mate to death as well as his small congregation, yet here he remained, doing his duty.

He's a great man who deserves better.

Noah looked over at his friend. Just the slightest extra pressure on the trigger and he could obtain his revenge. Wolf stood out there on the plain at that very moment, right in front of him at the entrance to the cavern. It must have been his private hell to let the man live.

"I wish we could help them, Nico. Maybe we should take out as many as we can and make a final stand."

"Be patient, Noah, my good friend. We won't have long to wait. We have to take what's left of this mess and make it matter for Tom and Isobel."

Noah turned his head towards the priest. He seemed barely recognisable, covered in so much dirt. The enemy could walk right over him and not be aware of his presence.

"I'll hold off, Nico. Then we'll give them hell."

Noah raised his weapon slightly, turned his head away and spat-out a globule of glutinous sandy saliva.

"I've got the recipe right here in my hand, but I'll leave Wolf for you, my dear friend."

Chapter Eighty Two

Tom spread his arms wide in a futile attempt to shield Isobel.

The enemies' bullets didn't kill me, but can I be sure about Izzi surviving?

"Leave her alone, Vogel."

The security chief's face contorted into a hideous looking scowl.

"This is personal, Fox. I killed your parents, so it's only fitting that I get to dispose of their offspring."

Isobel screamed at Vogel from under Tom's protruding arm.

"You're such a gutless creep. How many good people have you murdered by sneaking up from behind?"

"Plenty, but not all. I stood eye to eye with your father, when I blew his brains all over the floor."

Isobel pushed Tom aside; hurling herself so fast and so unexpectedly at Vogel that he didn't have time to react.

Tom raced to help, but before he covered even half of the distance, Vogel held her face down with his gun at her head.

"Time's up, Fox. Now you get to watch your girlfriend die."

———————

Tom placed his hands over his eyes and retreated several paces from the kaleidoscope of blazing light entering the cavern. For a brief instant, he thought the enemy came in with a powerful searchlight, then he understood.

Utilising a tiny gap between his fingers, he distinguished the shape of an Angel. The creature looked huge in the confines of the cavern.

It's just hovering; waiting for something and not attacking me. Why?

Slowly Tom's eyes began adjusting to the brightness. Within seconds, he could see well enough to distinguish two humans climbing down the ladder; a tough looking man with dark hair, followed by a younger leaner man who immediately assumed authority.

"Put down the gun, Frederick. This game is over."

Vogel began to laugh and Tom thought it sounded desperate; almost hysterical.

"Well if it isn't the chairman's brat and his underling in person."

"I'm not going to ask you again, Vogel."

"You can ask the same stupid question all day, but I won't honour it with an answer."

Wolf strode forward and gestured toward the Angel.

"You don't seriously believe we came down here to make a deal, Vogel?"

"I don't care. I've tasted the Prize, Wolf. Do you know what that means?"

Wolf turned and nodded to the Cobra.

"Yes, I do. There's only one agency that can kill you now. Look my friend, here comes your doom."

Tom witnessed no evidence of any communication between the Cobra and the Angel, yet before Vogel could move, the creature hovered above him.

"Iz. No."

Tom looked on in horror, as Isobel became engulfed in the same blazing electrical current.

───────────

Tom ran forward trying to rescue Isobel, but the heat drove him back. He could only watch, as the Angel continued his attack.

"Iz ...?"

He felt overwhelmed by the Angel's presence. Thoughts and emotions bombarded him without any normal sequential order, as if a tiny tear opened up in his consciousness, allowing the infinite to break in and rampage through his mind; the past, present and future arriving all at once.

I can't hang on ... I have to let go.

Despite the glare and the dissonance and all of the confused happenings inside the cavern, he connected.

His mouth opened and he cried out; moaning, screaming, shouting, yet he made no sound.

What's happening to me?

Tom never understood what people meant by spirit, yet without realising how, he opened a doorway and touched its source.

"Oh God ..."

This time, in that ecstatic, all-encompassing moment, he threw his head back and cried out with such voluble joy that everyone in the cavern, including the Angel, stiffened into non-action, but the enemy's surprise didn't last long.

The Angel screamed back at him with a tortured shriek of hatred that stung his ears and knocked him to the ground. In a flash it hung above him, but instead of attacking, it pulled away, shrieking.

Tom staggered to his feet.

I'm affecting this thing. It seems frightened ... Scared of me.

Then he realised that he no longer needed to shield himself from its glare; the creature's bright pulses diminishing to a meagre radiance and its hovering became uncoordinated and erratic.

Tom began to feel sick in the stomach, but before he could react to this clenching bout of nausea, he felt overwhelmed by a much stronger force. A strange vibrating phenomena, saturated mind and flesh, and wonder began to colour everything he perceived.

I can't stop ... I can't stop this. It's ... happening.

Then the seemingly impossible occurred. The infinite universe downloaded itself into the finite of his being, like all of the oceans spilling into a single drop.

The Angel feels this too ... He's desperate ... Panicked.

It backed as far away from Tom as possible, before it began lurching around the cave, jerking and bucking; its screeches forcing all of the other occupants of the cavern to the ground. Tom could see them writhing in the dust; hands clamped over their ears in a desperate attempt to keep the screams from bursting their eardrums, but he didn't feel their pain.

The Angel retreated and appeared next to the steel ladder at the cavern's entrance.

Yes ... I can see you now.

He recognised a human inside its failing light.

It's confused. It's never been threatened before and it wants to escape. No ... Wait ... Fear is driving it ... It comes.

Tom saw the creature's eyes widen and focus on him. Then it gave another ear shattering shriek and attacked.

Pain surged through Tom's body, as the pulsing current tossed him against the cavern's rear wall. He didn't fall. He remained pinned, suspended twice his height from the ground.

He'll hit me with everything he's got now; his deathblow.

The pressure holding him against the wall increased and the Angel screeched, as bolts of blue and white electrical current pulsed around it. Then all of the flashes of current came together, into one stream of brilliant light.

Hang on ... Survive this ... You can do it.

A force within his mind rebelled; rejecting his thought.

No ... Don't succumb to fear. Courage. Let go ... Surrender fully to the joy you're experiencing.

The light struck Tom and engulfed him, but rather than struggle, he allowed the Angel full access to his being.

"Iz?"

Through his agony, he looked down at Isobel. She lay in the foetal position with her arms tightly wrapped around her knees.

She's alive ... Just.

Wolf looked around for a possible means of escape, as he backed away from the rampaging Angel, but there didn't appear to be anywhere to go. After several steps, he collided with a figure of flesh and blood and realised he held the Cobra with a forearm jammed against his throat.

"Costa. Control this thing. Or we'll be killed."

"I can't ... It's not responding to my commands."

Wolf realised the searing pain could prove fatal if he didn't do something.

Move. Only indecisive fools fall victim to collateral damage.

He felt almost overwhelmed by the violence raging around him, yet he didn't panic.

Assess ... Evaluate.

He held the Cobra in front of him as a shield, as he gauged the environment.

Vogel and the girl are down. They look dead.

He spotted another glowing light, despite the glare emanating from the Angel.

The Prize ... It's close.

He wasted no further time on thought. He bent over as low as he could and darted to retrieve the canister.

Dive ...

His body struck the ground as a bolt of crackling light blasted the air above him. Somehow Fox continued to survive and seemed to be returning the Angel's fire, which detonated into ear shattering blasts somewhere between them.

Of course ... Fox must have used the Prize.

Wolf jumped to his feet and ran forward. He bent to retrieve it, but the cavern exploded with light and noise; the concussion driving him face first into the black soil of the cave.

He looked up through his fingers as another blast echoed around the wall.

This's it. I have to move or I'm dead.

He tried to rise; the whine of the battling current changing; a buzzing drone escalating to a pitch that assaulted the mind.

Oh no ...

The sound and light retreated from the Angel; sucked into a whirling vortex of dazzling colour before it disappeared with a pop, into a spinning dot of black.

Wolf noticed the black disk begin to crackle as he ran towards the entrance. Before he got there, it exploded, blasting the Angel and himself into the wall beside the steel stairs and all went blank.

He couldn't be sure how long he lay unconscious, but when he looked back down the length of the cavern he could see that no-one remained on their feet.

As he dragged himself up into a standing position, he spotted the Cobra. He remained alive; barely.

Wolf knew an opportunity when he saw it. He grabbed the man's smoking arm and lifted him up.

If I escape with the Prize and save Costa, I've got a much greater chance of survival.

He saw a flicker of light as he dragged Costa and the canister towards the surface. He didn't look back.

Tom sat on the soot covered floor and watched as Wolf struggled to carry the smoking body of his companion up the ladder. Then, like a phoenix rising from its own ashes, the Angel began to pulse. It turned towards Tom and attempted to scream, but it emitted nothing more than a tortured croak.

Tom perceived the dying creature beneath the light. It no longer hovered and its brightness continued to fade as he watched.

It attempted one last screech, then it turned and followed Wolf up the ladder, using the feet and hands of a man; the fraud exposed for all to see.

The cavern fell into darkness, yet Tom could still see the body that lay in the centre of the cavern.

"Iz?"

Chapter Eighty Three

Noah gripped his automatic weapon with sweaty hands; his finger trembling, as it engaged the trigger.

He spoke quietly to the man lying next to him and continued his vigil from their hide on the ridge.

"I can't stand this, Nico. What on earth is going on in there?"

They could see the radiance bursting from the cavern's entrance, even in the harsh light of the afternoon.

"I've never felt so powerless."

Both men struggled to contain their emotions, as their friends did battle without them.

"They're our life's purpose and only God knows what's happening to them down there."

"It's nearly time, Noah. I know we're going to die and I'm ready."

"Your Emma … She'll be there waiting. They'll all be there, but I'm not going without a fight."

"Nor I."

Noah reached out and squeezed the priest's arm.

"The light from the cavern's stopped. Get ready."

Noah could see a man labouring from the entrance, dragging another. Once out, he passed the injured man to a medic and limped towards a waiting helicopter.

It's Wolf.

Noah lowered his weapon.

This revenge belongs to you, my old friend.

———————

Wolf shouted at his troops to form around him.

"Why are you staring at me, you fools?"

Yes ... Of course, they're shocked.

They can't believe a mere mortal could survive such a thing, but he didn't have time for their adulation. Helicopter rotors spun, ready to take off.

He limped forward several steps and stopped; noticing the state of his female prisoners.

"Mother of God. What's happened here, sergeant?"

"Sir, I ... I'm not sure. Just after you went into the hole, the scarred one went crazy. Not long after, the other one started to jerk all over the place in some sort of spasm."

"Get them to a helicopter, we're moving out. Also, inform our captain and all of our flight crews that I want the cavern totally destroyed. Use every rocket we have."

———————

With trembling hands, the priest aimed his weapon at Wolf: the murderer of Em, his great love and all of his brethren. He could avenge her innocent blood right here, but as he evoked her memory, his rage began to battle with the goodness of her life.

"My dear, sweet, Emma."

She fought the good fight and she'd never condone my need for vengeance. She'd stay my hand; reminding me always of our great responsibility to the truth; never confusing justice with revenge.

"Alright you monster, cop this."

He squeezed the trigger and the weapon kicked. He saw the projectile explode into Wolf's thigh and nodded. He aimed low, as an initial warning; a declaration of war, which allowed him to act. He knew he could never commit murder, but he could kill to stop a killer.

Noah followed the priest's lead, firing a constant stream of projectiles down on their enemy.

"Stop them reaching the helicopters, Nico. We have to keep them pinned down if we can."

"It's too late for that."

The priest could see two already starting to rise into the air. As he spoke, they began to receive fire from several locations around the battlefield, as well as the two operational helicopters.

The gunfire ceased and the priest raised his head in surprise.

"Noah, look."

Both men watched as the Angel rose from the cavern; its light intermittent. It no longer moved as it once did. The priest thought it looked almost comic now, running like a man.

He turned away from the Angel and looked over at his friend, as Noah raised himself onto one elbow and started jabbing his forefinger towards the enemy.

"Fire at Wolf, Nico. He'll have the Prize. We can't let him get away."

Bullets fizzed by, landing all around them, but they continued their assault on Wolf.

Uta knew where Noah positioned himself and waited for the attack. It came much later than she expected and hit the SRP hard from the ridge.

There's only two of them and they're in the same spot. It won't be long until they're eliminated, especially with helicopters in the air.

Uta looked over at her sister.

She knows and she's ready.

"Now."

She kicked out at her captor at exactly the same time as her half-twin and they broke free of him. She knew he could catch them, but she also knew he focused elsewhere.

Why expose yourself to enemy fire? Why die for two unarmed women when you came here to fight?

Bound and exposed, they bounced towards the only possible cover: the cavern's entrance.

Uta turned for the briefest moment, before entering the gloom and laughed when she spotted Wolf. She could see his annoyance.

The priest saw another two SRP men fall.

I think I got him.

The bullet struck Wolf somewhere in the torso region, but a soldier dragged him away through the dust towards their aircraft.

"We've failed, Noah. They'll make it into the air."

"No … Wait for Wolf's helicopter. Aim all your fire in that direction. Don't stop. We can't give up."

Wolf sat forward in the seat behind the pilot and attempted to assess the full extent of his injuries. The thigh shot leaked blood, but didn't appear to be an immediate risk, unlike the wound to his chest.

Each time he spoke, his mouth bubbled with red froth and he coughed up globules of fresh blood.

A scorched and sooty figure slumped beside him. He braved a smirk and tried to speak. Wolf hardly recognised his rasping voice.

"A lung shot. You're a dead man, Wolf."

"You don't look so well either, Costa. I'd say we're both as good as dead."

We're not going to make it to our next destination ... No way.

He flinched in agony and grasped at the wound to hold in the pain, but the object in his hand hindered him.

The Prize.

The canister still contained a third of its original contents. He could swallow half and give the remainder to the Cobra. He disliked the man, but saving him established some insurance against retribution.

Chapter Eighty Four

Tom felt fatigued; most of his strength draining away in his battle with the Angel, but he raised himself to face the new threat.

"Get away from her, Vogel."

"I don't have to shoot you. I just want to, but I'll kill her first so you can watch before you die."

Isobel sobbed with pain as she raised herself from the ground to face her father's killer. Between the smudges of soot, Tom could see red blotches and scalded skin. He also noticed her smouldering cloths and singed hair.

"You don't get it, do you, Vogel?"

"What?"

"Didn't you see what happened to Tom? He cheated death."

"No-one cheats me."

Vogel let out a high pitched wail and pulled the trigger. The hammer clanged against metal, but the gun didn't fire. Then his eyes widened and his face contorted with hatred.

"I've changed my mind, Fox. I'm going to kill you first."

He removed a knife from somewhere on his person and shuffled towards Tom.

"Your body might spit out bullets, but if I cut off your head ...?"

Tom felt weak and unable to defend himself. He tried to back away, knowing Vogel intended to go through with his threat, but where could he go?

I think I'm about to find out just how invincible I am.

Then a noise halted Vogel's attack.

Two women appeared on the steel stair and bounded from the last rung to the floor of the cavern. Tom looked at the scarred face and felt sick with recognition.

Uta ... And the sister.

Tom saw Vogel move in his peripheral vision. He backed away from the approaching women, looking almost happy as he gathered up his previously discarded gun.

"Beautiful. No weapons and tied like hogs."

As Vogel faced off with the two devil-women, Tom saw Isobel scramble towards Vogel's dropped knife. Holding on to the blade, she flicked the dagger across the cavern, landing it beside a surprised Uta.

"Nice work, bitch. Once I kill Vogel, I can use it on you."

While the women cut their bonds, Vogel hurried to reload his weapon. He succeeded, took aim and fired twice.

Tom heard the two detonations and a click and knew that Vogel didn't have any more ammunition. He looked at the man's horrified face and then at the women. Both bullets hit their target, but neither woman fell.

Uta laughed as she tossed the knife from hand to hand.

"Now it's your turn, Vogel."

The three combatants began to circle and snarl at each other, but Tom focused elsewhere.

Helicopters.

He heard them approaching and the whoosh of the first rockets being launched.

No ... Get going.

Before Tom could move, the entrance to the cavern exploded. The noise and concussion throwing him onto his back. A black cloud of dust enveloped him as he struggled back to a standing position; obscuring everything, including the three circling killers.

Tom's foot found Isobel and he reached down in the darkness and lifted her up by the arm. His action hurt her, but he didn't have time to be gentle.

"Hurry, Iz. This way. My father made a map. There's a tunnel."

Another blast rocked the cavern and knocked them off their feet. Seconds later, he heard a loud crack.

The roof?

He jumped to his feet and began to drag Isobel towards the rear tunnel, but several metres short of the entrance, another rocket struck, bringing part of the main roof down.

Tom heard Isobel cry out and she fell to the ground.

"Iz? Iz …?"

She didn't answer. He fumbled in the dirt and found her arm.

She's not moving ... A rock ... Quickly, get her out of here.

He lifted her and tried to run towards safety, but he didn't get far. He experienced a thunderous roar that brought pain to his ears and the entire ceiling of rock came crashing down.

Noah watched in horror, as the first of the rockets struck the cavern.

"Sweet Lord, no."

Flying debris and columns of dust swirled over the plain, as the last of the helicopters flew close by to deliver its death. Noah could see Wolf's face peering at them through the side window.

"It's him, Nico. Wolf. Give it to him."

As the helicopter released its rockets, both Noah and the priest rose to their knees, and fired until their weapons clanged to a stop.

For a moment nothing happened; the helicopter sped away, seemingly untouched. Then they spotted the smoke. Wolf's aircraft caught fire and plunged into the distant plain; exploding into a fireball as it struck the ground.

Noah fell to his knees in the dirt, spent; hardly noticing as the priest rushed by.

"Come on, Noah. They could still be alive."

The big man stood and watched, as his friend ran and fell, and ran again. There seemed hope in the priest's actions. Imagined or not, it woke him from his trance.

They arrived at the site in the last of the days glow. Instead of an entrance leading to a cavern, they found a deep depression covered by rock and soil.

What's he doing? Can't he see it's useless? The whole area's caved in.

In the fading light, he could see that the priest displayed no intentions of giving up.

"We have to dig, Noah. We have to keep going."

The big man shook his head in anger.

What stupidity. No-one could survive under all of this rock.

"For God's sake, Nico. This is a grave."

The priest stopped digging and slumped onto his hands and knees in the dirt. The memory of all those who lost their lives seemed to drift above the sunken trough: his beloved Emma and brethren, Tom and Isobel and so many more.

"You're right. They're gone."

Noah heard the tremor in the priest's voice and struggled to control his own emotions.

"I suppose it's a fitting resting place. Against all odds, Tom brought us all the way to the Prize. Now he's buried in the place where it all began."

"No. Rubbish. That's sentimental nonsense, Nico. It's a crime that we survived and they perished. Two old men like us have no right to …"

The priest reached forward and placed his hand over Noah's mouth. Utilising the only sliver of light remaining, Noah followed his friend's line of sight and searched the horizon. Then he saw it. A brief glimpse of a silhouette coming towards them.

Both men lowered themselves to the ground and drew their weapons.

"Nico, don't shoot unless you have to. There might be more than one."

They waited in silence as the figure approached. Noah thought the footsteps sounded laboured and tired. He rose onto one knee, aimed his weapon and called out.

"Stop … Don't move. Not even a muscle or you'll die. Now, slowly raise your hands and come closer."

Nothing happened. The dark figure didn't move.

"No. That's not going to happen. I'm carrying an injured woman and she's someone you both love."

"Tom …?"

Noah found it difficult to form his words.

"Tom. Is that you?"

"I need a little help here. Iz's badly hurt."

Noah rushed forward and took Isobel in his arms and experienced a rush of warmth returning to his heart. He looked over at Tom and shook his head in wonder.

He looked so serious as he focused his attention on the priest's disjointed attempts to speak.

"How did you survive, young man? We saw you shot … And the cave-in?"

"Luck … God … Who knows?"

"We didn't see Vogel, but we did see the devil-twins enter. What happened?"

Tom pointed into the collapsed cavern.

"They're under there."

The priest shook his head very slowly.

"I still don't understand how you survived."

He watched Tom's expression grow into a smile and didn't understand when it turned into a chuckle.

"You don't get it, either of you?"

Noah's eyes widened and a similar smile appeared on his face.

"Nico. He did it. He got what we came for."

"No. We saw Wolf leave with it."

"Nico, old friend. Tom's done it. We've won."

"And, Wolf?"

"We saw his helicopter go down in flames and explode with the dying Angel on board. No-one could survive that."

As Tom put a hand on both of their shoulders and beamed, a gentle female voice came from Noah's lap.

"You did it, Tom. We won."

Chapter Eighty Five

The chairman and the Assembly board received live footage from the Raptor Park engagement. The continuous feed failed in the cavern, but Wolf filled in the details when he and Roberto made it back to the helicopters.

The Assembly board knew when Vogel and the two women sampled the Prize. They also knew when the Angel failed and injured their chairman's son.

The rocket attack brought all of the board members a moment of elation. They witnessed the collapse of the cavern's roof and rejoiced knowing it caused the deaths of Fox and the girl, as well as Vogel and the twin devils, yet the chairman himself felt a moment of panic.

My only living son ... almost slain.

The chairman watched as Wolf rescued a portion of the Prize and dragged his dying son Roberto to the surface.

No ... It couldn't possibly get any worse than this.

Then Wolf surprised him; administering the Prize and saving his son.

Thank you, my God, thank you. My son lives and I now possess the greatest power on Earth.

Antonio cried out. His joy turning to horror, as his son's helicopter and his life's work, plummeted from the sky.

No ... No ... No. This can't be happening.

Many hours later the chairman sat considering his fate.

How could I ever talk my way out of this? Impossible.

The last of the Seven Angels lay dead and the Prize gone.

It's a total disaster.

His hair felt damp with sweat as he pondered his doom. Tomorrow he faced the Assembly board with his official report.

I'll be removed as chairman and shortly after I'll be killed. Someone will brush past me and I won't even feel the slight contact to the skin. The chemicals will take effect within seconds, bringing on a massive heart attack that I won't survive.

He flicked a long strand of wet hair away from his face and patted it back down on his scalp, with the back of his hand.

The Black Cardinal is bound to the same fate. Once he's elected, they'll force him to capitulate and grant them their wishes. Then he'll suffer the worst of ailments; an untimely death.

Antonio always treated hindsight as an excuse employed by the weak, but now his own thoughts became dominated by it.

I only made one mistake and it cost me everything.

He grossly underestimated the son of Alexander Fox. Who could have guessed that Tom Fox could fight and defeat a vastly superior enemy? Against all the odds, he destroyed the power of the Seventh Angel and the entire Assembly.

Tom Fox ... Oh, how I loathe you.

Some, even amongst his own organisation, referred to him as a hero.

A hero ...?

Yes. It might be true, but even as I take my last breath, I'll never admit it.

Chapter Eighty Six

The world turned slowly towards the sun and the horizon glowed with the promise of the day's beginning. Not long after, a breeze sprang up. It blew through the salt bush and lifted swirls of previously disturbed soil; spinning them into braids of intertwining dust that fluttered and then dissipated into the warm, clear air.

Animals hopped and padded across the plain; heading for burrows and hides before the day's heat bore down on them. As the sun's rays fanned the sky, birdsong erupted amongst the eucalypts that flourished alone the banks of Spring Creek. Only then did the creatures of the day begin to emerge.

The grey, yellow-brown and black stripes of the death adder became more distinguishable as it slid from under its protective cover of leaf litter and silently made its way across the plain.

It stopped and waited.

A large red kangaroo bounded close by, followed by several others and the snake perceived the fear in their movement; determining vibrational information through its internal ear.

It felt a strong need to dig itself into the red gravel and hide. It flicked out its tongue and sensed the presence of an even larger animal; a scent it couldn't determine, but one that fit with the vibrations of fear in the animals hopping by.

It slithered away past several piles of rubble and into the loose dirt of a large sunken pit. It felt like the perfect place to bury itself and set an ambush.

Only the camouflage of its broad triangular head and the tip of its tail lay above the ground. The tip wiggled with the exact movements of a worm, which attracted the prey it desired.

Once again it stopped all movement and waited.

The death adder's tongue flicked in and out; picking out the scent of dried human blood and the same odour of fear that drove it into the pit.

It sensed movement underground; strange vibrations rising towards the surface. Then in the half light of dawn it saw a large human-like hand break the surface, driven up on the end of an extended arm.

The adder lashed out with the quickest strike of any snake in the world; regaining its original strike position after only one fifteenth of a second; its bite attempting to inject a lethal dose of highly toxic venom. It struck again and again at the creature, until the enormous arm began to glow. As more of it emerged through the earth, the snake connected the vibrations and scent of fear with the image of the creature and decided to retreat.

The death adder rose out of the hole and slithered under the overlap of a large rock. There it remained motionless, as the huge glowing creature broke through the surface and raised itself to its full height.

The End

Be the First

Be the first to hear about my new releases! Just sign up below.
I promise not to share your email with anyone else, I will only use
it to contact you and let you know about my new releases.
http://eepurl.com/-Z4Eb

Calling All Blood Prize Readers

If you enjoyed Blood Prize, please consider leaving a review at
Amazon. Your input will help other readers to share your reading
experience and would be very much appreciated by the author.

Rate this book at www.amazon.com

Free Adventure Travel Blog

If you would like to experience my free, serialised Adventure
Travel Blog, please join me on:
http://kengraceblog.wordpress.com

Social Media Invitation

You are also invited to visit my website, or follow me on
Facebook, Twitter or LinkedIn.
Ken Grace Books Official Facebook page:
www.facebook.com/OfficialKenGrace
Ken Grace Books Official Twitter page:
www.twitter.com/KenGraceBooks
Ken Grace LinkedIn Profile:
www.linkedin.com/pub/ken-grace/a2/a78/856
Ken Grace Books Website: www.kengracebooks.com

www.ingramcontent.com/pod-product-compliance
Lightning Source LLC
Chambersburg PA
CBHW051539250626
47157CB00001B/113